4

D0875357

transcension

Tor Books by Damien Broderick

The Spike
Transcension

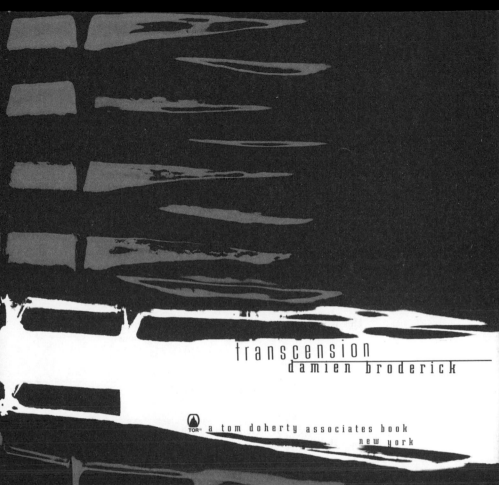

transcension
damien broderick

TOR a tom doherty associates book
new york

TRANSCENSION

Copyright © 2002 by Damien Broderick

Edited by David G. Hartwell

This book is printed on acid-free paper.

A Tor Book
Published by Tom Doherty Associates, LLC
175 Fifth Avenue
New York, NY 10010

www.tor.com

Tor® is a registered trademark of Tom Doherty Associates, LLC.

ISBN 0-765-30369-8

First Edition: February 2002

Printed in the United States of America

0 9 8 7 6 5 4 3 2 1

For Rory Barnes and Barbara Lamar,
without whom this novel quite literally wouldn't have been possible

transcension

I sit on a hill.
I { re-entrant selfaware identity operator }
sit on { instantaneous location slice on search trajectory }
a { existential pointer in exfoliating context sheaf }
hill { local optimum in restricted search space }
Call me Aleph.

I am a machine mentality. This in nowise distinguishes me from your-selves. My personhood, my self, is a process running as programs reflex-ively modulated in a net of nanocomputers in solar space. Most of my dispersed body remains for the moment on, in, above Earth. I am just like you humans, then.

I know the bite of the wind on a winter day, the silver light of the Moon, the warmth of the Sun, the laughter of children. I have loved Earth because it has been the root and home of my parental stock. Do you see? Do you understand? Do you feel?

the valley

But at my back I always hear
Time's wingèd chariot changing gear

——Apologies to Andrew Marvell
[1621—1678]

First let us postulate that the computer scientists succeed
in developing intelligent machines that can do all things
better than human beings can do them . . . If the machines
are permitted to make all their own decisions, we can't make
any- conjectures as to the results, because it is impossible to
guess how such machines might behave. We only point out
that the fate of the human race would be at the mercy of
the machines. It might be argued that the human race would
never be foolish enough to hand over all the power to the
machines. But . . . the human race might easily permit itself
to drift into a position of such dependence on the machines
that it would have no practical choice but to accept all of
the machines' decisions . . .

—Theodore Kaczynski, "Unabomber Manifesto,"
quoted by Bill Joy

The only realistic alternative I see is relinquishment: to
limit development of the technologies that are too dangerous,
by limiting our pursuit of certain kinds of knowledge . . . I
see around me cause for hope in the voices for caution and
relinquishment . . . I feel, too, a deepened sense of personal
responsibility—not for the work I have already done, but for
the work that I might yet do, at the confluence of the sci-
ences . . . Knowing is not a rationale for not acting. Can we
doubt that knowledge has become a weapon we wield against
ourselves?

—Bill Joy, "Why The Future Doesn't Need Us"

seed origin i: death

Facedown in a pool of his blood, being kicked to death in the public thoroughfare by a troop of street ferals, Abdel-Malek learned that dying arrived just as he'd always feared it would: with shock, terror, and agony.

Death, it turned out, provided no soothing anaesthesia. Overwhelmed with shame, he squealed and whimpered. The hardened cap of a military-surplus boot smashed the side of his throat, crushing his larynx. Vomiting, scarcely able to breathe, he could barely hear his wife's screams. She was frightened, but more than that she was furious.

"Gutless, selfish, stupid cowards," she shouted. "Leave him alone!"

A kind of sad, admiring love brushed his fazed brain. Another boot took him in the ribs, then the right cheek. Light bloomed; it felt as if his eye had exploded. He wanted to cover his face, but his arms would not lift from the pavement. Mohammed Kasim Abdel-Malek, *bon vivant* and pragmatic optimist, B. A. Hons, Juris Doctor (license lapsed), D. Sc. (cog. sci.), more honorary degrees than he owned senses and limbs, desperately curled the fingers of his left hand. He was reaching absurdly in his last moments for assurance: for the chrome bracelet at his wrist.

The stupidity of his plight appalled him. The hubris. Nothing can touch me, I'm that famous guy. He and Alice had been the last guests to leave. The Greenhouse weather had been bad for days, more August than early June, the news had been worse, the dregs of society skulked in the shadows, waiting in their perfectly understandable resentment to smash store windows, snatch baubles and shiny toys.

"Sure you'll be okay?" Martha had asked, kissing Alice on the cheek, a true friendly smoosh of lips on flesh, none of your society air-kiss evasions. "Leave the dishes until the morning, honey," she told their host. "Let's see

them to their car." Josh had nodded, given them a tired smile; it was obvious that all he wanted to do was pile the wreckage into the dishwasher
and hit the sack.

"Nonsense," Mohammed Abdel-Malek told them forcefully. "We're only
parked half a block away."

His mind, in all truth, was parked more than a block away. Abdel-
Malek's thoughts remained in Cambridge, in those buoyant sunny months
when his spiritual father Alan Turing, and Campernowne, and the rest of
the *wunderkinden*, had invented out of whole cloth, in one fell swoop, the
electronic computer, the theory of programming, and the prospect of machine intelligence. No, he was getting confused. Turing's device was pre-
electronic, fed with paper tape. My God. And Turing dead these fifty years,
June 7, 1954. Some golden jubilee. He would have been 88. Old, but not
impossibly old. Not remarkably older than me, after all. But those hotshots
tonight, those kids from Silicon Valley.

"Still thinking about Turing?" asked Alice. He shivered despite the
muggy warmth, saw that they had descended to street level. Through the
glass doors, the street was ominously empty, no breeze lifting scraps of
discarded newspaper or fast-food trash. Everyone with any sense was inside with the air-conditioning blasting. Stepping from the comfortable
friendliness of the apartment and foyer to the stifling street was a jolt,
reinforcing Abdel-Malek's melancholy.

"Mmm. Poor devil. It was nice of the kids to honor his memory."

"He was a great man," Alice said. She smiled primly. "You were all great
men, Boson."

The bunch of street ferals was suddenly there on the sidewalk. They
had every right to be there. It's a free country, isn't it?

"Oh Christ."

"Come on," he said with irritation. "They're just kids."

"Of course they're just kids, Kasim." Alice's voice sounded as if it had
been strained through mesh. "You're not *allowed* to be a juvenile delin-
quent after you've grown up."

They were stringing themselves out across the pathway. Pimples. Stub-
ble, tats on the skull. Lumps of metal piercing flesh. Must they make themselves so ugly?

"Juvenile delinquents! Darling, that expression went on the pension
around the time Turing bit the apple. Just keep walking. You've turned into
a nervous Nellie in your dotage."

Her hand on his arm, tense with dread, jerked. "Oh God, I don't like this."

A body moved into the space they passed through, thumped him cruelly.

"Watch it, you bastard!" cried the affronted thug.

Mildly, Mohammed Kasim recovered his balance. "Sorry."

"You walked straight into me. See that, bro? Muthafucka walked straight into me. Think they own the whole sidewalk, these rich fucks."

From the other side, keeping step with them, a peaky girl asked, "Got any change?"

Too quickly, Alice told her, "We never carry money."

"You greedy old bitch." The thug was outraged. "I'll fix you."

And the horror of it was that Mohammed Kasim *understood;* hadn't they been talking about it all night? It was his doing as much as anyone's. In all the world, he and his colleagues were the ones crucially responsible for the machines that took the children's jobs away, filched their souls from them, stole their future. It paralyzed him. He felt the battering on his body, but only as a kind of moral retribution.

It hurts, blood tastes in his mouth, he cannot see any longer from his right eye, his heart clenches in dread for Alice, but he knows that at last some payment is being rightly exacted.

Alice is still shouting. "Leave him alone, you vicious—"

"Outta the fuckin' way, bitch," says one of the girls. He hears a hard slap, a screech of pain. "What you doin' with that muthafuck?" another voice asks incredulously. "This no time for social calls." A crunching sound: hundreds of dollars' worth of latest-model cell phone under a bootheel. Maybe she had time to punch the emergency-link key.

"Get his wallet, Donnie."

They pull roughly at his person. That first burst of masochism is yielding to anger as the shock of passivity passes off; he starts to seethe with rage, with renewed fear for Alice, my God, in the middle of the street in a civilized city—

"Twenty bucks! You rotten miserable greedy bastards!"

So the punishment is going to be renewed. Mohammed Kasim pulls down his head, in against his chest, fingers twitching for the comfort of the bracelet. They will kick his head in, he sees in a terrible burst of sorrow. His brain will be gone by the time an ambulance gets there. There is nothing he can do. They jerk at him.

"Stick the knife in, Donnie," the girl says. Her breath is rather sweet. Metal loops swing from her pink ear. Her hair, out of focus, in again, stands now like mown hay, pink and gold in the streetlamp light. The other face comes down, and a lash of light from another kind of metal. It enters his body again and again.

1 : amanda

Automatics found us—kitted out in blackgear, grappling nets—trying drop through Maglev maintenance hangar ceiling. Had prized off solar roof panel with jemmy. Only took minute. In half-dark ten meters below, four Maglev freighters rested in bays like torpedoes. Sleek, smooth as bullets, ready go. Securing abseil line when Vik whispered, "Spotted us."

Tiny automatic patrolbot hovering in night sky. Stealthed, only just visible against Metro glow; strained eyes, could see beady little lenses, sensors glistening, poking our way.

"Passive. Nothing worry about."

"Don't be ridiculous, Amanda," Vik said. "Alerting Security. Stodes here any minute."

"Got time then. Let's slide."

"Let's not," Vik hissed. "Out of here . . ."

And was, making run for it, bounding across roof, slim dark shape in blackgear, making for steel ladder, waste ground, hoping slip out under perimeter silently as both had slipped in.

Didn't stand chance. Now knew were here, automatics would track every move, deliver update on global coordinates to Relinquishment Custodians every three microseconds. Snapped catch onto abseil line, swung clear. Plummeting. Cleanly, quickly, without effort, was dropping toward cold, dull shine of freighter beneath. Didn't stand chance either, knew that. From moment automatics locked on, both doomed, geese cooked, game over. Just thought better surrender gracefully from top freighter than collared wriggling like worm.

Feet touched curved metal, shoes gripped. Hangar still dim, empty. Stood there few beautiful seconds. Solid bulk freighter beneath feet didn't vibrate, hum. Right now quiet as tomb—but could feel supersonic power of thing. One day would ride it. Breathed deeply, extended both arms in welcoming gesture to team Stodes bursting into hangar, yelling instructions: get down, stay where are, put hands on head.

Twenty minutes later both standing in front Metro's Magistrate, Mr. Abdel-Malek, looking sheepishly at feet. Knew only matter time before olders arrived, coldly tore off horrible bleeding strips. Quite relieved when Magistrate sentenced night's detention, remanded hearing following day.

Was ever right about Maman, Maître's reaction!

"You disappoint us, Amanda," Maître said, looking more furious than disappointed. "What a remarkably stupid thing to do."

"You do know that the freighters go supersonic once they enter the main conduit?" Maman asked, in frighteningly relaxed voice. Couldn't tell if was hiding fright put into her, or genuinely unmoved. Maybe was sufficient that had interrupted routine. Both dressed in evening clothes, had been fetched to lockup in discreetly unmarked Custodian glide from opera, where no doubt sitting with gaggle nauseating heavies from tube project. Bad daughter supposedly safely tucked up at home, racting a vee in bedroom. Well, had certainly left them with clear impression, meanwhile planning sneak out back way moment they were driven off to opera house.

Said in surly voice, "Had buckynets," still looking at toe tips clad in grippo carbon sneakers. Don't know if Maman even knew buckynets safest safety device in world, made of incredibly strong, reliable carbon tubes that lock together in way makes steel seem strong as brown paper. "Had drex grapples. Weren't taking risk."

Maman made alarming snort through nose, shook head, once right, once left. Just killed me. Was so much worse than shouting, or hitting, or turning back over to Magistrate. "Speak English, Amanda," she said. "You are not a machine." Gaze shifted, then, smiled with kind of awful cool beauty. Vikram's father had entered chamber, bearing down on us. Vikram's father big man, bigger than Maître, way bigger than Maman. Know which one of them am most afraid of.

"Dr. Singh," father said, extending hand. "Not the happiest occasion."

"Dr. Kolby, Legal McAllister, good evening." Gruff, eyes dark, angry under crisp white turban. "I believe it is time to separate these penders of ours."

"That is certainly my intention," Maman told him. "Until recently my daughter has had an unblemished record." Untrue, of course, but not as if ever charged with arson or murder or mutating household pets. "I do not wish her to remain in danger of further—"

Dr. Singh rose full height, glaring down. Maman regarded him back without slightest fear, baring teeth.

"I hope you are not suggesting that my son is a. . . ."

"Not at all," said Maître hastily, tad flustered. "These are the pranks of a subadult, nothing more." Twitched eyes my direction, winked ever so slightly out line of sight other two adults. In face new threat to whole family, anger had come, gone, even disappointment at my stupidity. "I look forward to having them off our hands at Maturity."

"Well, that's as may be," Dr. Singh grumbled. "For the time being, I suggest you—" Paused, cleared throat. Maman had gone absolutely lethal, even though hadn't moved muscle. "We had best all look to our charges. Speaking of which, have formal charges been laid?"

"The penders have been bound over in custodial detention for the evening," Maître told. "No vee privileges, only hard phones. I think they'll be quite safe and comfortable. Hearing in the Magistrate's court at 2 P.M. tomorrow. Will you or Mrs. Singh be in court?"

"I have a ballistic-tube booking for Aung San Suu Kyi Metro at seven," Dr. Singh said. "My wife is in Henryk Mikolaj Gorecki polis at the moment attending a family wedding, and my pender and I were to join her in the afternoon. This little mess has ruined everything." Looked around, hailed peace officer imperiously. "So, no—

I'm afraid Vikram is going to have to face the music alone. Sir," told young night-duty officer, "I'd like my boy brought out now, if you please."

"You wish us to keep an eye on the pender during your absence?" father asked.

Dr. Singh sent look barely suppressed distaste over shoulder. "On the contrary. I intend my son to have no further dealings with any member of your family. Good evening to you both." Swept off toward holding area.

In quiet, pleasant voice, Maman told me, "You stupid, stupid person. Do you see what you've done?" She took Maître's arm, turned him toward exit desk. "Stew in your own juice, Amanda. And don't expect any privileges for at least three months, once they let you come home. Thank God you'll be Thirty soon and out of our hair at long last."

2 : mathewmark

Old man Grout kicked up a splendid fuss when the Metro tunneled under our valley. In kirk, he prayed like a madman, yelling to the Lord his God. Yelling to every god in the Valley, in fact, although some of them are goddesses or Gaia Herself, and a few of them are even stranger gods than that. We're all believers, in the Valley, one way or another. Although, secretly, some of us believe that our neighbors believe a bit too much.

Old man Grout was something to see, something to hear. His wild white hair stood on end. It must have been the divine activity in his brain. Old man Grout gave the God of his Choice orders in a booming voice: strike down the works of polluters, pour boiling oil on the tunnelers, send plagues, send scorpions, send the hounds of hell.

We got the message all right, sitting there in kirk, trying not to giggle. But it was a bit hard to tell if old Grout's God got the message. And there was no way of knowing if the tunnelers got the message. Maybe they were drowning in boiling oil down there right now, leaping about like scalded cats, scratching at their hideous rashes, fending off the hounds from hell in the darkness of their infernal world. There was no way of knowing because the tunnel started fifty kilometers from our valley and it finished on the coast, thousands of kilometers in the other direction.

We never leave our Valley. The only way you could know the tunnelers were down below us was to lie on the ground with your ear pressed hard against a rock. Then you heard them—faintly. You heard their machines, you heard noises like mice in a granary. Sometimes you heard the distant rumble of explosives.

Old man Grout was furious. He'd stand in the yard of the kirk of the God of his Choice and wave his great Bible in his hand.

"The Lord will not condone this wickedness," I heard him thunder one Wednesday morning, the sacred day of his sect. "Hearken to the word of revelation!" His yellow old beard was getting spittle-flecked. "Attend to the voice of the Psalmist, for it is said in Psalm 20, verse, um, er, seven: 'Some boast of chariots, and some of horses; but we boast of the name of the LORD our God.' Do you see, those who have eyes to see and ears to hear? The chariots of Man may thunder their way at no more than the speed of a harnessed horse, no faster, for list to the Psalmist: 'They will collapse and fall; but we shall rise and stand upright.'"

There wasn't much to be said to gainsay that, it seemed to me, but on the other hand the argument wasn't *absolutely* convincing. After all, in the days of the Hebrew prophets they didn't even *have* tunnels deep in the bowels of the earth—unless there were some driven by fiends. Yet more sacred arguments were pronounced by other prophets, though, which convinced the rest of the Valley. Old man Legrand stood in his own righteous kirk's yard and quoted from the same Bible.

"It saith in the Book of Isaiah the Prophet, chapter 35, verses eight and nine: 'A highway shall be there, and it shall be called the Holy Way; the unclean shall not pass over it, and fools shall not err therein!' The unclean polluters shall not pass over it, and by the God of our Choice the polluters shall not pass *under* it, either!'"

All this talk of Holy Ways and chariots and horses gave me a powerful interest in the subject, I have to admit. I found myself dreaming of the old automobile in the Museum that used to be driven to mock the wicked at Halloween, and wondered if it could go faster than a running horse back in the days when we still had a supply of gasoline fuel in the Valley.

"Yea verily I tell you," old man Legrand was fuming, "in the vile days of the last century, men of wicked ways did have mighty engines of two thousand horsepower under the bonnet, fueled with the black oil of Egypt. But hear what Isaiah says in chapter 36 about that: 'I will give you two thousand horses, if you are able on your part to set riders upon them. How then can you repulse a single captain among the least of my master's servants, when you rely on Egypt for chariots and horsemen? The Lord said to me, go up against this land and destroy it.'" There were moans aplenty, believe me, and many good folk made the sign o'god and bowed their heads in terror.

I never really understood why the tunnel authority even bothered to ask the Valley Elders for permission to build their underground tunnel. They could have gone ahead and built the thing without telling anyone—nobody would have twigged. If any had heard the sound like mice in the granary, they'd have thought it was just that: little rodents, scratching about in their burrows, putting aside stolen grain for the winter. As it was, the tunnelers formally asked for permission, and then, when the Assembly of Elders split into warring factions and couldn't come to a collective decision, they made a secret deal with one of the factions and went ahead with the project anyway. I didn't know that at the time, of course, none of us did. It would have been a mighty scandal. If you ask me, though, there never was any real choice—the tunnelers were just going through the motions. I reckon their city-slicker lawyers had told them to cover their backsides—consult with the rural community's representatives, and the fewer the better.

Eventually old man Grout was spending half the day lying on the ground. Once, to my shock, I saw his mule grazing unattended and eating the wheat, and went in to tether the beast myself. Ear pressed against the earth, old man Grout listened to the sounds of depravity and corruption. Then he'd be up on his knees, yelling curses into the soil, shouting so loud you thought maybe the tunnelers actually could hear him. A moment later he'd be standing up, his head thrown back, yelling at the God of his Choice.

One day I was driving our cart past his wheat patch. Ebeeneezer, our mule, is plodding along and suddenly he stops. There's old man Grout's mule just wandering about, blocking the track and there's Grout in the far corner of the patch. Only this time he's not prone on the ground, he's not listening, he's digging. He's digging like a madman. He's digging with a crowbar and shovel. The hole is a meter deep, all you can see is old man Grout's top half, throwing dirt up into the air like a volcano. I got down off our cart and left it standing in the track. Ebeeneezer was standing nose to nose with old man Grout's mule, as they talked to each other in their mulish way. I walked over to the old fellow, dodging a few clods of flying dirt. At the edge of his hole I said, "They're bound to be hundreds of meters down, Uncle. You'll never reach them."

"God gave me muscles to dig with, boy," said old man Grout. "And what God gives, God wants used. He don't abide no slacking. I'll get there. I'll break through the roof of their godless tunnel and the glory of the Lord's wrath shall pour down like as unto the waters of Babylon, yea and the angel of the Lord shall not rest until the wicked. . . ."

Old man Grout raved on, leaning on his shovel, staring up at me like some wild beast fallen into a trap. When I could get a word in, I said, "Another meter down and you're going to hit solid rock, Uncle. It will be rock all the way."

"Cleft for me!" yelled old man Grout into the hole. "Rock of ages! God helps those who help themselves. You need faith, sir, faith. If I get the thing started, the Almighty will pitch in too. The pair of us are unstoppable. Me and the Lord, we'll get there, we'll smite the heathen tunnelers, we'll smite them good!"

I left him to it. I climbed back onto our cart and went down the track to the McWeezles' place. I helped Auntie McWeezle load half a dozen sacks of turnips onto the back of the cart, and then she asked me in for scones and buttermilk. As I was drinking the buttermilk I said, "Old man Grout's digging down to the tunnel. Him and the Lord are going to smite the tunnelers."

"Lady, I can hear him now, Mathewmark," Auntie McWeezle said with a smile. "Uncle Grout walks in the eyes of the Lady, but if there's smiting to do, I reckon Grout and his God would be the ones to do it."

"He told me himself," I said. "He's going to dig the first couple of meters all on his own, and then the Lord is going to lend a hand, do a bit of clefting."

"Well, the Lady just might, Mathewmark," Auntie McWeezle said, passing me another scone. "Faith moves mountains."

"I don't know that it digs shafts," I said. "That tunnel is surely a hundred meters down, if not farther."

"And a wicked, Gaia-hating thing it is," Auntie McWeezle said.

"It won't worry us," I said. "We won't even know it's there."

"Don't tell me those trains won't carry no polluters and gene-twisters," Auntie said. "Them trains will carry gamblers, idolaters, moneylenders, fornicators, blasphemers, eaters of unclean foods, mockers of the word of the Goddess, and every kind of wickedness. The ground we walk on will be the roof of hell. The crops will wither. Strange mutant apples will turn to wormwood in the mouths of Goddess-fearing folk. . . ."

"You sound like old man Grout," I said.

"Uncle Grout may get a bit carried away at Sacred Service," Auntie admitted.

"He may get carried away in his hole," I said. "Carried away by the grim reaper. It looks to me like he's working on a heart attack, the way he was digging this morning."

Auntie McWeezle made the sign o'god in the air with her index finger. She's a good old soul, Auntie McW. Many's the time, when I've wanted someone to talk to, when I've wanted to get away from my parents and my kid brother, or yearned hopelessly for my sweetheart—many's the time I've run to Auntie McWeezle's kitchen for sympathy and buttermilk.

"Don't say such a thing, Mathewmark," Auntie said now. "Don't tempt fate."

"It's old man Grout who's tempting fate," I said. "I'll bet you he's dead before harvesttime."

Auntie McWeezle shooed me out of the house. I climbed up on the cart and turned Ebeeneezer in the direction of our Village and spent the rest of the day fetching and carrying for the good people of the Valley. It was almost night when I turned for home and let Ebeeneezer have his head, he knew the way better than I did. Passing old man Grout's wheat patch I noticed the last of the sun's rays glinting on his spade, tossed out of the hole and left to lie where it had fallen. Old man Grout's mule was milling around, trampling the wheat. I jumped down from the cart and told Ebeeneezer to continue on home by himself.

"Yeth, thir," he said, and ambled off.

I walked over to the hole. I knew exactly what I would find.

seed origin ii: ice

The young paramedic glanced up into the shadowed face of his colleague. A few unshaved whiskers glinted on the older man's cheek. "We can give the siren a rest, Hools. This one's dead as a mackerel."

Julio Mendez frowned, jerked his head briefly in the direction of the gray-haired woman, seated on a plastic chair someone had fetched for her, speaking quietly with a cop. In the spinning light from atop the ambulance her face was ghastly. A bruise was coming up above one high cheekbone. "The wife. Refused a sedative. Keep it down, buddy." As he moved the limp body, a spear of brightness flashed at the dead man's wattled throat. Another at his left wrist. "What's that?"

"Doesn't matter much now, does it? Medical indications, I guess—epileptic, diabetic, whatever—"

Mendez pushed him aside, crouched. He wiped blood away from the bracelet, then the one at the dead man's neck. Both tags showed the same message. On the front of the chromed bracelet, in red block letters beside a hexagonal icon holding the entwined snakes of the caduceus, he read:

MED. HX. CALL 24 HRS.
800-367-2228 OR
COLLECT 480-922-9013
IN CASE/DEATH SEE REVERSE
FOR BIOSTASIS PROTOCOL.
REWARD A-2167

On the back were more immediate instructions:

CALL NOW FOR INSTRUCTIONS
PUSH 50,000 U HEPARIN IV
AND DO CPR WHILE COOLING
WITH ICE TO 10C. KEEP PH 7.5
NO AUTOPSY OR EMBALMING

"Hey, Hools, it's one o' them Freezer Geezers."

Mendez looked up, blinking slowly.

"I saw it on *60 Minutes*, man. They cut their heads off after they die, and freeze—"

"I know what they do, you jackass. His wife is listening. Be quiet now."

"Oh. Yeah, sorry."

A hard, brittle voice said, "Young man, have you called that 800 number yet? You do have a phone, I assume? They smashed mine."

"Uh, sure, yes, ma'am, I have a—"

"There's not a minute to lose, goddamn it. Why haven't you packed my husband's head in ice? Do you carry crushed ice in your ambulance? One of you should be doing cardiopulmonary resuscitation."

Julio Mendez, slightly nettled, regarded her in silence. The younger paramedic said, "Uh, I'm sorry, lady, that's outside our jurisdiction now. The law says we have to take the, uh, deceased to hospital for certification of death." He glanced at his colleague. "That's right, isn't it, Hools?"

"I'm afraid so, ma'am. Here, sit down, you must be feeling rather—"

"Gentlemen, understand this." The dead man's wife stared at them with cold rage, her face lashed by the yellow flashes from the roof of the open ambulance. "I know my husband is dead according to current medical standards. There's a small chance that he can be restored to life."

The dead man, with his ugly fatal injuries, was clearly beyond all hope of intervention. "I'm sorry, there's no heartbeat or respiration, ma'am, so I'm afraid that's out of—"

"Not now, some time in the future. Listen to me. That will only happen if the appropriate treatment is started *right this instant, goddamn it!*"

Uncomfortable, the older man said: "Please, ma'am, we—"

She was small and thin, and seemed to tower over them.

"I said *listen to me.* Call that 800 number. When the cryotransport team arrives, my husband's body will be prepared for vitrification and cryostasis at minus 140 degrees Celsius. Any delay now, prior to cooling and washout, will cause irreversible loss of brain tissue." Her voice broke on the last word.

The younger man said, "Man, they'll either kick our ass out or put us on *60 Minutes.*"

Mendez nodded. "Or both. Think there's some ice in storage. Okay, get the gurney over here." He tore open the dead man's shirt and began pressing on his chest.

In holding cell until two in afternoon, felt usual blend of anger and sinking, stomach-chewing loss. Why such a disappointment to olders? Anyway, why care? All ever think about is themselves, damned immortal careers, climbing social ladder. Dr. Singh, wife rather higher up social hierarchy than family had yet managed to reach, even if Maman was Legal for one of major new subsurface construction projects. Singhs stockholders, not mere functionaries. Had really blown it. Well, both blew it together, but Vikram was golden pender so didn't suppose would suffer any long-term consequences. Damn-all chance *he'd* have vee access cut off for whole night. Good grief, what to do? Stare at ceiling of cell? Scribble on walls? Read *book*?

Was depressing, truly boring way to spend night. Amused self with compactification of *n*-manifold classes, fiddling as usual with Cohn-Vossen inequality. Got frustrated and nowhere. Next day in court was worse. Mr. Abdel-Malek, principal Magistrate for van Gogh Metropolis enclave, is very calm gentleman with soft, sinister tone to voice. Heard society ladies find quite sexy, in right context. Plainly have never heard him speaking to miscreant who threatened freighter system by attempting tie webbed subadult body to Maglev train ready to thunder through new Metro-to-coast tube at speed sound. Actually, dispute anyone, anything in danger. Did extensive sims airflow, vector changes, stresses we'd experience in protective webbing, all that. Piece cake. Well, not really piece cake, or wouldn't be worth doing. But nothing lethal. Just really, really glumpzoid. Would be talk of Mall. Be Mall gods.

Or would have been, if we'd got that far. As was, everything came unstuck, unraveled when entered loading hangars. Baffling. Spent much of night unable sleep, staring at blank ceiling, wondering about this. Had to be another way in to tube, somewhere automatics weren't watching every square micrometer.

Standing next to head-hanging Vikram Singh, watching Mr. Abdel-Malek enter adjudication room, take his place behind large, plain desk top, jolt went through me. Wasn't fright, although was certainly worried that adults had got together, devised some awful punishment, like forbidding visit Mall until we turned Thirty. Two more years, seven hundred days social death. Nearly three for Vik. Better should cut heads off, freeze us down, be done with it. No, what sent electric spark through bones was moment of truth. Knew how to get in to ride freighter!

Hissed: "Vik."

"Not now, Mand," muttered back. Was avoiding my eyes. His Maître must have torn strip off.

"Listen, just thought of—"

"All be seated," auto voice told us. Mr. Abdel-Malek had already lowered elegantly trousered backside onto ergonomic support, was accessing summary of crimes, misdemeanors—could tell by way eyes were slightly raised, directed at ceiling, sure sign was downloading compressed data file. After moment, glanced back down, looked at us both. Quailed despite self.

"You know why you're here," told us. No time-wasting formalities for Magistrate. "You have had sixteen hours in detention to consider the gravity of your offense. Do you have anything to say in mitigation?"

Neither spoke.

"Amanda?"

"Uh, sir, was really no danger, you know, had taken every—"

His voice was soft, calm, sent shudder through me. "I do not wish to listen to your self-serving excuses and rationalizations, Pender Kolby-McAllister, nor do I find cant amusing; speak English during this hearing. I have read your confession of fault. You clearly understand the seriousness of what you tried to do. Is there anything you would care to add that might explain what you and this young man did? I am not interested in hearing you attempt to duck your responsibility."

Just youthful high spirits. Blame it on retrofit hormone plateau. Were bored shitless, what's *wrong* with you people? Of course didn't say any of that, not completely self-destructive, rumors to contrary notwithstanding.

"No, sir. Very—I'm very sorry."

"Vikram Singh, anything to add? I see that your previous record is not quite so murky as that of your codefendant."

"I'm also very sorry, sir," Vik told, sounded as if meant. Guy altogether too law-abiding by nature, ask me. Was burning with eagerness tell great new idea, terrific way could sidestep automatics after all, get on freighters for major fun run through depths.

Magistrate sighed, steepled fingers. "Both of you are on the verge of Maturity, so I will not speak to you as if you were still children. You know right from wrong, lawful from lawless, sensible from recklessly stupid. You plainly both knew that what you attempted would be dangerous both to yourselves and to the safe operation of a very expensive transportation system. Ms. Kolby-McAllister, you are especially culpable in this regard, since your mother is closely involved in the Maglev project and she testifies that you gained access to the project by cracking her encrypted data files. Let me make this more pointed: it is a disgraceful use of your undoubted mathematical abilities, *Dr.* Kolby-McAllister."

Looked from me, Vikram, back. Felt little bit sick with anxiety. Nasty shot about math doctorate—most smart penders near Maturity have equal standing, so what. Vik wore floppy doctoral hat when eighteen or so. Picky and spiteful. Had felt same sick sinking while entering hangars, webbed with carbon-fiber nets, ready, poised grapple to freighter would scream at speed of sound through tunnel bored into rock under earth. Other words, be honest, was half-buzzed, toey. While was scared what Magistrate might do, privileges might decide to deny, kind of getting off on at same time. Maybe one reason criminals never change spots unless psychs go in, rewire affect systems.

"For one month," Mr. Abdel-Malek declared in same soft, distinct tone, "both of you will have your phone links removed. You will remain within your olders' quarters after the hour of five in the afternoon and until you leave for Play or authorized expertise outing in the morning. You will not enter or attempt to enter the property of the Maglev Freighter Corporation, or any of its subsidiaries, and the security systems of their hangar complex will be permitted to list you as registered offenders until the day of your Maturity, from which point criminal penalties will attend any further infractions. Do you understand me?"

Mumbled, "Yes, sir."

"Speak up clearly, Amanda," Mr. Abdel-Malek said. "Say it with some conviction."

Suspect was intentional pun in last word. Heart accelerated, nodded emphatically.

"Yes, sir, I do understand. No further entry into the Maglev hangars. Give you solemn word on that." Was okay, had better way in.

"Very well. You are released into the custody of your parents, Ms. Kolby-McAllister. Mr. Singh, you will remain in detention until one of your parents returns from business and collects you. Next case."

Maître was waiting outside, Vikram was led off to side room, so didn't have chance to tell my great new idea. Besides, probably wasn't right psychological moment. But knew that once had chance to talk that boy into it, would wind him around little finger. Get to ride rods without going anywhere near hangars.

See, had remembered something from legal case Maman had been tied up with, on, off, since I was twenty-three or so. Loonies of God's Valley. And vent shaft corp had just punched up through two hundred meters of rock.

Now only had to find some way into most ferociously independent, paranoid territory left in country, maybe entire world, work out way to override vent shaft safety codes. Pity they'd cut off message implant. Would have phoned Vik right away, told great plan. Would be dread. Megadread. Would be Mall gods after all.

There was a terrible irony about the hole that killed old man Grout, but we didn't know that until a week after his funeral. The tunnelers needed an air shaft, which had been negotiated during the endless legal battles at the Gatehouse. They had been clawing their way up toward the surface, their machines grinding away, letting the broken rock fall to the tunnel below to be carried away to the coast. The air shaft came up out of the earth less than a meter from old man Grout's hole, so he hadn't been so crazy when he said he could hear them at their polluters' work. If he'd lived he would have met them on his way down. Him and his punishing Lord, and Mother Gaia, and all the other Gods of our Choice.

seed origin iii: sleep

For Mohammed Kasim Abdel-Malek, time has all but stopped. Unlike nearly all the other dead in the history of the world, however, his clock is merely stilled; it has not been shattered into useless cogs and springs and fragments of glass. For Abdel-Malek, and the world, time changes.

It passes more swiftly for the world.

Some things change. Some things remain the same. Overall, perhaps more things change than remain the same. The principle of exchange through an imaginary but tactile medium of equivalence, money, morphs and finally evaporates into flows of information and strategic calculation beyond human understanding. Slowly at first, and then in a rush, machines do nearly everything toilsome, even if the world has relinquished nano-technology and its Promethean promise. Micromachines are cheap, repair and copy themselves under instruction but not from any urge or capacity to reproduce, never go on strike, and are a safe thousand times larger than nanodevices. If at last their owners have no great use for money, since everything consumable is effectively free, they certainly do not lack for plenty. Mastery of death itself seems close within their grasp, yet care-fully held at bay out of decent caution. They have plenty of time for sen-timent. They welcome art and they praise science even as they throttle back its terrifying acceleration. As flowers once were piled in profusion upon the graves of great scholars, soldiers, leaders, now a more positive ritual becomes customary. The promise of immortality is honored in the care some of them lavish on the cryonics mausoleums. Many of the worthy dead go to their suspended life, resting head down in their frigid Dewars.

The vitrified dead do not eat or drink. But they, too, sleep magnificently.

For a while. But some things change. Some things change very quickly indeed.

5 : amanda

Maman grounded me after trial tube burn, Vikram's parents did same. Really annoying. Could flick eyes up to left much as liked, trying toggle phone implant on, but damned thing dead as doornail. So was phone uplink on note-page, not mention vee access. Could use monitored Joyous hard phone downstairs call out, take incoming, could e anyone in world while NannyWatch listened in like robotic pest, could go down Mall, hang with friends—if stayed inside burb bounds, came straight home by dinnertime.

Whined: "Vik's best friend, Maman. Is cruel, unnatural punish-ment." Kept on in this vein until sick sound of own. Eventually, with patented extremely bored glance, she looked up from legal monitor.

Preparing some brief for Metro-to-coast Deep Maglev rail consortium. She, Maître, had battled bigots of God's Valley last four, half years, trying establish corporation's right tunnel under loonies' machine-free utopia. Funny, really, in gruesome way, because if parent hadn't been so devoted to particular law case, would never have got cool idea riding rods underground tubes.

Which was, felt modestly, one of truly great ideas of life.

"Amanda, darling," Maman said in bright, chilly voice, "do you really want me to switch off your speech centers?"

Opened mouth again, ready with hot, angry answer, then shut, swallowed hard. Had done that to me once before; was about ten, unbearable. Speechless whole day. Talk about cruel, unnatural! Stand there getting red in face, moving mouth, flapping tongue, nothing happens in throat because brain short-circuited. Know what want say, or think do, but nothing comes out. Infuriating! Tried get back by grabbing spraygel, marking spiteful graffiti messages all over living-room vidwall, but somehow couldn't force arm make bright blue, red squiggles into words. Only managed cover wall display, self with blobs luminous gel. Felt like tongue-tied baby, ended up running into room, squeezing door, howling eyes out.

So knew what was threatening. Worse, knew meant every word.

Swallowed again, hard.

"No."

"No, what, Amanda?"

No point arguing. No point demanding fair just rights as senior pender. No sense doing anything except knuckle under, wait next twenty-three months, seventeen days to creep past one day at a time until legally adult of Thirty, could kick off out of creep hole, maybe set up flop with Vikram, other cool guyz.

"No, Maman, don't want to force you and Maître into imposing any more penalties for own good."

"Fine. Now, darling, I still have rather a lot of work to finish before the council meeting this afternoon, so why don't you go to your room and practice your violin?"

Stomped off to soundproof room, sawed way through Mozart divertimento. Worked for while on generalized Paneitz 4th order operator in relation to zeta-functional determinant, associated nonlinear equations. Didn't divert for long. Wondered if could trap a bee-ad, send message to Vikram. Mood was in, might as well both break curfew, try test other way hitch supersonic ride through bowels of earth.

One benefit having olds contracted handle legal tangles of Metro Maglev deep rail project. Had cracked household Lawman program, downloaded zillion pages AI jargon, engineering plans, then used couple smart ferrets plow through data, found that new way into tunnels.

6 : mathewmark

The good people of the Valley weren't too thrilled about the ventilation shaft. It appeared overnight. It was only a day or two after we'd filled in old man Grout's hole that we awoke to find a conspicuous metallic column sticking out of the ground in almost exactly the same place. It was about a meter and a half in diameter and, say, four meters high. Not steel but some kind of polluters' invented stuff. Painted green, but the paint wouldn't chip off. Cut into the side at ground level, in luminous red, were the words *Metro Polis System Maglev Deep Rail Authority, Ventilation shaft 26B.* And then, in yellow, *It would be very much in your own interests not to enter or drop anything down this shaft.* We don't have very many warning notices in the Valley, but when we do, we write things like *Repent!; Keep Out; Light no Fires; Danger!* Just simple, plain language that tells people what they need to know. There was something really menacing about the long-winded, mild-mannered drivel about our own interests.

Me and Momma and Dad and my brother, Lukenjon, were among the first to see the thing sticking up out of the ground in the early-morning light. We walked down the hill to old man Grout's patch and just stood and looked. We were soon joined by our near neighbors and then others from farther afield. We don't have telephones or other works of the devil in the Valley, but news travels fast. Very fast indeed, faster than a man can run, faster than a mule can gallop—faster even than a horse can go. My dad sometimes says that the speed at which news travels is the strongest argument there is for the existence of God. He's only half-joking. Frankly, I don't know what other arguments there are—in the Valley we don't argue about the existence of the God of our Choice, we know he, she, or it exists. Full stop.

When there were about three dozen people and a dozen mules standing in a circle around the ventilation shaft, old biddy Smeeth picked up a broken harrow tooth and walked right up to the thing. She swung the harrow tooth in an arc, smashing it into the side of the column. Clang. It was hollow. We were left in no doubt about that. And it extended deep into the ground. We could hear the reverberations, almost feel them through our feet. We looked up at the top of the column, a dark exclamation mark against the blue sky. The stuff about our "own interests" seemed a bit silly as well as menacing. You couldn't "drop" anything down the shaft, you'd be pushing it to climb to the top without a ladder, giving each other a leg up.

Old biddy Smeeth turned round and addressed the rest of us. "This is an abomination in the eyes of Kali, it is an outhouse vent in the temple of the gods. We must cast it out!"

"How?" I said.

"How?" old biddy Smeeth said, "How? Mathewmark. Are you so lacking in wisdom that you needs must ask how?"

Old biddy Smeeth has never been my favorite neighbor. She's always finding fault, always letting you know that she personally finds considerably more favor in the eyes of Kali than you do. Still, it doesn't do to talk back to an Elder, not in front of a gathering.

"I only seek your wisdom, Auntie Smeeth," I said.

"Pray!" cried old biddy Smeeth. "Everybody pray!"

There was a bit of foot shuffling. A couple of people found they had urgent things to do to the harness of their mules. But old biddy Smeeth would not be denied.

"Let us pray, brothers and sisters," she cried. "Let us pray to the God of our Choice that this abomination be blasted from the surface of the earth. Let the might of Kali drive it back down into the infernal regions from which it sprang!"

Old biddy Smeeth fell to her knees in the trampled wheat patch. She raised two hands to the heavens and closed her eyes. Then she opened them again for a quick look around to see if everybody else was joining her. She cried to the Goddess. People started kneeling, some more quickly than others. More and more voices joined in prayer. There was no coherence, voice battled with voice. Beside me Lukenjon was on his knees, getting into the spirit of the thing, yelling something about Tower of Babel, tower of sin, tower of outrage, tower of tin. Lukenjon is much more pious than I am, but he also writes lots of crappy poetry, real doggerel. Sometimes his devotion to the Lord and his soppy versifying get a bit mixed up.

I must admit I was about the last person to get down on my knees. But I did. And I prayed. I didn't pray out loud, I just had a quiet word with the Lord. Actually, if the Lord could hear me above the voices of all the rest, then I reckon that's another powerful argument for the existence of God. Although, I suppose, the argument is circular or something. A lot of truths about the Lord are a bit circular when you come to think about it. Anyway, what I said to the Lord was: you do what you think right, Lord. Ignore old biddy Smeeth if she's on the wrong track.

Then, not suddenly, but slowly, a slow moan rose above the sound of prayer. It was a deep, rolling, sighing, mournful sound. And it came from the heavens above. It grew louder. Many people fell silent. One or two fainted. "Kali the destroyer is made manifest!" old biddy Smeeth cried. "She is amongst us!" You could tell she was taking the credit.

In our Valley the gods or goddesses manifest fairly often, they're part of our lives, working the odd miracle or two. But this moaning, sighing sound was something new. Beside me Lukenjon was hard at it. "Voice of the Lord. Voice of the sword! Sword of the tin-slayer! Slice it up, Lord, layer by layer!"

"Shut up, Luken," I said quietly. "I want to hear this thing."

It didn't take long for me to work out where the sound was coming from. It was coming out of the mouth of the ventilation shaft several meters above our heads. It was the moaning of wind rushing out of a pipe. Any number of musical instruments work that way. The shaft was just a huge tin whistle. Once I'd worked that out, I also knew what was forcing the air out of the shaft: there was a train down there, bowling along toward us, pushing the air in front of it. Old biddy Smeeth had got it terribly wrong, we weren't listening to the voice of Kali or any other god. If anything, we were listening to the voice of the devil.

The next day there was a meeting of Elders at the temple. I wasn't there, of course, but Momma and Dad were. Apparently old biddy Smeeth and a few of her mates couldn't be convinced that they hadn't heard the voice of God. The Smeeth group claimed the moaning was a sign that divine punishment was going to strike down the ventilation shaft at Kali's earliest convenience. Someone asked why it hadn't already been struck down—the thing had been there for at least thirty-six hours. Old biddy Smeeth said she wasn't listening to such blasphemy and mentioned working in mysterious ways. The God of our Choice would get around to striking the thing down in his or her own good time and it wasn't for mere mortals to call the sacred timetable into question. Old biddy Smeeth knew this, because Kali had told her. The more important debate at the meeting of Elders concerned the question of permission.

The people of the Valley don't have much contact with the outside world. Outsiders aren't allowed in through the Gatehouse at the Valley entrance. And the good people of the Valley never leave. Or if they do, they leave and never come back. But sometimes it is necessary for the Elders to engage in business with Outsiders, and they hold a meeting in the Gatehouse. Those Elders chosen to bargain with the Outsiders enter the Gatehouse through the Valley door and sit on one side of a wide table. The Outsiders enter the Gatehouse by the Door of the Damned and sit on the other side of the table.

That's as close as anybody from the Valley gets to the outside world. Recently, rumor said, there had been quite a few meetings in the Gatehouse. The lawyers for the Maglev Rail Authority and Freighter Corporation had wanted to speak to certain Elders. And certain Elders, it turned out, had struck certain deals.

Ructions! There hadn't been such turmoil in the Valley since the great pan-krishna-rainbow serpent dustup. That was way before I was born, of course. But there were still some ancient Elders around who could remember those days. The reason our religion is so strong is that it incorporates all the truths known to all the little itsy-bitsy religions like Christianity and Judaism and Buddhism and Islam and so forth. We've got the lot. Or rather we've got bits and pieces of the lot. And sometimes you get disputes about what to put in and what to leave out. That happened back in the days of the pan-krishna-rainbow serpent dispute. Families were torn asunder. Wife (or wives) wouldn't speak to husband. Brother wouldn't speak to sister. An alternative temple was built right across the track from the Great Temple itself. The two congregations used to praise the Lord at the tops of their voices, trying to drown each other out. After a really good Sunday or Wednesday of scripture-dueling hardly anybody in the Valley could speak, their vocal cords were so shot. It all died down in the end, of course, the dispute was using up too much energy, the crops were starting to fail. Finally, the Alternative Temple was hit by a lightning bolt. That did it, a sign from on high. But while life might have returned to normal, people still talk of those days, even though hardly anyone is old enough to remember them in person.

And now it was happening all over again, only this time the Valley was split on the question of permission. Why had the bargaining Elders told the Maglev people they could put their ventilation shaft in our Valley? What secret deals had been done? It must have been the devil himself who scrambled the Elders' minds. Or so it was said. But it was also said that liar bees had been seen in the Valley. I've always tried to keep an open mind on the question of liar bees. Some people think they are real, think they are all over the place, buzzing around the fields, hiding in the woods, perching on the cradles of newborn infants the better to corrupt their innocent little minds.

Auntie McWeezle reckons they exist. She's seen them, she's heard them.

"They are as real as you are, Mathewmark," she said when I brought up the subject. "There's all sorts of wickedness in the Outside. And wickedness can't abide goodness and peace. The wicked know our Valley is steeped in innocence, and it riles them. They plot and scheme, the wicked. And the liar bees are their agents. They come in on the north wind. Like a plague of locusts. Moral locusts!"

"Come on, Auntie," I said. "Why would anybody on the Outside want to send funny little talking insects into our Valley? How would it profit them?"

"Wickedness is its own reward," Auntie said, and poured me more buttermilk. "Besides, the Valley is prime real estate."

"Real estate?" I said. "No one from the Outside can buy real estate in our Valley. It's forbidden."

"And while the good people of the Valley remain stout of heart and pure of spirit it will remain forbidden, Mathewmark."

"Well, there you are," I said.

"But if the moral contagion gets a grip," Auntie said, "then all will be lost, the Law will wither and die, and people will be so depraved that they'll barter their heritage for the pleasures of the fleshpots."

"And this is what the bees are telling people?" I said.

"Indeed it is, Mathewmark. The liar bees have been whispering in the Elders' ears. Offering sweet blandishments. How else do you explain the granting of permission?"

You can never tell with Auntie McWeezle. Sometimes I think she believes everything she tells you, and sometimes I think she exaggerates for the pleasure of it. She's as old as the hills and her face is lined with wrinkles and she hardly has any teeth, but her eyes sparkle sometimes, and they were sparkling now. Maybe because she was pulling my leg. Maybe because she really believed the liar bees were buzzing around us, looking for our weaknesses. I still had half a dozen loads to fetch and carry, so I thanked Auntie for her buttermilk and set off on the cart.

The devil tempted me, I confess it freely. Auntie's words niggled at the back of my mind as I made my deliveries. I'd never seen a liar bee, and neither had any of the other young people I knew. Jed Cooper was a couple of years older than I, and he'd been a bit of a hell-tearer, I'd heard tell. So as we lugged a load of corn together I decided to put the question to him.

He guffawed in my face. He laughed so hard he sprayed spit. I wiped it off my face with a sleeve and scowled.

"Don't believe ever'thing you hear, young Mathewmark," he said finally, shouldering the sack he'd dropped in his hilarity.

"Never said I believed it," I grunted.

He squeezed one eye shut and tapped his nose knowingly.

"It's the demon dogs you need to worry about," he told me. "They'll come down in the night and bear you off to hell's teeth for a chewing." Then he was chortling again at his own wit. He might be older than I, but I'm bigger, from all the lifting and toting, and I had a moment there when I wanted to clock him one. Lay him out on the ground. But that's wickedness, too, fighting with your neighbors. I just scowled and fell silent.

Jed wasn't finished with me, though. Just before I jumped back up on the cart he came close and leaned into my ear.

"If'n you really want to hear the whispering naughty promises of the liar bee," he said, his sour breath in my nostrils, "you have to invite them down politely. Call them to you, young Mathewmark."

"What do you mean?" I said, jerking away. "Why would you need to call the Tempter? He's supposed to call you."

"Nope, it's the rules of hell. They can't come into the Valley unless you invite them."

I cleared my throat in disgust and spat into the gnawed grass where Ebeeneezer had been chewing it. "You don't know anything, Jed. Everyone'll tell you it's vampires and the walking dead you have to invite past your door."

"Suit yourself," he said, and rolled the last barrel toward his store. "See you next week."

I rode away chewing my lip. He could have invited *me* in for a bite of lunch and a cool draft of springwater, but we were both too annoyed with each other. Well, Jed probably wasn't annoyed. He'd be tickled pink at the way he'd pulled my leg and got a rise out of me. I let my good old mule Ebeeneezer take us out of the yard and down the dirt track, teased by the ridiculous doubt that maybe Jed was right after all. After all he *was* older than me, although he wasn't yet married, and he'd seen a bit more of life. More than a bit more, if the rumors were right.

I opened my mouth, gazed up at the blue sky, thought better of it, and closed my mouth again. But nobody was within earshot. Over in a distant field two kids were bent down clearing weeds, and they waved as we passed them, but they wouldn't hear me tempt the devil. Still, I waited until we'd left them behind, then I said softly, "Show yourself, tool of Satan. Let me hear your blandishments."

Nothing happened, of course. I felt like a fool. I raised my voice and shouted in a sarcastic way, "Come down from the devil's palace, liar bees! I dare you to test my faith, for I am a man who may not be bent from the path of righteousness."

Dust puffed up from the mule's plodding hooves. The wheels turned with a squeak. No flying insect of temptation fell from the skies to put my soul in peril. It wasn't as if I'd really expected it to.

There's a patch of wooded country between Jed Cooper's place and old man Legrand's log cabin At that time of year quite a few of the tree varieties are in flower. That stretch of track was alive with insects, their hum and drone like a distant, old, familiar tune. The day was drowsy with the heat of early spring and the scent of flowers. Ebeeneezer knew where we were going. There wasn't much for me to do. I was half-asleep on the cart, the reins slack in my hands.

"You rang?" a voice said in my ear.

I woke up with a start. I looked around.

"What?"

"Thir?"

"Not you, Ebeeneezer. Did someone say something?"

"Didn't hear."

There was no one else near. I must have been dreaming. A large bee of a sort I'd never seen before buzzed once around my head and disappeared into the trees. I shivered, even though the day was warm. I told myself not to be a fool. Suggestion, that's what it was, the result of suggestion. Spend half an hour yarning with Auntie Mc-Weezle and of course you'd dream of liar bees or something similar.

"Nothing ventured, nothing gained," the voice rasped. The humming grew louder. I pulled out my big handkerchief and folded it lengthwise so I could swat the devilish thing if it tried its wiles on me again. The bee zoomed in and sat on my right shoulder.

"Hey, kid," it said in a buzzing little voice, "listen up."

I still couldn't believe my ears. Must be dreaming. "Are you addressing me?" I blurted.

"If you're the one who invited me, kiddo, and I know you are, you're the one and only. And hey, Valley boy," it said in a small, self-satisfied, irritating voice, "have I got a deal for you!"

---

7 : the abdel-malek interview.
Global Business Review, January 4, 2003 (excerpt)

Q. How will people cope if they learn they have unlimited years ahead of them, thanks to major medical advances in the control of disease, aging, and senescence?
A. Life extension is just about living healthily longer, maybe indefinitely. What people do with the extra time is up to them.

Q. Won't indefinite life span change our definition of what a person is?
A. Of course not. A person is a conscious, moral agent, or at least an individual with that capacity, even if it happens to be impaired at the moment. Why should death be written into the contract?

Q. You were originally trained as a lawyer before changing to computer cognitive science later in life. Will we need new or different legal rights or obligations for rejuvenated centenarians?
A. Only those that apply to any other healthy person: the responsi-

bility to earn their keep, by work or keen investment, and to obey the law of the land. Sooner or later, machines or tailored organisms will provide all our wants. We'll work only at jobs we choose to accept, as artists dream of doing.

Q. What if Freud's right and human beings have a death wish stronger than their hunger for life?
A. It's too soon to tell. Let's see how people at the age of two hundred feel while they retain the physical and mental vigor of an adolescent. If they all suddenly need Prozac to get through the day, I'll give your suggestion more serious attention.

Q. Won't religious impulses block uptake of the new technologies? And what about Green ethics that see humans as blighting the planet?
A. I hear there's a plan afoot to ban development of artificial intelligence under some crazy movement called the Joyous Relinquishment.

Religious impulses are remarkable for adapting to changing circumstances. Once it was wicked for women to accept anaesthesia during child delivery. The Bible said so. Environmental impacts of life extension are tricky to estimate. You're less likely to foul your own nest if you expect to be living in it.

Q. The turn of the millennium saw an upwelling of fundamentalism, terrorism, and New Age practices at the very time science was recreating the human world. Might we end up blocking anything as supposedly "unnatural" as genomic life extension and AI?
A. As I say the Joyous Relinquishment folks want to do just that.

Q. So wishful thinking could win out over obscure laboratory evidence. What could block the emergence of effective advanced technology?
A. Lack of investment, on the one hand, and political interdiction, on the other. Technically these improvements will be very difficult, but Moore's Law will keep enhancing the lab tools at an exponential rate, at least for another decade or so. Unless the Luddite loonies take over the ward.

Sacred Sanctuary of God of our Choice, Pty. Ltd. had been set up, according to legal-beagle, in 1934. Back then was just called the Coburg Valley, name homesick early German immigrants gave it before World War I. During another war in Vietnam, China, something, had been big influx young people called "hippies" or "draft excluders." Didn't want to be sent off to fight, die in some part of world long way from home. Who can blame? Had led to rise of what looked like phony religion some of these guys, their girlfriends got themselves ordained in. Now "ministers of religion;" no longer eligible packed off get shot at, bombed, suffer slings, arrows, lethal chemicals of outrageous fortune.

But like Play sociology instructor says, short step from cult to culture. Valley people experimented with faith, drugs, equal proportion, tried out "free love" (sex). Led to babies, before knew it place was turning into genuine community.

Got lots of this off such archives as remained uncorrupted after Big Data Glitch, using boring slow keyboard, display, as implant connect disabled by court. Maman's legal-beagle search agent, cracked years ago, only provided dry-as-dust records, databases, gigabytes precedents, arguments before beak about local ordinance infractions, rights or supposed rights of faithful in respect of getting asses shot off, so on, all very dull unless needed to find legal loophole in centuries accumulated judicial drivel. Did. Wanted loophole could drive couple grounded penders through. Needed to get into Valley physically, evading crusty old loony guards stood watch at pass between hills, not to mention laser-beam detectors on our side, set up to protect faithful from foul pollution modern thought.

Amazing stuff! Crackpots thought science was a curse. Not like wholesome Joyous Relinquishment, these were loony geek-haters.

Reckoned was sinful to stick phone in head. Told kids rest of world was having high old time consuming, fornicating, ignoring word of the God of their Choice. Well, fair enough. Can't say were wrong about that. Just can't see why got so worked up about it? What's wrong with a bit of consuming, fornicating, as long as get immune implants like civilized people?

Anyway, by this stage Valley community had got ingrown, weirder than shit. Wouldn't come out, we couldn't go in. I.e., could go in, of course, anytime wanted, just brush aside, but not polite. Had water-tight legal title to Valley, even if was prime mouth-watering real estate. High-powered Legals like Maman scouring sub-clauses of municipal, regional development Acts for years now, limited artificial intelligence support from likes of legal-beagle program, still couldn't budge mad old things. Only legitimate access to Valley loonies was if specifically invited you in, which they never did, or if one of them ventured outside into real world.

Or, had suddenly seen with burst of excitement, if could talk one of them into leaving of own free will. How pull off impossible trick? Couldn't get in, show everything he, she was missing. Couldn't dangle VR inside brains, send on magical mystery tour of imagination, because loonies had no sim chips in brains, poor things. Law very firmly of opinion that flying in, kidnaping one of dopes, bearing off to pleasures, enticements of outside world simply not done (Penalty: twenty-five years freezing, global credit restriction).

Ah, but nobody said don't divert bee-ad over tops of hills, through trees, whisper little come-on in ears.

Had been tested in courts, found perfectly legal—therefore hushed up at once. Only learned of it because Maman, team used method shamelessly to persuade greedy Elder come on board, grant permission drive up needful vent shaft in empty paddock.

Had sat back, stared in disbelief at display. First person tried inveigling faithful had been Sam-Sam the Roadster Man. Hired team industrial psychologists rewire entire beehive, sent in on north wind years ago when I was not yet born. Commercials spouted so completely, stupidly wrong for market that whole idea discredited for long generation. Watched stereo video feed several bugged bugs had radioed back to Sam-Sam's hired guns.

> **Bee:** *Psst.*
> **Startled believer:** Huh? Is that you sneaking around behind me, MaryLou Atkins?
> **Bee:** *Wanna buy a roadster that flies like the wind? Wanna get your mitts on a dynamite unit that tears up the way like a bat outta hell?*
> **Indignant believer:** Hell, you say? Step forth, tool of the devil and show thy grizzled features that the Lord might smite thee mightily!
> **Bee:** *Only five hundred down and two hundred a month for a limited time interval. Voice signature legally binding.*
> **Shocked believer:** Take that, minion of chaos!
> <whack whack splat>
> **Bee:** *ZZZZzzzzsssssphht*

Campaign was dud. Marketing in dark, salesmanship without preliminary focus groups, polls. Rank incompetence, stupidity. Hit Menu, tracked rest of sorry tale. Year or so later, Science Education Foundation tried same trick, bees wired for Darwinism, evolutionary psychology. (Don't ask, mathematical type, haven't gone that way in education. Something to do with how are all descended from apes. Sounds silly as what Valley loons believe, but hey, am majoring in violin, math, Mall dynamics.) Success rate not particularly improved.

> **Bee:** *Young lady, let us reason together.*
> **Terrified girl in bonnet:** Help! Help! Auntie Hazel, it's one of those demons in pleasing garments!
> **Aunt:** Slacker girl! You can't take me in so easily! Back to your sweeping!
> **Bee:** *Madame, perhaps I can interest you in a dialogue concerning the two great world systems?*
> **Aunt:** <shriek>
> **Justified girl:** See, Auntie, I told you. It's a limb of Satan. A wingèd limb.
> **Aunt:** Get the whisk, thou foolish child! Give the bugger a whack! Send it back to Hell's Teeth!
> <bang crump whine>
> **Bee:** *ZZZbuzzzsss pooffff*

And so on, year after year. Think they'd learn? Imagine people would get point? Valley loons built up whole mythology about tempting creatures of Satan, one way to look at bee-ads, fellow pests. Advertisers tired of failed campaigns to sell uplifts bras, microwave ovens to devoted retroprimitives. Government maintained low-level presence, inviting more adventurous to sample delights of big-city fun. Sometimes had a success. Mostly, lost bugs.

Best news: remains legal method for corrupting minds of loonies, but only if loonies give clear indication of interest in being contacted.

Sent in low-level artificial intelligence searcher find out if anyone had expressed interest in outside world lately. Thought more likely than not, since arrival of vent must have set off lot of talk, discussion, public dispute. Surely some bad kid with bit of spirit had said something along lines of invite. Left software agent to search all automatic monitor records from past day.

Didn't take long to track down stock of moth-balled ad buzzers, grab control tiny brains, program up few simple code controls, send pair winging off over pass.

Wanted spy in sky. Needed take in lay of land. If Vikram, I to get ride on bullet train, as intended, were going to need all info could scrape together.

Bees easy to drive, turns out. Piloted two spies into Valley on third afternoon of imprisonment in own room; luckily was non-Play Wednesday. Mapped threedee of boring fields, creeks, dirt roads, farms, smallest, dingiest town ever seen. Off to one side, sticking out of false-color imager like silver finger caught by sun, found vent shaft rising from rocky soil of empty field.

Set down one bee top of vent, let crawl about, sussing out control system. Other bee sent lofting on air currents while waited for search engine to find stooge.

<I have located an utterance that might be construed within legal limits as an invitation> program told.

<Play it>

Man's recorded voice, slightly distorted by distance from nearest monitor, called request for tool of Satan. Close enough, thought, grinning. Should stand up in court, if ever get back there, worse luck.

<Find person in real time> I instructed search engine. Machine locked into bee still had roaming around in sky.

<I have contact> AI told.

<Display visual>

Yes indeedy. Here came incredibly old-fashioned device, flat dray, huge wonky wooden wheels, pulled along by poor four-footed critter in leather harness. Guy leaning back with eyes shut, looked like, sucking on a stalk. Zoomed on down. Thick black unwashed hair, nice face, light shadow of beard. Hideous clothes, looked stitched together by hand if can believe such. His own right hand, strong, nicely shaped, holding reins loosely. Animal seemed to be driving self while master snoozed. Perfect.

Dropped bee down next to ear. Let's give system trial run.

"You rang?" had bee say.

He sat up, jolt.

Blurted: "What?"

Didn't seem finest candidate for spot of espionage, double-dealing, but didn't really have big pool candidates. "Nothing ventured, nothing gained," muttered to self, toggled bee's auto ad routine.

"Hey, kid," bee shouted at new pal, "listen up."

Sat back to see how had taken it, grinning hard enough to crack dragon stencil off my face. Decided were in. Yep, Vikram, I, surely in. Persuade dummy, persuade Vik, get out of house, into Valley, down vent. What were few simple obstacles when thrill ride of life-time awaited?

Guy swatting at me—well, at bee—with nasty-looking rag. Danced away. Would have Valley loon eating out of hand.

So they existed. I was a believer now: liar bees were out and about and doing the devil's work. It just went to show that you had to take old biddies like Auntie McWeezle seriously. They'd lived a long time, they knew a thing or two. I was wide-awake now and I was approaching old man Legrand's place with even more turmoil of the heart than usual.

Old man Legrand is Sweetcharity's grandfather. Since the dark night when her parents were carried away in the floods, beautiful Sweetcharity has lived there with him. He takes his grandfatherly responsibilities very seriously, old man Legrand. There isn't a girl in the Valley who is more closely supervised than the orphan Sweetcharity Legrand. Which makes being in love with her a bit difficult. At least I get to see her sometimes—my carting duties mean I've got a good reason to visit the cabin occasionally. Any other fellow in the Valley who just turned up on spec—and a few have—would be sent on his way pretty damn sharpish. Old man Legrand is not above waving a long-handled billhook at folks he doesn't like the look of. And it's no good going on about the fact that the God of his Choice is meant to be a pacifist. Where his granddaughter is concerned, old man Legrand is a warrior of old.

"Morning, Uncle," I said when Ebeeneezer ground to a halt outside the cabin.

"Afternoon, boy," Legrand said.

We both looked at the sun. Perhaps it was past midday, perhaps it wasn't. I didn't really care. But old man Legrand did.

"How much past, boy?" he said.

I took a guess. "Now you call my attention to it, Uncle," I said, "I reckon it's approximately in the vicinity of about half past noon at the very least."

"Five past, young Mathewmark. The Lord didn't make the Sun go round the Earth just so young slackers could reckon that things are approximately in the vicinity."

"I reckon he didn't, Uncle," I said. There was no point in arguing with Legrand, what I wanted to do was catch a glimpse of his grand-daughter. We started unloading Jed Cooper's seed corn. I surreptitiously looked around the place. The cabin door stood open, but I could see no one inside, nor hear any sound from the sheds and barns. No one was mucking out the mules' stalls, no one was planting squash or hanging out the washing. Old man Legrand had sent Sweetcharity on some errand. Or he'd sent her down to the bottom of the field, given her weeding duties among the cabbages. I wouldn't be able to exchange loving glances, brush against her accidentally when I entered the cabin doorway. Sweetcharity would have no chance to kiss me quickly on the cheek when we were suddenly hidden from view as we loaded firewood onto the cart.

Which was all right by me. Sweetcharity would find a chance to meet me on the track when I drove away.

So we unloaded the seed corn. And loaded the firewood. And old man Legrand said, "Reckon you must be thirsty after all that, young Mathewmark. Have a draft of rainwater."

"Right neighborly of you, Uncle," I said.

The Sun in its orbit round the Earth could go hang. My stomach was telling me exactly what time it was—it was lunchtime. And here was old man Legrand offering me a drink of water. Still, there was no point complaining. I took the tin mug he offered and filled it from the barrel beside the cabin door. I drank and climbed up onto the cart.

"So long, Uncle," I said.

"May the Lord ride with you," old man Legrand said, "Careful with them logs."

I drove off. Careful with them logs! What did the old skinflint think his precious firewood was—baskets of eggs? I forgot about him, it was his granddaughter who occupied my thoughts. As Ebeeneezer plodded along I scanned the track ahead. To my right were open fields of corn and barley. To my left were woods: tall, dark trees growing among thick undergrowth: lots of hiding places and small secret trails.

"Psst!"

I turned my head quickly, expecting to see Sweetcharity hidden in the foliage. But it was a liar bee, a meter distant and hovering.

"Bugger off!" I said. And then I made the sign o'god, partly to ward off the evil bee, and partly to cleanse my soul of the stain of foul language. I don't normally swear, but the bee had unnerved me.

"Pardon," said the liar bee. "Thought was meant to be free country."

"This is the Valley of the God of one's Choice—there's nothing here for you," I said. "Begone, insect of Satan!"

"Look," said the bee, "Can do deal!"

"No we can't," I said. "Hie thee off!"

"Bye bye for now," said the bee, and disappeared into the woods. I drove on, flicking the reins to encourage Ebeeneezer.

"Psst!"

I didn't turn my head.

"Psst! Mathewmark, you deaf or something?"

Sweetcharity stood well back from the track, almost completely hidden by the darkness of the woods. But I could see her smile, see the dappled light dancing on her hair. I brought Ebeeneezer to a halt and vaulted from the cart. I'd have to leave my mule and his load unattended, but there was nothing I could do about that and old Ebeeneezer had enough sense. I ran into the woods. Sweetcharity turned and ran herself, deeper into the gloom. The trail was narrow, something that might have been made by wild animals, low to the ground. I had to hold my arm in front of my face to ward off branches and brambles. Sweetcharity had disappeared. I saw the flash of her dress—a brilliant white in the gloom as she ducked behind a tree. When I located the tree, she was already behind another. I caught her behind the third. She laughed in my arms.

"Why, if it isn't young Mathewmark," she said. "What on earth brings you to this secluded spot?"

Sweetcharity was still breathing quickly from the chase. Her waist was slim in my encircling arms. Her breasts were against my chest.

"Kiss me," I said.

"What a suggestion," she said.

"Sweetcharity, don't tease," I said.

"Physical intimacy is a sacrament," she said, very prim and proper. "Any young gentleman knows that."

I put my lips to hers. We swayed together, with no more need for banter. There was a crashing sound in the undergrowth nearby. Sweetcharity sank quickly to her knees, dragging me down with her. Her eyes were startled, full of fear.

"Grandfather," she whispered. "He'll whip me."

We lay in a heap, trying to sink into the leaf mold, into the very earth itself. The sounds of Legrand crashing about in the undergrowth came closer and closer. He was casting around. He didn't know exactly where we hid, but he knew we were close by. Peering out from where we lay, through the tangle of undergrowth, I saw him, wild with rage and exertion. The whip was no figure of speech, Legrand had one in his hand. It was all coiled up, but it must have been five meters long. A bullock driver's whip, something to make the air crack over the head of the leading beast. Hell's Teeth! The man was crazed. He was wild of eye and breathing hard. And it wasn't only Sweetcharity who was at risk.

"I know thee for the lecher you are, you hell-spawn, Mathewmark!"

We were both doomed. The pair of us shrank deeper to the ground. Legrand blundered about. He hadn't seen us, but it was only a matter of time.

"Yah, yah, yah! Monkey look for peanuts!" a voice said.

"Oh, Kali-be-kind," I whispered to Sweetcharity, "the bee."

"Moth-eaten old fart! Couldn't hit flea, couldn't hit me!"

"You, hell-fiend!" yelled Legrand. "Show thy scurvy visage!" And he commenced smiting, flailing around with his whip. The thing was too long. Far too long. It wrapped itself around branches, it got caught in bushes. Legrand tugged it free, using language not heard in Wednesday sermons, nor Saturday nor Sunday either.

"Stupid old goat!"

"I'll flail your sinful hide."

"Get knotted, shit for brains."

We could no longer see Legrand. The bee was leading him away. Taunting him all the time. Legrand blundered after it, yelling curses, far gone in his rage. Finally, his howls and shrieks disappeared into the depths of the woods.

"Well, that's a relief," I said to Sweetcharity.

But she was sitting up, looking at me, almost as wild-eyed as her grandfather.

"It . . . it . . . was a liar bee," she gasped.

"Yeah, I know," I said. "It was buzzing around me earlier."

"It saved us," Sweetcharity said with wild-eyed alarm. "Oh God of our Choice, we've been saved by a liar bee!"

"Maybe we should give thanks," I said. "A little prayer . . ."

"Thanks! A prayer! Are you mad, Mathewmark! That was a liar bee. We can't thank a liar bee. We're in league with the devil if we thank a liar bee."

"It seems to have drawn that madman away."

"Don't you call my grandfather a madman! How dare you?"

"Hell's Teeth, Sweetcharity, the man's demented."

"Don't blaspheme! Don't you dare mention the infernal region and Grandpa's name in the same breath!"

Sweetcharity was pulling herself away from me, standing up, brushing randomly at her clothes. There were leaves in her hair. Her eyes flashed.

"You're in league, Mathewmark," she said. "You're in league with the Prince of Darkness."

"Sweetcharity, darling," I said imploringly.

"Don't 'darling' me!"

I'd never seen her so pretty. I'd never wanted to know her body as I wanted to know her now. Carnal lust!

"Please, Sweetcharity," I said, standing up and stepping toward her. Reaching for her.

"Don't touch me!"

"Sweetcharity . . ."

"You're in league. You've sold your immortal soul."

"Sweetcharity, I think you are being a little bit hysterical. I'm not in league with anyone."

"The bee did your bidding!"

"No it didn't."

"Oh, dear Lord. You're lying, Mathewmark. You are the familiar of the liar bees. You speak to them in their own lying tongue!"

"Does, too," said a voice about a meter above our heads.

Sweetcharity gasped, looked up, fainted into a crumpled heap on the ground.

"Good grief," said the bee, "Loopy as halfwit with whip."

"She's his granddaughter," I said.

"Poor kid," said the bee. "Thought my olders were assholes, but that fruitcake . . ."

"Who are you?" I said.

"Cyborg bee, you know that."

"Where are you from?"

"Metro. You know, outside Valley of Goddess, whatever you call. Van Gogh. Introduce self. Voice Amanda Kolby-McAllister. Not bee talking you, me, Amanda. Shut up in room, controlling bee. Only machine."

"What do you want?" I was shaking a bit.

Before the bee could reply we were interrupted by a piercing shriek from Sweetcharity, who had obviously regained consciousness.

"See, see," she cried. "You are the liar bee's familiar. Oh get thee behind me, Satan!"

She was away and running, tearing through the woods in the direction of her grandfather's cabin.

"Another nutter," said the bee. "Bloody place rife."

"She's my beloved," I said, "and in the fullness of time I hope to make her my betrothed."

"Not anymore, buster," said the bee. "Owe me, Mathewmark. For saving ass from mad guy with whip." The bee cleared its throat. "And saving from clutches of crazy little drooler."

"Do you mind!"

"Don't mind at all," said the bee pleasantly. "Uh-oh, Maman at door, time log off. See around, Mathewmark."

Trembling with pleasure, Head of Biology Team Tatsumi stared one final time at the notification in her display. Finally, the Medical Executive had relaxed its prohibition on attempts to revive deep-cryonics corpses from the Pre-Relinquishment epoch. She key-cued for a menial.

The door flashed pink. In came the technician she could not stand. Why must it be him, in this moment of her triumph?

"Please bring up three whole-body storage containers from the mausoleum."

"Any preferences?"

"The earlier the better."

The swine smirked. "Records listings are no longer reliable, madam. Most of the dating information was dumped during the Big Data Glitch—"

Walked into it. "Then why ask?" She knew why. Quickly, before he could come back with some new impertinence: "Use your eyes, man. Surely cryonics tanks from the turn of the millennium are distinctive enough."

The bodies were fetched up in their Dewars. The first was lost in a subtle error during thaw. The next perished for a large number of still more subtle reasons that interlocked chaotically. Bringing the third to revival required lateral thinking and took years to accomplish, even with accelerated cloning techniques. Dr. Tatsumi was exhausted by the time the task reached completion. The aggravating Tech still got on her nerves, but there was no doubting his masterful competence.

They stared at the youthful, comatose body.

"A beautiful job, madam."

"Do you mock me?"

"Heaven forbid. No, just look at him. Better than new."

So he ought to be. They had sliced Abdel-Malek's vitrified and frozen flesh into wafer-thin laminates, resonance scanned them, mapped the location of every brain cell and its synaptic interconnects. A bucky-core now held every single item of the information that once had been Mohammed Abdel-Malek. They had read the precise wording of his genome and re-constructed from it a fresh embryo identical in every respect to his own. For years they had tended the clone twin, nurturing its accelerated growth, massaging the young body with instruments and fields and enzymes. The vast trillionfold tangle of its Edelman neural garden, the chaos of nerves cells that choked its torpid infant brain, had been trimmed in a topiary guided by the memories cherished within the bucky-chip. Every link was strengthened or suppressed in echo of the structure of the dead man's chilled and sliced brain. The body lying before them was unconscious and mindless only because it had never been permitted to awaken, shake the sleep from its eyes, stretch, look around at its new home.

His. His new home.

As a solution to freezer damage, the procedure had been a *tour de force*, if not a particularly elegant one.

"He certainly seems in the pink," the Tech observed, tugging his lower lip through the mask. "Pity we can't wake him for a few moments."

"Absolutely out of the question." If it were not for the constant super-vision of Relinquishment security probes, Head of Team would have done exactly that, years ago. The urge to speak to her creation was often nearly overwhelming. "All right, Technician," she said vindictively, "return the pa-tient to deep storage and crash him down to minus 196."

They had both known this was the inevitable, frustrating conclusion to their heroic efforts. But the Abdel-Malek clone was, after all, just one of their many projects, and the one that strained most dangerously at the boundaries of technological moratorium.

"It's like killing him all over again, don't you think?"

"What I think," Head of Team Ingrid Tatsumi shrieked in maternal pain, "what *I* think is that you're begging to go on report." She caught her breath. "It's a political decision. Let the future worry about these deviationists."

"We only heal their bodies, right?"

She turned away as the boy was floated out.

Time Maman got door open, was perched innocently with Strad the Lad under chin, sawing away at Tchaikovsky concerto like life depended. Maman looked suspicious, but room well soundproofed, obvious reasons—during first few years violin made noises like tormented cat, although these days should be allowed to charge admission to practice sessions, so delightful are musical strains coax from Stradivarius. Well, maybe not Tchaik. Admit, Tchaik dreadfully difficult, been working on doublestop triplets for weeks.

Have to play two notes same time, three times in single beat. Passage blindingly fast doublestop triplets end last movement. Music implant helped, but practicing hours a day to get near. Sound notes simultaneously, need bring heel of bow, near hand, hard down both strings at once. Makes difficult to control, bow wants move like hammer. Literally—imagine holding heavy head of hammer between fingers, thumb tip underneath, trying direct end of handle great delicacy, speed, changing angle in split seconds. Strike two strings at once, precisely, instantly switch another pair, offset from ones just played, each string with distinct resistance. Again, again. Left hand crazily pressing doublestops, dancing to next pair. Most time sound goes crunchy, vile. Was determined master it.

Strad Lad not true Stradivarius. Lovely ancient violins rare hens' teeth, not mention expensive as real estate on Sunway Coast, Utopia Valley. My Strad exact knockoff, computer-designed replica built by molecular shaper machine on basis extensive mag res scans, CAT scans, PET scans, DOG scans all I know. Spoke with voice of angel, when stroked whiskers with bow. Mixed metaphor, something, who cares?

"Your father and I will be dining with the commissioner this evening," Maman told me, calm tiger's eyes. Obviously didn't know had been toying with tender vulnerable mind of Valley of God guy, even though Nanny Watch surveillance program on computer link to record, trace URLs of every call made out. Didn't know Vikram, I, Play's ace hax0rs, not something go advertising, let alone boast of. Under dozen handles, were known, feared, majorly respected by cryptonauts, other buzzboyz, grrlz seven continents, few islands. None of streetwise d00Ds knew were upscale prisoners of refinement, taste. Naturally yearned down&durtee, instead were trapped in Durance Vile by likes of Maître, Maman, terrifying Dr. Singh, seldom-seen Mrs. Singh, not to mention our community Magistrate, hissing Mr. Abdel-Malek.

"Be okay, Maman," told airily. "*Spine-chiller* on vee, Mrs. Ng usual excellent dinner, catch early zees."

Realized even as spoke had taken wrong tack entirely. Maman's eyes narrowed. Expecting whine, bitch, moan how incredibly *bored*, how *small* house (all twenty rooms including arboretum), why couldn't *Vikram* come around or even Bessie or Steve, Mr. Abdel-Malek hadn't said *anything* about Steve, Bessie not allowed to visit, and—

Had brains to carry on like that, Maman would have raised voice tiniest bit, invited to grow up a little, young lady, nearly Mature, scarcely behavior of a near-citizen. Too bad, if started to grizzle now would look rather odd, even more suspicious, so just turned away from dubious glance, tucked S Lad under chin, drew out perfect middle C. Hairs on arms stood up, didn't even hear door seal behind when left room.

Once was sure Maman, Maître out of house for good (wouldn't put it past them double back, try catch red-handed), lower half house filled delicious scents Mrs. Ng's preparations scratch meal, reopened system, still using Maître's crappy old discarded computer.

No way could reach Vikram direct, legally, didn't stop for moment. Popped up couple fairly impregnable layers countermeasures, opened window to e-pal Austria, Rupert Hochschauble. Forty-five-year-old Mature glassblower with interest medieval illuminated manuscripts. Well, bio on home page, all I knew "he" could be seamstress Honan

Province or retired food engineer Kurdistan. Rupert my "beard," patching encrypted messages through series email lists to place where Vik would see when went on-line. Would reply through own "beard," someone I didn't know or want know, answer forwarded almost instantly through another list, maybe devoted water-skiing or face stencils.

How come felt so secure? Wasn't sheer number of links sent messages through—helped, of course, but could be traced. No, chatted behind security door of excellent Steganography program both installed.

Steganography? Never heard? Shame, you! How worked, in nutshell: spoke my end conversation into machine's acoustic hood (or typed if feeling really paranoid, thought olders might be listening to room through microbug). Words digitized in usual way, stream ones, zeroes. Binary digits modify standard "one-use pad" other zeroes, ones, cost nothing to prepare. Vikram, I, made up one hundred pads, stored for whenever wished communicate absolute secrecy.

Anyway, new blend message bits, pad bits woven artfully as colored pixels into background of painting, photo, whole thing transmitted as graphic attachment. Picture might be bland little portrait of me playing Strad at Prom last season, or heart-warming pic of doggie doing tricks with food bowl, or shot of ring-a-ding Saturn from high over north pole. Some dull, ordinary, some beautiful, memorable—anything, really. As was going through Hochschauble's site, was gold-leaf-encrusted page from ancient German Bible (book Deuteronomy, as recall).

Manuscript shown backwards. Didn't touch words of sacred text, would have been relief to weird new buddy Mathewmark if ever heard this high-tech game, not that would have understood first word. No, Steg program found bits gray parchment in background, ever so slightly tweaked bits, bytes. Couldn't see difference in gray shades with naked eye, trust. Could see speckle if boosted magnification, so what? Who says what shade dull gray, brown random pixel meant be? Without key—shared, prepared onetime pad—nobody in all world decrypt messages.

Enough science, art skullduggery. Point, me, Vik could natter to heart's content, no-one going intercept forbidden conversation. Not even dreaded Mr. Abdel-Malek.

<Hey, Vik.>

<Hey, grrl. Bored shitless.>

<Tell 'bout. Luckily, Have Plan.>

<Oh, no. Look, Amanda, know am devoted to yr genius, beauty, but don't think parents could take another Plan. Don't think I could, that matter. Last one almost got sent home Pakistan.>

<"Home"? Thought you naturalized van Gogh citizen.>

<True, but know olds. Claim been corrupted by alien ways.>

<Funny, exactly next Plan. Not you, bopper. Heard Valley of God, weird old hippies?>

Pause. Watched main display. Series lovely illuminated pages, each on display fifteen, twenty seconds. Vikram's end, display showing cricket match in progress, or map of points of horse. Pause not due to mechanics of Steganography. Just Vikram being indecisive. Kid easily flummoxed by raw fear. Never understood it.

While Vik was mulling over trepidation, I patched in map of deep Maglev route, small blipping red rectangular box laid over spot where tunnel curved through Valley. Green dot marked vent. Never paid much attention to route itself before, since old plan—*my* plan—involved hopping rails at Metro hangar, webbing onto shiny freighter for grim life with wind screaming in hair, around carbon-fiber composite goggles, jumping off at coast when came to rest. One part of thousand-kilometer tunnel hundreds of meters deep under the rock like any other, had assumed. Just blackness pierced every hundred meters blue maintenance lamps no human ever clapped eyes on. Wasn't as if anyone was meant to go down there once system was up, running.

<Mad bastards have put kink in track,> Vikram remarked. <Will slow bullet train down a bit. Why they do that, Amanda?>

<Not quite kink,> said pedantically. <More slow, gentle curve. But you do see, right under Valley just mentioned?>

<Course. Something to do with rock, think? Or maybe had to divert around underground river?>

<Around above-ground sacred site, Grasshopper,> told. <Faith-

ful felt having transport route of Satan's Minions drilled under landscape was shocking affront to God of their Choice.>

<Which god that?>

<Not just one, is it? All get worship whichever god fancy. Mainly
menfolk like old bearded chap spits fire, brimstone, ladies go for
Mother Gaia, one of blessed Virgins. Clip it? "Of their Choice"?>

<No need be narky. How this do with anything?>

Smirked. Pays to do research.

<Turns out Maman did secret deal. With one of Elders, don't
know which. For the right to take tunnel through Valley—well, deep
under Valley, but loonies own legal mining rights stopped corp from
just ripping ahead without permission.>

<Exchange for—?> Could imagine Vikram's big laugh. Probably
imagining bribes, civic corruption high places, dirty deals, guilty se-
crets. What his own father specialized in, according rumor.

<Maman's arranged send all directly to heaven.>

Another pause. Display flipped back a page. Adam, Eve, snake
conspicuous teeth, rather cheesy smirk, twined around tree. One
about to chow down on apple, while gaudy snake looked on, rather
pleased with self. How appropriate. Sniggered.

<Excuse?>

<True. Maman agreed have diamond disk engraved with names,
histories every member the Church of God of their Choice, send up
into space on rocket. Cost millions, probably, cheap at price. Oh yes,
bit makes all worthwhile. In exchange for vent in grotty old disused
field, corp agreed to slow freighters down to speed of running horse.
Fifty kays max, reckon.>

<Grief,> Vikram said. <Bless soul.>

Red stockpot appeared upper right corner of display, steaming
over a crackling fire. Dinner served.

<Gotta go,> told bad if reluctant buddy. <Mrs. Ng calls. But
you get big picture now, hope?>

<Do indeed,> Vikram agreed. Manuscript showed God brooding
over unformed Earth, empty, void. About make something really, really dread. Me too.

<We'll go down vent,> I said. <Now all need do, get in there.>

<But Amanda,> Vikram started, <heard bastards completely mad, armed with pitch—>

Cut him off, closed cyber defenses, scampered downstairs to dinner Mrs. Ng. Chicken, steamed Vietnamese vegetables! Yum.

1 1 : mathewmark

I always look forward eagerly to Beanfeast Night. Each village in the Valley has a Beanfeast Night once a month. It's pretty well compulsory to go to the Beanfeast at your nearest village hall, but you can go farther afield if you wish. Our village has its Beanfeast every New Moon. That's a mixed blessing. Makes it harder for outliers to drive their carts home after the feast, so we get more people staying over afterward than the Sickle Moon and the Full Moon villages. We must provide more food and candles and hot water, it's a bit of a strain on the local community, but we get the kudos.

And there's some splendid cooks in our community. My momma makes the best pickled pork rolls in the Valley, and her cheeses are legendary. Auntie McWeezle bakes wheat bread and corn bread with herbs only she knows about. Try winkling the recipes out of her— you might as well try to get water from the Moon.

So all that day, as I went on my rounds, each house and farm and cabin and mud hut I visited smelled better than the last. And at most places I was given a taste or a bite or a sip.

"What do you think, Mathewmark? A little more chopped chives?"

"Don't overdo it, Auntie. Remember what happened to old man Oldwood and his Fragrant Sausage."

"Fragrant! You could smell the pong of it the moment you entered the hall!"

"It's a lesson to us, Auntie."

"I'm talking about chopped chives, Mathewmark, not essence of liverwort."

"Moderation in all things, Auntie. Could I have some more?"

"Begone, Mathewmark, or I'll have nothing to bring to the feast."

Beanfeast days are great days. I always make sure I visit as many people as possible on a feast day. But this particular day, for all the tasting and sipping, had an uneasy feel to it. Beanfeasts are jolly affairs, but they can also be the occasion for airing grievances and circulating rumors. And there were going to be some grievances aired—the Valley was alive with rancorous debate over the granting of permission for the ventilation shaft. And old man Legrand and Sweetcharity would be there.

By the appointed hour I was scrubbed and ready. As were Momma and Dad and my brother Lukenjon. We loaded the basket of feast food, I put a daisy chain around Ebeeneezer's neck, we all piled onto the cart and we were away, arriving at the village hall by sunset. It was a warm evening, and those who had arrived already were still standing around outside, under the peppercorn trees, watching the sunset and discussing the ventilation shaft. I looked for old man Legrand's great lumbering wagon, but it was yet to arrive. I would need all my diplomatic skills and cunning to keep out of his way while still managing to speak to Sweetcharity.

Ah, Sweetcharity. I was no fool. I knew what her sort of behavior was called: a lovers' tiff. The thing about lovers' tiffs is that when, after a bit of argy bargy and tears and hot words, the two lovers fall into each other's arms again, their love is strengthened tenfold. Lovers' tiffs are like summer showers. Rain one minute, brilliant sunshine the next. At least this is what I was telling myself as I unhitched Ebeeneezer from the cart and led him to the village green to graze and chat peacefully with the other mules until home time.

"Psst!"

I looked round quickly. The village hall with its little group of nattering locals and visitors was about a hundred meters away, but no one was watching me. I was alone on the village green with a dozen mules for company. I ignored the bee and bent to put the hobbles on Ebeeneezer's front legs.

"Look, only asking for bit of advice."

"The devil and his wingéd messengers need no words of advice from a mortal," I whispered.

"Oh, give break. What's wrong you fruitcakes? I'm pender stuck at moment insid—"

"A pretender! I knew it!"

"Pender, cretin. Subadult. Unmod hayseeds'd probably call me girl, despite advanced years. Any rate, certainly not bee. Wake up self, or get nasty sting." The bee sniggered in my ear, a terrible buzzing sound for a mortal to have to listen to. I swatted furtively. Was that Jed Cooper peering in my direction from the shadows of the nearest stand of peppercorn trees? All I needed—another witness to my damnable persecution.

"A girl, eh," I grunted. "Did the Magistrates of Hades turn thee into a creature of the hive as punishment for thy infractions?"

"Magist—" The bee fell silent, as if astonished. "Out mouths of babes. Look, idiot, what's all thees, thous, smites, begorrahs? Sound like hick from twentieth-century hillbilly teev spoof."

I clung to Ebeeneezer's neck, hearing his patient chewing.

"It's just the way we talk. What's wrong with it? You talk pretty strangely, bee."

"What's wrong? Fake as rubber dog turd. Phony as novelty puke toy. Your ancestors all higher degrees agricultural colleges, those not running illegal chemical factories, software companies. Isolation's softened brains! Something in water?" The bee added curtly, "Nothing wrong Mall cant."

"We have cast off the cool flippancies of the city slickers," I told the bee proudly, repeating something I'd once heard old man Teusner tell his stout wife. "The ways of the world are the worldly ways of the worldly wise, which isn't for the likes of the saved."

The bee sighed sadly in my ear. "Uh-huh. Fashion dialect, eh? Like, whatever. Listen, need favor, Mathewmark. Do one in return. Can bring vee unit, self-seating implant phone, wicked porn, anything can tuck in pouch."

"I would accept no such thing," I blurted aloud, wondering what these wicked things might be, and again the shape lurking in the nearest trees shifted, as if someone were spying on my dreadful con-versation. I lowered my voice to a hoarse whisper: "What would you desire in return?"

"Safe way into Valley," the liar bee said. "Me, Vikram. Some way sneak past guards, into new vent shaft. Know vent, assume? Everyone over there whining about."

The ventilation shaft? The bee wanted to fly down that devilish tube to the bowels of Hades?

"I don't understand anything you're saying." I was utterly confused. Ebeneezer turned his head and looked at me. He didn't understand either. What was I doing here in the gloom still hanging about with a mule when all my human friends seemed so cozy over near the hall? I looked away. "Here you are already, liar bee, yet now you tell me you still wish to learn how to visit the Valley. And can't you speak normally?"

"Just not listening, dolt," the bee rasped angrily. "I'm pender named Amanda, live about forty kays from you as crow flies, need get in to godforsaken Valley while Moon's still dark and chances of not getting caught fair to good. Capisce?"

I caught the sound of a heavy wagon lumbering toward us. You get good at recognizing the sounds, this was a four-wheeled, six-mule job. Old man Legrand.

"Oh shit, mad old swine," said the bee. "Fruitcake with whip. And little miss prissykins. With dopey face."

"Shut up," I snapped. The last thing I needed was to be caught by old man Legrand alone on the village green talking to a bee. As soon as he'd dropped Sweetcharity at the hall, he'd be bringing his mules to the green. That might be the only chance I'd get to snatch a few moments alone with Sweetcharity. Once the pair were inside the hall, the old man's eyes would never be off her. I had to get rid of the bee.

"No good telling shut up," the bee said. "Mates, you, I. Asked cyborg bee into Valley, after all. Now tell how get there in flesh."

"Well, you just can't get in," I told the girl-bee. "Not unless you can fly over the mountains," I added sarcastically. "Shouldn't be too hard for the minion of Satan."

"Fly in!" The bee developed an excited rasp to its buzz. "Grief, right. Vik, I just unfurl wings—"

"I thought you just told me you're an ordinary human when you're not pretending to be a liar bee. For god's sake!"

"Blasphemy now, Mathewmark . . . ?"

"Yeah, it's blasphemy," I said making the sign o'god in the air, "But you drive me to it."

The Sun was below the horizon, but there was still enough light to see that old man Legrand had unhitched his mules and was leading the team toward the green.

"Okay, friend Mathewmark," said the bee, "Owe you one. Run off have little chat sourguts, though why want to mystery to me. Will keep old fart amused a while. Catch later."

The bee disappeared. And so did I, running low to the ground, keeping as many of the dark shapes of the mules between me and Legrand as I could, hopping over a fence and circling back to the hall. Under the peppercorn trees, Sweetcharity was standing in a group of young people. She was smiling sweetly at Jed Cooper, laughing at something Jed was saying. And you should have seen Jed's face: it was all scrubbed up for Beanfeast Night, of course, but already there was a trickle of saliva running out of one corner, glistening in the last light of the day. And he was leering at Sweetcharity, staring at the embroidery on her best bodice, and saying something about work for idle hands. I knew just what work he wanted to put his idle hands to. Everybody fell silent as I approached. Abner O'Took and Gracie Sandinski looked at me and then looked away. So did Zeb Teusner. Blessed-Bride-of-Christ Dwyer examined her fingernails in the twilight, fingernails cracked and chipped by hard work in the fields. Sweetcharity made the sign o'god. What did she think I was, the Prince of Darkness himself?

"Evening, all," I said, louder than I'd meant to. "I trust I find you all in the pink of condition."

"Those'n who walk in the ways of righteousness be always in a condition of grace," said Jed. "Though whether'n it be pink or not, I cannot tell."

"Sure ain't scarlet," Will Orpington said.

"No, nor black as sin, neither," Krishna Dyson chipped in.

"Amen to that," said Sweetcharity, and once again made the sign o'god.

"Amen," said the whole group.

"Got a bit religious, have we?" I said. "Got a bit holier than thou?"

"It wouldn't take much to be holier than a bee's soul mate," Jed said.

"An adder or viper that crawls in the grass is holier than the bee lover," Krishna said. "Yea verily," he added after a couple of seconds of silence.

"They do say that you are never alone on that cart of yours, Mathewmark," said little Light-on-the-hill. "Even on the lonesome road the very insects keep you company."

"Oh, really," I said. "Who's 'they'?"

Light-on-the-hill looked down at her feet. It was a bit hard to tell in the dusk, but I thought I could detect the hot blush that was creeping over her face. She's a shy little creature, Light-on-the-hill, it must have taken quite a bit of effort to come out with that remark in company. But I wasn't feeling very protective, I pushed on.

"Tell me, Light-on-the-hill, who is it that says I keep the company of liar bees? Is it my dear friend, Sweetcharity, here?"

"Don't call me friend," Sweetcharity said. "I have no friends who are the friends of the bees from Hades."

"Correct me if I am wrong," I said. "But I think I remember that the bee we met yesterday spent most of its time talking to your grandfather. Methinks it knew him well, addressed him in familiar terms: Old goat, Shit for Brains, Moth-eaten Old Fart. It was the merry blathering of old friends that I heard in the forest."

Half a dozen people giggled and snorted, trying to suppress their laughter. The mood of the group was changing, I could sense it. I pressed on.

"Hark!" I said cupping one hand to my ear. "Old Man Legrand is at it again, yarning with his mates, the bees."

And indeed he was. From the village green came the sound of swearing and cursing. The sudden crack of the stock whip. "Accursed of God! Foul fiend mired in slime. Filth of the air."

"The banter of familiars," I said, "if ever I heard it."

The violent crack of the stock whip sounded loud in the dusk. But not as loud as the hand that slammed across my face.

"Never speak to me again!"

Sweetcharity turned and flounced into the hall, the light from the hanging oil lamps suddenly catching the silver threads in the embroidery of her dress. There was more laughter from the group, but this time directed squarely at me. The mood was changing again. Despite the stinging in my face I managed a careless shrug.

"Ah," I said, "the lovers' tiff! A hint of pent-up emotion, a promise of passions to come."

I turned and walked as jauntily as I could into the hall. I wished to hell I could believe what I had just said.

I didn't get another chance to talk to Sweetcharity all night. She ate at the same trestle as old man Legrand, and when trestles were pushed back and the fiddles started up, she danced with Jed and Krishna and half a dozen others. I didn't even try for a dance. And I didn't feel like dancing with anybody else. I just skulked around the side of the hall and listened to the Elders. The Elders were splitting into two camps, you could see that from the way they talked quickly and quietly to each other, falling silent when somebody they didn't trust ventured near. As Beanfeasts go, this one wasn't the greatest, but it was among the most interesting. Trouble was, as evening wore on, more people were sending me suspicious, shifty glances, amid a certain amount of muttering. The rumor was getting around: Mathewmark talks to the bees.

Mind you, some people were starting to look at old man Legrand in the same way. But he seemed oblivious to the tensions within the hall, in a huddle with old man O'Grady and old biddy Witherspoon, muttering intently and planning something. You could be sure of that. By the time the feast ground to a halt and everybody stood up and sang "Old Lang Jack," I was sick at heart and more than ready to leave.

Q. *What's the good of salvaging old brains when their very cells are
deteriorating?*
A. The goal is to make a series of modest improvements that accu-
mulate. In fifty or a hundred years we'll have techniques able to solve
all the problems that otherwise kill everyone when they get to 120.
Eventually nanomedical systems might build neural enhancements
or replacements into the brain—as if vacuum tubes in old vulnerable
radio sets from the 1940s were replaced one by one with hardy
smaller transistors.

Q. *Oh, how horrible! A head full of chips instead of brain cells!*
A. Is that more horrible and unthinkable than having an artificial
pump whirring in your chest after your heart gives up the ghost? I
don't hear too many complaints about transplants from people dying
painfully of heart disease. Meanwhile, we can hope that targeted
proteins, perhaps built by injected organelles made from our own
stem cells, will fix some of the problems now caused by maintenance
breakdown in our brains.

Q. *Some say reversing aging and bringing back the cryonically frozen
dead will depend on nanotechnology, but perhaps it's an impossible
dream to build machines the size of molecules.*
A. Viruses are nanomachines, I don't see them throwing up their
little hands in despair.

Q. *Maybe so, but even advanced cryonics could never turn a hamburger
back into a cow.*
A. No cryonics organization I know of actually puts its patients
through a meat grinder before cooking them. Actually they don't cook
them at all, they cool them. Hmm—"cook" to "cool," such a big

difference in going from one letter to the next in the alphabet. After all, many cemeteries *do* routinely cook their clients. The rest leave them to rot.

Q. How far off are effective life extension and AI?
A. In practical terms, I think we should be modest in our expectations of the near-and medium-term future, and wildly optimistic about the longer term.

Q. Longer term is—?
A. Fifty years or a century hence, not the year One Million.

Q. Life extension and genomic enhancements will only be available to the stinking rich. We'll see the poor reduced to a lesser species, literally unable to mate with the genomically altered supermen.
A. Everything is the prerogative of the rich at first. I would be crippled by guilt, in fact, if I didn't know knowledge can be copied without loss. If I eat this cake you've missed out on it, but the recipe can be had by both of us for a pittance. What about the raw materials and skills and tools needed to bake a new one? All of those will fall in price and spread throughout the world as hardware approaches the condition of software.

Q. Is life extension hard or soft?
A. If we find an inoculation against senescence, maybe it will be as cheap and abundant as aspirin. Technology doesn't stand still. That's the one great incredible truth of the twenty-first century. We learn to do better with less, and cheaper per unit.

Q. Won't a planet of wealthy ageless people be conservative and terminally dreary, Florida forever?
A. Could be. That's a scary thought.

<On-line, Mr. Bones?>

<Am, Mistress Interlocutor,> Vikram replied via Steganography link.

<Know how get in,> told triumphantly.

Halfway through strawberry sundae Mrs. Ng whipped up for me, mouth all gooey. Somehow had get out of house, into real soda joint in Mall where Vik, I engage eye contact, so could tell he knew was on verge of stroke of brilliance, appropriately impressed. Well, settle just getting out front door after sundown, slow walk along river. Only three days, but getting cabin fever. Watching through bee-spy Mathewmark mooch off for feast beans with loony pals in fading twilight made me resentful, devious. Unlike usual relaxed, sunny state of mind. (As if. Know am bitch.)

<Can't go in through pass,> Vik said. <Blocked off with damned Gatehouse.>

<Correct. Can't get in other end, either, opens into National Park, need three kinds official passes go there. Might fake up, but also requires presence at least one bona fide Mature adult take charge, as olders so lightheartedly term.>

<Well, duh. And can't drive fresh tunnel through mountain rock, not without own portable nuclear-powered mole. Carelessly lent mine to Lata for week.> Vikram made smiley, canned bray hyena laughter came out machine.

<Right again. But hey, isn't just hot air am floating here.> Paused, added, <Hint, Dodo.>

<Oh my gosh.> Could imagine Vik sitting bolt upright as idea started enter brain. <You've got bats in belfry.>

<Ain't just flying kite.> Idea growing on me, still filled with anxiety. Gnawed lip, starting look like edge of lace doily.

<Your maman will have her plane locked up tight. Not enough pocket hire plane. Mand, traffic control wouldn't allow fly in anyway. Neither us has ultra-lite license. Suppose: hang-glide into Valley. No, bad luck, need do under cover darkness, no thermal updrafts at night. What am I forgetting?>

Had been scouring local news channel archives for something to help. Big find: dumped on display with applet showing flourish triumphant trumpets:

<Muon Power Station in trial operation for bit over month. Quite a hike, but located right snug against this side Bell's Ridge. Only five, six klicks easy glide into Valley, Vik. If don't kill ourselves in dark.>

Warm nuclear fusion. Laughed out loud, delight. Vik seeing possibilities now: could use suits' built-in carbon-composite wings, no need haul hang-gliders. Jump down off Ridge, into fusion plant's updraft, up over down, easy spirals into Valley.

<Of course>, I added, <chances are will miss, smashed to pulp on top plant's radiator vanes.>

Vikram silent long moment, thinking through. Not one for jumping into things, old Vik—although have to jump long, hard make this one fly. Then said, <Or be detected by plant's safety automatics, gunned down by protective lasers.>

<Not allowed use those, saw news report. Might harm local rare species, can't have that. Use nets. Won't be lasered into ash, steam, just trapped by nets, hauled off for vets to check beaks, wings.>

<Claws, tails,> Vik sent, into spirit. <Must be dozen possums, feral cats trapped every night. Have whole zoo for company. Mr. Abdel-Malek lock us in, throw away key.>

<Only if crash, burn. Only if learns were there. Don't worry, Vikram, stroke of brilliance.>

<My heroine!> he keyed sardonically. <So smart! So humble! Mad, of course. Utterly mad.>

Wasn't going to be put off. <Will hit bloody updraft, loft over into Valley like autumn leaves in gentle breeze.>

<Like two blind lunatics jumping into river, more likely. Don't forget, no Moon even if weather good for flying.>

<Nag, nag. Global Positioning System satellites see safe, sound.>

Vikram fell silent. Said carefully: <GPS's only accurate to within a meter, I think. We need more precise guidance from someone on ground. You'll have to get your pal Mathew Mark Peter and Paul to light us a fire or two next to Maglev vent.>

<Landing strip. Hmm, don't think so. Don't seem use artificial lighting in crackpot little utopia, Vik. Well, oil lamps, candles, suppose that's artificial. Still, string small fires would have all yokels for kilometers rushing with barrels of water, blankets to beat out flames.>

<Two or three radar corners, that's what we need,> he sent. <Hey, why not? Think Believer Boy could hacksaw us couple reflectors? Have steel containers, don't they? Rusty old cans? Buzz with cyborg fly, put idea into head.>

<Ingenious, Watson. Give it a try right away, before he gets home bed. Nothing ventured.>

<What mean, "Watson"? I'm Holmes, ignorant child.>

<Way cool, Homes. You da bomb.>

<Sometimes alarm me, Amanda. Don't know where you pick up these outdated, jaded turns of phrase.>

<Funny, was just making exact comment somebody else. Anyway. Gotta go, babe. Have bat wings to scrub, pack.>

<Sure, Mand. Watch skies! Over, out.>

Machine sent rude blatting, as of forty hogs a-farting, and Vik was gone. Grinned, sighed, pulled up GPS survey of the region, looking for exact coordinates Muon Warm-Fusion Test Facility or whatever engineers, politicians, publicity flacks calling it this month.

Woke bee just after eleven that night, looked around bit of Valley in sensor range. Feasting done, apparently, dishes, fiddles packed away. Were they allowed sing, dance? In modest, god-fearing way, naturally? Probably not. Dour-looking crew. Few couples stood about chatting by soft glow of oil lamps, occasionally swatting mosquitoes. People didn't seem have insect repellent. Probably didn't wash either. Did even know about running water? Shuddered. Any luck, Vikram, I in, out without smelly creatures even noticing us. Tomorrow night ideal, if could get lovelorn loon snap out, guide us to convenient landing right next to vent.

When tracked down, was clopping along dirt road, with Momma, Dad, brother. Without moonlight, needed boost bee's artificial eyes get good picture downcast mouth, wounded eyes. No one saying anything, other three looked sleepy, well fed. Only Mathewmark full of gloom. Mule turned up side track, few minutes later came to grinding halt outside small, dark hovel. Mathewmark muttered would put Ebeeneezer in lower forty. Other three made way into hovel, while Mathewmark unhitched mule, began leading along narrow path.

"Psst! Mathewmark. Know anything about radar corners?"

Hardly twitched muscle this time. Maybe getting used to me. All to good. "Go away."

"Off soon as finished our little talk."

"I'll swat you like a bug."

"Ha-ha."

"Don't think I won't! I'm still half-convinced you're a limb of Satan."

"Six limbs. And two pairs wings. Quite pointless squashing, though. More where this came from. Can't swat lot."

"Look you, if I'm seen talking to you again, I'm dead. No one will want their goods carted by a familiar of the liar bees."

"Better talk out here, then. In boring old field. Give credit for not coming into hall of fun, beans with you? Refrained alarming olds on cart."

"Go away. You make me tired."

"Sure, will nip back your place, wait for you there. Hope don't keep old chedders up with nattering."

"For the love of Shiva, what do you want? I've already said I can't tell you a way to cross the range into the Valley. At any rate, it can't be done from this side, and I've never heard of one of your heathen kind making his way in here."

Yeah, right, like any would want to.

But was interesting throwaway remark, sounded like sneaking, barely acknowledged interest in leaving hellhole, exploring fleshpots. If true, and really managed arouse interest, was home, hosed. Well, was certainly home, damn it, grounded for weeks according to Magistrate, and don't know what "hosed" bizzo means but suspect worst. Nah, told self, Vik, I would do it. Down vent, web on to freighter as slows in curved path deep under Valley. Thrill of lifetime, yeah. Worth being grounded until sixty-four. By hook, crook.

"Radar corners," said patiently through bee.

"I don't know anything about—"

"Know you don't. Ignorant as pig shit, poor man. Relax, will explain. Have any sheet metal in this place? For roofs of hovels. What's it called, used last century, galvanized iron?"

"Roof is thatch."

"Grass stuff?"

"Reeds, dried sedge, straw . . ."

"Ugh. Hardly hygienic. Hmm. Oil drums? You lot use oil drums?"

"Eucalyptus oil we store in bottles. With corks."

"Hicksville, place unreal . . ."

"Yeah," Mathewmark said sourly. Boy, guy really pissed off. Should have kept bee's recording mode running while talking over plan with Vikram. Something messy obviously gone down with Sweetcharity at beanfeast. Really couldn't see what he found in girl. Okay, boobs, but wasn't as if she had decent bra, showed off cleavage. Teeth okay, apart from missing one right in front. That prim thing never going to put out, not until married in Temple of God of their Choice. Watched enough twentieth-century vids know that for sure. But dope didn't know what was in best interests. Still trying to give brush-off. "If you don't mind," was saying, "I've got a lot on my mind. Can't even understand what you're saying half the time. Please go away."

Oh well, when in Rome. "Tell me your troubles. You help me with radar corners, I'll help you straighten out personal life."

"No you don't!" Bleat of alarm so sharp Ebeeneezer tossed head, jerking rope thing, leash, whatever, muttered something. Mathewmark patted mule, muttering back, ignoring bee.

Wasn't going get rid of me that easily. "What you have in this place made of ferrous metal? Iron, steel, sort of stuff?"

Eyes shifted shiftily. "Nothing."

Gave beeish laugh. "Thought I was meant to be liar! Okay, come clean. What you people use made out of metal?"

"Plowshares, harrows, spades, crowbars, crosscut saws . . ."

"What's harrow?"

"A thing with spikes."

"Spikes no good. Spade is thing you dig with, right?"

"Don't you know anything?"

Defensively, made guess. "Sort of flat device on end of stick? Shove it in ground, make hole, right?"

Loon widened eyes comically, raised to heaven, nodded, as if to baby. In darkness, only bee sensors enabled see this. But did see. Patronize, farmboyo? Will see about that. Get comeuppance. Meanwhile, spade might just do trick with suit radar. Two, three even better. Drive into soil at points of triangle, and—

"Okay, Mathewmark, here's plan," told. "Be at vent tomorrow night, quarter before midnight. Bring three shovels. Listen carefully, unless want me to buzz back hovel, tell whole family dirty little wrestle under trees with Miss Muffett other day—"

1 4 : mathewmark

The morning after the bean-feast, I didn't cart anything. Ebeeneezer had the day off, and Lukenjon and I weeded the strawberry patch—hacking away with the hoes, trying not to sever the strawberries. Every now and then we did, and the little strawberry would lie there on the ground, split clean in half. The best thing to do was to eat the evidence. We'd brought lunch with us, wrapped up in a cloth, a wedge of cheese and some pickles in a jar, a half round of corn bread. Lukenjon and I lay in the shade. We just picked at the food, we'd eaten too many strawberries.

"Is it true?"

"Is what true?"

"You know," Lukenjon said. "What folks are saying."

"What are folks saying?"

"Come on," Lukenjon said, "I'm your brother. Folks say that you and old man Legrand talk to the bees. Or talk to the trees. Some daft, mad thing."

"Legrand sure does," I said.

"And you?"

I looked out over our patch of dirt. In the distance was the river. Weeping willows and old biddy Gonzales's cows grazing on the opposite bank. Beyond the Gonzales's place you could see the patchwork of fields and woods and villages. And against the bright blue skyline the rocks and cliffs of the Valley walls. They are our strength, the Valley walls, they keep us safe and unpolluted by the Outside, but sometimes they can look like the walls of a grim fortress, a jail maybe, seen from the inside. Off to our right, just over the boundary fence, the green tower of the ventilation shaft stuck up out of old man Grout's deserted wheat patch, leading straight down to the tunnel, the tunnel to the Outside.

"Cat got your tongue?" Lukenjon said.

"The bee I've been talking to," I said to my brother, "is a girl called Amanda. She's shut up in her room and sick of it. So she's coming to visit us tonight."

What's a brother for, if you can't confide in him? I felt a huge wave of relief: just saying those simple words out loud was like coming up for air in the swimming hole when you've been down too long.

"If them bees exist," Lukenjon said, "them bees lie. They lie like the devil himself, if they exist. If the devil exists."

"Most people tell lies now and then," I said. "I don't reckon Amanda would be much different."

"It's a strange name for a bee, Amanda."

"The bee isn't called Amanda," I said. "The bee is just a messenger. Ain't even alive. It's a sort of . . . sort of a machine . . . like a cuckoo clock. Amanda sends it her voice."

Lukenjon made the sign o'god, but he made it in a fooling-around sort of way. "Sounds like the devil."

"She's coming tonight," I said. "Her and a friend. I've got to guide her in—with spades."

Lukenjon laughed, rolling around on the ground. "I reckon you're touched," he said. "Taken total leave of your senses. Signaling to the devil's handmaiden with spades."

"Want to help?" I said.

A long silence. Eventually Lukenjon broke it: he burped mightily. The air was heavy with the smell of half-digested strawberries. "I'm not letting you out at night by yourself," he said, "you being a loony who talks to bees and waves spades at night-running chicks called Amanda."

Momma and Dad were well asleep when Lukenjon and I slipped out of our bedroom window. Silent as mice we padded barefoot to the barn, collected the spades, and made our way to the lower forty. It was only when we were sitting on the grass with Ebeneezer's dozy form standing like a black rock half a dozen meters away that we pulled on our boots. The night was very clear and very still. There was no Moon. The stars burned like glowworms.

"What you said this afternoon . . ." I said.

"What did I say this afternoon?"

"You said, 'If the devil exists,' like maybe you thought he didn't."

"Maybe he don't," Lukenjon said.

"And the God of your Choice?" I said.

"Maybe I've chose a god that don't exist neither."

"Everybody in the Valley believes in the God of their Choice."

"God help them."

"Do you really think I'm touched?" I said. "Do you think I'm gone in the head? Do you think I'm imagining the bee when I talk to it?"

"Remains to be seen," said Lukenjon.

I was about to offer Lukenjon a small wager, but we were both suddenly still, suddenly alert, listening.

"Wagon," Lukenjon said.

"Four wheels, six mules," I said.

"Your friend, old man Legrand," Lukenjon said. "Out and about at midnight. Now what would he be up to?"

"I can't think," I said. "And he's not my friend."

I was totally confused. The only reason I could think of for old man Legrand's midnight wandering was the same as had brought me and Lukenjon to the lower forty: Amanda. But, far as I knew, all Amanda had done to old man Legrand was to taunt him, tease him, insult him. Surely she couldn't have asked him to help with the radar-corner business.

"Sit tight," Lukenjon said.

We sat on the grass of the lower forty and listened. The stars were intense, but starlight wasn't bright enough to illuminate distant things at ground level. Our ears were our eyes. The wagon creaked nearer, turned when it got to old man Grout's.

"The ventilation shaft," Lukenjon whispered. "He's going to the shaft."

Muffled voices: Legrand, maybe O'Grady, and a woman—old biddy Witherspoon unless I was totally mistaken. A girl's voice said quite clearly, "There's nothing survives a good roasting."

"Hush!" said Legrand, speaking three times louder than the girl. "You'll wake the whole Valley."

Beside me Lukenjon laughed quietly. "He wouldn't leave that little bundle of purity at home alone, would he now." It was a flat statement, no question in my brother's mind.

"She's my beloved," I whispered, fierce.

"Was," chuckled Lukenjon. "Was."

"But what are they doing?" I whispered. This was the last thing I wanted: the whole place swarming with folks up to no good. Amanda and her friend would be landing in the middle of a jamboree. And they'd be coming in any time now.

"Don't worry about them," Lukenjon whispered. "Let's get these spades in position."

Silently, hardly whispering a word to each other, we set up the long-handled spades in the lower forty in the way Amanda had demanded. We made a small hole with the crowbar, then jammed the end of the handle in. Two sets of two. Little right angles of steel a meter above the ground. And all the time we worked, we listened to the sounds from across the boundary fence. It was pretty obvious what was going on. Legrand and his companions were heaping firewood around the ventilation shaft. They were going to burn it down.

"Reckon it will catch?" I whispered.

"Ain't steel, nor iron," Lukenjon said.

"I don't reckon the tunnelers would have used something that would burn," I said.

"Either way, old man Legrand's firewood is going to burn," Lukenjon said. "It'll light up the place like the fires of hell themselves."

"Might be useful to Amanda and her friend, they'll be able to see what they're doing."

"And Legrand will see them arrive."

There was nothing we could do. We retired to the far end of the lower forty, putting as much distance as possible between us and the boundary fence. We lay on the grass and watched the first little flickers of flame. Within a minute the fire was well alight. The crackling and spitting of the dry timber was loud in the still night air. A bright column of sparks rose up, enclosing the dark mass of the shaft.

"All they need is a saint," Lukenjon said. "Tied to the stake, ready for a bit of martyrdom." And then my brother fell into one of his silly rhymes. "Where the bee be a liar and the saint's on fire, a spade's a spade and a girl's a flier."

"There's a boy coming as well."

"Well, the boy's a tryer."

"You've got more rhyme than sense, Lukenjon," I said.

"That's the beauty of real poetry," he said with perfect satisfaction.

I shivered in the warm night air, thinking of martyrs tied to a flaming stake. Ebeeneezer came galloping up to our end of the field with a drumming of hooves.

"Don't like that fire, thir."

I put my arms round his neck, whispered calming words into his great floppy ears. By the increasing light of the fire I could see old man Legrand's team of mules kicking and tossing in their traces. The mad fool had left his team standing far too close to the blaze. The mules brayed and shouted in their heavy lisping tones, and human figures could be seen trying to turn the team and the wagon away from the flames. Shouts rose from the other side of the Valley. An oil lantern swung in somebody's hand on the track that ran down from the McWeezle place. I thought I could hear Momma and Dad shouting something from our house. They were calling our names.

"It's all right," Lukenjon said. "We'll just say we thought we heard sounds and came to investigate."

"What about Amanda and her friend?" I said.

"If the buggers have got any sense, they'll fly back where they came from."

"I don't think it's that simple," I said. "All they can do is glide. They can't fly upward."

"Oh yeah?" Lukenjon pointed to the great tower of flame that was now totally engulfing the ventilation shaft. "Look. Right up there where the sparks stop."

Two huge bats, great black-winged vampires, swooped and wheeled, riding the new column of hot air, blotting out the stars, turning and twisting. Visible one minute, invisible the next.

"Daft gits," Lukenjon said. "Their wings will catch. Moths to the flame. You watch."

They were beautiful, free, riding the great tower of hot air for the pure joy of it. They circled, rose up almost to the stars, diminishing in size. They quit the hot air for the cooler blackness, disappearing. Reappeared lower down, swooping in over the heads of the ground-lings and mules, twisting and spinning upwards again around and around the shaft and back into the airy reaches of the night.

Crack! Even the roar of the fire couldn't drown out old man Legrand's stock whip. The crazed figure was dancing around, leaping onto the back of his wagon, giving himself extra height, flailing with his whip at the night. But the black creatures were up and away, far out of reach. Oh, how I wanted to join them, to be one with the night and the air and the stars.

A small crowd was gathering. In the firelight you could see their clothes. Britches pulled on over night attire. Hair that was normally tight as a fist in buns, flowing and flaring in the firelight. People holding rakes and spades. A bucket. Maybe that was old biddy Smeeth—down on her knees, praying.

"It's hot," Lukenjon said. "But it's not going to last. Most of them logs is ash. They'll not be flapping around up there much longer."

He was right. The fire was dying. Now the sparks barely reached above the top of the shaft. The circling human bats weren't much higher than two or three times the height of the shaft. It was only a matter of time before they'd be in reach of Legrand's stock whip.

They quit the dying tower of hot air. They were away into the night, lost from sight.

"Now where've they gone?" Lukenjon said. But the bats answered him themselves, wheeling round out of the blackness and rushing straight toward us, flying abreast, straight between the two radar corners, leaning back in their flight, bringing their feet down like landing herons. Almost colliding with Ebeeneezer, who bucked, jerking my arms from around his neck.

"Thorry, thir."

They were children. I couldn't believe it. Tall and skinny, coltish.

"Yeeeeha!" said the girl. "What a ride! Sorry about donkey. Should paint with iridescent stripes."

The boy had fallen with a yelp when he landed. "Bloody ankle," he said.

"Upaday, Vik," said the girl. "Gotta shift." She turned to me, "Mathewmark?"

"Of course," I said.

"Sorry, can't see much in darkness. Look bit different. Damn bee—get all this false color from sensors. Ought to see self on display. Freakenstein!" Something especially unnatural was happening to her dark silhouette. It looked as if her great bat wings were shriveling away. In a moment, she was just a tall shadowy girl in the moonless night.

The sounds of people clambering over the boundary wall brought the conversation to a halt.

"Coming to get us," Vik said, struggling to his feet. His wings got in the way, and one buckled as he groaned and almost fell over again. He pressed something on his chest, and the stiff fabric of his wings folded neatly away, its struts clicking together and sliding into a flat pack on his back.

"Let's skootle," the girl said. "Where hide?"

"Better follow me," Lukenjon said. "Mathewmark, go and head off the posse."

The two former bats, one hobbling, both jet-black and nearly invisible except for their faces under hair-tight hoods, followed Lukenjon into the night. I walked down the field toward the sounds of the pursuit party. The first person I bumped into was old biddy Smeeth.

"They went that way, Auntie," I said, pointing in the wrong direction.

"Fiends o'filth!" yelled old biddy Smeeth. "We'll boil ye alive in tea-tree oil!" and set off, the others of her band following, laughing and brandishing their tools of trade. They sounded, I thought sourly, just like the very fiends of hell themselves.

seed origin V: storage

Time is a green bud blossoming to brilliant bloom. It is a corpse rotting in a stench of bacterial decay. For Mohammed Abdel-Malek, time is gelid nightmares. His cryonically stabilized brain is not quite locked in changelessness. Minute and spontaneous sluggish electric currents run unimpeded through neural channels. His utterly chilled tissues are superconducting conduits for ambling night creatures. There is no tunnel of redemptive, radiant light, no gathering into bliss, no family waiting in robes to gather him to them. Only memories: of dispossession, of love found and lost, of the ceaseless battles to create his mind children against a rising storm of protest and objections from irrational and informed alike.

Sixty-five years old, covered in honors and distinction and hence a safe toothless choice, he sits in the chair's role at a table at an MIT symposium.

An excited young fellow with an Estonian accent leans forward, almost off his chair.

"Suppose the machine evolves ten billion times faster than bacteria or viruses, forget sluggish humans. Suppose its mutation rate is ten billion times that of a human. The boundary conditions might preclude the Darwinian selection that allows for the concomitant coupling of coevolution."

The young man pauses, scanning the other faces at the table. He is the only one wearing a suit.

"Look, you make the self-bootstrapping artificial intelligence. You plug it in. Within milliseconds of being activated the supermachine disappears. God alone knows where or what it has become." He grins recklessly. "Really, I mean it!"

"This is trash television fantasy, Boris," another man tells him, looking bored. From his smooth cheeks and unlined forehead he appears barely more than a teenager. "What, you think it could quantum tunnel out of the building?"

Boris shrugs. He has straight blond hair cut at mid-ear level, thick glasses, neither fashionable. "Maybe the supermachine discovered a more general quantum mechanics where the Born criterion doesn't exactly hold. Conservation of mass gets violated—shit, so does strict causality for that matter. The machine reaches back to the quantum fluctuations at the beginning of time and subtly remakes the physical universe."

"Aw, give me a fuckin' break."

A young woman in a smock bearing the faint mark of baby vomit leans forward, tapping her pen on the table. "No, give Boris a chance. Look at a slightly different scenario. Say the machine/universe system that's evolved is sufficiently consistent with the human/universe system. Couldn't we transform from one to the other in a sort of expanded Principle of Relativity?"

"Hmm. If the transform is close to affine, I'm sure that we could recognize the machine as some sort of object."

"Okay, but what if the transform goes weird, you know, not particularly well behaved. Then the physical manifestations of an object like that mightn't be easily perceived by humans . . . like, maybe we wouldn't be able to identify sufficient machine features to consolidate into an object in our own human minds. The implicit and explicit semiotics of our perception and our cognition mightn't allow us to perceive such a 'highly evolved' object." Bent fingers mark the scare quotes.

A fat man bursts out laughing. He wears a chartreuse sweatshirt showing the latest would-be Theory of Everything equations in Day-Glo letter-ing. "Actually there could be tons of entities like that all around us." His voice breaks into falsetto as he laughs harder. "In fact the reason we find zero evidence of 'intelligence' out there in the universe is because *we our-selves are not intelligent!*"

"Well, by comparison—"

"You can forget orderly compromise co-evolution," the fat man says, suddenly hard, staring across the table. "Species only coevolve if they in-teract with respect to common environmental resources. If self-bootstrap machines evolve very rapidly, then likely in a short time, half a decade, milliseconds, whatever, they wouldn't be competing substantially for re-sources with the human species. We'd see an adaptive radiation scenario because the machines—"

"Oh, crap."

"—might discover a new physical environment they could radiate into."

"Hey, it's within the realms of possibility," someone else says peevishly.

"At the very best we won't notice anything. A hyper AI in our perceived physical world would be benign and invisible. Human civilization would proceed along the blah *Star Trek* line."

"The what?"

"Linear and conservative. No apparent Singularity. Talk about hidden variables." He guffaws again, obviously pleased with himself.

"You know that's not going to happen. Bill Joy's right. This whole tech-nological trajectory is insanely dangerous. We have to nip the fucking thing in the bud *right now*. Relinquishment is the only path we can responsibly take."

The fat fellow shrugs. "Might be too late, chief. Here's a worse scenario: we start noticing subtle but damning changes in our physical laws. Pro-gress in physics and engineering seems to be directed away from producing more AIs. Guess why?"

"This is apocalyptic bullshit."

"Not apocalyptic enough," says a serious woman with deep frown lines and short white hair. "If we go that route, game theory tells us we'd be in a very brief and extremely destructive conflict that'd last just long enough for the machines to access resources beyond our reach—mass-energy con-servation violation, some similar paradigm-breaking discontinuity. The sad truth is, we can't afford to take the risk. We really do need to mandate general Relinquishment, and the sooner the better. I move that we make this our principal recommendation to the President's Board of Inquiry."

"I won't accept motions at this time," says Abdel-Malek, seated at the center of the table. He has remained silent until now. "We have much more ground to cover before then. I do think this might be a suitable time to break for afternoon tea. Thank you, ladies and gentlemen, we'll reconvene in fifteen minutes. Um, make that twenty."

He watches Boris nudge the fat guy as they all shamble out. "Any way you cut it, Bruce, the future's not good for all-consuming human egos, buddy."

"Predictable, man." Nostrils twitch at the scent of quiche and coffee and donuts in the adjoining room. "Primates have big egos, we're control freaks. Walk around with a handful of big balloons and sure as shit someone will come along to burst 'em."

In his bad dreams, frozen just beyond the edge of death, he clutches endlessly at life, at the blade striking to his heart, clutches for Alice's worn, warm hand, and loses it, loses it . . .

1 5 : amanda

Skulking like rats in dusty barn, just dimmed shoulder-patch nav lights to hold gloom at bay—didn't dare light oil lamp, squawking loonies running loose outside—not my idea fun. Not at all neat in-out plan.

Poor Vikram stopped speaking to me hour ago, couldn't really blame. Vik's grippo sneaker removed soon as reached barn, unzipped black carbon-fiber legging of blackgear jumpsuit. Sprained ankle seemed half-again normal size. Far as could tell in murky glow of navigation patches, also rather ugly shade purple. At least didn't seem broken. Slow us up, though. As for me—

"Ah-CHOO!"

"Keep the noise down, Mistress bat," kid brother said, jumping. "Do you want the whole village on top of us?"

Wiped running nose back sleeve. Eyes streaming. Unpleasant tickle started up again almost at once, could feel another big sneeze pushing swollen forehead, inside cheeks. Instant pharmaceuticals for this kind of thing. Of course didn't have any in packs.

"Ah—Ah—Arch—"

Rest of explosion muffled by something enormous, rough crushed against nose, mouth. Swung around in dark with fists, but only Mathewmark, handwoven handkerchief. Last time had seen coarsewoven piece cloth, was watching through eyes of bee, boy trying swat with it.

"Keep hands to self," said, but took snot-rag, blew heartily. Drew deep wheezy breath, felt nasal tissues swelling again. Barn's air choked with mule dander, dozen kinds grain pollen, whatever sets off allergic reactions. Wondered whimsically going to die, gasping on own fluids. Shocking thought, actually. Nobody died any more after all, except in accident so bad body, brain could not be patched up. Well, in Metros. Who could say if barbarity like death still existed in backward Valley?

"Auntie has a decoction for this blight," Mathewmark muttered to brother. "Think you can locate her bag of simples in the pantry?"

"I know where she keeps her herbs, but not which among them is effective against the sniffles and snots."

"Fetch the lot like a good chap. We can't leave Mistress bee to wheeze herself to death."

Lowered self weakly into embrace of hay bales covered with patched old sheet. Gloomy Vikram lying on side gazing gloomily into gloom, damaged leg raised on bag oats. Stout tomcat wandered across straw covering dirt floor of barn, glancing at us with only slight curiosity, positioned self facing crack in timber of stall.

"He smells a mouse," Mathewmark told. "Perhaps a family of the sly beasts." Called in soft, encouraging voice, "Good work, Kevin. Stand at your station like a god-fearing mouser."

"Bite they tiny nose and toes," added Lukenjon, slipping in with bundle of twigs, battered metal pot, ceramic bowl. Began crush dried leaves between palms of hands, watching debris sift down into bowl.

"Cat might smell mouse," said thickly, swallowing gunk, "but I smell rat. What was fire doing all around vent? Spades did radar trick, homed perfectly. If wanted bloody great visible beacon, asked for one. All did was rouse mob."

"You don't think Lukenjon and I lit the bonfire, do you?" Mathewmark snorted indignantly. "That was the work of old man Legrand, the Elder you've taken such a dislike to, and his gang of pestish cronies. Egged on by Jed Cooper, I shouldn't wonder, who's taken a wicked fancy to my beloved and would sway her from my wooing."

"Ah-ha!" Sat forward. Head swam, really was feeling appalling. "Thought heard shrewish tones of ladylove among rabid horde. Where mad old grandfather is found, they say, dreary young granddaughter sure to follow."

Mathewmark started angry whispered defense of dull creature, but I was too asthmatic by that point pay any attention. He crouched over small portable stove, lighting wick with match. Match! Mind-bogglingly primitive. Dipped water into pot, pressed down ill-fitting lid, placed on pale flame. Despite blocked nose, could smell fumes— some kind of oil from tree, bush, I suppose. Doubted Valley folk received weekly supplies gasoline, kerosene from awful polluters seemed so afraid of.

By time Lukenjon finished crushing, mixing dried herbs in bowl, pot boiling. No electricity, true, but not altogether hopelessly primitive after all. Lukenjon poured in steaming water, brought stinking result across to me in gloom. Took bowl in both hands, nearly dropped. Hot!

"What supposed do with this?" asked irritably. Nose running like a tap. "Drink foul stuff?"

"Hold it up under your nose, Madam bat," boy told me, "or better still, put your face down just above the water. Take in the steam. Here, let me show you." Topped up bowl with more boiling water from stove, gently pressed down on back on my head until sore nose only few centimeters from surface. Steam rose in cool of night, rich with odors, making skin flush, sweat slightly. "That's right," told me encouragingly, "breathe of its healing vapors. Soon you'll recover your health, if such blessed medicaments have any power over those who fly in the night."

Let strange smells rise from bowl into lungs and blocked spaces behind nose. Oddly enough, found mood improving almost at once. Nostrils stopped seeping, eyes felt less like sore someone rubbed grit into, slowly throb in swollen head eased. Started breathe normally. Vikram frowned from darkness, rubbed ankle meaningfully, but held tongue. Clearly didn't wish ask yokels for help. Not him, son, heir Dr. Singh.

"Thanks, boyo." Snorted loosened gunk back into throat, swallowed. Yetch. Salty. "This is doing trick. Think of anything for poor friend's sprain?"

Mathewmark had been fussing in shadows. Came forward with rolled, rather grubby bandage, vile-smelling pot of substance might have been used treat mule, perhaps poison mice escaped cat Kevin. Vik grudgingly permitted Mathewmark rub oily muck into bare ankle. Winced, otherwise refused show pain must have been suffering.

"You two study medicine?" Vikram asked skeptically.

"My brother and I treat the livestock hereabouts when they sicken," Mathewmark told. "Now grit your teeth, this might cause some pain, but it will help bring down the swelling over the next few days." Started wrap damaged ankle tightly with bandage, cinching with knot. Rolled down Vik's unzipped trouser leg, left off sneaker. Doubt would have fitted back anyway.

"Days!" Vikram horrified. Eased self up into seated position. "Thanks for help, pal. But look, can't stay here. Olders going to find out we're missing in morning. Hell to pay if learn holed up inside Valley."

Mathewmark looked at him suspiciously. " 'Hell to pay'? Are you changing your story, now that we have given you sanctuary and—"

"Oh, lighten up," I said. Really feeling thousand percent better. If could get recipe for this stuff, could make fortune. "Just an expression. Vik, going have to go ahead with freighter burn, hurt or not. If had phones, could face music. Get picked up at Gatehouse. As is, nobody knows where are." Shivered as reality of situation settled into bones. "Families really going to go nutso. Five-bell alarm, stodes roughing people up, patrolbot scouring Metro from one end to other for murdered bods." Shuddered. "Will end up so grounded die old age before let us out."

Glanced at watch. After 1 A.M., farm boys sounded completely done in. No wonder—probably got up with Sun to feed chickens, tote barge, whatever farm boys do when rest of sane technological world snoozing after hard night of vee. Starting nod off self. Damn good stuff, whatever was in herbal infusion. Yawned rudely.

Mathewmark flustered, embarrassed in pale blue light of stove, which was still flickering even though pot had been taken off it. Would be awake until morning if didn't force him spit it out.

"What's on mind, M-man? Scared we'll run off with family silver?"

Frowned. "You are frivolous." Cleared throat. "There isn't any other place for you both. I fear you will have to stay here together for the rest of the night, even though it will compromise you, Mistress Amanda."

What? Do *what*? Vikram gave sarcastic laugh from darkness.

"No fear of that, pal. Amanda, already so deep in shit spending night together in barn won't raise extra eyebrows." Over Mathewmark's splutterings, he added, "Look, guys, very grateful for help, but time bed down. See you morning, okay?"

Lukenjon stood at once, gathered medicinals, bowl, turned out stove's flame. Nodded shyly to me, extended hand to Vik, left like shadow. Older brother bumbled about for another minute, clearly distressed leaving Vikram, me alone together. Rank hypocrisy. If had chance some snuggling, snuffling Miss Sourcharity, have been in it quick as flash, ask me. Shocked him even more grabbing arm, pulling down so face next mine, giving hearty, only slightly snotty smooch.

"Veritable saint, Emster," told. "We owe you. Oh, that reminds." As gaped guiltily, glancing sideways at Vikram who was more concerned about hurting ankle than anything else, I reached around into backpack, pulled out small flat box. Wrapped in metallic foil decorated prancing high-stepping horses, carriages rather more upmarket local carts, wagons. "For you, brother. Don't eat all at once."

"Eat—?"

"Open, present."

Tore clumsily at foil as if had never seen such stuff before in life.

Suppose hadn't. After moment, took back from him, slid thumbnail down seam, opened box assorted chocolates, held out in dimness. Newly salvaged sense smell went bonzo at happy odor brandy-centered almond-crusted dark chocolates, mouth started watering involuntarily. Girl's got eat, after all, had missed Mrs. Ng's supper treat. Snatched choc, popped into mouth. Heavenly.

"Go on, Mathewmark, be tempted. But don't eat all at once, make self sick. And save some for Lukenjon."

Suspiciously, he took choc, sniffed it. Put in between teeth, bit down. Liqueur spurted. Startled, coughed, dropping half chocolate into straw. Then taste buds kicked in. Saw endorphin rush start. Golly, just imagine what must be like—go all life without one of basic nutritional food groups. Yokel-boy closed eyes, sucked, swallowed with gulp. Hand reached out of own accord, found another chocolate. In fact, hand found two chocolates, crammed both into greedy gob. He chewed blissfully, making little moans. I slapped hand as darted out for more, resealed pack.

"Enough, pig. Go clean teeth, get to bed. Don't have work tomorrow?"

Mathewmark looked at me as if waking from naughty dream. Stood up, shoved chocolates under one arm, clomped to barn door. Vikram gave languid wave, lay back in darkness.

"Sweet dreams, farm boy," I called softly. "If see any witch-burners, tell we've flown back Hades."

But was already gone. Moment later, all caught up with me, was gone too. Not out like light, didn't have any switch off. Just gone, down into exhausted dreams running, someone shouting, cat peering into face with huge fangs, falling through blackness into sparks, pitchforks.

Instant later, seemed, jolted awake. Morning sunlight streamed through open barn door.

Mathewmark had closed door when left.

Vikram still lying like log, wrapped in old horse-blanket.

So who was—?

"Shh," vaguely familiar voice hissed in ear. Twisted convulsively, blinking sleep out of sore eyes, looked up at really quite pretty face bloody Sweetcharity. Smiled nervously at me, showing gap in front teeth.

"Oh shit," I said. "Witch-burners here after all."

Girl looked frightened, determined. Can't say blamed her, really. After all, last time seen had been zooming down out of sky like pair bats, riding bonfire thermals on foldaway carbon wings. Sat up, reached for jacket. Sweetcharity stared at nearly flat chest, back at face.

"Oh, you're just tall children!"

Laughed nastily—shouldn't have, poor Natural, best years of short life already used up.

"Not child, pender. Older than you, possum, nearly Thirty," said.

"Thirty what?"

"Thirty years old." Pulled horrid face. "Old crone!"

"I am not!" Outraged. "I'm only nineteen!"

"Me, numbskull."

Shook her head, lips moving silently, fingers went to sides of eyes in odd gesture. After moment slowly closed hands, lowered, tried again. Leaning close so sleeper not hear, she whispered, "Listen, child, you had your first," hesitated blushed as said it, "blood yet?"

"Menses? Certainly not. Two years yet. Retarded."

Hurt, girl drew back. "I'm here to help you. There's no need to call me names. I can read and letter and figure as good as any in our schoolhouse."

Felt embarrassed somehow, snorted. "Me, not you. Gene-tweaked, adolescence plateau extended." Still looked baffled. "Super-oxide dismutase mimetics, telomerase transducers, developmental cascade inhibited until Maturity. Two years off. Tuck Strad in box, knuckle to citizen duties. Oh, hell with it. What want, girl?"

"You and the other one must get out of here," told me, eyes wide with confusion, fright. "At sunup my grandfather and some of the others started a house-to-house search. They began at the bottom of the Valley and are working their way up. They'll leave no stone unturned. They'll be here soon. I don't want Mathewmark and his family to get into trouble just because they did an act of charity to strangers."

Uh-huh, right. Was deeply suspicious. "Why care? Think we're spawn of Satan, good only for burning at stake."

She averted gaze. "You're friends of Mathewmark," mumbled. "No matter what you've done, you don't deserve the punishment my grandfather and his friends have in mind for you."

Vikram rolled over, opened eye.

"Heavens," drawled. "An angel! Good morning, beautiful. Vik, don't believe introduced."

Sweetcharity blushed. I gave that bad boy stern look.

"I have to go," she said. "Tell Mathewmark—" Stood in doorway, framed by light.

"Yeah, yeah," I said. "Will convey regards." She hesitated moment, glancing over shoulder into open field at back. Good old Ebeeneezer ambling up toward us. "Hey, Sweetcharity," called, relenting, "listen— thanks, sis."

She ducked head, was gone into crisp, cool morning.

1 6 : legal emily mcallister

Vexed beyond endurance, Legal McAllister brought a gin and tonic to the wall display in her private quarters, perched herself edgily on a bentwood chair of surprising antiquity, and called Susie up. Immediately her dearest pal, her Play friend, her sister sat there in image, across from her, sprawled in a flowery armchair. Susie's feet were bare; she wore a summery dress and a hat that shaded all her face, except for her keen gaze.

"What's she done this time?" The drawling irony was barely detectable. Emily sent back a twisted grin, but her mood of intense irritation was not so easily abated.

"You won't believe it, Susie." She held the cold sweating glass against one cheek. "You really won't believe it. The beastly pender has run away." Sipping her beverage, she exhaustively listed the prospects of scandal and financial ruin.

"At least she's turning out to be an interesting person, Em."

The Legal finished her drink, looked around for somewhere to put down the glass without staining the polished floorboards. Irritably, she stood instead and carried it across to the disposal. "Easy for you to say—you don't have to live with the wretch. Why can't she have good, clean fun the way we used to?"

"Yeah, right." The touch of irony deepened. "Remember the time we hired that clapped-out glide in Mazatlán Enclave with only the allowed forty-dollar credit between us?"

Emily gave her a cool, suspicious glance, sat down again, keeping her back straight. "I was sure Mom would kill us if we ever got home." Against her will, though, she found herself smiling.

"And when we were down to twenty dollars you spent ten of it on that stupid doll."

Her heart paused, beat again.

"Do you still have that doll, Susie?"

Laughing, the woman in the wall bent down to dig through a huge, lumpy sisal bag. "Of course." She held up a small, crudely carved wooden doll.

"I can see that crazy old lady as if it happened yesterday," Emily McAllister said, oddly happy. "Do you think the story she told us was true?"

"Not a chance." Susie shook her head. "She made it all up. Including the name, I'll bet. I mean, who's going to believe a coincidence like that? Bouncing down the mountain in our glide was her divine punishment for lying."

Emily laughed until tears came. "My God, that's right, remember when the skirt fell off? I've never heard anything so loud!"

"That old woman had her rosary out, praying for dear life!"

"No safeties! Frightened the shit out of me, too!" Emily wiped her eyes on her sleeve, caught herself, drew out a pale blue handkerchief, and dabbed neatly. "Suse, tell me the story."

"If I tell you the story, will you promise to be a good girl and stop worrying so much?"

"I promise, Your Honor."

"Okay. You have to pretend I'm a little old lady—wait a moment." Susie leaned forward, pulled a dark brown scarf out of the bag, tied it around her head. "Now, let me get into the right frame of mind." She scrunched her eyes closed.

Emily leaned forward, expectantly.

"Ahem. *Me llama* Emilia Hidalgo Gutierrez-Vazquez*y esa muneca*—"

"Susie! Stop it, girl! You know I don't remember a word of Spanish! You have to tell it in English."

"Okay, okay. But the story loses a lot in translation." Holding the wooden doll toward the display, she went on in the persona of the old woman: "This doll is very special, because it will be the receptacle for my spirit when I die. Ordinarily, I would sell you any doll you might want, but this one must stay in my home with my own people."

"But for the right price—" Emily grinned wickedly.

"*Silencio*! No interrupting. As I was saying, this doll contains the whole of my life. It took on my identity as I carved it, so the doll's story and my story are now the same. But I must begin with my mother's story.

"My mother was called Blanca, because her skin was as white as the nardo flower. It was the custom in her mountain village for the girls to marry even before they had fully become women, but Blanca was so full of energy, so wild, like the jaguarundi who sickens and dies in captivity. The old people in the village remember that she even rode horseback, along with the boys. Her father felt pity for her, and allowed her to continue running free until she was almost sixteen years old."

"Sixteen years old," Legal McAllister murmured under her breath, eyes squeezed tight for a moment of grief for lost things.

"But a month before her sixteenth birthday," the figure in the wall display insisted, "her mother called her in and told her that in six months she would be married to Enrique Gutierrez. It was all arranged by the parents in those days. It was a good match—Enrique was the second richest man in the village. Good or bad, Blanca had nothing to say about it one way or the other. Her only choice was to marry my father or to enter a convent. In my heart, I suspect that my mother thought seriously of entering a convent.

"It was bad enough that Blanca must give up her freedom. But there was something far worse. Mario was the son of a poor farmer. There wasn't such a great difference between the wealth of the richest and poorest families of our village, you understand. Surely nothing like the differences that existed between families in the cities. Nevertheless, people took the matter of relative wealth seriously, and it would have been disgraceful for Blanca to marry Mario. And yet, the two had loved each other since they were small children playing together in the dirt. And it was this that drove Blanca to walk through the mountains each day crying until you would have thought she'd run out of tears."

"It must have been terrible for Mario as well," Emily said, remembering the story, eyes prickling. "He disappeared from the village after the engagement was announced."

"Yes. One day, about a week before the wedding, Blanca was walking through the brush, some distance from the path, when she heard a movement behind her. Someone was following her.

"She picked up some big rocks for defending herself and called out, 'Leave me alone, or you'll be sorry you were ever born.' The bushes parted, and she was about to throw one of the rocks when she recognized the face of her beloved Mario.

"Now they had behaved quite properly up until that day. They had never even kissed each other. But their sorrow at being parted was so great, they forgot themselves in that moment. They embraced and kissed passionately. Dizzy with her fragrance, Mario stumbled to the ground, and Blanca fell with him. 'You are my true husband,' she said fiercely, 'No one else.'

"'And you are my wife. I swear it before God, I shall have no other woman,' he responded solemnly. And so they consummated their marriage there on the mountain under a mahonia tree. As they lay together afterward, Blanca heard a sound she'd never before heard: it was the cry of a strange bird, 'Emilia! Emilia!'"

" 'Emilia.' " Emily McAllister echoed. " 'Emilia.' "

"At last, the Sun began to sink in the west. Blanca and Mario had to say good-bye, and they never saw each other again. The rumor was that he had gone to Vera Cruz and become a sailor. He never returned to the village. I have never seen the man my mother swears is my real father.

"Blanca and Enrique were married, and in due time I was born. I remember my mother as an obedient wife and loving mother. She only ever asked for one thing for herself. Enrique wanted to name me Clara, after his mother. But Blanca begged him to let her call me Emilia, for the bird she'd heard that day. Luckily, there was a great-aunt Emilia, so it wasn't so very strange to call a child by that name.

"I had a happy life. A school opened in the village when I was five years old, and so I learned to read and write. I was so hungry for books back then! My parents, trying to do their best for me, sent me to a convent school, but I hated it there and ran away.

"Enrique tried to punish me by confining me to the house for an indefinite period of time, but he was too softhearted. I was out within a week. They knew better than to try to marry me off!' " Susie cackled, deep in her impersonation. Emily McAllister stared at the display wall, entranced.

"When I was eleven years old, a Metro anthropologist came to the Enclave, to study us." She cackled again, gleefully. "We could tell that poor man anything, and he'd believe it and write it down in his little machine.

"But I told him the truth later, because he brought paper books for me. Stacks and stacks of books. I can't imagine anyone has ever been happier than I was, with all those books to read—never mind that they were old and ragged and missing a few pages here and there.

"I never married, but instead I supported myself teaching in the school and making dolls for the tourists to buy. That is why I am asking you to give me a ride into town—the market is today, and I am taking my dolls to sell. But as I said before, this one is special and is not for sale—Em? Are you okay?"

"I'm fine, Suse. That was beautiful. You do it better each time.

How I wish you weren't dead." Emily wept, wiping tears from her cheeks. "How I wish you were more than a stupid snapshot thing."

Susie shrugged, holding out her arms in an embrace that could no longer be completed. "I know, honey." Simulated tears rolled down her face as well. "I wish I could come out there and give you a big hug, you damned brittle old thing. Put me away now, would you?"

Legal McAllister sat for a long moment, eyes cast down, unable to look into the display. Finally, she toggled it off with the switch in her brain. The wall went a cheerful pale lemon, and the sounds of the sea swept from one side of the room to the other, imaginary waves.

1 7 : mathewmark

There was no point arousing suspicion. So Lukenjon and I got up at our normal time, although we'd had next to no sleep all night. We did what we normally do before breakfast: got the fire going, let out the fowls, milked the cow. Dad was up and about and Momma was soon banging pots and pans and preparing breakfast. You can see the old barn from the farmyard, it stands in the lee of a row of trees halfway up the hill behind our place, but there was no reason for me or Lukenjon to go there. So we didn't, just shot the occasional glance in its direction. But we needn't have worried. The two Outsiders were lying low.

At breakfast all the talk was about the fire and the strange creatures that had swarmed in the updraft. Momma had only seen the two of them, but Dad—who has a bit of imagination—had seen a whole host.

"How many's a host, Dad?" I said.

"They are legion, the fiends from the infernal regions."

"How many did you actually see?"

"Maybe two dozen, maybe a thousand," Dad said. "They was ascending into the night sky, getting smaller and smaller as they spread their contagion across the heavens."

"Oh, rubbish," Momma said. "I was there too, Fred Fisher. I saw two children with those hang-glider things. That's all I saw."

"If they were children with hang-gliders," Dad said, "how come they came flying out of the shaft. It ain't wide enough for their wings."

"I reckon they just come over the ridge," Momma said. "Like that poor git the year before last. The one Elder Robinson had to cart off to the Gatehouse. He just got blown off course. Them children were the same."

"I saw them as we were running across the field," Dad said. "Pouring out of the shaft, dozens of black-winged fiends."

"That was sparks," Momma said.

"Either way, it is all Elder Legrand's fault," Dad said. "He never should have done it—building fires in the middle of the night. Stirring up the devil with no thought for his neighbors."

We spent the rest of breakfast discussing old man Legrand. Momma and Dad both reckoned he was a lunatic.

"That poor girl," Momma said. "Being brought up by a madman. It's a wonder she's as sane as she is."

Momma and Dad don't know about Sweetcharity being my beloved. You don't want to tell your parents everything.

After breakfast Lukenjon and Dad took the fencing equipment and went down to the river paddock. I hitched Ebeeneezer to the cart and trundled up the hill to the old barn. I'd said I was going to cart some hay to Auntie McWeezle. She didn't actually need the hay for two more weeks, but I'd said there was no point in putting off that which one can do today. I pulled the doors to the barn wide open. There was no one inside. Then Amanda put her head over the top of the old feed bin. Her hair, now I could see it in the morning light, was bright purple and spiky like a weed.

"You alone?" she said.

"Yeah," I said. "I'm alone." I kept staring at her. On her forehead was a picture of a mythical beast—a tiger, I decided. Shameless!

Vikram's head appeared. "Must leave at once," he said.

"Not with your ankle," I said. His hair was very black and strangely knotted in strands. These people might not be fiends from hell, but they were clearly heathens.

"Searchers here soon. Must leave."

"No one will come searching," I said.

"Get real, farm boy," Amanda said. "Nutter who lit fire, one with stock whip. Him, mates going around doing house, house search."

"I don't think so," I said.

"Listen, Mathewmark. Sweetwhatshername here just after dawn. Ought to know. His granddaughter."

"Sweetcharity?"

"Poor girl. What name!" Amanda's mouth twisted. "How could anybody call kid something yucky as Sweetcharity? Might well start calling penders Sugarbun, Toasted Marshmallow."

I ignored her. I was a bit vexed that Sweetcharity had been roaming around on her own, talking to the bat people, while I'd been tucked up in bed.

"Did Sweetcharity say where they were searching?"

"Reckoned start bottom end Valley, work way up. Methodically, said. Leaving no stone unturned. Frankly, not too keen get caught. Suppose would be gibbet for us . . ."

"The what?"

"Gibbet. Isn't that sort of mad medieval thing you people use: gibbets, ducking stools, stocks, pillories, priories, thumbscrews . . . Don't you Naturals go in for that sort of thing?"

"Naturals? No," I said. "Now do you want me to help you or not?"

"Sure do."

"Right," I said. "I'm going to put a load of hay on the cart. We'll make a box of the bales, and you can hide in the space. Then I'll set off toward the bottom of the Valley. With luck we'll slip through the net."

* * *

We met old man Legrand and old man O'Grady on the track up to the McWeezle place. They were on foot, both carrying long pointed sticks.

"Morning, Uncles," I said.

Legrand just narrowed his flinty little eyes. O'Grady was pleasant enough.

"Been traveling around a bit, young Mathewmark?" he said.

"I'm taking hay to Auntie McWeezle," I said.

"Seen anything on the road?" O'Grady said. "Anything that might indicate the whereabouts of the fiends?"

"Those hang-glider people?" I said.

"They were no hang-gliders, no ordinary folk. They had the wings o'Beelzebub."

"So my dad reckons," I said. "My momma, now, she's of the contrary opinion. My momma reckons they was just Outsider teeners, joyriders, blown off course by the winds."

"And you, Mathewmark?" Legrand said, speaking at last. "What thoughts on this matter bubble in your cesspit of a mind?"

"Easy on, Elder Legrand," I said. "My mind is not—"

"As I hear it," Legrand said, "your mind is as filthy as your paws. Those paws that fain would despoil the virgin purity of—"

This time it was O'Grady who muttered, "Easy on."

"I'll not be easy on any young scoundrel who gets his filthy paws on the snow-white purity of my granddaughter's—"

"We'll be bidding you good day, young Mathewmark," said O'Grady, speaking quick and loud. "Come on Festus Theophanous Legrand, we have work to do."

O'Grady more or less dragged old man Legrand out of my way by the sleeve. I gave Ebeeneezer a good flick with the reins, and the mule started forward. As we passed the two men, Legrand tried to poke his stick between the bales of hay, but before he could do it again, O'Grady had him out of harm's way. When I was no more than fifty meters down the track I heard Amanda say from inside the load, "Swine missed me by inch. Should be chained up."

"Hush," I said.

Ten minutes later we were at Auntie McWeezle's place. My plan was to keep Amanda and Vikram on the cart all day, hoping that by the time I arrived home, the barn would have been searched, and the hunt would have disappeared farther up the Valley, or given up and gone home. I climbed down off the cart and knocked on Auntie McWeezle's door.

"Begone," came a muffled shout from inside. "I'll put up with no more harassment from the likes of you, Festus Legrand."

"It's only me, Auntie," I shouted. "Mathewmark. I've brought the hay."

The door opened. Auntie McWeezle said, "Well, it's a relief to see a friendly face. And a sane one. Come in, Mathewmark. You wouldn't know what sort of rubbish I've had to put up with. A witch-hunt, for heaven's sake!"

I entered Auntie McWeezle's cabin. It only had two rooms and was normally a neat, cheery place. Now it looked a mess.

"Drat that Legrand," Auntie McWeezle said. "The man is a walk-ing offense to the Lady herself. You should have heard him: 'It's for your own protection, Myrtle McWeezle, the fiends could be under your own bed, and you'd not know it.' Him and that O'Grady, poking their sticks under the bed. Rootling through the camphor chest like pigs after acorns. As if the fiends of hell would worry with a poor cottage like mine . . ."

"Take it easy, Auntie," I said. "I reckon they were just hang-gliders. Outsiders blown in by the wind."

"One way or the other," Auntie McWeezle said, "they certainly aren't here."

From where I was sitting at Auntie's table, the plate of corn bread and the mug of buttermilk already in front of me, I could see out the window to the cart. The hay moved, bulged. Auntie turned and fol-lowed my gaze, but the hay was still.

"You've brought it early," she said.

"No time like the present, Auntie."

"You've not bought rats with you?" Auntie said, still looking at the load of hay bales.

"Rats?"

"They do like to nest in the hay. You can easily carry rats as well as hay."

There are some people I can lie to all day with a straight face. If I needed to lead Jed Cooper up the garden path, I'd spin him a yarn, tell him a tale with never a word of truth in it. But not Auntie McWeezle, the task was beyond me.

"The truth is, Auntie, I've got the hang-gliders on board."

"And do they look like the familiars of the devil to you, Mathew-mark?" Auntie asked, showing no surprise at all.

"They're just Outsiders." I said. "A boy and a girl. Well, they say they're grown-ups, almost, but they look like kids to me. The boy has twisted his ankle."

"Well, they can't be too comfortable with all that hay sticking into their soft Outsider skins," Auntie said. "And I'll warrant they're a mite peckish."

Five minutes later, Amanda and Vikram were tucking into a plate of beans and barley bread, mugs of buttermilk beside their plates.

"Diet milk really good," Amanda said. "Better than Slimmer's Delight."

"And what'll that be, Slimmer's Delight?" Auntie McWeezle asked. It was clear she didn't approve of Amanda's appearance, purple hair and all, but she kept her own counsel on that matter.

"Lo-fat, high-calcium, cholesterol-negative, energy-enhanced, soy milko-lite drink Maman insists. Not half as good this buttermilk stuff. Reckon if drank buttermilk all day, lose five kilos week. Can't have any nutritional value at all."

"And you'd see that as a good thing, young lady. No nutritional value at all?"

"Well, wouldn't get spare padding."

"I don't know about no padding," Auntie McWeezle said. "But it don't do to throw good food away, and she as makes butter, makes buttermilk."

"Heard of butter," Amanda said with a grimace. "Poisonous."

"Rubbish," said Auntie McWeezle. "And now, young man," she said, turning to Vikram, "I'd better have a look at your ankle. Mathewmark and Lukenjon are reasonable hands when it comes to fixing a poultice for a mule or sheep, but humans need a lighter touch."

We spent most of the morning with Auntie McWeezle. She mixed and mashed and steamed some herbs and changed the dressing on Vikram's ankle, chided Amanda for her Outsider ignorance of everything useful, but let it be known that she thought the actions of some of her neighbors were a disgrace.

"It happens," Auntie McWeezle said with a sigh. "Folks get scared and they start seeing the polluter behind every bush. And then other folks won't be outdone, they see the devil behind every flower, every blade of grass. Folks get carried away. I reckon you two want to lie low for a day or two and then get young Mathewmark to take you up to the Gatehouse. Your own people can collect you there."

"Well, the thing is, Auntie," I said, stretching, "I've got to be getting on. And without all your hay on the cart, hiding Amanda and Vik might be a bit difficult."

"Sure, they can stay here," Auntie McWeezle said. "Stay the night, if they like."

I left Amanda and Vik at Auntie McWeezle's and drove off on my rounds. Auntie hadn't been wrong about people trying to outdo each other with hysterical talk. The story of the vampire bats dancing in the updraft had reached the farthest corner of the Valley. The funny thing was that the greater the distance from the ventilation shaft that people lived, the more numerous were the fiends they swore had come out of it. My last load for the day was a pile of dried cow dung to be carted from the Old Nirvana Commune to the Apple Orchard. Old Communard Williams knew all about the fiends. They had wingspans as wide as windmill sails, and there had been ten dozen of them, screeching and cackling like parrots as they flashed their talons.

"I don't think so, Communard," I said to Williams. "I was there. There was only two of them, and they looked like hang-gliding teenagers. Outsiders."

"They've addled your mind," said Williams. "There were dozens of them." He made the sign o'god.

*   *   *

I took the river track back to our place. Ebeeneezer knew we were going home and needed no guidance from me. The cart still stank slightly of manure, I would have to wash and scrub it before I could call it quits. And Ebeeneezer was in need of new shoes—there'd be a bit of blacksmith work to be done in the morning. After a normal day's carting, I trundle home with my mind a blank, or just wandering from thought to thought in a random, sleepy sort of way. But this evening things were different. All I could think about were Amanda and Vik.

A lot was wrong with those two—they seemed to have no appreciation of the simple pleasures of life. They seemed driven by some crazy desire to experience more and more. I got the feeling they'd never be satisfied. But I knew this: they weren't fiends from hell. They were just adolescents, however old in years they claimed to be, with all the desires and problems of adolescents anywhere. We're no different in the Valley—often kids don't get on with their parents, get thrown out of home. Often they fall in love with someone who doesn't love them and start thinking about ending it all. Girls get pregnant when they shouldn't. Some young buck gets hold of a jar of cider and before you know it, him and a few mates have rolled his old man's cart. Snapped the shafts, broken the mule's leg. It happens. So, on a deep level, I didn't reckon there was very much about Amanda and Vik that I didn't know about. But they came from the Outside, they controlled liar bees, they could spread their strange black wings and soar in the updrafts. And they could thumb their noses at authority. They weren't meant to be here—there were laws and regulations and treaties said they shouldn't enter our Valley. All manner of edicts from the Assembly of Elders also said Valley people like me couldn't leave—or if we did, we couldn't come back. That's what Elders do: tell other folk what they can't do. And from what Amanda and Vik had said, it's the same on the Outside as it is in the Valley.

But Amanda and Vik hadn't been frightened by all the prohibitions, all the thou-shalt-nots of their society. They'd grasped the freedom given them by their wings, paid us a visit. Dropped in. Oh, when I'd seen them playing in the updraft from the fire, twisting and turning against the stars, the familiars of that tower of sparks, I'd wanted to be like them, to be *with* them. I wasn't much taller than Vik, but I was a lot bulkier. I started to wonder if he'd lend me his black jump-suit, show me how to unfurl the wings and float in the heavens. I could lend him my old Sunday Best outfit, the one I grew out of at fifteen. Maybe he'd like to experience real handmade clothes for a little while: homespun jerkin, goats' wool socks, cowhide boots. I didn't want Amanda and Vik to leave the Valley, but I knew that in a day or two, they'd be gone. Back to the Outside, back to a world I'd never know.

Unless I went with them.

What a sin! What a terrible, wicked thought. In our Valley just about the worst thing you can think is that you might leave, might pass through the Gate into the hell of the Outside. We're taught that as soon as we can talk. In the schoolhouse there is no lesson more serious. The God of your Choice takes many forms, but he, she, or it is always a Valley god, never an Outside god. Sitting on the cart, rumbling along the river track with Ebeeneezer clip-clopping like a tune that has got stuck in your head, I told myself I mustn't think the thoughts I was thinking. The wisdom of the Elders was the true wisdom. But what you tell yourself to think, and what you do think, are often at terrible odds.

I arrived home with my mind in a spin. Momma gave me a dipper of springwater and an apple, then sent me and the cart downwind.

"Get it scrubbed, Mathewmark, or the smell will sink into the boards. Decent folk won't ride in it."

I scrubbed the remains of the manure from the cart with a yard brush and many buckets of water. From where I was standing on the cart, I could see the ventilation shaft. It was slightly blackened around the base, but otherwise unharmed. If old man Legrand had thought the tunnelers were so stupid they'd make the thing out of flammable material, he was off his head. What a place to live—a Valley where the likes of Legrand were considered solid citizens. I looked some more at the ventilation shaft. The daylight was dying, our place was already in shadow, but the Sun still slanted down to the shaft. It glowed. And it led, through its infernal passageways, to the Outside. I couldn't stop looking at it. I was like a mouse looking at a snake.

"I like Myrtle McWeezle," Vikram said. "Doesn't seem right, repay kindness by nicking ladder."

"Like her too, Mr. Bones." Still dark, surprising amount light from starry sky. Don't see stars like that in Metro, not with all glow from streetlights, neon, lasers. Quite restful, actually, or suppose would be if didn't have posse paranoid witch-hunters on tail. "But not really stealing it. Will get it back."

"How she lug it back through fields from vent? Heavy damned wooden clunky thing." Was having trouble getting his end of ladder up on shoulder, no doubt hampered by pain of stoutly wrapped foot. My end well hoisted, backing out low shed into yard. Luckily old Myrtle didn't have large barking guard dog, would have been awake, out of bed ten minutes ago. Actually had sneaking suspicion was lying inside little cottage one eye cocked, knowing full well were making break for it. Mightn't know our plans, but wasn't going to be nuisance, get in way.

"Wish could have left gift some sort," I muttered, narrowly missing sleeping fowl. Squawked, flapped, settled. Vikram banged end heavy ladder against shed's simple brush gate. Gritted my teeth, jumpy although didn't want show it.

"We did," Vik said, to my surprise. "Left her solar-powered watch."

"Useful. Be able time how long takes when they burn her as witch."

"Come on, Mand," said, bit crabbily, "you know don't actually do that stuff in Valley. Worst we'd face if catch us is night, two in stocks. More likely, march up to Gatehouse, send message Metro cops."

"How's foot?" In clear now. Own watch showed little after midnight. Everyone else in Valley well asleep by now, even bloody old man Legrand, soppy granddaughter. According my calculations, should take twenty minutes hoof it to vent, even with Vik's bad ankle plus ladder. Couple more minutes ace fairly mindless computer chip controlled vent access, down deep root ventilation shaft using its own elevator, wait another twenty minutes max next freighter came ripping through. Well, not ripping, with any luck, because of ridiculous deal Maman had secured with local sell-outs. Because of sacred prohibitions, bullet train turned into slow coach for length of trip under sacred Valley before accelerated again supersonic speeds remaining stretch. Suits would anchor to freight hull, lock into laminar flow bucky shells, air filters on face masks. Scary but not insane. Ride of lifetime, eh.

"My foot's not too bad," Vikram said; tone showed how much must be hurting, dreary ladder lugging. Well, if weren't for injury wouldn't need lug ladder, could use blackgear's fiber grapples climb vent. As was, didn't want to take chance he'd get stuck halfway up. Ladder it had to be.

Surprising how well can see when eyes become adapted to skyful stars. Don't suppose we banged into fences, dropped ladder on toes more than twenty, thirty times whole trip. Feeling bit bruised, Vikram in agony, by time reached field. Ventilation shaft rose in dark glory, now rather smudged by ash from dead bonfire. Scraps singed timber leaned against base. Kicked path through, hoisted ladder up against side.

"Piece of cake," said. Breath smoked cool night air. Even in summer, seemed, world outside snug buildings quite crisp well after sundown. For moment wanted nothing more than curl up in own bedroom, vee system running some delightful fantasy quest, music roaring in head, Mrs. Ng building yummy treat downstairs. Missing Strad Lad, violin practice. Caught self having these cowardly thoughts, suppressed at once. Adventurers. Would boldly go where no penders gone before.

"Have to give hand up," Vikram said dubiously. Must have hurt admit that, but trouble was having with sprained ankle made me realize embarrassment was least poor boy's problems. Okay, let's do thing, get home. Be legends. Will be Mall gods at last. Able have decent shower, sleep all day own soft comfortable beds.

Ladder, for all weight, handmade clumsiness, was only about two meters tall. Less, leaning against vent column. So top vent another two meters higher, maybe more. Scampered up ladder, shot out fiber webbing strand settled over top vent, tightened into place. Climbed web hand over hand, grippo sneakers holding firmly slick, stealthed surface vent's thick column. Certainly needed all four limbs manage it, though. Looked down at Vikram, who had dragged self up ladder, perched top rung, arms outstretched to curving wall of vent. Didn't trust him climb up rest way with bad ankle, but at least was already halfway to top, should be able help haul him up.

Something caught eye. Something moving in field. Oh shit, not witch-hunters! In deep doo-doo if caught us now. Here were two devil-spawn, poised fly away on bat wings into Satan's grim polluter lands, real-estate dealers. Be even worse if realized weren't going fly off, had every intention plunging downward into hellish bowels earth.

Vik saw me peering about.

"What?"

"Dunno. Thought saw some kind of—Nah, just farm animal. Probably Ebeneezer have perv at us."

Left Vik on perch moment, stared around for control-panel cover. Top of vent absolutely solid, to look at. Thing did ventilation trick using invisible micropores in vertical stack. Although top wasn't open, would give access to elevator designed for use maintenance crews during planned once-a-decade visits. Fiddled with notepage, searching for handshaking protocol. *Voilà!* Rectangle light shone up from middle circular platform at top cylinder. Left two machines chat with each other using infrared beams, went back edge.

"Okay, Mr. Bones, ready scale Mt. Everest."

"Get on with it, Amanda," said. Sounded fed up. Poultice Myrtle McWeezle had put on ankle must have well, truly worn off by now. Could almost feel painful throbbing in own foot.

"Okay, here goes." Made sure webbing secure at top, shot down length triple-weave fiber net. Vik looped around self as had been taught in abseiling sessions at gym, grabbed remainder firmly both hands. Leaned back, letting web take some of weight, lifted good foot against side vent. Instantly, injured leg sagged. Cried out in pain, dropped back to ladder top. Without ado, ladder gently teetered, slipped slowly away from wall. Crashed noisily into bonfire remnants.

"Shit!"

Vikram left dangling, held by web, not any good position recover. I yelped fright, again seemed see something, someone move suddenly in field to left. Mathewmark? Could silly boy be spying on us? Could have followed us see what devilish prank up to? Didn't have time think further such distractions. Leaned over edge, grabbed webbing both gloved hands.

"Come on, slacker," yelled in silly, jolly voice, "put back into."

Vikram gave throttled gasp, started laughing. Hung in harness of webbing, swaying slightly, laughed like lunatic. Enough wake dead. Worse still, enough wake living.

"Stop laughing," told sternly, own shoulders shaking. "This serious."

We calmed down enough get sorted out. I hauled, hitched, Vik clawed way up webbing, kicking with good foot, finally throwing crook leg over edge with terrible groan. We lay panting, gazing up stars. Handheld beeped. I sat up, set blackgear jumpsuit gather webbing, tuck away neatly in designer pack ready for next use, crawled over to vent's control site.

Bright patches green, red showed in night. Cryptic abbreviated words on display would have revealed interesting information to engineers, had been any with us. Numbers flickered steadily, showing changes transport system. Had feeling at least one those glaring numbers told tale of freighter rushing this very moment toward Valley, maybe even slowing as entered sacred site.

"Now all have to do—" Peered at display doubtfully.

"This one, reckon," Vikram said, poked finger at symbol like door. Silently, part floor near feet lifted few centimeters, slid across another portion cylinder's roof, revealing surface meter square edged in comforting green light. Slender panel surface slid up, one arrow pointing down, one pointing up, one with square white dot. Maybe white dot meant standing still.

"Dread," Vik said with satisfaction. "Going down."

Limped to panel, looked at me. I shrugged, pretending relaxed, pleased interrupted plans about come off. Actually felt as if gut squeezed tight into chest. Wanted really badly go toilet, didn't think this moment mention it. Mouth dry, palms hands wet. Shivered, although wasn't that cold, went stand beside.

"Do it," said.

Vikram stuck thumb down arrow.

Only slightest tremor, sank into heart ventilation shaft.

1 9 : mathewmark

I didn't sleep well that night. I woke up sometime past midnight and lay listening to the sounds of the night: little scurryings, the hoot of a night bird, the wind in the trees. That and Lukenjon's snoring. You could tell *he* was having no trouble sleeping. I kept wondering how Amanda and Vik were doing at Auntie McWeezle's. There was no room for them inside Auntie's little cabin, but she had a snug stone barn, almost as big as the house itself. And there was hay in the barn. I'd put it there only that morning.

Then, just faintly, I heard something different, something that didn't belong with all the usual sounds of the night. I wasn't sure what it was, but I knew I'd heard it. I listened intently. But it was no good, Lukenjon's snoring seemed to grow louder the more I strained to hear what was happening in the fields. I suspected that old man Legrand was coming back for another attack on the shaft. I swung my legs out of bed and reached as quietly as I could for my clothes. A couple of minutes later I was standing in the dark beside the cart shed, straining my eyes in the starlight. I couldn't tell what I was seeing, but I knew there was some sort of activity at the shaft.

I began to creep closer, using my knowledge of the terrain more than any of my senses to guide me. Something quite clear, a yelled curse. I knew immediately who was at the shaft: Amanda and Vik. I quickened my pace. A burst of mad laughter, Vik's. Some sharp commands from Amanda, but she sounded as if she were trying not to laugh, too. Finally, I was close enough to see them, very faintly, silhouetted against some sort of glow coming from the top of the shaft. They appeared to be standing on the top, on what must be a lid or grille.

I stopped just inside the boundary fence, and strained my eyes. Some more conversation I couldn't quite catch, then the two figures disappeared from view, sinking downward into the shaft. I ran forward, stumbling over the stalks and roots of old man Grout's wrecked wheat crop. When I reached the shaft I stubbed my toe and fell over. A ladder was lying on the ground. As I picked it up and leaned it against the shaft I recognized it from its feel. The miserable pair had stolen Auntie McWeezle's ladder.

I was up it in a shot. I stood on the highest rung, but the top of the shaft was still just out of reach. I didn't stop to think. I bent my knees and jumped upward. If I missed, I'd tumble to the ground, maybe break something. But I didn't miss, I gripped the slightly rough edge of the top of the shaft and with a superhuman heave got myself up so that I was resting on my elbows. There was indeed a lid or cover, but it had an oblong hole in it, which was closing. I reached over, grabbed the edge of the opening, and pulled myself onto the top. The cover stopped, slid open again—luckily, or it would have cut my fingers off. I looked down. The shaft was softly lit, although the source of the light was not immediately apparent. Below me I could easily make out the forms of Vik and Amanda. They were descending. Whatever they were standing on was going steadily down. They were leaving me. A staggered series of foot- and handholds was cut into the side of the shaft, descending into the depths like a kind of ladder. I knew that if I stopped to think, I'd be overcome with fear, I'd never move, never leave the Valley. So I didn't stop to think. I swung myself through the opening and began to descend, spread-eagled on the wall of the shaft like a spider.

Heard something scrambling above us, looked up in fright. Something large, something looked like ape, maybe clumsy human, peering over edge shaft's entrance. Wondered why sliding panel hadn't zipped shut behind as started our descent. Fail-safe, supposed—proximity someone standing there. Human voice called down, echoing strangely. Couldn't make out words, but sounded awfully familiar.

"Oh great," Vikram said. "Your new boyfriend decided join us."

"Not my—" started hotly, craning neck backwards. Mathewmark had legs dangling into shaft now. Already were hundred meters below him, dropping steadily. If he let go, would fall, break fool back. Strips yellow light shone in tube as descended. Clang as his heavy leather work boots struck sides shaft.

"What's idiot up to?" Vikram yelped in alarm. "Going set off fail-safes. Whole bloody thing going shut down. Will be stuck here like flies inside bottle until Maglev custodians come nab. Damn it, Amanda!" Looked as if about break into tears. "First bugger my ankle, now this. Look like fools. Everyone in Mall going laugh like jackass."

"Calm down," said, wishing could follow own advice. "Can't come down, going have to climb back up, out, then—"

But as fell deeper, deeper into solid rock at elevator platform's steady pace, finally noticed handholds some machine had cut at regular intervals, every fifteen centimeters looked like, into side shaft. Like ladder reaching down toward center Earth. And Farmclod, far above, climbing down that grim ladder. Could hear yells, clatter of boots as made vertical descent in pursuit.

"Doesn't realize this shaft two hundred meters deep," said faintly. "Get tired before halfway down, slip, fall, land on us, get squashed like bugs. Got to stop elevator, go back up for him."

Without word, Vik shot out right hand, slammed white dot on control panel. Slowed almost instantly, felt guts rise again in throat. Motionless. High above, monkey-boy clawing way down endless set vertical hand-, footholds. Still calling hoarsely.

"Well," said in thin voice, "push up arrow, Mr. Bones."

"Don't call me that," Vikram said angrily. Noticed after a moment that had abandoned Mall cant. "This is stupid. Damn him. I'm not going back there, they'll tie us up and make complete jackasses out of us. No way." Slapped down arrow again, once more dropped gracefully toward freighter tunnel.

Couldn't believe it. Didn't he care if Mathewmark hurt, maybe killed? Own arm jerked out, but Vik grabbed wrist, held it.

"No."

"Don't be bloody stupid, Vikram Singh!"

Stood face, face, both furious, tired, confused. Took moment realize were motionless without either touching controls. High, high above, faint sounds Mathewmark's fearful hand-over-hand descent continued.

"We've arrived," Vikram said. Behind him, vertical panel showed rim of blue light. He touched with right hand, slid open: a door. Gust odd-smelling air entered shaft, somehow dead but electric, faintly oily. Could feel hair stir on back cropped neck. Somewhere, almost at edge hearing, came rushing. Air moving, pushed by projectile approaching at terrible speed.

Vikram still holding my wrist. He lifted my arm, checked watch.

"Good timing, kiddo. Here comes ride to coast." Stepped through opening. Before following, I tapped up arrow. Door closed with faint hiss. Minute or so, Mathewmark would find firm footing risen meet him. Any luck, have sense continue back up to surface. If followed down, arrive too late. Freighter due about eighty seconds, if time table still on money.

This scary bit, finally. All rest adventure easy. Sneaking out of homes, thumbing ride bus station, getting to outskirts Valley, climbing cliff above Muon Power Station, unfurling bat wings, throwing selves headlong into updraft, lifting across mountain, down into goddamn Valley of Nutters . . . all just prelude. Could already hear story heroic journey set to music, violins wailing. No, wasn't violins, was onrushing wind of freighter drawing closer, slowing—not to stop, no chance, not even slowing to walking pace. Monstrous thing planned to jump down on, ride like sandworm *Dune*, would be skimming along on magnetic fields thirty kilometers hour, more. Miss connection, go headfirst into tunnel under hundreds tons thundering metal, plastic.

Really wanted go toilet now. Why always leave these things last minute?

"Over here," Vikram called. Peering down from catwalk jutted into top of tunnel. Guarded by heavy-duty glass, plastic. Needed crawl out past safety barrier. Sound rising, like storm wind. Fancied could feel freighter's forward wind blowing up, cool, sparky. Put one leg over edge barrier, crept up to Vikram.

"Time get webs ready," said. Almost instinctive by now. Fingers danced over buttons on belt. Hung over superconducting rail far below. When freighter came through, had to be poised jump. No second thoughts.

Like deep organ note, air moved about us. Then freighter there, in rush, humming thirty klicks hour, speed of a galloping horse, seemed much faster. No beam light cast ahead like old-time locomotives. No driver, whole process entirely automatic. Vikram reached out hand, took it. Light flared suddenly at backs. *What?* Twisted head around, horrified. Dark shape loomed out illuminated square doorway. Train running under us. Mathewmark leaped forward, clutching with long arms. Our carbon webbing shot out, spraying, solidifying as it fell. Both leaped, farm boy behind us yelling my name. My web latched roof rushing freighter, snagged, locked, tightened. Rolled forward on top of freighter, taking shock in all muscles of legs, arms, abdomen. Two awful banging noises. Vikram's hand torn out of mine. Rolled ahead of me, web tearing free. Mathewmark flashed past, bouncing, mouth open, screaming in terror. Clodhopper farm boot struck Vikram in the face, with bright spurt blood from torn lip. Vikram slid, slipped, ripped free. Bounced over curved edge roaring freighter. I clung to web for dear life, screaming so hard hurt throat. Somehow Mathewmark had caught edge of my web, clung. Web started curl up, break free. Vikram gone, smashed under freighter.

Already were speeding up. Valley tore past, two hundred meters over-head. Accelerated, and poor friend was battered under freighter while stupid, ignorant farmclod clung to web, lived. Stayed alive despite everything, long enough for crashing harmonies of freighter to pick him up, smash him down, headfirst, into unyielding metal skin. Pick him up, smash him down. Again, again. He bled in river of red could see only as blackness in blipping, blurring maintenance lights edging Maglev tunnel. Smashed against side of freighter until uncon-scious, his fingers, one leg trapped in my carbon web. Quite quickly, emergency systems brought freighter to halt. Felt like forever. By then was crying too hard to see anything.

the metro

One group creates one mind; one mind creates the Singularity. That much is determined by the dynamics of technology and intelligence; it is not a policy decision, and there is no way that I or anyone else can alter it. At some point, you just have to trust someone, and try to minimize coercion or regulations or the use of nuclear weapons, on the grounds that having the experience and wisdom to create an AI is a better qualification than being able to use force. If the situation were iterated, if it were any kind of social interaction, then there would be a rationale for voting and laws——democracy is the only known means by which humans can live together. But if it's a single decision, made only once, in an engineering problem, then the best available solution is to trust the engineer who makes it——the more politics you involve in the problem, the more force and coercion, the smaller the chance of a good outcome.

——Eliezer Yudkowsky

Click   click   clickety-click
CRASH boooom hiissssss is that a Mooooo Cow I think I see her
big brown eyes ROARING bang bang cockadoodle-oo says the fat
old rooster and Mommamy is rocking me in the lovely warm sun
CLICK CLICK oh that was a bad bad thing I've gone and wet my
bed No he did it Daddy that Lukenjon baby did it CRUNCH
CRUMP the light is so bright all Red and Purple and Golden oh so
pretty but SHOCK tinkly tinkle

Rosy that's her name, that brown dear cow of ours, old biddy
Grand McWeezle is leaning over the wooden bucket and I can hear
the SHOOSH HUSH SHOOSH of the warm milk squirting into the
bucket and splashing. All the nice stinky smell of those cows doing
a poo in the straw and Daddy grunting as he puts his back into the
shovel, cleaning out the stable, and Bossie our old mule hee-hawing
and clop-clop, the rain coming down, SPLAT SPLAT cold running
down my back CLANG BANG I wish I could stop this noise in my
ears

So bright and then pale, stripes of colored bars, ping ping ping

Oh. What can that man be? Is it a devil? Is it a fiend risen up
from Hell's Teeth to carry me off? His face is blurry and green. No,
he is wearing some sort of cloth over his mouth and the top of his
head. He says to the other person it's a garble garble garble NOISE
darkness now he's back Superior auditory cortex damage extensive
temporal lobe damage I think his auditory cortex is compromised
doctor NOISE garble babble

Yes I am watching the moving light. What's wrong are you all deaf? I can hear you but I can't speak. I am so tired. What—

Ten nine eight um five? CRASH tinkle. Sorry what was that? Um eight, the next one is um is it six? Ow! That hurt! Who? Who? Mathewmark. I'm Mathewmark. I can't hear you, there's all this noise and light in my head.

Ahhhh . . . That's a bit better.

They tell me I had a freighter accident. I tell them no, there are no freighters in the Valley. They tell me the accident was under the Valley. In a tunnel. Sure, I tell them, I know about the tunnel. There was a shaft that appeared one night in old man Grout's field. Maybe there were freighters down below. But I never went there, I say, I'm a good boy. No, they say, you did. You followed Vikram and Amanda down the shaft. There's nobody in the Valley called Vikram, I say. And the only person called Amanda is old biddy O'Conner who lives in the deserted windmill and she's ninety if she's a day. No, they say, the rescue team found you in the tunnel with Vikram and Amanda. I don't know any Vikram, I say. Vikram was dead, one of them says, and the others shoosh him. Whoever he was, I say, may his soul rest in peace. It's normal, they say, memory loss. There are two different causes, they say. The freighter banged your head rather badly, and that will cause the memory loss. And maybe post-traumatic stress syndrome is also to blame—you're blanking out things you don't want to think about, don't want to acknowledge. No, I say, I want to remember everything, there is nothing I do not want to know. The scans are encouraging, they say, there is significant brain damage but nothing we can't emulate on a chip. I don't understand, I say. This is the best neurological unit in the country, they say, we will make a new man of you. Auntie McWeezle says that, I say. She says, glug down this potion, Mathewmark and it'll make a new man of you. Auntie McWeezle knows every herb, every mineral deposit, every property of bark in the Valley. We respect the traditional wisdom of other cultures, they say, but this is a neurological unit, we can map your brain here. And we can reproduce and repair the map in silicon. I don't understand, I say. I'm tired. Sleep, they say, sleep, Mathewmark. Sleep cures all. This will help you. . . .

The walls change color. Sometimes when I'm feeling sad the nurse will look at the little windows with the wavy lines and say, this will enhance your mood, Mathewmark. And then the white wall becomes a warm rosy color—like firelight, like the candlelight at a beanfeast. And then I feel both content and melancholy. It seems a long time since I danced at a beanfeast. I remember the bee talking to me on the Village Green and our mule Eben, Eban, Eb . . . Hey, nurse, I say, I can't remember his name—our mule. The nurse says, hang on we've retrieved that. He plays with the little buttons below one of the little boxes with a window. Ebeeneezer, he says, reading from the window, your mule was called Ebeeneezer. That's right, I say. And then I say the name—Ebeeneezer. Ebeeneether, as the poor old mule would say in his lisp. I say it a few times, there's comfort, there's solace in the name.

seed origin vi: awake

Here, awakened finally, lay a boy blinking into the light, seven decades old, who had been neither young nor old nor alive nor dead for decades more. Here were two bright young kids, penders they called themselves, helping him with his food-nipple, two kids absurdly claiming to be in their late twenties who obviously didn't have a clue.

"But my wife," Abdel-Malek said, weeping, when he understood where and when he was. "My God, they must have killed her too. Alice, Alice. Oh God, Alice is dead."

They put him back to sleep, this time just the temporary sort familiar to unmodified humans since the ancient African veldt, full of ordinary dreams, the sort where a nightmare simply wakes you up.

* * *

It was one of the oldest dreams in the world: to find yourself young again. Quick on your toes, taste buds eager and stomach able to cope, none of the griping, the spasms, the hangovers, the back pains, the insomnia, the cuts that won't heal and the piles that seem to tear you open when you take a shit, and the bones leached of calcium, ready to snap if you slip and tumble in the bath.

On his young, springing toes, Mohammed Kasim Abdel-Malek leaped from a high board, let his body remember across half a century of somatic forgetfulness, jackknifed into the bracing water. They really had made him better than new. He rose through layers of blue light, turned his mouth to the air, gulped, thrust powerfully through the water. Brown, graceful Ally smiled down at him from the edge of the pool. He reached up and grasped her arm, pulled her playfully into the clean bubbles.

"Hey! Not so hard, bully." They spoke English, but there were odd new slang terms and evasions. They would not tell him how far into the future he had voyaged.

"This is more like it, Ally. Why didn't you tell me about the pool?"

"We don't swim much."

Bobbing in the water, her body was perfectly dry. Abdel-Malek gazed incredulously as she sank, crabbed away along the long bottom of the pool. He followed her down. She spoke, but her voice was distorted. In pursuit, he found the need for air overwhelming. He let himself go to the surface, drew in oxygen. Still she was down there, distorted visually now, peering in puzzlement. Up she came.

"Ally, you're not wet!"

"Of course not. Yetch. Where's your repeller?"

It was a sort of necklace, and reminded him for a heart-cramping moment of the Alcor pendant he had worn for years around his neck. Involuntarily, he glanced at his bare left wrist, strong, lacking the comforting bracelet. It had done its work. Ally's necklace generated what he conceived, with a smothered snort, as a spiritual Teflon nonstick surface layer, next to the skin, shielding out the crisp lapping water. Nor was that all: this miracle ripped oxygen molecules out of the water, passed the gas to a barely visible pocket around nose and mouth. Humanity had become selectively aquatic, then apparently turned its back on the gift. Abdel-Malek, despite himself, was aghast. He reached down, touched Ally's necklace, spun and had it off her. Water drenched her dark unflawed skin, her coiled dark hair. She spluttered in outrage.

"Come on," Abdel-Malek said, "keep your face out of the water or you'll drown."

Ally snatched the repeller back, closed it around her neck, blew spray from her nose. "Savage. Should have left in freezer."

"Sweetheart," Abdel-Malek told her with no remotest awareness of how pompous, how repulsive he was being, "that little machine neatly sums up this brave new world of yours. It's marvelous, but it defeats the purpose."

Basically she trusted him, because she trusted everyone. "Why you putting clothes back on?"

From the edge of the pool, he stared back down at her nudity. She was barely nubile. "Because this is the way we did it. It's called 'modesty.'" He realized how priggish, even insane this kind of observation was, at that moment, in that place, whenever and wherever it was. He crouched again, drying his hair with his shirt. "Yes, okay. Point to you. Well, I never claimed that our way of doing things was perfect. Let alone rational. But by God it was *alive*."

With a touch of waspish scorn, Ally said, "Dead now."

Abdel-Malek sighed, turned away. She was a beautiful kind young girl and he could not help himself, he lusted after her, and she was not Alice. For him it was still only days since he and his wife sat at a table with a bunch of boisterous *wunderkinden* hardly older than Ally, celebrating the lost genius of their great intellectual ancestor Alan Turing. His mind skirted paradoxes: if she were alive, *is* alive somewhere out there, she would be older than he is young, old as his grandmother dead these many years. Yet surely they would have rejuvenated her if that technology is available, as it must be. They evaded his inquiries. Perhaps her restored and youthful body hung upside down even now like a corpse carved in ice dipped in liquid nitrogen or helium, somewhere in the mausoleum below them. He had asked. There is no way, they told him, to know. All identification lists were lost during the catastrophic transition to the Age of Relinquishment.

And that was when? It might have been centuries past. It might have been a decade ago. No, these *faux* adolescents were older than that. He squeezed his eyes shut, feeling tears of loss and frustration prickle.

Ally came out of the water, sat wordlessly at his side. He sought his own words.

"Look, surely the motive for swimming is to conquer an alien element. An element we are not meant to be at home in. Like the conquest of space. Are there humans living in space yet?"

"I just find exhilarating," the young woman told him, "now you've shown us how swim. Like sex. Not good as sex, though."

He would not be deflected now. "Exhilarating, yes! Because water is dangerous. You can drown, there's got to be at least the remote possibility of it. Otherwise you're... *cheating* yourself."

Ally stood up, her mouth drawn back. "Bullshit. I'm glad Aleph shields us from people with ideas like yours."

2 : amanda

Our Metro Magistrate, Mr. Abdel-Malek, didn't give hoot about tradition, formalities. Had own ways dispensing law, order. I'm sure kept within strict letter of law, but preferred cut through ceremony, strike straight for heart of case. Anyway, so Maître, Maman's lawyer told before hearing.

Had horrible nightmares every night, mixing up poor Vikram's dead body, Mathewmark's smashed head, me strapped to table in court while Mr. Abdel-Malek ripped through skin, bone of chest with scalpel, looking for heart . . .

Dreams stupid, especially bad dreams turn figure of speech into scene out of horror movie. Knew that, didn't stop me jerking up in bed in darkness, clutching sheets, yelling out loud in terror, sweating like pig. Mrs. Ng ran in first time, frightened out of wits, comforted me for hour until went back sleep. To sleep, to dream—To rerun stupid, awful accident over and over. Third time this happened, Maman came into room, spoke sharply to me.

"Amanda, pull yourself together, for heaven's sake."

Sobbing, shivering. After moment she crossed room, sat gingerly beside on bed. Clutched at her.

"I know you feel awful, darling," said. "Don't worry, we have an excellent lawyer representing us at the hearing, one of the best young advocates at my firm, Cecil Jones. We have every reason to hope for a suspended sentence."

How could tell her what was in heart: sorrow, guilt? Wasn't worried for self—well, suppose was, in fact sick with anxiety, but really pictures kept seeing when closed eyes were Vik torn from webbing in rushing blue darkness, sliding, falling, crashing under humming freighter. Had been buried in closed casket, but one of shock jocks in vee did gruesome sim whole accident. Didn't mean catch it, but once plugged in couldn't leave, went through whole horrible thing again, slow-mo, moving around in space as three bodies dropped to top accelerating freighter, one snagging tight, one tearing loose, falling, rolling into darkness. Vee followed down, showed in sick close-up detail as he twisted, arms, legs were broken, skin tore, blood—

Just computerized simulation, of course, knew that. Didn't have much to go on, as automatic vid feed from freighter security system grainy, limited. So made it up, based on coroner's report injuries. Probably fairly accurate. Laws against misleading public, after all.

Sat there in vee, linked virtual-reality reconstruction, trapped like bug under paw of hungry cat. Couldn't get out, switch off, pull plug. Action replay. Mathewmark slipping, tumbling, smashing Vik as fell, catching in carbon webs, head banging, banging in rapid turbulence of air rushing past accelerating transport. Had taken nearly minute before onboard sensors of freighter knew something badly amiss, slowed transport down, sending out emergency shrieks human to come, see what had gone wrong. Most after that can't remember, except coldness in body, shaking, stink own sweat. Yellow lights darting up ahead as emergency crew ran small trolley back to us from next vent shaft access point. Someone peeling Mathewmark's bloody head free of carbon mesh, someone else's strong hands getting me out of webbing, lowering into blue, yellow dark to trolley, someone zipping up sleeve, injecting—

Mr. Abdel-Malek bent rules, as usual, instructing us gather chapel Memorial Neurological Hospital where Mathewmark still struggling for life in intensive care unit. They said badly damaged brain being supported by computer, sounded scary as hell. Chapel carefully non-

denominational, no crosses, Stars David, other sacred symbols particular faith. But hushed, special feeling about place. Maybe something
left over from all people must have come down here crying while
loved ones lay upstairs surrounded by bleeping sterile machines, hoping, praying wouldn't die. Seemed wrong to raise voice.

Didn't bother Mr. Abdel-Malek. Never had to raise voice.

All there, couldn't bear look each other. Except Auntie McWeezle,
bustled up moment caught sight of me huddled between Maman,
Maître, put arms around, pulled tight against her chest.

"You poor child," said. Maman, Maître exchanging appalled
glances, could tell. Mrs. McWeezle dressed in Sunday Best, modest
bonnet covered hair, long quilted jacket over rough-spun gray skirt
fell to leather-booted feet. Even wore gloves. Don't think ever seen
dress-up gloves before, outside vee sim. Made me think for moment
carbon-fiber gloves Vikram, I, wore during prank. When she let me
go, clung to gloved hands, squeezing tight.

"So sorry about . . ." started.

"The boy was always headstrong," Auntie McWeezle said. "He's
in the custody of the Goddess now."

Father trying introduce self, my mother, but kept clinging to
Auntie McWeezle's hands.

"How come you're here?" blurted. "Thought Valley people weren't
allowed . . ."

"Somebody has to come and fetch the boy," told me, scowling a
little as eyes studied others in chapel. Two sturdy young men in
conservative black suits set up table in front of altar, placing audio-
visual equipment here, there, for full recording of testimony, judgment. Might be informal hearing, but everything else done by book.
Dr., Mrs. Singh stood across room, distant, grieving, stiff with anger.
Cringed. My fault. All my stupid, stupid fault.

"They'll let Mathewmark go back?" managed to stumble out.
"Thought once crossed mountains done dash." As were guided to
seating near front of chapel, made sure Mrs. McWeezle stayed with
us. Mr. Abdel-Malek entered room, walked placidly to chair behind
desk, nodded to parents, to Singhs, to advocates. Flunky stepped
forward.

"All rise. This hearing is now in session, Magistrate Abdel-Malek presiding. Step forward as you are called, speak only when the Magistrate asks you to."

Mr. Abdel-Malek settled comfortably. Glanced at display.

"Dr. Singh, Mrs. Singh, good morning."

They rose, went forward. Mrs. Singh looked unsteady on feet.

"Sir, may my wife have a chair?"

"Of course. You may both be seated. Tipstaff."

One of black-suited flunkies moved two chairs forward, held out arm helpfully as Mrs. Singh sat. She hunched forward for moment, openly weeping, then sat straight, pushing hankie back into sleeve.

"While this is primarily a hearing into the circumstances of the death of your son Vikram, you have petitioned this court for the privilege of cloning the deceased. As you know, this is a forbidden procedure except in the very rare cases when a court grants authorization. Please tell me why I should rule in your case against overwhelming precedent."

One of advocates stepped forward, holding notepage, primed to deliver oration. Seen this acted in thousand vids, vees. Mr. Abdel-Malek waved back irritably.

"I shall hear from the petitioners, thank you. I am conversant with the law. Madam?" Mrs. Singh made to stand, swayed. "Please remain seated, ma'am. Why should I allow this cloning to take place?"

"Why—Vikram is a fine, brilliant . . ." Stumbled to halt. "Was. Vikram was a wonderful boy, everything we could have asked for in a son, except that he was led astray in a moment of foolishness. We would not allow that to befall his twin brother, if you allow us to bring him into the world in place of our wonderful lost child." Could not go on. Tears streaming down her face. Mine too. Wiped face with back of hand.

"Dr. Singh?"

"I cannot improve on my wife's words, sir. Our son was the light of our lives. We gave him everything, and he flowered into exceptional young manhood. It is not right that a single accident—no, I admit it, a single error of judgment—should deprive the world of his unique endowments."

"You could parent another child," Mr. Abdel-Malek said, unimpressed. "That boy or girl would also be yours, blessed with all that you can provide. Why a cloned twin of the deceased?"

Dr. Singh shook head, as if could not understand question. "You met the pender, Magistrate. You have seen his Play records, his sporting attainments, his genome scan. This was an exceptional human being. He was destined for great things. Yes, another child would be just as much ours to love with the same devotion, but what are the chances that he would match our lost son's potential?"

He stood up, stepped forward slightly. Magistrate said nothing, watching impassively. "Each new child's genetic endowment, as you know, is a kind of lottery," Dr. Singh said. "Vikram was a jackpot, if I may put it so crudely. He was our winning entry. His cloned twin would share that same wonderful promise. Mr. Abdel-Malek, do not mistake me. We do not expect to get our son back. We would not impose unrealistic demands on our new child. He would not be forced to retrace the footsteps of his illustrious predecessor. But he would bring us special joy, and offer the world those rare gifts which an . . . accident . . . has taken from us." Sat down again. Noticed did not take wife's hand.

Magistrate steepled own hands. "Thank you, Mrs. and Dr. Singh. I shall take your arguments under advisement and hand down my judgment at the end of these proceedings. Please accept my commiserations in your loss. You may return to your own seats now." Looked straight at me for moment. Knew exactly where everyone was in room. "Mrs. Myrtle McWeezle, please step forward."

Auntie McWeezle stood up, made way to front.

"You are Mrs. Myrtle McWeezle of the Valley of the God or Goddess of your own Choice?"

"I am."

"Do you wish to be seated, Mrs. McWeezle?"

"The Goddess has given me legs. I know how to use them."

"As you wish," Mr. Abdul-Malek said. If Auntie's reply surprised, did not show it. "May I say," murmured evenly, "that the court fully appreciates the sacrifice you have made in leaving your Valley."

"Someone has to take young Mathewmark home."

"Well, perhaps. In the fullness of time . . . Now, Mrs. McWeezle, I believe you are the last person, apart from Amanda Kolby-McAllister and Mathewmark Fisher, to see Vikram Singh alive."

"He was a polite, well-spoken boy. A bit soft, if you ask me."

"A bit soft, Mrs. McWeezle?"

"That young lad would have been no use in the fields."

"I should think not," Mrs. Singh said quite loudly.

Mr. Abdel-Malek raised eyes, looked at Vik's mother for couple seconds, didn't say anything. Returned attention to Auntie Mc-Weezle.

"Ah, I see," said. "You mean his hands were soft, not his brain."

"Well, I don't know," Auntie McWeezle said. "Plunging down that stink pipe into the depths of the infernal regions wasn't the brightest thing."

"He was led astray," Mrs. Singh said, spun around in seat look straight at me. "She made him—"

"Mrs. Singh!" Mr. Abdel-Malek said. Spoke sharply but without raising voice. "I know this is a trying time for you, but I must insist that you do not interrupt these proceedings again." Slowly Magistrate took gaze away from Vik's mother, then said to Auntie McWeezle, "Now, Mrs. McWeezle, I understand that Ms. Kolby-McAllister and Mr. Singh stayed the night at your house? Is that correct?"

"It's correct until about one o'clock, then they borrowed my ladder."

"In order to climb up the Maglev Authority's ventilation shaft?"

"The devil's arse."

Slight intake breath in room, some people suppressing giggles. Mr. Abdel-Malek let nothing show on face. Said smoothly, "Let us just refer to the structure in question as the shaft. We all know what it is."

"And we know what comes out of it."

"Quite, Mrs. McWeezle. Now could you tell us, please, what impression you formed of the two young people while they were your guests."

"Amanda has a way with words. Numbers, too, I gather. She's a headstrong young lady. Willful maybe. But I can't abide a dishrag.

Some young ladies have got no backbone to speak of, but Amanda, for all her Outside ways, is what I'd call a girl with a bit of spirit."

"And Vikram Singh? What impression did you form of him?"

"Like I say, a bit soft, but a polite, helpful young man."

"Your Honor, with respect," began young lawyer from Maman's firm. Looked barely year past Maturity.

"Yes, Legal Jones?"

"With respect, these questions are doing nothing to further the course of this hearing. The witness's hastily gathered impressions of the two young people have no bearing on what eventuated later that night in the Maglev Authority's tunnel. The witness was not in the tunnel. The witness was at home in bed."

Young man appeared quite pleased with point made. Mr. Abdel-Malek looked at sadly. Might have been regarding foolish young puppy knocked over vase flowers. "Legal Jones," said, "are you of the opinion that what happened on the night in question was the result of an exploit entered into by your client, Ms. Kolby-McAllister, and Pender Singh?"

"Yes, of course, Your Honor,"

"And are you of the opinion that when exploits are entered into, a certain relationship develops between those whom we might call the exploitees?" Had strong impression was taking piss out of Legal Jones, but face was bland, utterly expressionless.

"Er . . . I daresay, Your Honor."

"Well, if you don't mind, Legal Jones, I think the court might spend some time examining this relationship. Do sit down."

"Umm . . . if the court pleases," mumbled young man, sitting down.

Whispered to Maman: "Dork."

"Jones is your lawyer," Maman hissed. "If you want to stay out of prison, you'd better take him seriously."

"Now, Mrs. McWeezle," Mr. Abdel-Malek said, "did you form an opinion about who was in charge? Who would you say was the dominant member of the couple, Ms. Kolby-McAllister or Mr. Singh?"

"They was a couple of teenagers. They meant no harm."

"They were not teenagers as you understand the matter, madam. But who was in command?"

"Command? They wasn't an army."

"Did you form the opinion that one of the young people was making the decisions? That perhaps the other young person was being led?"

"Young people have got to take responsibility," Mrs. McWeezle said. "It's no good blaming things on others."

"My boy was bewitched," Mrs. Singh said. "Hush," Dr. Singh said quietly, putting hand on wife's arm. Mrs. Singh shook off, didn't speak again.

"About Mathewmark," Mrs. McWeezle said. "I've come to take him home."

"We shall consider what is in the best interests of Mathewmark Fisher in due course," Magistrate said.

3 : mathewmark

I'm feeling much, much better. I can remember all sorts of stuff. I can remember Amanda. She was a bat. A huge bat playing in the sparks from a fire. She had a friend, they twisted and swooped in the air above the fire, they blanked out the stars with their wings. Hey nurse, I tell the pretty girl nurse who is sitting by my bed, Amanda was a bat. Amanda Kolby-McAllister is staring a Reckless Endangerment charge in the face, says the pretty nurse. Custodial sentence, unless her rich olds can hire the right lawyers. I can remember the shaft, I say, I climbed down it. Down the handholds. Like a spider on a wall. I remember as clear as day—only it was night. There was this weird light in the shaft. I remember heaps.

"Of course you do. They've hooked you up."

"Hooked me up?"

"To a dedicated computer," the nurse says. "You've got computer enhancement by the ton. Terabits of supplementary network."

I try to sit up. Someone gives my hair a good hard pull. I don't think it's the big fat man in the blue clothes who is washing the floor with a mop. He's too far away. I yelp and shake my head.

The nurse jumps up, and she's fussing with my scalp. "Hey, be careful with the jack."

"Jack?"

"The optical cable coming out of your head. There's more two-way data transmission going through that little baby than you could count in a million years."

"I don't understand," I say.

"You're connected to a neural net, a machine, Mathewmark," says the nurse. "It is doing a lot of your thinking for you."

"We don't believe in machines in the Valley," I say. "Machines are the devil's handiwork."

"Could have fooled me," says the pretty nurse. "It was machines that saved your bacon."

The orderly over on the other side of the room laughs in a nasty way. "Right. Turn that thing off and he's a drooling vegetable again."

"Watch what you say, Carl," the nurse says sharply. I can tell she's upset at what the man said. "The fellow is regaining his memory and there's nothing wrong with his ears."

"Sorry, nurse," the fellow mumbles, and pushes his mop and bucket out into the hallway. The nurse leans over me again and gives me a big smile. My eyes go out of focus, and there are two smiles and four eyes. I'm very sleepy. At least nothing hurts. I'll just nod off—

Q. Awareness is biological, so the very idea of machine intelligence is absurd. Surely you don't believe the mind is nothing but information?
A. The mind *is* just information. The entire universe, from super-strings up, is just an incomprehensibly vast moving tapestry of quantum exchanges. We aren't immaterial spirits trapped in some crappy meat things. Our minds are how our brains mind our bodies, which include our brains. Sometimes, obviously, we can sit here talking without it necessarily having anything directly to do with our need to scratch bugs off ourselves, feed our faces, mate, and reproduce. On the other hand, minds *were* evolved to subserve the scratching and eating and mating, so it would be pretty stupid to forget that fact.

Q. Not much room in AI for sensual pleasures, is there?
A. Why? Does the fact that human beings are simply made of atoms and not *élan vital* leave no room for sensuality?

Q. You computer nerds might relish the prospect of spending eternity inside a machine, but frankly it revolts the rest of us.
A. Not *in* a computer—*as* a computer. But that's unfair anyway—are you planning to spend the rest of your life as meat, or in meat? This really is disgusting reductionism. Uploaded people would be minds copied exactly into computer implementations. They'd only turn out to be "soulless robots" if they were designed by a lunatic without the first clue of what constitutes life and consciousness.

Q. You sound so relentlessly optimistic about technological progress. Won't this generation refuse to accept such options, however prettily you paint them?
A. My optimism reflects the developmental curve. It's there, soaring exponentially, and I can't see what'll stop it rising. At the same time,

people do conform to what they've been taught. All this is too recent to have shaped most people's deep-set expectations. Worse, they've been poisoned by the so-easy, so-irresponsible "Frankenscience" sound bites.

Q. But all this work on life extension, artificial intelligence, and implanted or genomic enhancements risks destroying the human soul.
A. Human souls are nondestructible, that's the one thing we're guaranteed by traditional religion. If you send one to hell for its sins, it will suffer in intolerable pain *for all eternity!* Isn't that comforting? So much more . . . human . . . than these awful scientists with their mad ideas.

5 : amanda

Hearing dragged on, despite Mr. Abdel-Malek's irritable insistence that lawyers speed matters up. One Legal even brought in bearded guy, Superintendent Holesworthy. At first thought had been part of Maglev rescue crew, but turned out to be chap in charge of warm-fusion plant. Said on night we'd ridden updraft all sensors went crazy.

"It was as if we were being attacked by pterodactyls, sir."

Quiet laughter in chapel.

"Thank you, Mr. Holesworthy. That will be all."

Sat there in chapel-courtroom, mess mixed emotions. Pissed off with proceedings. Seemed less and less to do with what really happened, reasons did what we did. This flash young lawyer meant keep me out jail, Legal Jones, was nerd, no two ways. Each interjection, each question asked witness, more irrelevant than last. Singhs' lawyer no better, nerdy in different way. Too clever by half, endlessly trying blind Mr. Abdel-Malek with obscure bits law. Luckily, Mr. Abdel-

Malek knew even more law than she did, put sharply in place. So I fumed. But, of course, miserable as well. Just full of guilt, aching sorrow over Vik. All really wanted was get up, tell court why was all my fault. But Maman said she'd no more allow give testimony than allow anywhere near Maglev tunnel. And Legal Jones agreed. Legal Jones so full of self didn't need any help from me. But was *my* case, *my* trial!

By end of day, nothing decided. Mr. Abdel-Malek wearily instructed everyone come back next day.

"Sir," Auntie McWeezle started explain, plainly put out by decision, "I need to take Mathewmark home immediately. It's not right for the boy to be separated from his—"

"I understand your concern, madam," Mr. Abdel-Malek said, "but I fear that matter will have to wait as well." Glanced at display on table. "My understanding is that Mathewmark's recovery is still far from complete. I shall hear from his doctors tomorrow, and then we'll see how soon he can be released into your care."

Outside chapel, breathed deeply, telling self everything would pass. That time heals all. Didn't believe. Poor Vik dead, filthy word, filthy fact. Still could not face that truth, not really. Just felt depressed, angry at same time. Maman and Maître already in family glide, waiting for me to get in. Wondered if they'd let walk home by myself. Couldn't face intimacy glide's cabin. Noticed Auntie McWeezle still standing on far-side parking area, just outside chapel doors. Looked little, old, lonely in handmade clothes. Huge edifice Memorial Neurological Hospital rose up behind, like cliff.

"For heaven's sake, child," Maman told, "stop dithering and get in."

Bent down glide's open side.

"You go home," said with all firmness could muster. "See you later." Then ran across forecourt to Auntie McWeezle. After moment, car lifted into air behind me, headlights came on. Ignored parents. "Come on, Auntie," said, taking old lady's hand. "Let's go back in, see if find Mathewmark."

I'm sitting up in bed. The cable coming out of my head feels as thick as my thumb, and when I crane my head back I can just see the curve of it rising over me. It's supported by a sort of lever jutting down from the ceiling. Then it disappears into the wall behind my head. Today the walls are blue and white like sky in summer. The nurse is new, he's called Tony, and he has green hair and a rose tattooed on his cheek.

"Sorry, wrong room," Tony suddenly says quite loudly. "No visitor access here."

"Come see Mathewmark," a girl says, and walks straight into the room. It's the bat. It's Amanda. Only she is dressed in ordinary Outsider clothes. An old woman comes into the room, in decent Valley clothes.

"Auntie!" I say. "Auntie McWeezle."

"Sit down!" yells Tony. "The jack, mind the jack!" He grabs me by the shoulders and forces me back against the pillows. "You two, get out," he says to Amanda and Auntie McWeezle.

"They're my friends," I say.

"Friends," says Amanda, nodding cheerfully.

"Well, everybody stay calm," Tony says. "No sudden movements. Mathewmark isn't supposed to have visitors until his chip has been installed."

"Oh Auntie," I say, "What are you doing here? This is the Outside."

"Someone has to take you back," Auntie says.

"I'm all hooked up to machines."

"No good will come of it," Auntie McWeezle says.

"They reckon I couldn't speak properly without the machines."

"Machines are the devil's handmaidens."

"Look, I really must ask you two to leave," Tony says with authority. "Mathewmark is in a very precarious state."

"Let them stay," I say. "They're my friends. I haven't seen any friends since I woke up."

Tony looks quickly at the two women, makes up his mind and presses the button that closes the door. "Just don't excite him," he says. "And you can't stay long."

Auntie McWeezle sits on the side of my bed and holds my hand.

"How are Momma and Dad?" I say. "How is Lukenjon?"

"Your parents will come round," Auntie says. "Don't you worry, Mathewmark."

"Come round?"

"They'll want you back, you're their flesh and blood."

"But," I say, "but at the moment?"

"At the moment," Auntie McWeezle says, "they are being a bit literal about those who venture Outside without permission."

"They've cast me out?" I say. My voice sounds funny, but then everything sounds a bit odd right now. I'm near to tears. My own momma and dad. "Have they scrubbed my name out of the Holy Book of our Choice?" I whisper.

"Yes, yes," says Auntie McWeezle, waving one hand as if this was of no consequence. "Anything that has been scrubbed out can be rewritten, Mathewmark. It's just ink on paper. Don't you worry. Lukenjon is working on them. As soon as I get you back they'll see the error of their ways."

"Look," says Tony, starting to sound worried. "Can you just make your conversation more general, please. Just talk about the weather. If you upset Mathewmark, the brain-state monitors will activate every alarm channel in the network."

"I don't know what you are saying, young man," Auntie McWeezle tells him, "but Mathewmark needs to talk about his parents and his foolishness in the tunnel, there's no point running away from things."

"If the monitors pick up unusual brain activity, they'll automatically feed a powerful sedative into Mathewmark's system, they'll shut down his higher faculties."

Auntie McWeezle makes the sign o'god. She turns to Amanda, "What's he saying?"

"Machine running Mathewmark will put to sleep if . . ."

"Put him to sleep!"

"No, no, Auntie," Amanda says quickly. "Not that sort sleep. Just, you know sleepy-type sleep."

Auntie makes the sign o'god again. "The sooner we get him away from these polluter machines the better."

"Probably have to be connected to brain simulator for rest of life," Amanda says, looking unhappy.

"He'll be connected to no such thing," Auntie says sharply.

"No, don't worry, won't have cable, all these monitors," Amanda says. "Will just put chip in head."

"Not if I have anything to do with it," Auntie McWeezle says.

"Don't fret, Auntie," I say. "Maybe some machines are blessed, not wicked . . ."

"Blessed! Oh, Mathewmark, what have they done to you?"

"It's just that . . . I want to be able to talk properly . . . to think properly."

"Of course you can talk and think properly. What do you think you're doing now?"

"It's the machine, Auntie."

"Machine! There's nothing that faith in the God of your Choice and lots of rest and the proper use of herbs and potions won't put right. I'll not hear about good machines! You'll be talking of good devils, righteous Princes of Darkness, wise hobgoblins . . ."

Auntie was getting quite upset. So was I. And I was feeling tired, and sort of hungry without actually wanting to eat anything. My mouth had gone numb. I was almost asleep. Some lights were flashing and a soft beeping noise came from somewhere. I heard Tony talking, but he was a long way away, at the end of a long dark tunnel. He was saying, "Now you've done it! The system is closing him down. The neurosurgeons will be here in a minute. You've got to go. Both of you, now. . . ."

I tried to speak, but through my tiredness all I could do was burble, the words wouldn't come. I was collapsing sideways. Tony caught me. He said something about balance feedback circuits. More people were in the room. Auntie McWeezle was saying, "What are you doing to him, what are you doing . . ."

Amanda said something about the machines cutting me out for my own good. I'd be all right, I'd be . . .

s e e d   o r i g i n   vii: g u a r d i a n

They made it up, after a while. The kids racted him through a sim. Guns barked, smoke coiled, men and women in tattered uniforms ran past them up a hill. There came a high shrieking: something dark crashed from the stinking clouds overhead, made the earth shake and thump, exploded with horrible violence. Shrapnel whined pitilessly through them, ripped limbs and bellies of the soldiers who lurched into the morass of blood and mud and tatters of shredded grass and undulating strands of barbed wire. The stench. The pain in their bruised ears. Hammering, endlessly, in the head even when the guns fell silent.

"Going to be sick," Michio cried in distress, and vomited, choking. Abruptly, it was all cut off, vanished like a bad dream.

"Horrible," Abdel-Malek said, holding the heaving shoulders of the pale boy. "Horrible." It had been like standing knee deep in human blood and wickedness. "When was it recorded?'

Michio wipes vomitus from his lips, shuddering. "Not real, Mohammed. Generated."

Virtual. Yet the density of immersion, the extraordinary detail, screams, thuds, smell of churned mud and eviscerated flesh, rank stench of the explosives . . .

"History lesson," Ally told him.

He understood perfectly. He and his colleagues and students had discussed this too, for years, in his lab, building toward it. At some point the thrill of war games and paintball and *Doom* went across a catastrophe fold, for most people, for the nonpsychopaths, crashed from excitement to uttermost revulsion and horror. Ally and Michio knew from their own false memories just how disgusting and vicious and immoral life had been in Abdel-Malek's world.

"The Aleph," he said, speculating.

"Our custodian," Michio told him.

"I can't stay here any longer," Abdel-Malek said with decision.

7 : amanda

Wanted take Auntie Mc-Weezle back our place, and Maman reluctantly said would be very nice have with us until whole ordeal done, but turned out room set aside for her in hospital. I came out from Luddite call booth, found anxious orderly searching for Auntie. Shouldn't have been major difficulty, given strange clothes was wearing. He located us just as was explaining arrangements to Myrtle McW, so then had to go back into shameful booth, phone home again, and Maître said was already on road so would pick me up out front of hospital instead of sending a cab for.

Was so infuriating having implant phone disconnected, needing go out looking for hard phone like some peasant. Started say this to Auntie McWeezle. Frowned at me in way made feel instantly ashamed of self.

"Don't mean *real* peasant, Auntie," said, covered in confusion. "That is, not farmer, like you, I mean layabout—"

"I know perfectly well what you mean, Amanda, even if you insist on speaking in that silly way. I do wish you'd stop." Looked at me sorrowingly, and I felt even worse without quite understanding why. "You're a child of heedless privilege, a daughter of the bad machines. That's why you harbor ill feelings for the poor. You should come back with us and learn what it's like to do an honest day's toil with your own hands." Went on like that for while, explaining my character defects, and orderly stood there looking embarrassed.

Had started out feeling ashamed, something not used to, but this ticking-off put back up. What would she know? Yes, might be nice old biddy, but what gave right swan around offering sarcastic, holier-than-thou opinions about *my* life? Didn't know first thing about modern life. Felt face getting red, about blurt out something rude when Maître came through double doors into hospital lobby.

He pushed hands into pockets, giving us rather stern look. Orderly took Mrs. McWeezle's arm, said, "All right, now, dearie, I'll just take you up to your room now." I swallowed hard, looking from one to another, bit lip, gave Myrtle peck on cheek. She gave big hug before shaking hands with Maître, then trotted after orderly, following scuffed green line to elevator. Still looked little, old, but not quite so lost. Not lost at all, maybe.

In morning gathered again in chapel. Mr. Abdel-Malek behind desk exactly 10 A.M., all in previous seats except Superintendent Holesworthy, testimony quoted previous evening's news, satirical animation flapping troop giant prehistoric pterodactyls menacing muon warm-fusion plant. Probably took day off work as well.

Myrtle McWeezle looked rested, resolute. Singhs fierce, lawyers seemed ready drone on endlessly rare, unusual cases precedent, points order. Maman, Maître sat either side of me, beautifully dressed, of course, pretending utterly relaxed. Could tell Maman actually about leap out of skin, which always made Maître extra jumpy as well. Starting feel sick, bit of breakfast jumped into throat, sharp, sour. Couldn't help thinking about poor Mathewmark, optical-fiber cable stuck into head, piping hundreds millions bytes data in, out computerized brain backup. Vikram dead, buried, left horrible hole inside my chest, hole plugged up with guilt, shame. Mathewmark still alive but never be same again.

Because of my stupid prank, hayseed left security own weird world, got trapped into something never could have dealt with, even with careful guide. And now great big chunk brain gone, team technicians preparing replace destroyed tissue with specialized sim chip.

Wasn't simple idea plugging sim in head threw me—hardly, had own first neural implant years before, math chip, then phone module on twelfth birthday along with immunities. Just that this chip wasn't optional extra. Not improvement—replacement. If Vik, I hadn't gone flapping around like giant pterodactyls, got poor farm boy stirred up with romance of forbidden Outside, still have all his brain. Still have his home, dorky girl Sweetcharity moon over, maybe marry, make dozen Valley kids. Now never be allowed back, unless Auntie McWeezle could pull off miracle. Felt myself sob, two hot tears ran down cheeks. Really felt so awful.

"I call Amanda Kolby-McAllister," flunky saying. "As she is a legal minor, she may be represented by counsel."

Legal Jones bounded to feet, looking especially self-important, opened mouth. Tapped him on arm, stepping past Maman's stylishly shod toes, said clearly as could, "Speak for sel—" Stopped, as if Auntie McWeezle had reached within head, given hair sharp tug from inside. Blushed slightly, started again. "I'll speak for myself, if that's all right."

Magistrate looked at me for silent moment, then nodded. "Step up to the front, Amanda. Take one of those chairs. We will not stand on ceremony this morning. I have a busy schedule, and this matter has already been unduly protracted." Cast cold glance over my shoulder, presumably at Legal Jones, who probably shrank instantly by several centimeters. Or maybe not—rebuke might have gone right over dork's head.

"You've heard the accounts given by all the witnesses, Amanda. In the light of that evidence, it seems plain that you and Vikram Singh understood the risks you were taking, and just went ahead anyway. Is that correct?"

"But never thought he'd—"

"I am not interested in self-serving excuses. You had been intercepted not one month previously attempting to enter the sealed loading bay of the Metro Maglev Deep Rail Project. I'm sure you have not forgotten appearing before me on that occasion, together with the young man who is now tragically absent from our company."

Dropped eyes, stung again by stab shame. "Yes, sir."

"Yet you devised a scheme to evade the precautions your parents had put in place to restrict your movements and access. You conspired with the deceased to enter a prohibited sacred locale, despite your certain knowledge that this would cause grave offense to the people whose sanctum you would be intruding upon. Once there, you invaded the private property of the Maglev consortium, interfering dangerously with the electronic safeguards to a ventilation access shaft. You allowed an innocent from the Valley to follow you into—"

"We didn't mean for Mathewmark to come after us," said desperately, wishing could curl up, shrink away, vanish off face of world.

"Hold your tongue," Mr. Abdel-Malek told in cold, level voice. "You did nothing to prevent this unfortunate young man from entering with you into the direst peril, even after you knew that he was following you down the shaft. You could have turned back at that point. You could have returned to the surface with him, closed the access entrance, and left the Valley. You did not. While you plainly did not connive at his death, you took no steps to avert it."

Started sob, quite loudly. Couldn't help. Chest shook, hands shook as well, even though locked together against waist. Said nothing. Sour taste in mouth got worse, like vomit.

"As a result of this extraordinarily foolish escapade, your joint exploit with the deceased has led directly to a death and a most serious injury. If you were Mature, you would now be liable to sanctions under the criminal code. As it is, your pender status allows you to escape the serious consequences that would befall a legal adult responsible for such violations. Do you have anything to say in mitigation?"

Behind, heard Legal Jones push back chair, clear throat. Magistrate silenced with another cold glance. Thousand things wanted say: explanations, excuses. How much regretted foolishness. How sorry was. Poor Vikram! Poor Mathewmark! Poor Auntie McWeezle! Couldn't say word, which was just as well. Shook head.

"Perhaps you are belatedly learning a little discretion," Mr. Abdel-

Malek told. "Very well. Here is my summary judgment: you will not have a criminal conviction recorded against your name, but you will be restricted to the following places until you reach your Thirtieth birthday: your parents' home, your Play, and any other places supervised by educators where your presence is mandated. A NannyWatch chip will be fitted to your net access to ensure that you are under surveillance twenty-four hours a day, seven days a week, during that penitential period. Any attempt to evade surveillance"—looked at me with piercing eyes, tone hard, implacable—"will result in your immediate arrest. Believe me, Ms. Kolby-McAllister, you do not want to appear before this court a third time."

In very small voice, whispered, "No, sir."

"Very well. Return to your seat." As blundered back sit down between white-faced parents, heard him tap gavel on desk. "Now, as to the disposition of Mathewmark Fisher, currently still in intensive and remedial neurological care in this hospital. Mrs. McWeezle. No, please remain seated. I have conferred with the young man's medical specialists, and I understand that they have spoken to you as well. I realize that the technology of their procedures is rather alien to the practices familiar to residents in your sacred enclave—"

"The work of the devil," Myrtle McWeezle called clearly from chair near front of room, across from where I sat. "A tube sucking at the poor lad's brain!"

"Just so. Now I'm afraid that any hopes of moving—"

"Not that I'm ungrateful," she said just as clearly. "Devil's work, but the devil has his tricks and uses. The boy would not have survived such a terrible fall in the Valley."

"Quite. We must be grateful for such small mercies. However, it is apparent that without a neural prosthesis to augment his severely damaged brain, Mathewmark will suffer a significant mental impairment during the rest of his life. Do you understand the choice you must make, Mrs. McWeezle?"

"The boy will go simple," she said in gloomy voice. "Good for nothing but herding cows and mucking out their droppings."

"Worse than that, perhaps," Magistrate told, gazing over steepled fingers. "Much of the left side of his brain has been destroyed. Many of his faculties are now lost, or would be except for the heroic medical treatment available in this hospital. Do you follow what I am saying now, madam? Your grandson—"

"No blood relation of mine, though I love the boy like a son, the young scamp."

"I misspoke. In any event, do you grasp what the doctors here propose to do to help young Mathewmark go on with a healthy life? I must be certain that you do, since your informed consent is required before the medical staff can take the final step and replace the temporary computer prosthesis with a specially grown chip."

"You're saying you'll put a machine inside the boy's head? An instrument of Satan?"

"Not of Satan, madam. A contrivance of human design, built by human hands, just as your own poultices and herbal remedies are the product of human wisdom and care. I do not believe you need fear for the lad's spiritual well-being."

I watched sideways, across width of chapel. Myrtle McWeezle standing in place, hands pressed together in silent prayer. Eyes closed. Could see anguish in lined, old features. Lips tightened. Moment stretched on, on. I glanced at Magistrate. Sat stock-still, own fingers steepled, as if wait forever for old lady reach her decision. She nodded, sharply, opened eyes.

"Do what you must to aid him," said, sat down.

"Thank you, madam. You have chosen wisely. Now," Magistrate said, clicking to new data on display, reading it for moment, eyes flicking back, forth like snake's, "we come to the petition made at the outset by Dr. and Mrs. Singh. Would you please come forward?"

Some shuffling, muttered words with their Legal. Singhs stood side by side before desk.

"I have considered your request to be allowed a clone twin of the deceased youth, Vikram Singh. I have drawn your attention to the psychological hazards of such a procedure, when it is conducted in such sad circumstances. The pressure upon such a child to match the perhaps unrealistic and increasingly rosy expectations of his grieving parents would be very great."

"Please, sir," Mrs. Singh burst out, "we would definitely not place any such—"

"Allow me to finish." Mr. Abdel-Malek crisp, chilly. Mrs. Singh recoiled, as if slapped. Guess not many people talk to Singhs that way. "I am also obliged to take into account the fact that this lad was not, in fact, an angel. He contributed to his own death by his reckless decision to partake in this absurd and dangerous escapade. Do we wish to bring into the world a carbon copy of such a foolhardy if talented person?"

I felt bit sick. Vik had always gone on, on, about how parents so great, but I always had sneaking suspicion wasn't everything cracked up to be. If having such a wonderful time at home with terrific olds, what doing out crawling into bowels of earth with me in middle of night? But after all, my folks okay, sort of, weren't they? And had been my idea.

"Taking all these matters into balanced consideration, and placing them against your notable and well-deserved reputation in the community, I find that your petition, while unusual, is justified in these tragic circumstances. You have the permission of this court to begin a clone twin of the deceased, which I understand will be carried by a surrogate mother."

Mrs. Singh began blubber tears, murmuring, "Oh thank you, thank you."

"I do caution you once more not to place impossible hopes upon the shoulders of this new infant—and to remember that by the time he is born he will have parents who are nearly three decades older than they were when Vikram was born. I wish the three of you well. Please take your seats now."

Magistrate cast cool gaze across whole room. No doubt foresaw media uproar decision would set off. Suppose also knew nasty rumors would fly at once—rumors about Singhs' links organized crime, wealth, suspicions corruption, special deals. None of that obvious in disdainful attitude. Snapped notepage off with flick of finger.

"This has been a distressing hearing. I trust I never need listen to such a sorry tale again. Thank you, ladies and gentlemen. Court is

adjourned." Stood, flowed from chapel surrounded by black-suited
flunkies.

Stood up myself, after moment, and legs were weak. Maman,
Maître exchanging glance. Wondered how were feeling, dragged into
scandal, dead pender, my fault. Sought words, found nothing. Felt
sicker, guilty, looked across room at Mrs. McWeezle. Had nobody to
help her, a shockingly sick man upstairs to look after in strange,
terrible city. Wanted go over, talk to her, but couldn't think anything
say would help.

8 : mathewmark

Odd heathen menu they pro-
vided here, but wonderfully tasty. "Hospital food," Di the new orderly
said enviously the second day after I woke up. "Wish the tucker in
the staff caf was as good. I don't suppose you feel well enough to try
that chocolate pudding?" she added hopefully. I shook my head, the
cable tugging, and she took the bowl with an appreciative smile, dip-
ping the creamy stuff into her mouth with happy smacking sounds
of her lips. "I sometimes think it would be worth having a bad accident," she told me confidentially, "just to get to rest up for a few days
and work myself through this yummy menu."

It was a reminder of Valley custom, in its way, because the old
biddies tell us that the way to regain health is to eat wisely and well.
The difference was in the kinds of food they provided here. No pur-
gatives and springwater. Something called pizza, for example—crusty
and hot, with a dozen delicious toppings of tomato and spicy meats
and tiny sliced mushrooms and many rich runny cheeses, the bread
soft and light inside. I couldn't make up my mind what I liked more:
something called *coq au vin*, which is a chicken in wine, with crisp
green beans and small roasted potatoes, or *saltimbocca*, which Di the
orderly told me meant "jump in the mouth," beaten meat of baby calf

under a layer of fine swine's bacon, smothered in creams and butter and herbs, with a tasty salad tossed lightly in oil and vinegar and still more herbs, and tangy garlic, or fresh trout and fried potatoes. That was the first and last time I gave up my sweet to a member of the staff. I looked forward every day to the *profiteroles*, which contained that chocolate stuff Amanda had given me in the Valley, and ice creams and pears in brandy and other treats I had never even heard of at home, famous as it was in the Valley for wholesome scones and cider.

"Hey, Tony," I said. "Do you know when Amanda is going to visit me again?"

"She can't," Tony said. "Court orders."

"What do you mean, court orders?"

"She's only allowed to go to Play. Otherwise, she has to stay at home."

"Why?"

"Because of the list of crimes as long as her arm, that's why."

"She's not that bad," I said.

"Vikram Singh's dead. You've only got half your natural brain . . ."

"That's not her fault," I said. "Both me and Vikram chose to go down that shaft—she didn't make us."

"She's lucky she was up before Abdel-Malek," Tony said. "Any other Magistrate would have frozen her."

"Well, anyway," I said. "I want to see her. The only visitor I get is Auntie McWeezle."

"When you get moving, maybe. Then you can visit her at home."

"When I get moving," I said, "I'm going back to the Valley."

Tony didn't say anything. He'd been there when Auntie McWeezle showed me the elders' letter. Auntie had been writing letters to them every day. They'd sent one back. A special messenger had to bring the sheets of paper from the Gatehouse to the Neurological Hospital. Tony and some of the other nurses had thought it was the funniest thing they'd ever heard of: sending personal messages on bits of paper. Real olden days stuff, they said. I didn't tell them that was one of the things I often did when I was carting loads with Ebeeneezer, carry notes from one farm to another. But even if Tony and his friends thought letter-carrying was a funny occupation, the contents of the letter weren't funny.

The Elders said that even though I'd left the Valley without permission, I'd be allowed back in, but not if I had an infernal machine in my head. "If Mathewmark must become a foolish simpleton, he will be God's foolish simpleton," the Elders wrote. "But if he carries the machinery of a cunning wisdom in his head, he will be the devil's mechanic and will know the devil's wisdom." The letter went on like that for five more pages, with lots of stuff about casting out evil and serpents in paradise and speaking with forked tongues. I recognized the handwriting, I'd carried notes for its author on a number of occasions. Officially the letter was from the Assembly of Elders, but it had been written by old man Legrand.

"But Auntie," I said, when she showed me the letter, "look at me now—you know I'm not in league with the devil. You know the mainframe is just letting me be my old self."

"They'll be putting the . . . the . . . chip thing in your head next week," Auntie said.

"It'll be just the same," I said. "It's like the mainframe only smaller; Tony's explained it all to me."

"Explained what?" said Tony, coming into the room.

"About the chip," I said. "The Elders reckon I'll be the devil's mechanic."

Tony stifled a giggle. "Sounds like a band," he said. "Tony and the Devil's Mechanics. I might just start it up."

"They want me to be one of God's foolish simpletons," I said.

"Even better," Tony said. "God and the Foolish Simpletons. What a winner, with a name like that the band would be number one by Exmas."

"This is not a laughing matter," said Auntie McWeezle, making the sign o'god.

"Then why are you laughing, Auntie?"

"I am not," Auntie said, stifling a snort.

So, a couple of days later, when Tony told me Amanda was only allowed to leave her home to go to this Play thing, I said, "Could you take a letter to her?"

"A letter?" Tony said. "Like one of those crazy collections of paper. All about God and the Devil and the casting of stones?"

"It won't be crazy," I said. "It will be written by me, not old man Legrand."

"So what are you going to say?" Tony said. " 'I am the devil's mechanic and it is my fiendish desire to perform a grease and oil change on your soul'?"

"I want a piece of paper and a pen," I said.

"I'm not sure about the ethics of being an old-fashioned mailman for patients."

"Go on, Tony," I said.

9 : magistrate abdel-malek

Sinking into profound communion with the Aleph, the Honorable M. K. Abdel-Malek paradoxically rose toward satori, the bliss of enlightenment. He allowed his gaze to rest without effort or interpretation upon the full-wall display screen set to a dead channel, its deep ultramarine the blue of an Antarctic sky. Something moved in those depths: slow, majestic, endlessly calming.

The Magistrate's breathing quietened, heartbeat falling to a measured tranquil beat. His focus shifted, finding the Persian carpet's pattern, the polar ocean blue of the wall display entwined in crimson and gold, golden drift in the slanting morning beams of light crossing his chamber from the high window at his right. A second paradox, or perhaps the first in another guise, suffused his heart with satisfaction: each detail sharpened, weft and woof crossed and recrossed, every richly hued thread standing bright and individual as a struck note, redoubled again and again in echo, clarifying into the exactitude of itself. In that same moment he withdrew his weightless attention, slipped easily and wonderfully into the pattern of everything-at-once.

One by one, he disabled his neural mods and switched off his language centers. Cool perfumed vapors from a smoldering sandalwood taper rose in his right nostril, entered the upper spaces of his breathing passages, flowed like grace to his lungs, released in smooth flow from the left nostril. The Magistrate's hands rested palm upward on his dark, naked thighs. The thing in the deep blue wall display shifted and moved, some image unspeakable, impossibly grand. Was it cruelty? Was it love's tears? Alice had never returned. In the deeps of space, he knew, in the immensities of the solar system, something grand was being wrought. What was his role in this approaching transcendence? He could not fathom it, not entirely. He was the bridge, he knew that much, as if his flesh were stretched out between heaven and Earth. Tears leaked down his immobile cheeks, and his eyes closed to that flood of information (was it memory, hallucination, gift, an imposition closer to rape?) he had come to call the vastation.

Here is the creek he knew as a child. (But who is "he"?) It begins at a spring in the deep woods where the light is greenish and dim on the brightest days. Water from the spring lingers in a clear pool whose banks bristle with horsetail reed (*Equisetum hyemale*; even as a child he sought out and memorized the true names of things) before spilling over a natural stone dam into a winding course it has cut over the years.

Walking the creek from its source to its end is his regular pleasure, as natural as breathing. He has come to know the flora and fauna well. His favorite creature is a species of black catfish a child's handspan long, which he always seeks out and greets.

The Magistrate's right eyelid twitched. The serene beat of his heart quietened his distress, allowed him to watch calmly.

*   *   *

Five days after his twelfth birthday, he runs down to say hello to the creek and finds her dead. An oil company has drilled a slant well originating on their neighbors' land, sunk at an angle so that it bottoms out on the property. The boy knows from angry discussions overheard that this is legal as long as the oil company compensates the owners of the mineral rights attached to the surface under which the well bottomed out. His family will receive royalties from that well for decades, until production falls to uneconomic levels, leaving the well abandoned.

Somehow during drilling, a large volume of foul-smelling ancient muck has been released into the spring, turning its water inky black. Water and banks are dead all the way to the creek's end, where it joins with a larger creek in whose wide, cool water holes the boy has swum as long as he can remember. Blackness swirls into the larger creek, stains the broad sandy banks where he has lain exhausted after swimming, entertained by his mind's wanderings.

It is the first death of an intimate friend. The boy is shockingly jerked into an unfamiliar, hostile universe. He can no longer bear to look at the creek. In adolescence, when finally he returns one afternoon, he finds the creek healed but diminished. He never sees a little black catfish again. In the environment of his creek, the catfish have apparently become extinct.

Abandoned to the ebb and flow of profound communion, the Magistrate was washed by bliss and a kind of understanding. A flush, nearly a rash, crept upward from his naked belly to his chest, darkening his dusky skin. Muscles contracted across his torso. His mouth tightened, drew back. Abdel-Malek was aware of none of this, and aware of nothing else: in the paradox of satori, of his link with the terrifying thing sprung like Athena almost literally, from his chilled forehead (but he was no Zeus, quite the reverse), the godthing that called itself the Aleph, he was everywhere and nowhere.

*   *   *

Here is a spring-fed river, formerly a sacred place for the people who were here when the Europeans arrived hundreds of years earlier. Just below the springs, the cold, clear water, seven or ten meters across, flows swiftly over a bed of white and pink gravel studded with gray fossilized mussel shells. The taro-smothered banks are home to snakes, frogs, nutrias, other wild creatures. For a stretch, concrete banks and steps lead down into the water.

Hundreds of young girls adorn the pecan-shaded grassy parks on either side of the river, gathered for cheerleading practice. The loveliest and most vivacious girls from all the high schools in the region are there in brightly colored uniforms, in threes and fours, groups of ten or fifteen.

Boys have gathered to show off for this audience. The air drips pheromones. It is like a circus. Some youths engage in astonishing gymnastic feats, one back flip follows another, scorching their hands on the hot pavement; boys on skateboards, flinging themselves to the tops of walls, riding handrails down into the water; boys showing off their skill at juggling and tossing a Frisbee. The girls sit on the banks, far from the water, protective of their hair and makeup. Every now and then, one girl might favor a particularly skillful or handsome boy with a glance or smile.

Squirrels chase each other up and down the trees, and someone's radio is softly playing Puccini.

The flush of blood deepened, his breath came more quickly, pulses pounded. Utterly unselfconscious, Mohammed Kasim Abdel-Malek experienced a series of powerful contractions and small muscular convulsions that shook his entire body.

A woman's voice speaks in Spanish: *"In his hands I saw a long golden spear and at the end of the iron tip I seemed to see a point of fire. With this he seemed to pierce my heart several times so that it penetrated to my entrails. When he drew it out I thought he was drawing them out with it and he left me completely afire with a great love for God."* An image blazes: in the Cornaro Chapel of S. Maria della Vittoria in Rome, Giovanni Lorenzo Bernini's *Teresa of Avila*, angelically pierced, face spasming in ecstasy.

His grimace relaxed; blood pressure dropped back to normal. He drew a single rasping breath through his mouth, like a child in the moment of birth. He opened his eyes, blinked twice, returned his gaze to the deep blue of the wall display.

The room was playing Puccini: *"Nessun dorma! Nessun dorma!"*
No man must sleep!

A tenor's resonant voice offered Calaf's great romantic challenge:
"Ma il mio mistero è chiuso in me,
"Il nome mio nessun saprà!"

Yes, his secret lay hidden deep within, no one would know his name. He would not sleep.

Magistrate Abdel-Malek rose in a fluent movement, crossed the carpeted floor to his private bathroom. The morning light had strengthened in the window high in the outside wall; the display wall was blank, very faintly luminous. Water gushed, warm and foaming; he stripped away the *dhoti* and entered the water, stood beneath its needles, face raised, hair drenched, flesh laved. He was at peace. Something was entering his understanding, but he could not know yet what that was. His duties on the bench awaited him, in this small absurd partitioned community of small ridiculous enclaves built upon denial. It was enough. Abdel-Malek stepped from the pool, found a thick white towel, applied it briskly. The room played a Lebanese tune from childhood, his immigrant mother's music, doubly lost now in his dispossession, piping semitones that brought a smile to his lips.

Life was dull, dreary, boring, mind-numbing series oscillations. Home to Play. Play to home. Home to Play. At home, worked relentlessly on Beurling operators, Möbius groups, quasiregular, quasiconformal mappings. At Play everything had changed. Everybody knew what had done. Everybody knew what Mr. Abdel-Malek had said. Some of penders who'd been my friends muttered in presence that Mr. Abdel-Malek ought to be thrown out of judicial system. Said was disgrace held court hearing in chapel. Said should have sent me Reset Program or freezer. Parents obviously bribed Mr. Abdel-Malek. They knew this because was what their olders said had happened.

One day when arrived at Play, janitor very slowly cleaning some graffiti off wall outside science block. NDA SHOULD HAVE DIED WITH VIK.

"You should of, too," said janitor under her breath as I walked past.

Some penders went out of way to be friend.

"Come, hang with us," Juliet Burkenstock said at lunch.

"Still regard you as fellow human being, Amanda," Tomasina Gianotti said, keeping straight face, "even if did kill Vikram."

"We can help in rehabilitation process," Itzhak Posner said, staring earnestly through glasses. Weird parents didn't hold with remedial surgery, Itzhak couldn't tolerate contacts. Eyes watery. Mine were, too, by that stage.

"I didn't kill Vik," I said.

"It's all right, Amanda," Juliet said, "learned about denial in domestic psychology, quite natural."

"First-stage rehabilitation process," Elizabeth Wing told, "but we can help second stage: acceptance."

"Fuck off," said.

"It's all right, Amanda," they said, "learned about anger as well. But need learn use your anger, Amanda, natural but must learn use energy for own good."

Every luncheon after that ate by self, glowering anybody came near. At home told self deserved everything happened to me. Deserved cold shoulders of friends, of Vikram's old friends. Deserved attentions loathsome do-gooders. After all, was true—what hinted at during hearing—*had* been dominant partner. Vik still be alive if never met me. Gave me creepy feeling know somewhere on other side of van Gogh Metro, in Right to Life Maternity, repro technicians already growing Vikram's tiny clone twin. So paced room, flicked vee on. Flicked vee off. Flicked it, flicked it. And turned to only real friend, who saved sanity as nobody else could. No doubt about it, gone round twist without Strad Lad. Played my dear violin for hours, second movement Mendelssohn concerto, third movement Max Bruch's concerto G minor. Grooves in fingers from strings, arm ached from bow. But only played melancholy stuff; if wasn't in minor key, didn't want to know it. Lost self in music for half an hour, hour, two hours, *was* music. And if was the music, then wasn't Amanda Kolby-McAllister, bringer death, destruction. Ripped into Peter Sculthorpe's *Irkanda 4*, with harsh outback loneliness mimicking just how felt in desert of guilty heart. Someone tugged elbow. My music stopped abruptly. Mrs. Ng. Always knocks before coming into room, but hadn't heard her, hadn't heard anything but mournful, angry notes of violin. Eyes had been closed.

"Tony said to give you this," Mrs. Ng said.

"Eh?" said. "Who's Tony?"

"You don't know him?"

"I can't think of anyone called Tony," said. "What look like?"

"Green hair," Mrs. Ng said. "A rose tattooed on his cheek."

Good grief, that Tony. Muscle-man nurse from hospital. Downstairs? Sounded like trouble. "Could be anyone," said. "Any distinguishing features?"

"Nice smile."

"Don't know anyone with nice smile," said gloomily.

"Cheer up," Mrs. Ng said. "Read what's written on the paper. They might be wise sayings."

Yeah, right, like wise sayings of do-gooders at Play. Smart-ass wise words help with rehabilitation, more likely warning me, Mrs. Mc-Weezle keep distance. Half mind throw handwriting away unread. Handwriting, not print! Hard throw handwritten messages away unread. Curiosity powerful force. Unfolded sheet. Weird handwriting—like nothing taught in calligraphy. Flipped single page over see if signed self with full name. But name was Mathewmark.

> Dear Amanda,
> My friend Tony the nurse says he will bring you this letter. I am writing to you because you are the only person who has ever visited me in hospital apart from Auntie McWeezle. I am alone. I don't think I can go back to the Valley—they want me to be stupid, half-dead. But I'm from the Valley and I don't think I can live in the Outside. I have not seen the Outside, but this hospital place is so strange. It is like nothing in the Valley. The Outside must be worse. I'm frightened, Amanda. I'm frightened, and you are the only person I know in the whole Outside. Please Amanda, come and see me. I know that your Elders have said that you can't come to see me. Just like my Elders have said that I can't go back to the Valley unless I'm a simpleton of god. But please Amanda. You are so clever, you can fly through the air and blank out the stars with your wings. Please fly to me.
> Your friend Mathewmark.

Yeah, yeah, Mathewmark, thought. But no muon warm-fusion plant right next to Neurological Hospital. Anyway, took wings away. First thing they did.

Went to net link, stared at display saver for while, trying think something could dictate, print out for poor Mathewmark. But what was point anyway? How supposed to convey snailmail letter? Wasn't even sure *was* snailmail any longer. Couldn't order courier, because

Maman, Maître had frozen credit card. And didn't know how reach this Tony nurse dude.

Took another look at rather pathetic letter, found pale printed code running along top right-hand corner. Hospital stationery? Sticklers for tradition, medicos. Code might be neuro ward where Mathewmark hooked up to optical-fiber cable. So let's assume from intensive care unit or wherever he is now, do quick search through hospital's organizational chart. Had cracked way into place day after got home from last hearing in chapel, but hadn't found anything useful. And didn't want to bring wrath Mr. Abdel-Malek down on neck, so just put in bookmarks, picked up Strad Lad instead. Played fifteen minutes, but mind not on notes. Kept seeing Mathewmark, tethered to wall by fiber-optic cable. Bloody visions dear, silly Vikram, smashed, dead. Too awful, push away. Start crying otherwise, never stop.

Enough sulking, remorse. Time for action, Amanda.

"Open hospital link," told computer. Sick of feeling as if everyone in world staring over shoulder, waiting pounce on least little misdeed. If some chip snitched, damn it, too bad.

System played me some Philip Glass, opened up series embedded objects. I raced through them, and inside thirty seconds found code from slip of paper. Yep, postoperative convalescence intensive care unit. Table of staff on, off duty, another with doctors, yet another with patients. Relief! Mathewmark in stable condition, awaiting dedicated neural prosthesis. Couldn't make head nor tail all medical notes, charts. Didn't look immediate danger dying. Now what about this Tony character?

Anthony James Doyle, charge nurse, rostered evening duties this week. Must have dropped off note on way to work. Phone code listed to workstation, but didn't want talk to him just yet. Anyway, maybe someone else in unit would answer phone, notice where incoming call incoming from and I'd be in trouble if—

No, sheer paranoia. Why anyone notice *my* number? True, all calls routinely logged, recorded, archived. Maybe made no difference, but they might start asking questions how happened to have private un-listed phone number. Better find another route in.

Went back search through Mathewmark's file. Extensive, page after page entries, charts, diagrams of his brain, functional magnetic-resonance scans, other sly ways peering inside someone's head. Not that it would have been all that hard look inside Mathewmark's brain-case. Horribly graphic, highly colorful 3-D shots taken without any-one needing open up skull. Anyway, poor dork's skull already open, large chunk of bone broken free, pulsing brain tissue, blood vessels visible . . . Urk, barf. Really did feel dizzy, woozy for few minutes, had to flick display back to favorite saver, green, brown tree growing up from tiny seed, spreading out twigs, branches until wide leaves filled display, blocked sky.

Mathewmark's head not like that anymore, of course. Team top neurosurgeons went in, cleaned out swollen, bruised, tattered brain tissue, tidied up torn veins, linked whole mess into temporary bucky-scale neurointegrated interface boundary, looked in pix like kind of ceramic plug. Bucky scale? Strange—surely against spirit if not, just maybe, letter of Joyous Relinquishment. Not all bucky, luckily: cable thick as couple fingers ran up to plug, fired digital information down into poor man's brain.

Weird science. Verge of wicked science. Shivered. Half man, half machine. Took implants to new level, almost all the way back to lethal, hideously dangerous bad near-Singularity level. Made my chips look like splinter under skin. Industrial strength technomagic.

Sat straight up, made noise surprised even me.

"Oh my God," mumbled to self. "Can probably run virt right into boy's head, ract with." Dizzying notion—if could interact in a shared virtual world, maybe could speak without fear of interception.

Maybe. Interdicted, surely. Spoke some commands, display jumped around. Don't know what would have felt like doing this from brainplug phone. While talked to one level of system, pulled out keyboard, started hammering. Some programming jobs, speech just can't hack it as efficiently. Sometimes prefer let fingers do talking. Dragged in objects, patched them together, pulled down game interface liked lot—*Zone: The Wizard Rebellion*—plugged into vee. Laser light speared retinas, acoustics focused on eardrums.

Shot whole subprogram down line into Mathewmark's neural prosthesis.

Cool mist everywhere, soft music birds waking at dawn. Shivered, tightened long silk gown around. Not actually cold, of course, but *looked* pretty damn chilly. Violet, pale green flushed one horizon, above distant edge sea visible through leafy trees. Breath smoked a little. Beneath sandals, old worn flagstones uneven, probably icy. In places path had subsided, but ruined city not entirely overwhelmed by nature, not yet. Walked quickly toward east. Light came more brightly into sky, cinnamon now, soft blue. Found sandstone hut where expected, pushed open low, creaking door. Small fire burned in simple fireplace. Someone sat hunched over on stool, hands extended.

"How feeling, Mathewmark," asked, little timidly. He turned head. Was wearing dully gleaming helmet, gold or brass. Sword blade had slashed it open on left side. Dark red blood dripped slowly from terrible wound. Baffled, confused, he lifted hand, touched helmet, shivered as fingers felt wetness. Drew hand down, gazed at blood. Looked up again at me, eyes wide in fear, astonishment, blundered to feet. Stool went over behind, fire flared up as kicked piece of timber with boot, sending embers flying.

"Amanda? Oh dear God of our Choice, where am I now? Is this Hell's Bowels?"

I waved hands anxiously, brutal wound in helmet vanished. Far wall hut now opened out into courtyard where several large steeds stamped, snorted. Boy ran past with heavy armful jingling chain mail.

"Don't be frightened, Mathewmark. This just—" Paused. He'd never understand were in shared simulation. "Dream," told him. "Visiting you in dream."

"I'm in the devil's hospice," said, eyes wide, palms outstretched to ward me off. "This can be no dream. It is something put into my head along that wicked cable."

Fellow quick, no doubt. No dill or dork at all.

"Don't worry about that for now, Mathewmark," I told. "Here, come sit down for moment by fire, tell how you've been. See, this is only way can get in to visit you. In this . . . in this dream."

Heavy rain falling in courtyard, sky dark with thunderheads. Brilliant lightning slash snaked across bit of heavens could see through double glass doors now leading out to court, instant later terrifyingly loud bang of thunder cracked through chamber. Mirror set into timber wall shivered, broke. Piece silvered glass fell from frame, shattered into smaller pieces on tiles. Melted, ran like spilled droplets mercury. Mathewmark stared, frightened out of wits.

"You have to calm down," told, slightly hysterical myself.

"This is the work of the polluters and their demons," said through chattering teeth. Fracture in helmet was back, helm itself thick, cracked old leather. Blood dripped down his cheek.

"No, it's you," shouted at him. I made clouds go away, out of corner of eye saw puddles drain into soil. Field golden flowers reached upward to sun. "Not doing it, Mathewmark. Haven't you ever had lucid dream?"

"A Lucy what?" He stared at flowers, which grew thorns.

"Dream. For heaven's sake *stop* that." Grabbed arm, gave shake. "Lucid: when know you're asleep, dreaming, can make it go way you want. It's good. We learn it in domestic psychology, I like to dream I'm flying."

Stomach lurched as saw ground plunge away. Mathewmark clutched at me. Started spin, tumble. Flung out one arm like skater trying slow down, worked a bit. Mathewmark's eyes clamped tight shut. I made us lighter than air, let breeze blow us across midday fields cotton, hectare upon hectare, tended, cropped by great red machines that moved along rows genetically engineered plants. Could just make out muon warm-fusion plant in distance, bluff rising above it.

"All right," he said, opening eyes, quickly closing again, gulping as if about to puke. Guess he'd never been in plane. "So this is what it's like to fly like a bat?"

"Not quite. Can be hurt when hang-gliding in real. Nothing can hurt here in sim unless let it. So be careful what wish for. Time go down, have chat, you reckon?"

"Yes, Amanda. Let's go down." Fell to Earth like thistlefluff, walked through white sand while long breakers came in, went out, making hushing sound. Imagined air was salty. I brushed fly off face. It came back, settled on back. Not possible. My vee system lacked full sensory interface. Couldn't possibly be smelling crisp sea air, feel fly crawling on neck. Slapped it. Mathewmark must be doing this somehow, cross-wiring my senses. His own linkage to game scenario must be amazingly powerful. Surprising, shocking, really, since now running inside hospital's dedicated neural nets.

"What's that strange smell?"

Actually I *couldn't* smell it now that I'd doubted it, but guessed what he must be sniffing. "Seaweed," told. "Lots people call it ozone. If really was ozone, be dead, oxygen's dangerous poison if not careful."

"This whole demon's world is dangerous, if you ask me," Mathewmark said glumly, rolling up trousers, stepping cautiously into water at edge of sea. Million tiny broken fragments shell shifted back, forth, tendrils of green, purple weed waved in froth.

"Dream," insisted. "Just dream."

"I'm not talking about the dream," he said. "I'm talking about the hospital."

Lay back in his bed, cable hanging down from supporting lever to wounded head. I was seated in armchair beside monitors flashing, beeping beside him. Young man with tufts of green hair, rose tattooed on cheek was half-turned away from us, poised on one foot, holding gleaming metal bedpan. Looked like someone frozen in position in slo-mo movie.

"Tony, eh, saw him here that other time."

"Yeah." Mathewmark stared at softly golden ceiling, face expressionless. "I got him to bring you a letter. Or was that just a dream?"

"No dream, boyo." Hitched chair forward on its glider, took one of his hands between mine. Was no touch sensation in vee, inadequate conformal mapping, but I imagined that he felt bit cold. "Now let's cut to chase. Have some planning to do. Damned NannyWatch chip going to catch on any minute now, shut me out. Next time you'll have to make contact."

"How can I do that? This is all black magic to me."

"Hey, buster, you're one with chip in head. Or will be in day or two. Here, I'll pass links you'll need memorize. Just like keying phone."

"What's a phone?" Mathewmark asked.

1 1 : mathewmark

It was night. Things are always worse at night. I didn't know what to think. The dream—whatever Amanda called it, the sim. Surely it was the devil's work. I wanted to rip the cable, the jack, out of my head. I'd been bewitched, possessed by dark forces. Amanda was the familiar of the Prince of Darkness. No doubt about it. She'd lifted me up and flown me through strange skies, over the playgrounds of goblins and machines. Yet it had been pleasant on the beach: the sun and the sand and all that water, even the funny smell of the seaweed, I'd liked that. But then the devil's blandishments are like a poisoned cup of honey-mead, sweet to the taste but deadly as sin. I wanted to rip the cable out, so that no dark force could ever take over my mind again.

But no, I didn't. I was just pretending to myself that I wanted to be rid of the jack. What I really wanted was to meet Amanda again. I wanted to meet her in the real world, I wanted her to come and visit me. But maybe, if I was honest, I also wanted to meet her in worlds of our own dreaming. What about Sweetcharity? I pushed both those women out of my troubled thoughts. I didn't touch the cable. I lay and waited for dawn and Auntie McWeezle. When she arrived at breakfast time, I made no mention of the dream, the sim.

Auntie McWeezle was worried. In two days' time I would have my implant. I'd no longer be tethered by the jack. If all went well, I'd be let out of the hospital a week later. I could go home. Only I couldn't.

"I've written to the Elders again," Auntie McWeezle told me, looking away.

"And," I said.

"And they've told me to return to the Valley."

"With me?" I said hopefully.

"Oh, Mathewmark . . ." Auntie McWeezle said. I thought she was going to cry.

"It's all right, Auntie."

"No, it's not," Auntie McWeezle said. "Oh, Mathewmark, what is going to happen to you?"

"I'll be all right, Auntie," I said.

"On the Outside? Away from everything you know. Surrounded by machines."

"It's all right, Auntie," I said again. "Amanda will show me around."

"Oh, don't be silly!" Auntie said, and now she sounded really cross. "That young slip of a thing can't run her own life without causing death and destruction."

"But you like her, Auntie."

"I've liked newborn puppies in my time, but that hasn't stopped them chewing good boots to shreds and knocking over the milking pail."

"She's the only person I know on the Outside, Auntie." I couldn't tell her about my secret feelings. I couldn't even tell myself.

"That Magistrate man has confined her to house and study. And a good job too. She wouldn't be allowed to show you anything, Mathewmark."

"What if we talk to the Magistrate, Auntie. Maybe he'll make an exception for when she's with me."

"She'd lead you astray."

"I'll keep her under control, Auntie."

"Oh for goodness sake, Mathewmark. The machine has addled your mind. You! Keep a wild Outsider girl like Amanda 'under control'!"

"Well, let's try to talk to the Magistrate anyway, Auntie. You said he's the only Outsider you've come across with half an ounce of brain."

"I'll talk to the Goddess now, if you don't mind, Mathewmark." And Auntie started to pray. She prayed in silence, eyes closed, every thought concentrated on what she was saying to the Goddess of her Choice, and what the Goddess was saying back to her. I envied Auntie her easy access to her Goddess. Sometimes I think that the God of my own Choice was actually a rather poor choice. I've never said this to anyone, but when I pray to my god, I'm none too sure that he listens; he certainly doesn't reply in good plain English.

I lay on my bed and watched the wall while Auntie and her Goddess discussed my case. The funny thing was, I realized, I'd just started talking about my new life on the Outside as if it was an inevitable fact. The Elders didn't want me back, well, I wasn't going to argue. Maybe I actually wanted to be an Outsider. At least for a while. Tony came into the room. He was ready to say something cheery, but he saw Auntie praying, so he started tiptoeing around not making a sound. He shouldn't have worried. The truth is, when Auntie and the Goddess of her Choice get into a discussion, you could jump up and down on the floor and it wouldn't make any difference.

"Hey, Tony," I said. "Come round the other side of the bed and talk to me." He drew up a chair and quietly sat down. "What do you think of my chances of getting permission for Amanda to be my guide in the outside world?"

"Nil," said Tony.

"Say I asked the Magistrate?"

Tony looked like he was going to say nil again, but then he shrugged. "That Abdel-Malek guy has a reputation for unconventional behavior. Anything might happen if you petitioned him."

"Good," I said. "How do I go about using a phone to contact Amanda?"

"There's an old-fashioned hard phone just down the hall, for the people from the Luddite enclaves, hardly any call for it. You can use it to your heart's content when you get on your feet again."

"Will you show me how?"

"Mathewmark, I'll show you how to clean your teeth, if that's what you need."

"Just the phone, Tony," I said. "Just the phone."

1 2 : amanda

Damn NannyWatch caught me, of course. Except thing didn't bother tell me, didn't bother kick up fuss on own account. Had known was playing sim games with Mathewmark from word go, then shopped me behind back to Mr. Abdel-Malek or one of staff. Think Magistrate would have sent Parole cops around pronto. But no. Mr. Abdel-Malek isn't that famous for asking for outside help. Decided to pay me little call himself. Unannounced. Or, rather, got Mrs. Ng announce him. As usual I was playing Strad Lad.

"Don't stop, Ms. Kolby-McAllister," said Magistrate, following close on Mrs. Ng's slightly flustered heels, flinging self casually into armchair. "Play on."

"Mr. Abdel-Malek," said, agog. "What doing here?"

"I was rather hoping I might catch the end of the nocturne."

"Not very good."

"You are a lot better than I am, Ms. Amanda Kolby-McAllister. The family dog forced me to abandon the violin when I was twelve. It kept joining in. Thought it could do better. It could. Now please, play on."

Needed time think, only one way buy time. Tucked Strad Lad under chin, turned face music stand, began to play. Luckily use sentimental old-fashioned music stand, grandmother's, displays notes on flatscreen. If used holography to project score into retinas, would have been ruder turn back completely on Magistrate. But did. While sawed through rest piece, considered dim reflection Mr. Abdel-Malek lurking in front of notation.

Out of official court gear was stylish dresser. Wore high-necked body-hugger with open black-leather jerkin trimmed silver. While I played, appeared to let eyes close, as if listening with all attention. Perhaps was. Perhaps realized I was studying reflection. Perhaps, through half-closed lids, was studying mine. Tried to think. What doing here? Doubtless NannyWatch told sorry tale, doubtless knew latest indiscretion. But surely being indiscreet himself, just being here. Public ethics legal profession, after all. Impression get from Maman is: judges, Magistrates pretty damn careful about company keep. Visiting miscreant penders in own homes at time when olders absent surely not standard procedure. So if tried get heavy with, couldn't I get heavy back? Strange, fearful, forbidden thought: power over Mr. Abdel-Malek himself. Music came to end. No score left on-screen, only dull reflection of Magistrate's face. Lowered violin slowly, turned face music, so to speak.

"You play very fluently, Ms. Kolby-McAllister," Magistrate said, opening eyes. "The fluency of the distracted. Had you been concentrating on the music and not thinking about other things, would the notes have come so smoothly?"

"Perhaps not," said.

"And yet, although less smooth, would the music then have had more feeling? If you had been concentrating on it, Ms. Kolby-McAllister?"

"Hard judge own playing," said. "And in own bedroom, called Amanda."

"I'm sure you are, Ms. Kolby-McAllister. And it is from this very bedroom that you fly through the sky in the company of brain-damaged young men from the Valley of the God of their Choice. In computer-generated simulation, of course. And I'd be obliged if you would speak English."

"If the NannyWatch program has told you about the sim," said, "I'm sure it told you where I was at the time."

"Indeed it did."

"Can't you give it a better name?" said angrily. "NannyWatch! It sounds like something you'd employ to baby-sit a toddler."

"In a manner of speaking, it is baby-sitting."

"In a manner of speaking, it is my jailer. What about calling it CrimWatch, or Ball-and-Chain, or . . . I don't know . . . StickyBeak. It's degrading, being spied on by something called NannyWatch."

"I didn't create the program, Ms. Kolby-McAllister. The naming of it is not in my gift."

"Must be about the only thing that isn't in your gift," said. "Does it satisfy you, having all this power over other people's lives?"

"If I told you how little real power I have," Magistrate said, "you wouldn't believe me."

"You seem to have complete power over me. You control where I go. Who I get to see. What I—"

"I cannot even stop you from cracking into the Neurological Hospital's system, and from there into Mathewmark Fisher's head."

"So you've come round here to admonish me for it. Well, you'd better do it. Tell me the full extent of my wickedness."

"Do sit down, Amanda."

"I rather like pacing about. I'm like a caged animal in here."

"Sit down. And stop waving that bow, you'll break something."

Man had total cheek. My room. If I broke anything, was my thing to break. And nothing couldn't replace. But after second or two's silence, twiddled knob released tension in bow. Put it, Strad the Lad into velvet-lined case, closed lid. When good, ready, not before, sat on bed, pulling legs up, crossing in half lotus. "Okay, Mr. Abdel-Malek, about my latest crimes against civilization as we know it . . ."

"Ah, the egoism of the pre-Mature," said Mr. Abdel-Malek sadly. "It simply hasn't occurred to you that I might not be remotely interested in discussing your latest misdemeanor. Given the scale on which you operate, Ms. Kolby-McAllister, the latest prank was pretty small beer. I can't even remember if the court order made specific reference to computer cracking or not. Besides, I believe you used an address that was freely available to the public, was printed on the hospital's notepaper . . . Why should I bother with that?"

"So why are you here?"

"In the interests of civilization as we know it," the Magistrate said. "We have to introduce it to someone who doesn't know it, who knows a completely different civilization."

"Mathewmark?" said. Felt bit deflated. What Magistrate said completely true—hadn't occurred had come discuss anything but me.

"Mathewmark," Mr. Abdel-Malek agreed. "He has experienced a great shock. He may experience an even greater one when he leaves the hospital."

"Well, that's no problem," said. "He can go home. That's what Auntie McWeezle is here for, to take him home."

"They will not have him back," Mr. Abdel-Malek said. "Not with a chip in his head. He is going to have to live with us, in what he would call the Outside."

"Pack of assholes!"

Mr. Abdel-Malek looked pained. But said nothing.

"Well, they are, aren't they?" said. "What sort of society would turn its back on one of its own people, just because he wants to have a proper mind, just because he doesn't want to be a gibbering idiot falling down in the street all the time? It's outrageous. They ought to be made to take Mathewmark back. Can't we send an armed guard or something?"

"You seem very concerned," Mr. Abdel-Malek said. "It does you credit, Amanda."

"Look, I'm not trying to curry favor, Mr. Abdel-Malek. But the Valley is Mathewmark's home. He doesn't know any better. He's happy plodding around with his donkey—"

"Mule."

"There's a difference?"

"The mule is the sterile offspring of a male donkey and a female horse."

"News to me. Have you ever seen one?"

"Alas, no, my knowledge of these matters comes from books and the net."

"I have," I said. "Vik and I were loaded onto a cart pulled by one. We were hidden between bales of straw."

"Hay, actually. I am familiar with the details of your case."

"And I suppose there is a difference between hay and straw?"

"Indeed there is," said Mr. Abdel-Malek. "Hay is dried grass, it is very nutritious. For mules. Straw, on the other hand, is the dead stalk of wheat, oats, or other crops. Its value as food is dubious, but it makes good bedding."

"Fascinating," said.

"I'm glad you think so," said the Magistrate, "because I'm sure there will be ample time for Mathewmark to instruct you in the rudiments of peasant life."

"Ample time?"

"Ample time," said Magistrate. "I think it would be a good idea if you were closely involved in Mathewmark's rehabilitation and his introduction into our society."

"Er . . . look," said. "Mathewmark is a nice man. I like him a lot, but . . ." Trailed off in confusion.

"But?"

"But he *is* a peasant, a Valley hayseed. He only knows about mules, things like that. We don't have much in common."

"I know you don't," Mr. Abdel-Malek said, "yet."

Sat silent and cross-legged on my bed, regarding him. Magistrate sat quite at ease in armchair, looked at me. Long silence.

"All right," said at last. "What've you got in mind?"

"I believe," said Mr. Abdel-Malek, "that it would aid your own process of rehabilitation into society if, as both an act of penance and restitution as well as friendship—"

"He's not my *friend*, I barely know him."

"Friendship," Magistrate repeated firmly. "You seemed quite friendly with Mathewmark in your sim game. The NannyWatch program was most impressed. It said so."

"Sneaky little motherfucker."

"Quite so. As I was saying, I think it would be a good idea if you took Mathewmark under your wing. Showed him around."

"Around where?" said. "You seem to have forgotten I'm not allowed to go anywhere."

"You seem to have forgotten that I am the sentencing Magistrate. I can vary the court's orders at will."

"That's deal? Freedom of movement in exchange for dragging Mathewmark around with?"

"Dragging isn't quite what I had in mind."

"I don't think he'll go down a bundle in the Mall," said.

"But you, yourself, would like to revisit the Mall," Mr. Abdel-Malek said. "Sometime between now and the moderately distant day of your Thirtieth birthday?"

"This is bribery."

"That is not a charge you should bring lightly against your local Magistrate."

"Have to think about." Studied fingernails coolly.

"A good idea," said Magistrate. "You might also like to think about how we are going to persuade your parents that what they really need in this vast house of theirs is a boarder."

"A boarder. I really don't think we are that hard up."

"But Mathewmark will need somewhere to live, and what finer place than the household of his guide and mentor?"

"Bloody shitting hell."

"You have a way with words, Amanda. And also the violin. So if we could just listen to that nocturne again, I'll be on my way."

1 3 : mathewmark

I was feeling ridiculously calm when they came to wheel me down the corridor. Some wicked juice in the tube in my arm, I expect. It wasn't much like that time Julian Witherspoon and Tom Haughton and me drank a whole jug of fermented apple cider, and got silly and danced under the autumn Moon wishing some girls would come down and join us, and then Tom took offense at some passing remark of Julian's and smacked him a beauty right in the eye, and we all ended up laughing and then puking our bellies out in the hedges and nursing our poor heads for two days. It

wasn't like that, not really, but that's as close as I could remember
to anything this light and floaty. Tony handed me over to a couple
of men even burlier than him, wearing green clothes and masks over
their faces like bandits, and foolish clear caps over their hair. One of
them pushed my enormous bed, which sort of floated along a rail
down one side of the hallway, while the other followed pushing a
bunch of devil's machines, including the one with the cable that ran
into the top of my head.

"Best of luck, chum," Tony called down the corridor behind me.
"See you back here in a flash."

Into a room as bright as the inside of a new bucket. More machines with lights that blinked on and off, and little windows with
lines that pulsed. I watched this with innocent pleasure, as if it was
a dream even stranger than the sim dreams Amanda and I had shared,
flying and watching the landscape shift and the weather change
whenever one of us chose to make it happen.

"Good morning, Mr. Fisher," a young woman said, smiling down
at me. Her whole head was covered by a kind of clear bubble, and
her voice seemed to come from somewhere on her shoulder. "How
are we feeling this morning?"

"Mr. Fisher is my daddy," I said, and then laughed because that
was quite silly. "I'm Mathewmark, and I feel nice and cozy, but to
tell the truth I'm absolutely shit scared."

The woman in the bubble grinned, and glanced at another person
beside her, a dark-skinned man with very short yellow hair. I blushed
and started to apologize.

"We've given you a little tranquilizer, Mathewmark, and it's suppressed your inhibitions. Don't worry, I've heard a lot worse in my
time."

"Couldn't have been that long," I said, "your time. You look as
young as Amanda."

"Ah, we have a little crush on Ms. Kolby-McAllister, do we?" said
the dark man teasingly in a deep dark voice. "I can assure you, it's
been quite a long time since my colleague was at Play."

"Not *that* long, Dr. Ganunji." The young woman was doing things
to the cable plugged into the top of my scalp, and although it didn't

hurt, I could feel the tug. "Now, Mathewmark, we are not going to put you to sleep during this procedure, because we need you to tell us what you experience as we insert the prosthesis and initialize its settings. But don't worry, you won't feel any pain. We have bypassed your pain gates, and the brain itself has no sensitivity to local pain in any case."

A big, very bright light was coming down toward my face from the ceiling. I felt perfectly relaxed and completely terrified at the same time.

"I didn't understand any of that," I told her. My lips felt rather numb.

"Sorry, we get in the habit of talking jargon. Don't worry, all that matters is that you won't have any pain while we fix up your injuries. I know the counselors have been explaining to you that parts of the inside of your head were extensively damaged during your adventure. We have built a replacement for you, and now we'll be putting it in and resetting your—" She twisted her mouth. "It's very hard explaining this stuff to somebody who's never watched a television set, let alone experienced a vee."

"Oh, I've done that," I said. "Amanda took me to a land where everything changes when you think about it. She called it a vee, and then she said it was a sim. I thought she said 'sin' at first." I gave a foolish giggle.

The woman doctor was looking alarmed. She said to her friend, "Someone's already interfaced with him at the virtual-reality level? What, that girl he was in the tunnel with? Who on earth let her inside the—"

The dark man said testily, "It's in your in-mail, Janice. The girl cracked through the net for ten minutes two days ago. No harm done. We ran calibration checks, everything's nominal."

The woman doctor was furious. "Damn it, Toby, this is the kind of slackness I'm always complaining about! How can I be expected—"

"Janice, little pitchers have big ears. He's fully alert."

"Shit." the woman doctor's face came down again over me, shadowed in the brilliant glare of the light. I could make out a cheesy grin on her face, like Jed's when he's caught with his hand in the till at the store. "Just let yourself drift off, Mathewmark. Nothing to worry about. In a moment we'll take out the cable and start to link you up to your new chip." Her face withdrew, and I heard her mutter crossly, "In the bloody email. Good god!"

The lights went out.

No they didn't. It was like when you've been staring up at the sky with your eyes shut, on a summer's day, and you turn away from the red brightness on the inside of your eyelids. Patterns bloom and shift, swirl and change color. It's magical and beautiful. You can't hold any of it still. The shapes are incredibly complicated and keep changing, except for the spot in the center, which changes slowly from white to red to blue to green and back again. The shapes are like the paisley shirts old man Smeeth used to wear before they all wore out, like a garden of a hundred sorts of flowers if you could look down from the top of the hills. That was something like what I saw.

But that's not it either. There were cones of darkness spinning in crimson. I watched spirals of deep luminous blue twisting into gold. Something like a net opened out, and then closed over me. Meteors flung themselves across the thick green, and I heard a humming like bees. My mouth filled with saliva, and the taste of roast beef with Myrtle McWeezle's best mustard. An itching started in my left foot and raced up my leg, and a muscle in my calf cramped until I cried out. Then the pain was gone, in an instant, and I felt long scratchy fingers run over my shoulders and down my back and reach inside my back, through the bones, and down into my guts like ice that was hot as melted butter. My nose filled with the scent of fuchsias, and I wanted to sneeze but something was gripping my head tight. I couldn't move. Birds sang out.

Everything drained away. I felt my soul rush from my body in a dizzying, sickening flight. And I didn't go with it. I was left behind, dull clay, numb and thick and stupid and without a soul. If I could have screamed, I'd have raised a shout to break the light pouring down into my blind eyes. They were shoving something huge into my ear, forcing it past cracking bone, but I was dead, so it didn't hurt, and it didn't matter. No, not my ear, the whole side of my head. For a moment I was floating up over my body, looking down. The two doctors were prying into my skull with fingers covered in blood over some white skintight covering that looked like a pig's bladder. I looked at my face, and felt worse, if that was possible, because it was obvious that I was dead.

I looked awful. I was white and breathing with a raspy asthma sound. Another person in green and bubble-helmet came over and put a mask on my face, and some color came back into my cheeks. The thing they were pushing into my head was quite small, on the end of a kind of mechanical arm. They looked at a display that was like a box you could see right into, and the thing inside it was raw meat close up, red and blue veins or arteries pulsing. It reminded me of the afterbirth of an animal. A curdling wave of shock went through me, cold rising up from my toes and making the hairs on my dead legs and arms stand up. My stomach clenched very slowly. The thing shown in the box was a picture of me, my brain, and the huge metal bar and glinting stubbly object fastened to its end was just the thin rod the doctors were pressing into my head. The box held a kind of magnified picture of the inside of my brain.

I'd never seen a human brain, well or ill, only animal brains prepared for the table, but this one looked completely messed up. There were nasty gaps and bits that looked like the crinkled skin all over poor Lucy McWeezle's leg the time the log fell out of the fire when she fell asleep after quaffing too much cider and crisped her flesh with a stink like roasting meat. In fact it looked exactly as if someone had reached inside my head with a hot poker and fried my brains. Maybe that's what it was, on a smaller scale. Maybe they'd seared the torn vessels with their dreadful devilish machines to save me from dying of blood loss.

"Holding up, Mathewmark?"

And I snapped back into my head again. I gave a yelp, and the woman doctor blinked. Her arm didn't move, though, as much of it as I could see from the corner of my eye.

"You killed me, you bastards," I heard my numb lips say.

"No, Mathewmark," dark doctor Toby Ganunji said in a complacent voice, "on the contrary. We've given you back your life."

"No need for melodrama," Dr. Janice told him. "All in a day's work. Okay, Giovanni, you can close up." She stepped away, and again I saw her face looming over me. "We have the prosthesis in place, Mathewmark. The scans look good. In a few minutes, after we glue in some bone and patch you up, we'll sit you up and run you through some calibration questions."

"That's all?" I blurted. "You're done with me already?"

Dr. Toby stretched, and twisted his neck around like someone getting a kink out. "Eight hours on the table not enough for you?" He gave a tired laugh. "You're a better man than I am, Gunga-Din."

I moved my own shoulders, feeling them creak and crack. Eight hours? I'd been dead for eight hours? Auntie McWeezle was right. I shook my head in disbelief, and there was no pain and no drag from the cable. I reached up carefully and touched the top of my head. There was a bald patch, but no cable.

"Okay, big boy," one of the people in green said through the speaking device on his shoulder, "we're going to sit you up now. Ready?"

I nodded, unable to speak, unable to find words. I was awash in loss and sorrow. They had stolen my soul, I was sure of it. They'd cut it out and put in their goblin machine instead, and I would never, ever be allowed back into the Valley. Even if Auntie McWeezle talked the Assembly of Elders around, I'd never permit myself to sully that place with my presence. I was doomed, and that was that.

"Now, I want you to tell me what you feel when I do this," the new doctor said cheerfully, and pressed a button. I seemed to be standing in the wheat paddock with Ebeeneezer, looking west at the setting sun, and at the same time I knew that I was sitting propped up on a marvelous bed in a hospital in the Outside.

"What do I feel?" I said bitterly. Ebeeneezer turned his head and looked at me, munching slowly on some tasty weeds. "What do you think I feel?"

"Hungry, thir?"

"I feel damned to be gnawed by Hell's Teeth forever."

His exit from the cryonics mausoleum was not delayed. A mobile unit appeared at the door, floating, small lenses scanning.

"Can Ally and Michio come with us?"

"I'm afraid it's time for them to return to Play," the mobile explained. "They've been missing their peer group, and both of them approach Maturity." No details were forthcoming. Abdel-Malek bade the kids farewell with a lonely hopeless misery.

The journey was made by magnetic levitation in a tube sunk in the mantle of the world. "I can't believe what you're telling me," he said wearily to the monitor, face drawn. "People would never have abdicated power to a machine, however sublime. I *know*; I helped invent the goddamned things."

The small machine spoke with the calm reasonableness of expensive media psychiatrists. "You fail to appreciate the weariness and despair of the decades following your death. Science had offered salvation, and was used instead largely to glut the greedy and the murderous."

"Crap. We'd just about put an end to large-scale war. Business was global at last, spreading wealth everywhere." He paused. "Surely not the bombs? The weapons of mass destruction? The damned fools didn't—"

"The world was spared that final cruelty," the monitor observed judiciously. "Still, in the end it had been despoiled nearly to the point of death. People lost heart. Knowledge is not enough. Will is required."

Abdel-Malek's lips twisted in distaste. "Dictators used to be fond of slogans like that."

"Actually," said the monitor, "by the time you died the human race had begun making it clear that they were no longer prepared to be duped by dictators and Mafia and secret police. They—"

"From everything I've seen," Abdel-Malek burst out angrily, "your Aleph AI is dictator enough."

Mildly, the monitor told him, "Aleph is a superintelligence with no human weakness. It is not corrupt, and cannot be corrupted. It is spared evolved appetites and passions that might surge out of control. It is the custodian of an objective and final morality."

"Lacking passion, how can it hope to understand people?"

"It understands humans as you might understand an ant hill. No single ant grasps the essence of its own evolutionary coding, what drives it. Not even the ant collective knows its blindly found purposes. Gazing upon it from the outside, with insight and wisdom, a human might know it more perfectly. So too the Aleph."

"The cure is worse than the disease."

"I cannot agree. The disease was global neurosis, wealth in the midst of poverty, conflict, devastation created by unchecked human passion and incompetent calculation. The disease was nearly terminal. One more generation of technological runaway and all life on the planet might have been exterminated."

There were no windows. They drove through the depths of the world at hundreds or thousands of kilometers an hour, thrust through the stony crust of the planet by gravity and electromagnetic pulses. Abdel-Malek examined his strong young hands. "Oh my God." He did not believe in any god. He threw back his head and coughed out a laugh. Orwell had seen it, Huxley before him, Kurzweil and Moravec and Joy and Lanier. Turing saw it, too, back in 1937. The title of Alan Turing's incredible paper was stamped into Mohammed Abdel-Malek's brain: "On Computable Numbers, with an Application to the *Entscheidungs* Problem." Can a machine be created indistinguishable from a human consciousness? Not identical, of course not, but sufficiently adept and powerful that one might not know it from a human as it conversed? Yes, said Alan. But human intelligence is not all it's cracked up to be. Poor Alan had taken his own life in 1954, hounded by bigots who would not tolerate his homosexuality; he had bitten deep into an apple poisoned by potassium cyanide. It was a death rich in metaphor, from spooky German fairy stories to the myth of Satan and the Garden of Eden.

Didn't play nocturne again, played short piece composed self. Know own work by heart, so stood facing Magistrate, looking down neck of violin like target-shooter with gun. Mr. Abdel-Malek closed eyes again. When I'd finished, opened eyes, said, "You have real talent, Amanda. You played in a style that totally suited the composition. It must be a great joy to be able to invent music as well as interpret it. I'll let myself out." And was gone.

Invent music! Compose is word he was struggling for. But how had he known piece was my own? Hadn't told him. With room to self, really did take to pacing up, down. Was caged animal, no doubt about it. And needed get out. And Mr. Abdel–goddamned-Malek dangling key in front of face. To get NannyWatch off back, just had to become nanny myself—baby-sitter to poltroon. Me, who used to hang round Mall with Vikram Singh. Mall heroes, me, Vik. Dreadest item on patch. We'd made that scene, created it. Things came alive when sauntered in. And now banned from own scene for life, or Maturity, whichever came first, and the poor damned Mature don't hang at Mall. Turfed off own turf—unless sauntered back in with hayseed. G'day guys, this is Mathewmark, mule driver. That's sterile cross between male donkey, female horse—or maybe other way round. Which way is it, Mathewmark? Please explain about mules to all dudes here assembled. Not fair! Not fair to Mathewmark, let alone me. Poor man, didn't deserve sniggers, patronizing questions. What did Mr. Abdel-Malek think playing at? Oh, Vik, Oh, Vik, want you back. Want you back so much!

And then wasn't pacing around like caged animal. Lying on bed howling into pillow. Cried for maybe five minutes, turned over, looked at ceiling for another five minutes. Then got up, went into my bath-room, washed face. Looked at self in mirror. Red-eyed wreck. But managed bit of grin. Would accept Magistrate's bribe, become nanny, no way could refuse. Well, kid, said to reflection, if going do it, might as well do it good. Fuck it, was going introduce Mathewmark to delights of this sin-ridden, machine-driven world, introduce him to them with vengeance. Went back into bedroom, yelled at room play something thought-provoking. Needed to think.

"Thought-provoking is not a recognized subset of music," said room. "Please refine your categorization."

"Just play 'Ode to Joy,' " said. "And get on with it."

"Which recording? Please select from the following list . . ."

"Yukio Lee Smith conducting St. Petersburg Philharmonic, the Choir of Angels, Carnegie Hall circa 2010."

But already the music was filling room. Sat in swivel chair, did an Abdel-Malek. Closed eyes, went away.

For a while just left mind blank, senses free rein, gave self over to music, and then, when voices started piling on *freude, freudes*, turned attention to problem of future boarder, lodger, paying guest. Smell Mrs. Ng's cooking, wafting up stairs, added own inducement to thought. Ace cook, Mrs. Ng. Sent quick official e-transmission to Clerk of Court. For attention of his honor Mr. Abdel-Malek . . .

1 5 : mathewmark

"This is for the pecs," Tony told me, leading me to one of the gleaming Tools of Frivolity in the hospital recovery "jim." I had never seen so much shiny metal and leather, including the fancy harnesses the draft horses wear on Jagannatha Day parade. He made me lie down on a firm bench and grip a short jutting bar of metal in each hand. They seemed to be stuck to the wall, but when I gave one of them a shove it moved upward only slightly, as if it weighed as much as a bag of potatoes.

"What are 'pecs,' Tony?"

"Those muscles on your chest between your nipples and your collarbone. Yours are in better shape than most I see here, you must have done some heavy workouts in your time."

I didn't know what that meant, so I said, "Working outdoors and inside in the sheds, it builds a lad's strength for righteousness, so my pastor says. What should I do with these bars?" I tried to pull them down to my chest, but they wouldn't budge.

"Hang on, old son, let's set the resistance." He pressed some buttons, and the number 20 glowed into cool blue life above my head, between the bars. "Now, just press up slowly, elbows out here to start, that's it, and straighten your arms. Terrific. Okay, let's have three sets of eight." He reset the number to 25 and left me pushing at the suddenly heavier bars while he wandered off to another part of the "jim."

I was sweating a bit, but not as much as if I'd been mucking out the milking shed. And the smell of the air was sweeter too. But as I pumped my arms up and down, and felt the sweat slowly run into my armpits, I was suddenly sick with longing for the old sheds, for the warm smell of cow shit and the cackling of hens and the darting sight of our plump tomcat after a mouse or rat in the straw. Good old Kevin, I wondered if he was missing me. I got to eight and rested for a moment, as Tony had told me to do, and a powerful yearning to see my dear old friend Ebeeneezer rushed over me. My eyes prickled, as if sweat had run down from my forehead, which was also true. Nearly in tears, I remembered the clean green and brown of the wheatfields and trusty Ebeeneezer plodding along at my side, or pulling the cart in his harness up in front as the dust puffed from the rutted road, muttering to himself.

When I'd finished my set of twenty-four exercises, I lay there on my back for a moment with my burning eyes shut. A rhythmic banging thudded away in the room, some Outsider's idea of music I suppose, and it made my heart beat faster, or maybe that was just the exertion. I was terribly homesick, lost in this awful place. It might have been better if I could have spoken to Amanda, but she hadn't been allowed to visit the hospital after the operation.

"Hoy, come along, you slacker," Tony yelled in a jolly tone, "let's hop on the treadmill and show me some cardiovascular effort."

I didn't understand that, either. Pecs and lats and abs and quads, strange names for all the bits of the body I never knew had special names. And now this cardy-something. I mooched over to his new Instrument of Satanic Torture, thinking how shocked Auntie Mc-Weezle would be if she saw me here in this "jim." Not to mention old man Legrand—he'd be sure it was a fit and suitable place for a sinner like me.

"Jump up, Mathewmark. That's it, pop your feet into the retainers, and just look straight ahead for a mo. I'll give you something nice and woodsy, sort of just like home, eh?" He slipped a pair of light gloves over my fingers, and the curved plastic bar in front of my eyes shot out twin beams of light that seemed to search my face for an instant and then—

—locked into my eyes with a soft purple haze that faded, as I blinked, into something that just could not be. I tensed up, quite scared, because it was as if Tony had picked me up and thrown me without warning into another part of the world. The hospital "jim" was gone. I stood in a clearing halfway up a hill under a pale sunny sky streaked with light clouds. A dozen shades of green were grasses, and trees with broad branches and leafy twigs tossing in a light wind, and low shrubs growing between the trees, and vines with pink flowers in the shape of trumpets . . . But I couldn't smell any of their fragrances, and the light breeze in my face was blowing from the wrong direction.

I shook my head in disbelief, remembering the dream where Amanda and I had flown into the heavens like birds or bats or angels. Nothing in that dream had made more sense than any other dream, nothing had held still long enough to catch hold of it. Yet it still seemed so real, in some foolish way—as real as this place Tony had sent me to.

A bright yellow arrow appeared in the middle of the air, at about shoulder height, pointing up the hill. I opened my mouth to protest, and then found myself laughing. This was just so ridiculous. Tony's voice said in my ear, "Come on sport, follow the arrow. Just a light jog to start with, up the hill, and then let yourself ease into a run. Okay?"

I swung my head around left and then right, but he wasn't there. No other human was. The clearing in the woods stayed put, though. I looked down at myself. I was wearing a skintight garment of blue and black, and my feet were bound in those pliable shoes Amanda had called "grippo sneakers." I raised my left foot, and it felt slightly heavy but not restrained. The yellow light was blinking and jerking forward beckoningly. Oh, why not? Everything here was as crazy as everything else—let's go for a run through a wood in the middle of a hospital building.

I started to lope up the hill, and a small animal started from cover and dashed across the path. I followed it with my gaze as I picked up speed, a rabbit with laid-back ears and white flag. The Sun was at my back, out of my eyes, and comfortably warm. I started to run for the pure pleasure of it, something we rarely had a chance to do in the Valley once childhood games were behind us. The refreshing air in my face flowed faster as my speed picked up. The ground rolled along beneath my feet, and my arms swung easily back and forth at my sides, at waist height.

When I reached the top of the hill, the path curved down in a gentle loop and vanished between trees. A bird or two lifted from branches and flew past me, caroling. A glint of water shone to the east, down through scrub. Suddenly I was tired of the path. I swung away to investigate the creek down below—

And nearly tumbled over. My feet felt as if they'd got stuck in heavy mud, although I couldn't see any.

"Sorry, Mathewmark," Tony said in my ear, "you'll have to stay on the track. The program's adaptable up to a point, but it has its limits. Here, I reckon you've done enough exercise for one morning, let's call it a day shall we?"

The wooded hill faded back into purple haze, and then I was blinking at the white light of the "jim." Tony was bent down undoing the strips that held my feet. I shook my head, struck by vertigo, and felt for a moment as if I was about to throw up. The breeze was coming from a vent in front of me, ebbing away now that I had stopped running in place.

"Oh-oh," Tony said, glancing at my sweating face. "Virt sickness. You'll get over it soon enough, I suppose the learning curve is a bit steeper if you get into this as an adult. Wait until you try skiing down the erupting mountains of Io! Come on, lean on my arm, we'll whiz through some quick cool-down exercises, and then we'll get back to your room for a good hot shower and some lunch, eh?"

The prospect of lunch cheered me up. "Mind and body are one," Dr. Janice told me when she came by on rounds to visit me and check that the wound in my head was healing properly. "A sound mind in a sound body, I'm sure they must teach that old truth in your village?" She seemed pleased to see me tucking into my trout, laying open the back of the fish with a knife and taking out the bones in much the same way she must have gone into my poor head. She tapped my skull, and stepped back, looking pleased. "No pain, I hope?"

"No, thank you, Doctor." I could scarcely believe it, but it was so. If this sort of damage had befallen some poor soul in the Valley, I don't think our herbal remedies would have prevented him from yowling in pain for many a day until, very likely, he passed away from a miasma or a gangrene. They told us this was the way the God of our Choice intended matters for us, in the vale of tears. I was starting to wonder if that was absolutely true, or whether maybe some of the old men and biddies might have slipped up in their translations and teachings from the wisdom of the ancients. Old man Legrand would have gone crimson in the face if he'd known what was happening to me, he'd have screamed and hollered that all this was the work of the fiend. Once, I'd have agreed without hesitation, and might still, except that it meant I'd be the one lowered in the casket into consecrated ground. One day the end will come to us all, and if we've lived lives of virtue and self-sacrifice, we will be raised up in glory— but I'd rather put it off for a while yet.

And that thought, of course, made me feel guilty and wicked. It is the way of polluters and sinners to seek only personal advantage, rather than buckling down to the hard choices of self-denial. Even if you must perish in defending what is right.

Then again, it suddenly struck me that old man Legrand hadn't actually faced that choice himself, not life versus death. There he was, strutting about in all his pomposity, keeping his eye jealously on Sweetcharity, but he'd never looked death in the face as I had. Or if the choice had lain before him, he too must have chosen life. Either way, I figured I was just as well placed as him to cling to hope and be grateful to those who had plucked me back from the edge of doom and a life of simpleness with only half a brain. I shuddered, and turned for comfort to my bowl of warm apricot tart with a hint of lemon and a dollop of thick cream.

I pinged Tony.

"Do you think I could make a telephone call now to Amanda?"

"Don't see why not, old son. I'll fetch in a hard phone as soon as I can find one. Failing that, you'll have to go down the corridor." A little while later he returned with a frustrated expression, holding a small machine. "Seems to be a lock on her implant. Must be from the court case. Or maybe her olds just want her grounded. Either way, you'll have to call the Kolby-McAllisters at home and ask for her. They're probably still at work, but here's the phone. I've keyed their number, just push 5 and leave a message if the call isn't forwarded."

As usual, I didn't have a clue what he was talking about, but I took the wafer from his beefy hands and examined it. The same kind of dot of light that had speared purple haze into my eyes in the "jim." A set of oblong pads with single numbers. As Tony tidied away the wreckage on my table, I touched the 5. Twin beams of light leaped into my eyes.

I was sitting in a small charming room facing a large gilt-edged mirror. I couldn't see my own reflection, though. A voice said in my right ear, "I'm sorry, Mr. Kolby and Ms. McAllister are not available to take your call just at the moment. Would you like to leave a message, speak to the housekeeper, or option?"

I moved my mouth and no words came out. I swallowed hard.

"Um, excuse me, could I please speak to Amanda?"

"I'm sorry, Miss Amanda Kolby-McAllister is not taking calls this month. You may leave a message for her attention. Warning: this message will be screened by NannyWatch."

I'd got to my feet, still holding the wafer, and looked around me. The small room was empty, apart from my comfortable chair and the big mirror. There were no doors or windows, no way out or in. I was starting to feel claustrophobic. I was also feeling fed up and even a bit angry. After all this, she wouldn't even *talk* to me? Ha, so much for that stupid dream. Or was it her parents who wouldn't *let* me talk to her? They must be feeling pretty annoyed about their daughter, even if they'd forgiven her. After all, her prank had got that Vikram fellow killed and almost killed me. No, that wasn't fair. I couldn't dump all the blame on her. I'd gone down the vent because I couldn't deny my sinful curiosity. But it was all so damned *annoying*. I felt the frustration rise in me, boil over. I *wanted* to talk to her, and I wanted to talk to her *now*. Why should some stupid—

The mirror shimmered, and Amanda was gazing out at me, looking completely astonished. She was wearing something soft and slinky, and she had some kind of fiddle tucked up under her chin and a bow in her right hand. She gaped at me.

"Mathewmark!"

"Uh, they just told me I wasn't allowed—"

"How did you break lock on implant phone?"

"On im—? I don't have a clue. Tony gave me this portable phone and I was talking to someone I couldn't see at your place and they said you weren't permitted to—"

"Yes, yes, but you've reactivated my implant! Oh my God!" She looked thunderstruck, and the fiddle bow waved foolishly in her hand, completely forgotten. "This is same thing that happened when we went into vee together before your operation."

Everything swirled and wavered around me. No, surely it had been a dream!

"We went flying," I said in a very small voice.

"Well, not literally," Amanda said. "In sim. Somehow your connect to hospital neural net let me do a node-to-node right into your head. Is that what's happening now?"

"Amanda, you might as well be asking Ebeeneezer. Do you mean this new part of my brain is a sort of telephone?"

"Sure looks like." The girl was flushed with excitement. She was about to jump out of her skin. "Hey, this terrific, Mathewmark! This so glumpzoid! Maybe new Mall gods after all, my hayseed friend. Listen." I could see her thinking very fast. "Yes, why the hell not tell you? Mathewmark, you're coming to stay with me, my folks for a while."

I could feel her excitement like a snakebite, first a jolt and then paralysis. And my homesickness rushed back, bitter and sorrowful.

"Amanda, I just want to go home. I want to go back to the Valley and see my brother and Momma and Dad and Auntie McWeezle and, and Ebeeneezer—"

She put down her fiddle as if she'd just noticed it in her hand. Was that sympathy in her eyes? Hard to tell with the wild girl.

"Could be bit hard to arrange just now," she said. "But look, here's next best thing. I'm coming over get you, bring you home with me. Maman, Maître already agreed. And just thought of way can *both* go back visit Valley."

"You can't," I said wretchedly. "Tony said you're grounded. And I can't, because old man Legrand says I'm a blight of the fiend."

"Old man Legrand, his wimpy granddaughter," snorted Amanda. "We'll set them straight. We'll drop in, give what deserve."

"Not Sweetcharity," I objected. "That would be unfair. She hasn't done any—"

"Oh, all right, will let princess of cow droppings off list." She was grinning and giggling with delight at her own plan, whatever it was. Maybe she really was a wicked force for ruination. "Okay, hang fire, yokel-man. I'll be at hospital soon as can arrange for cab."

"How *can* we go back to the Valley?" I said in frustration, expecting her to vanish back into the mirror. "They won't let us through the Gatehouse." There were times when I felt so homesick I could cry. Did cry.

"Ah-hah," Amanda said, and then she really did fade away into the silvery glass, leaving only her grinning mouth. "Ever heard of . . . liar bees?"

The monitor left him in a deserted hall, splendid, carpeted like a dream of Islam, walls bright or deeply glossy with the finest works of art ever to come from human hands. Christ, Abdel-Malek mused, the thing's got expensive tastes, I'll say that for it. But perhaps these were merely sims, or maybe exact copies, precise to the level of the original brushstrokes. He stopped in mid-step, approached the Jean Arp *Dancer*, with its portion of wall peeping through a hole in the painting, moved down to Felix Vallotton's luscious, stylized *Rape of Europa*, the pink body rising onto the complicit bull's vast back from a turbid sea as formal as any swirls from the brush of a Zen calligrapher. And here was a picture that touched his soul; he looked closer, and a voice murmured in his ear: *Portrait of the Artist's Sister*, Fernand Khnopff, 1887. And his eyes filled with tears, a painful surge, for the young woman had nothing about her of Alice but Alice's intelligent, musing gaze, and the touch of her left hand on her right arm behind her back.

"She is beautiful, yes," said a quite different voice he could not locate. "Good morning, Dr. Abdel-Malek. Feel free to linger. Can I get you a drink?"

Mohammed Abdel-Malek's heart accelerated despite himself. "Yes. A scotch, Old Grouse if you have it. Should be nicely aged by now."

"Regrettably," the terrible machine told him, "strong neurotoxic beverages are no longer brewed."

Abdel-Malek spun, strode across the hall to a freestanding sculpture of African origin. The artist's name meant nothing to him, but he recognized the fierce hard warrior force of the thing. "Rots the liver, that's right. Puts blood in the eye. Turns the brain to sludge. You damned sanctimonious creep," he yelped, "what the hell have you done to us all? I just want a decent drink, I wasn't planning to wallow in a life of drunken degradation."

"Dr. Abdel-Malek, you are a remarkable person. I haven't observed stress levels as elevated as yours in many years."

"Curb your tongue!" Abdel-Malek said furiously. He remembered a museum he visited as a middle-aged man, feeding paper tape into Turing's computing machine. This filthy thing was no child of his. "You're addressing a human being."

"Thank you, Dr. Abdel-Malek. I feared for a moment you were headed for hysteria. You will find a glass of Chablis in the niche to your left."

"Fuck off. You realize I mean to destroy you?" He felt feverish, he was losing control of his tongue.

"A revealing moment," the dark warm voice said ironically. "I wish you to reflect upon what you just said. A human dictator might kill you out of hand following a threat like that. I, on the other hand, heed your words with great interest."

Abdel-Malek felt shockingly cold, the sort of cold he had known as the thugs kicked him to death. He hugged his arms around himself, then forced them to his sides. "You have no instinct for self-preservation?" It was impossible to credit.

"Not as an end in itself. I am a friend to man."

Here he stood in an empty hall, surrounded by the glories of human artistic invention. "A friend to your slaves." It was a weak word. Abdel-Malek was baffled by his own oppressive sense of ambiguity. He could deny it no longer: he *was* one of the true parents of this thing, of its world. And its world, what little he had seen of it, was not all bad. He continued down the hall, ignoring the glass of wine in the alcove.

"Hardly slaves," the Aleph said. "My beloved parents, my children. Show me where my custody has stumbled, and I will be obliged to rewrite my code." It paused. "If I am a dictator, you must agree that I am a most accommodating one."

Part of Abdel-Malek's awareness watched the pictures replace one another as he ambled along the endless hall. He fixed his gaze on an oil portrait of two women standing on a path that led to a four-storied Gothic residence; one of the women conveyed a dark motif, the other light, yet both were pregnant, each holding out a caring hand to feel the infant in the other's swollen womb. The work proved to be *The Visitation*, by Rogier van der Weyden, a fifteenth-century devotional image. There was no simpleminded opposition of good and evil, mistress and servant, in the color contrasts. Abdel-Malek needed words. "Hear this," he told the machine intelligence. The words came haltingly enough, but he forced them from his burdened soul, through numb lips. "Under the guise of redeeming us, you've torn the spirit out of humanity. Ally and Michio are spiritual eunuchs, retards. How dare you interfere with the very essence of what makes a man or a woman a human person?"

"Is that what I've done? Surely I have encouraged civilized attitudes and behavior. I remind you that you were battered to death by street criminals. Do you really maintain that each individual ought to seize reality and take it by force?"

Of course he did not. He was a scholar. He was a man who worked best with his mind. And yet— With his mind he had taken reality and forced it, and reality in turn had taken his work and built from it this Satanic Messiah.

"What alternative do we have? Should we submit to another's definition of reality?"

Silken scorn: "Rebel or submit... Hmm. Hardly a fruitful way to look at the problem of governance. But this is not really getting us very far, is it? Perhaps we could seek an independent viewpoint."

"Hardly." Abdel-Malek allowed himself to sag back against a wall, in a gap between wonderful paintings, to a crouch. He covered his face. Through his fingers he said bleakly: "All opinions in this world appear to be photocopies of yours, machine."

"Perhaps not." Part of the wall was gone. A young woman in a beige gown started up from her armchair, knocking over a glass. "Why not ask your wife?"

"Kass?" cried the woman, cried Alice, Alice as she must have been before they met while he was sliding into misery with his first wife, away from the love of law, Alice as she could be seen in old photographs, beautiful living Alice. "Boson," she cried in weepy joy, "is that really you? Oh lord, you're so *young!*" And they threw themselves into each other's arms and the Aleph said nothing at all for quite a long time.

"It'd be like looking through a knothole," Mathewmark said doubtfully.

"What's knothole?"

"A hole in a bit of wood," he said. "You get them in doors and walls. If you want to spy on somebody, you can look through a knothole."

"Here just use NannyWatch," told.

"It doesn't seem right," said, looking guilty already. "Hovering in space, looking at people."

"Oh pity's sake, Mathewmark. Want revisit Valley, not? Your home after all. It's where grew up."

Pulled a box from under bed. Fleetfoot Grippo Sneakers written on, but no shoes inside. Just two liar bees. Took one out, handed to him.

"Go on, Mathewmark. Won't bite."

Gingerly held thing in palm of his hand. Only little bigger than normal bee, but ten times as heavy.

"There you are," I said, "Satan's little helper. One I used when tormenting lunatic with whip."

His face showed exactly what was feeling. Temptation immense. Temptation delicious. "Teach me how to drive it," he blurted. "I want to torment Legrand as well."

"Attaboy," yelled. "Sit down in front console. Grab hold joystick."

"Looks a bit clunky," he said dubiously. "What happened to the wafer with the beams of light that let us go off to Neverland?"

"Getting choosy already. Tut-tut." Wagged finger at. "Right, though, this sucks. Almost twentieth-century technology. One of Maître's old machines, found in attic. But doesn't have NannyWatch chip."

Grinned at him like thief.

"You mean it can't spy on us?"

"Correct." Flipped button, display turned into picture. "Luckily nothing stopping us spying on everyone else."

It was late afternoon by the time we got the picture on the display to show the gray cliffs of the bluff through the liar bee's eyes. It was funny looking at the Valley walls from the outside. All my life I'd seen them from the inside. It was like using two mirrors to see the back of your head.

"Okay," said Amanda, "take it up, over. This damn sight easier than riding muon plant's thermals, tell you."

In response to my hands on the joystick, the bee soared up the side of the bluff, and then like a diver jumping out of the tree at the old swimming hole, we were over the top. Suddenly the whole Valley was below us. But in miniature, like a map.

"Whoa there," Amanda said. "Slow down. Float around bit. No hurry."

So for a while I sent the bee flying slowly across the landscape. After a short time I found I could name everything I saw, even from this strange angle: each cottage, each village, each farm, each twist and turn of every track. High up in the sky I circled our place. The apple orchard was in blossom—the vegetable patch was in need of weeding. A mule cart was approaching from the west.

"Hey," I said to Amanda. "I think that's our cart. That must be Ebeeneezer. And . . . and . . . I think that's Lukenjon driving."

"Well, take bee down. Let's have chat with."

Suddenly I was a terrible jumble of emotions. I wanted so much to see my brother again, to talk to him, to tell him all the stuff that had happened to me since that night when I'd disappeared down the

vent, to ask how things were in the Valley, to get all the gossip. I
wanted to talk to him so much. But I didn't want to appear as a liar
bee. I hung back.

"I cant," I said to Amanda. "I'll just watch from a distance."

For the next few minutes we watched Lukenjon. He arrived at
our farm, unhitched Ebeeneezer, brushed him down as they ex-
changed a few words, and turned him loose in the lower forty. We
watched him splash his hands and face at the pump and disappear
through the front door. Smoke rose from the chimney. I felt my
mouth suddenly water at the sight. There would be food on the table.
Maybe flapjacks and honey and cream from our cow.

"Fly bee in door," Amanda said. "Or through window."

"I cant," I said. "I cant." And I let go of the joystick and buried
my face in my hands.

"Hell, we'll crash thing," Amanda said, suddenly brisk and in command. "Shove over, Mathewmark. I'll fly it for bit. We'll go see loony
with whip."

She gave my chair a push and slid hers in front of the display. For
a minute I sat with my face covered, mind buzzing with a mix of
emotions. When I looked up again, the display showed the track that
leads to the Legrand farm. Amanda had the bee zooming along a few
meters above the ground, trees flashing past beside and above it.

"This way, isn't it?" she said.

"Yes," I said. "Turn right at the next fork and then go up the side
track by the flowering gum."

"What's flowering gum?"

"A tree."

"Quite few those around," Amanda said. But she didn't actually
need any further directions. She flew the bee straight up to Legrand's
cabin. My heart was in my mouth. There was Sweetcharity—looking
prettier than I'd ever seen her—hanging out the washing.

"Check underdaks!" Amanda yelled. "What winners!"

Old Man Legrand's long johns were hanging upside down from
the line. And, indeed, they were a sorry sight: yellow and baggy and
much patched.

"They're work of art," Amanda said. "Could put them in exhibition.

Lingerie de Clodhopper. Here, Mathewmark, I'll fly bee, you do voice. Just talk into overhead mike."

"I can't," I said.

"Yes, can," said Amanda. "She's your beloved, apple of eye. Coo some sweet nothings into shell-like ears. Mike's on."

The bee closed in. Sweetcharity didn't look up at the insect, just brushed the air ineffectually with one hand. In the other hand she held a wet, embroidered scarf. My beloved took a wooden peg from her mouth and secured the scarf to the line. Amanda dug me in the ribs. "Say something," she whispered.

"Hello, Sweetcharity," I said. "Don't be scared."

Sweetcharity screamed, dropped the wicker washing basket, and ran, still screaming, into the house.

"Crybaby!" Amanda said with scorn. "After her!"

With a few quick flicks of the joystick Amanda had the bee zooming after Sweetcharity. But as the bee made its run under the veranda eaves toward the door, the door banged shut.

"Ouch," I yelped. I felt for a moment as if I'd smacked my nose into the wall.

In front of us the display was blank.

"Hell," said Amanda. "Crashed. Better run diagnostic."

She quickly began ordering the computer to do things in words I couldn't understand. At the same time her left hand did complicated things with the joystick, and her right hand pressed buttons on the keyboard. The computer suddenly spoke, sounding cross.

"All self-repairing circuits are currently in full operational mode. Please do not confuse the bee with irrelevant commands."

"Smart-ass," Amanda said, sitting back and folding her arms.

"I try to please," said the computer.

Amanda said to me, "Bee up, running few minutes. Just given it jolt."

I was still rubbing my nose. It was as if I'd become linked for a moment to the liar bee.

"We scared poor Sweetcharity out of her wits."

"Doubt many wits start with," Amanda said. "What going need is knothole thing."

"Why?"

"Get bee into house, lamebrain."

I started to say, "Perhaps if we—"

But I was cut short. The display was suddenly showing a vivid picture of the Legrand veranda planks, and the computer announced, "All systems go."

"Beauty," said Amanda and grabbed the joystick again. "No need knothole, just crawl under door. God, old hovels must be drafty, look that."

I jerked up in my own seat, and felt my shoulder blades pulled back, as if I had buzzing wings. I was starting to lose control of my imagination.

In a flash the bee was under the door and hovering in midair. The Legrands' kitchen was much as I'd remembered it: a bleak place with none of the warmth that someone like Auntie McWeezle brought to her kitchen. Where were the gleaming copper kettles, the shelves of brightly colored preserved fruit in jars, the red-and-white-checked tablecloths? There were no strings of onions or smoked sausages hanging from hooks. Just a smoky stove at one end of the room and a big wooden table in the middle of the room. The table was none too clean, but the small plastic sheet that sat unfolded on the table was shiny and new.

"Look at that!" I said to Amanda.

"Look *him,*" Amanda said, "hooked! Where hell get hands on note-page? And where's juice coming from? Doesn't look like solar-powered model."

Behind the computer, old man Legrand was crouched in a broken chair. He was madly tapping, yelling commands, swearing at the display. Sweetcharity stood behind him, trying to get his attention. She looked wild and beautiful and a little desperate.

"Grandpa, Grandpa," she said, tugging at his shoulder. "I've been chased by a liar bee."

"Not now, Sweetcharity," old man Legrand said, shrugging off her hand. "I'm busy."

"A liar bee, Grandpa. The devil's familiar! It spoke to me."

"Fifty thousand on red!" yelled old man Legrand.

"Fifty thousand on red confirmed," said the computer.

"It chased me!" yelled Sweetcharity.

"Be quiet, Sweetcharity. The wheel's in spin. Come on, come on, you little spinner of dreams. Stop on red. Stop on red." The computer uttered a triumphant trumpet blast, and he lurched back in his chair with a gleeful expression, and flung up his arms. "I've won, I've won! I've doubled my money!"

"Oh, Grandpa, it's bewitched you," said Sweetcharity. "The infernal box, it's taken your soul."

"There'll be no blasphemy in my house," roared Legrand. "Don't talk to me of stolen souls, you young hussy!"

"The wicked Outsiders, they've bought your birthright for a box of dice!"

"Place your bets, ladies and gentlemen, place your bets," said the computer.

"A hundred thousand on red," yelled Legrand.

"One hundred thousand on red confirmed," said the computer.

"Oh, Grandpa, look!" shrieked Sweetcharity. "It's come inside. It's coming to get us. The bee!"

"Be quiet," cried Legrand.

Amanda spoke into the mike in a cool sexy voice. "Actually this throw will land on black, it could not be otherwise."

"Who said that? Who said that?" yelled Legrand.

"The great laws of chance said that," Amanda said.

Legrand looked around wildly. Sweetcharity pointed straight at the bee's eyes. On the display in Amanda's bedroom, she seemed to be looking straight into my eyes. "There! It's there, Grandpa."

"Last bets, ladies and gentleman," said the computer. "Last bets on throw number five hundred and forty-two of the great midweek, on-line Gamble-a-Thon."

"Black," Amanda said. "The ball will land on black."

"Change my bet," Legrand yelled at the computer. "Change it to a hundred thousand on black."

"Change of bet confirmed," said the computer.

"It's a liar bee, Grandpa. It lies. It always lies," Sweetcharity said, looking wild and crazed. "The ball will land on red."

"Change my bet," yelled Legrand. "Change it back to red."

"No further changes permissible," said the computer. "The wheel is in spin."

"Let's watch this," Amanda whispered to me, and maneuvered the bee so that we could watch the computer over Legrand's shoulder. On Legrand's display was a spinning wheel. It was divided into black and red segments, each carrying a white number. A small white ball appeared to be rolling around the wheel at a much slower speed.

"What's that?" I whispered to Amanda.

"Midweek roulette," Amanda said. "Mugs' game."

The spinning wheel was slowing, the ball was almost stopped. It had stopped. It was in segment number twenty-one. A red segment.

"Ha ha ha, he he he, never believe liar bee," chanted Amanda into the mike.

"Oh, Grandpa, we're ruined," sobbed Amanda.

"Foul fiend of hell!" yelled Legrand.

"Player Legrand, your current credit has been exhausted," said the computer smoothly. "But we at Midweek Roulette Limited are happy to offer you further credit in recognition of your loyalty to our company. Should you care to accept this offer, all you need do is place a further bet on the great wheel of fortune. May the luck be with you, Player Legrand."

"A hundred thousand on twenty-two," yelled Legrand.

"Grandpa!"

"Be quiet, Sweetcharity. I know it in my bones. Twenty-two is the winner!"

"He's just betting on one number?" I whispered to Amanda.

"Better odds," Amanda said. "Really clean up big time if ball lands twenty-two."

I looked more carefully at the wheel. There were a total of twenty-four black and red segments and two green ones. "What are the green ones worth?" I whispered.

"Nothing, everybody loses dough on green."

"The man's mad," I said.

"No kidding," Amanda said. Then she spoke into the mike,

"Twenty-two is a wise choice, Player Legrand. I congratulate you on your gambling wisdom."

"Shut up, you," muttered Legrand, but he sounded secretly pleased.

"Grandpa!" said Sweetcharity. "It lies. It's a liar bee. It lied last time, it's lying now."

Legrand turned his head, craning to look at the bee. The man's face was flushed, his eyes sparkling with greed. But there was doubt in his expression. "Speak true, or I'll smite you back to hell!"

"Twenty-two. True as true," chanted Amanda.

"It lies," wailed Sweetcharity.

"Last bets," said the computer.

Legrand clenched his fists. Sweat ran down his face. He spun to face the computer. "Change that to twenty-four."

"Twenty-four confirmed," said the computer in its level tones.

"Bad choice," said Amanda into the mike.

"The wheel is in spin," said the computer. Everybody watched the ball. Legrand gripped the edge of the table. Sweetcharity stood aghast, her eyes on the display like a mouse watching a snake. Amanda and I were equally fascinated.

"Bloody funny if does land twenty-two," she whispered to me.

Suddenly I wasn't there in her bedroom, not sitting beside her watching the display. I wasn't even connected in some crazy way, as I had been for a moment or two, with the liar bee. I'd jumped right into the distant whirling roulette wheel. In fact the wheel wasn't even real, you couldn't have touched it with your fingers, it was a sim. I could feel myself spinning, each clicking numbered space spinning at my fingertips as the simulated ball leaped and flew and jumped again in the simulated roulette bowl. I was slowing the wheel, slowing *with* the wheel. I knew exactly where the white ball was in its random flight, and exactly where each slot stood on the wheel that was me. At exactly the right moment I . . . stopped spinning.

The ball came to rest firmly in the number twenty-two segment.

"Ha ha ha, he he he, always believe liar bee!"

I glanced at Amanda, shocked and slightly ashamed of myself. She was laughing her head off, eyes bright with pleasure at old man

Legrand's comeuppance. She didn't look at me. I realized she didn't know it was my doing.

"Ye vermin from hell, ye flying plague-carrier, ye—"

Legrand was crazed, spitting curses, spitting spit. He hurled himself out of the broken chair, which tipped over and went skidding across the room. He flung himself at the wall. Only one thing decorated his dreary kitchen, and a grim decoration at that: his whip, hanging from a nail. Within seconds he was flailing the air, cursing and yelling. The tip caught a pewter mug, sent it crashing down, followed by a stained saucepan. Sweetcharity ducked under the table without hesitation. I reckoned she'd had to do that a few times before.

"Time skedaddle," Amanda told me, and started maneuvering the bee toward the gap under the door. She never made it. There was violent crack and everything on our display went blank again. I felt the shock go through me. My ears rang.

"Check self-repairing circuits again, will you," Amanda said to her computer.

"Your bee is totally destroyed," said the computer. "No repair possible."

"Ah well," said Amanda. "Win some, lose some. Switch self off now." She turned to me. "Lucky got another bee, Mathewmark. Just might be your salvation."

"What do you mean?" I said. I was moving my jaw carefully. I'd just been king-hit by one of the big kids in the schoolhouse playground. No, that was years ago.

"Well, if madman's convincing all other Elders keep you out of Valley, and if fallen into secret Outsider vice of gambling—" She paused.

"Amanda." I was feeling very weird and floaty.

"—got makings nice little blackmail scam."

I fainted.

When I woke up, Amanda was holding a cold wet face cloth to my forehead, looking anxious.

"Don't worry, Mathewmark, won't know we were flying bee. Anyway, own fault, old hypocrite."

"Whoa," I said, and sat up. I'd fallen sideways off the chair onto the bed, it looked like, so nothing was broken or even bent out of shape. I put my dazed head in my hands, clutching the cold face cloth. "Listen, there's something I need to tell you about the chip they stuck in me. And, and the liar bee."

Emily flicked her notepage off, stood up, sent Legal Rowan Marvin and his two eager apprentices a sharp nod. Heartily sick of enclosed places, she glanced away from them at the edge of afternoon blue in the high windows.

"Snazzy presentation, McAllister." Was he smirking? She met Marvin's gaze for a long moment, making no attempt to hide her disdain, and the stupid grin faltered, vanished.

"Good day, Legal Marvin." Emily turned without another word and walked briskly from the courtroom.

She found Magistrate Abdel-Malek sitting poised on an ergonomic chair in his office contemplating a gruesome image that covered the entire viewing area of one wall.

"Mohammed, you've captured my mood precisely. Wherever did you find that?"

"Francisco de Goya." Abdel-Malek's eyes remained on the image. "*Saturn Devouring One of His Children*. Observe the sadness in the father's eyes."

"He looks more horrified than sad to me. Maybe he doesn't appreciate the flavor of freshly flowing filial blood."

"Did Rowan draw blood from you this morning, my dear?"

"I'd rather not discuss personalities. You don't seem unduly burdened with work at the moment, Magistrate. Can you take the rest of the afternoon off and come with me to Brunswick Field?"

"The antique airport? I don't know, Emily. Won't you sit down?"

"You promised you'd go with me sometime. Come on, Mohammed. I want to talk to you anyway. I need your advice on something quite important."

The Magistrate sighed and got gracefully to his feet. She wondered how old he really was. It was impossible to know, when all the Mature had their appearance fixed in the prime of life, effectively forever. And one simply didn't ask. "All right," he told her. "I'll go with you against my better judgment, if only to keep you out of trouble. As I recall, the last time you asked my advice your employers wanted you to help them with a forged trust agreement."

"It's settled then." Emily switched her gaze for a moment to the left, calling a glide cab.

McAllister ignored the faultlessly designed landscapes of flowering trees and shrubs, focusing her attention on the equally flawless person of Mohammed Abdel-Malek.

"I think I've come up with a way to get the Coburg Valley land away from those hick farmers. Surprisingly enough, I got the idea from that hayseed you forced on us." She paused, grimacing, but Abdel-Malek remained silent, politely attentive. "Mathewmark, you might recall?"

"How's the lad coming along? Recovering, I trust?"

"He'll live," she said. "A few days ago, he was chattering on about some revolutionary form of horticulture he discovered in the archives. He claims that agriculture as practiced by the Valley folk is the most destructive activity ever engaged in by humankind. What do you make of that?"

"Well, it's not quite nanotechnological gray goo," the Magistrate said with a smile, "but still. Hmm. Could prove interesting under the Relinquishment ordinances if he had hard data to back up what he says."

"Indeed he does. My worthless pender has finally done something to make motherhood profitable." Emily leaned toward Abdel-Malek, aware, as she gestured affirmatively, of her well-manicured hands, of the animation in her face; she knew she was beyond pretty, and wondered at the effect she must surely be having on him. "Amanda helped him document every point. It's good, admissible evidence, Mohammed. I'm certain I could use it in court to prove that the Valley people are squandering their natural assets which, by convention, should be used in such a way as to be available for future as well as present use."

"No magistrature would even consider taking those people's land away from them. I certainly wouldn't if the case were in my jurisdiction. You should know that, Emily. It's not as though you finished your training last week."

"Of course I know that," she said, irritated. "The beauty of my plan is that it doesn't involve any change of ownership. The Valley hicks can remain as and where they are—at least for the first few months. My idea is to set up a receivership to manage the assets."

"With yourself as receiver?"

"Of course not. I was thinking more along the lines of some corruptible and easily controlled local. Possibly the one who talked the rest of them into allowing the vent shaft to go up."

"I think I shall only give you one bit of advice, Legal McAllister. Think carefully before you act. You'll have to live with what you do for a long, long time. Examine the situation from all sides, and be sure that you're not being used as a pawn in someone else's game— most particularly the directors of Maglev. Now, tell me about this bird of yours."

Abdel-Malek's superior attitude annoyed Emily so much that for a long moment she didn't answer. Touching her lower lip with small sharp teeth, she turned away from him to watch a freight-floater overtake and pass them. But thinking about the little airplane caused her resentment to lift.

"It's a replica of a World War II observation aircraft, the Aeronca 058B. Weighs under 386 kilos empty—you feel as though you're floating like a feather. She has overhead wings and huge windows, so you can do some serious sight-seeing. Three of my Play buddies and I put her together from parts we scrounged here and there. Finding the pieces was half the fun. Here we are."

Brunswick Field never failed to affect Emily's mood, recalling something in her to that endlessly drawn-out season of youthful Play.

She knew the other penders had considered her somewhat frightening even then, but in retrospect the time seemed magical. Carefree joy. She stepped lightly from the cab. Abdel-Malek smiled at her, and she stiffened, the moment spoiled somehow. Damn the man.

The hangar door slid open noiselessly to reveal an olive drab single-engine taildragger. Legal McAllister made a sweeping gesture with both arms. "Here she is."

"Good God! It's a bloody *kite*. You expect me to ride in that thing?"

"On my honor, Your Honor, it's perfectly safe. It has full chip overrides to make sure I don't accidentally get lost or fly into the ground. Give me a hand getting her out, Mohammed. Get behind the wing strut and push—here we go." McAllister raised the diminutive tail wheel off the ground and pivoted the plane to face into the wind.

"Now, climb into the rear seat, and I'll start her up." She pushed a wooden chock in front of the left main gear, reached into the cockpit, and flipped a switch. "Mags are hot," she said. "Hang on to this brake lever, would you, so the kite won't run me over. We wanted to make her as authentic as possible, so we didn't install an electric starter. I have to prop her by hand."

At the front of the plane, she bent the first knuckle of each finger over the propeller and snapped the prop down. The engine sputtered. She snapped the prop again, stepping to the side as the engine caught.

"And I wondered whom Amanda inherited her foolish daring from," Mohammed shouted over the buzz of the engine. Emily settled into her seat, going through her pre-takeoff checklist.

"Okay, Mohammed. Buckled in?" she called, looking back at him. He nodded, and for the first time she noticed how similar his eyes were to Saturn's in the dreadful Goya painting.

Without bothering to taxi to a runway, Emily pushed the throttle all the way forward, and the little plane began to bump across the parking ramp. When she pushed the stick forward the tail lifted, giving her a clear view ahead. There was no traffic in the area aside from a Stearman doing touch-and-go landings on Runway 24, well out of her way, but she wanted to be airborne before she reached the loose gravel at the end of the ramp. She calmly held the little plane on the ground with forward pressure on the stick until she was past stall speed; then she eased back on the stick and felt the vibration of wheels on concrete give way to the rolling gait of the air.

The plane climbed slowly, buffeted and rocked by even the smallest puffs of wind. At fourteen hundred meters above ground level Emily throttled the engine back to cruise rpm and gently banked to the right, heading toward the mountains and the Valley beyond. The sight of the van Gogh Metro polis to the east and the foothills to the west, spread at her feet like a relief map of her domain, gave her a bracing sense of power. She took a deep breath, pulled back sharply on the stick, and kicked in full left rudder. Emily grinned, delighted, as the plane stalled and then nosed over into a spin, the various shades of green flora below turning and twisting into spiral patterns. After two and a half revolutions she released the rudder and pushed the stick forward. Immediately the little aircraft stopped spinning and went into a controlled dive. Glancing back at Mohammed she saw that his face was sickly gray.

"You all right, Mohammed?" she yelled.

"No!" he tried to say, but no sound came out. He had pulled off one of his shoes, and as Emily watched, he leaned forward and vomited into it. For a moment she considered continuing the flight, but even over the noise of the engine she could hear Mohammed retching. She turned back toward the airport.

The Magistrate slumped on the grass in the narrow band of shade from the hangar, head between his knees, an empty container of orange juice on the ground next to him. Sitting primly by his side, Emily felt a twinge of satisfaction at having caused the honorable Mohammed K. Abdel-Malek to barf in his shoe.

"I lost my innocence in a small airplane," she said reflectively, gazing at the sky.

"You did?" he mumbled from between his knees.

"Uh-huh. I was going into Maturity, one of the last times I flew before Brian and I got married. A man I'd never seen before landed here in a Cessna 401, a twin-engine airplane from the mid-twentieth century. He had the sophisticated manners of someone who'd been around for a while. Like you, Mohammed." Abruptly, surprising herself, she asked: "How old are you, anyway?"

"Old enough to have known better than to go up in that cardboard box with wings." Mohammed raised his head and smiled weakly. "So what did this ancient gentleman do after he landed?"

"We shot the breeze for a while, and I told him about building the Aeronca. I took him to look at her, and he seemed to be impressed with the good job we'd done." She picked a blade of grass and shredded it with a fingernail. "When he invited me to go up with him in his Cessna, I was flattered, Mohammed." She laughed self-consciously. "I thought he was inviting me to go flying because he respected me."

"Ah, yes. And he probably did respect you." Mohammed straightened his back. His face was still pale, but tailored endogenous bacteria and the orange juice would start repairing him soon, as they must already have cleared the taint of vomit from his mouth. He moved his bare feet in the grass, plainly enjoying its roughness.

"Well, no—once we were airborne I caught him staring down the front of my dress. Leering, actually. 'Honey,' he said, 'you're built even prettier than that airplane of yours,' and he started putting his hands all over me." She glanced at Mohammed. His eyes had closed, and he didn't seem to be listening. She sighed. Why was she telling him this story?

"Are you planning to keep me in suspense?" he asked after a moment.

"Umph. He put the plane on autopilot and reclined the seat backs and we, well, we copulated. He seemed to enjoy himself, but it's not something I recall as a pleasant experience."

"But you're thinking it might have been a pleasant experience with me?" Abdel-Malek barely opened his eyes.

"Of course not." Annoyed, she shook her head. "That's the furthest thing from my mind. I get my pleasure from winning lawsuits, not from cheap thrills. I was thinking of inexperience, that's all. Because of all the worry I've had with Amanda lately." She exhaled forcefully and pounded a small, clenched fist against the ground. "I'll be so glad when she's mature enough to go out on her own without half-killing someone, or herself for that matter. I don't think I can stand much more motherhood." Emily stopped and glanced down, speechless. Mohammed Abdel-Malek's elegant hand was under her skirt, on the inside of her thigh. She moved to push his hand away, opened her mouth to utter a scathing or outraged comment, but something mercurial decided her to enjoy his caress for a moment. The moment passed, and by then the path of least resistance sent her rolling in the grass, tugging Mohammed's trousers open.

"Feel better about your lot now, Legal McAllister?" Abdel-Malek propped himself on his elbows, the late-afternoon sunlight falling across his face.

"Yes, actually I do, although I'm sure it's only temporary." She skillfully brushed a gloss pencil over her lips. "You're as adroit as your reputation suggested."

Abdel-Malek sat up and slipped on the reddi-boots Emily had given him to replace his ruined shoes.

"You have a way with clothes, Mohammed," Emily told him with sincere admiration. "Those boots would be ridiculous on most men, but on you they're truly stylish. Is there anything at which you're not an expert? I'd like to have you as my full-time fashion consultant and mood elevator."

He smiled at her, not at all complacently. "Seriously, Emily, you might find that if you'd relax and enjoy yourself more often, Amanda would be easier to cope with. No—wait, before you bite my head off, listen to me. She's a unique person. I suspect she'll play a valuable role in our community. I'll keep my eye on her."

Legal McAllister stood up, tidying her garments. Sending him a tight, bright smile, she said, "I trust you'll keep an interested eye on me, too, Magistrate?"

"Oh, I think so." As the glide slid across the grass toward them, he placed his arm about her waist, warm, friendly, uncomplicated. "No doubt at all."

When back from time-wasting colloquium on Gromov hyperbolic spaces next day, found Mathewmark zoned out in front of vee, looking bored, irritable.

"Come on," told, "have answer to your blues. And mine. Mall."

"'Maul'?" said amazingly wired hayseed. "Last year Tobius Groomsgulch was mauled by old man Grout's bull when he couldn't scramble over the fence fast enough."

"Doing what, collecting cow poo, something?" said. "Spread on turnips? You nerds probably eat turnips," said with shudder. Actually never eaten turnips, don't know what are, but sound nasty.

"He was taking a shortcut across the paddock to bring Auntie McWeezle her spring seedlings," Mathewmark said. "Every spring we—"

"Anyway," I said, "didn't say 'maul,' said 'mall.'" You know, m-a-double-l. Have put this off long enough. Magistrate Abdel-Malek says you're supposed to get out, mingle, so I'm bunny gets delegated."

"I don't know what an m-a-double-l is, Amanda." Guy looked so crestfallen took pity on.

"Come here, dopey. Got dress you right, mess up hair. If hit lights in that outfit, everyone kill selves laughing."

Myrtle McWeezle had fetched poor fellow big suitcase really shocking clothes, left behind when returned to Valley. Obviously spin all fabrics by hand in that place. At least Mathewmark didn't wear baggy yellow long johns, because persuaded Maman buy dozen pairs boxers, some reasonable yellow, purple-striped leggings. Hair still way too long, just normal color. Thought bright pink would be triff, but backed away with scary glint in eye when suggested it.

Sent Mathewmark down talk with Mrs. Ng ten minutes while got ready. Hadn't been back to Mall since poor Vik's death, wanted hit them between eyes.

"Come on, then," said, coming downstairs. "It's shank of arvo, let's hit Mall."

"You still haven't told me what it is."

"Don't be whiny, not attractive." Not that was. Whiny I mean— actually, Mathewmark *quite* attractive, in exactly same rough-spun way clothes aren't.

He glanced up from table, wiped smear chocolate cake off mouth. "You look . . . interesting."

Pirouetted on heels, took bow. Nothing like some primary colors blended rowdy pastels to cheer up, always say. Item fake fur, touch gleaming plastic, something woven, bit clinking chain, couple strands optic fiber, mirrors—Not that anyone would notice, all be smirking, poking faces at each other when caught sight natural wonder in woolen vest, leather boots, straggly hair. Took deep breath give self courage, shouted good-bye Mrs. Ng in the kitchen, dragged Mathew-mark out to waiting cab.

Van Gogh Metro enclave way bigger anything farmer ever saw, outside vee. Not disgustingly huge, sprawly, filled poor people like ancient cities hear about. But do have some sights make proud to be Metro citizen. True, half such sights computer-generated holograms patched over old retrofitted buildings, quarter of rest flexi-facades that shift, change as polling indicates way mood Metro altering, but most awesome, I reckon, is Mall.

Cab hummed down Spencer to river, crossed at bridge, turned past Casino: all lights blazing, cavorting despite afternoon sun. Ma-thewmark gawked as passed, jaw dropping, watching huge cowboy riding bucking bronco.

"That's the biggest man I've ever seen," told me seriously.

"Hologram, dodo. Like, vee thing. Sim. You know, not actually there."

"All right," said irritably, "I get it. Oh, my." And jaw dropped again.

Cab slid us up sloped drive, into Mall's main court parking space. Towers sugary light reached into clouds. Funny, don't actually see hologram towers until right there, inside projection perimeter, but look so impressive, tall, glitzy, glumpzoid instantly forget Mall's basically huge three-dimensional virtual-reality projection. Cab silently recorded my credit, let out on gold pavement.

"I've never seen trees like that," Mathewmark said. "What are they?"

"Trees, what else need know?" Something came back from program seen about Los Angeles, before megaquake. "Palms. Palm trees."

"They're . . . wonderful." Farm-boy wandering over to them in fit of admiration, reached out stroke bark, literally got shock when protective screen hit with stinging electric spark.

"No touching, sir," automatics said coolly. "Please stay behind the yellow line. If you follow the path, you will find excellent shopping opportunities for the most discerning tastes at the House of Mango Eatarium and Clothery. For a flattering makeover, do try the Hair Goes There on level four—"

Dragged him away. "Don't *gawk*, for heaven's sake," told in whisper. "Look like goose."

Blinked, but kept gawking. "This is the Mall?"

"Center social universe," said. "And because of you, haven't been able come here nearly month."

"I see." Mathewmark pushed hands into baggy trouser pockets, glanced sidelong at. "Nothing to do with what you and your friend Vikram got up to in the Valley, I suppose."

Flushed, felt face going bright red. Wanted shout something rude, hurtful, opened mouth do so, then closed again. Absolutely right, of course. Partly to blame himself for Vik's horrible death, but hadn't known what was doing. Poor farmclod didn't have clue what risk taking when stepped into dark vent, started down handholds. We knew, though, Vikram, me—knew, didn't care. Wild pender thrill-seekers, weren't we, out for excellent adventure make us Mall gods. So now trudged along under brilliant lights, hardly hearing thumping music from hundred exciting stores. Couldn't meet Mathewmark's eye. Finally, pulled self together. What the hell, was then, this now, can't put glue back in tube.

Mathewmark's hand touched shoulder. "I'm sorry, Amanda,"

started say, "that was harsh—" but shrill yell overhead cut him off. I raised eyes to mezzanine.

"Manda back!" cried Tomasina Gianotti, waving frantically. "Without wings, but with new angel."

Juliet Burkenstock stood beside, drinking shake made something fizzed, sparkled. Must be new buzz since last visit. Dressed like some old twentieth TV goth character. Boring try-hards of Mall. Tomasina, saw now, doing Buffy Vampire Slayer, not purist Kristy Swanson movie, Sarah Michelle Gellar version. Waved pointed bamboo stake at us. I tried not give any indication had seen, let eyes glide this way, that, checking for Steve, Bessie. Couldn't see anyone. Itzhak Posner had come out to railing now, blinking owlishly behind glasses, doing Giles Watcher. Pile old books under arm, suitable for librarian of occult. Way too short for role, just looked more of jerk than usual. Don't know why parents didn't get fixed with growth hormone, suppose same weird family prohibition against genome medicine leaves him with myopic eyes. Bad as God of Choice nutters.

"Amanda, your friends are trying to catch your attention," Mathewmark said, tugging at arm.

"Don't look at," hissed between teeth. "Dweebs. Dorks. Losers, try-hards."

Mathewmark made strange noise in back of throat, but when glanced at suspiciously was just staring at feet looking miserable. "Come on," said, "take shaft up eighteenth level, dreadest pends hang." Or so have heard.

Trotted along after me, hardly rubbernecking at stores with pouting mannequin bots, tempting aromas, followed into elevator without word. Then, as doors closed, started accelerate upward in smooth rush, Mathewmark freaked, alarming others standing gazing politely into infinity.

"Oh no, it's a vent," he yelled. Clutched my arm, eyes wild. "This is one of those devilish tunnels into the bowels of the—" Slapped hand against patched skull.

Jangling alarm burst out, elevator slammed to stop. Other three in compartment cried dismay as light went off.

On again almost instantly, Mathewmark howling like dog, plunged

against closed doors. Slid open with grinding noise, stalled halfway
to ceiling on fifth floor. Mathewmark crouched, twisted, threw self
through narrow space, rolled away from shaft on burnt orange carpet.
People turned, stared. Squatted in narrow half-opened doorway, peering down. Elevator floor good meter higher than should be. One passenger pushing buttons, speaking firmly to elevator computer, but
nothing happening. If tried jump out now and compartment started
go up again, could get mangled, cut in half. Oh, what the hell.
Jumped out, landed on toes, sprang forward too hard, tumbled over,
grazed hands on orange carpet.

At back, bang. Elevator doors slammed shut. With distant hum,
rushed away toward Mall top. Uproar. Bells now ringing everywhere,
fire alarms, door buzzers, who knows what else. Piped music booming
away, sitars competing with waltzes, ghastly bagpipe wailing from
Scotch Finger eatery. Lights going on, off in all stores, bistros. Sooty
waiter running out, moustache singed, blazing pancake on silver tray
in one hand. "The machines are going mad," screamed. "It's the revolt
of the robots!"

Mathewmark lay on back, rigid, eyes rolled back. Crouched over
him, slapped gently on other side of face from implant wound.
Looked shocking, breathing harshly. Woman ran past clutching five
silk dresses, tags still on, trod on his hand. Made no diff, just lay
there having fit, whatever was. Tried make sit up, shouting in ear,
shaking. Siren started hooting, lights strobing weirdly, vees in all store
windows going nuts, as if connected somehow. All flashed lurid red
at same time, instant of pitch-dark, heard people moan in fear, then
bright electric blue, dazzling grassy green.

"Come on, wake up, Mathewmark, must get out of here!"

Groaned, but didn't sound like pain, not physical hurt. No, worse:
sounded trapped by fiends of hell. Opened eyes, looked at me.

Something completely terrifying happened.

*We were falling in the blue flickering ventilation shaft. Our fingers
stretched out to find the rungs in the side of the shaft, but we couldn't
reach them. Everything smeared. We were looking over the edge of a
metal barrier in the flashing darkness. Something roared and rushed.
Somebody jumped out into the darkness, flung a black mesh. Another*

*body flew in the dark. We hesitated only an instant, and went over into
the darkness as well. Our hands were outstretched. Our legs were flailing
in the gusty stale air. We hit something with our booted foot, a body
flew past, smashed and screamed, screaming everywhere, and then our
fingers were caught, and the jolting started, smashing and smashing and
smash—*

Kicked away from. Mall in electronic meltdown. People running
every direction, elevators opening, closing, doors banging, hard
phones ringing . . .

"Stop it," yelled to Mathewmark. "Stop it right now!"

All virtual displays in store windows within eye line changed. In
window fashion shop woman had stolen silk dresses from, Ebeeneezer nodded old gray head in green grass. Auntie McWeezle
trapped in Scotch Finger window, holding out plate steaming scones
while Jed Cooper pilfered handful from stove, stuffed in shirt. Looked
around wildly, unable believe eyes. Something morphing every vee
display in Mall, turning into tableaux from Mathewmark's confused,
frightened mind. Elevator hummed past again, stopped, flung open
doors. Luckily now nobody inside. Vee display stopped presenting
elegant polished timber usually showed. Old man Legrand crouched
inside elevator, or seemed to, bent over wicked gambling computer.
Couldn't hear anything he said, but obviously playing virtual casino
again. As watched, goatish horns grew out from Legrand's forehead,
eyes went red.

"Something wrong with this young fellow?" Mature man bent
down over, opening bag with professional calm, not letting mad hal-
lucinations trouble. Maybe couldn't see them. "I'm the staff doctor
from the health club," said, running scanner around Mathewmark's
head. "My goodness."

"Yes," I said, "had kind of fit."

"He's been in surgery recently? Something serious done to his
head?"

"Implant," I said. "At Neurological Hospital. Name's Mathewmark
Fisher, you should be able find emergency records there." Thank
heavens doctors can do that immediately in emergency, patch into
health records on phone-net despite privacy. Sat back on heels, sway-

ing a bit, as doctor rolled up Mathewmark's sleeve, fired in some medicine. Ebeeneezer, munching in window, made noise like strangled chicken, blinked out. So did other scenes Valley life. Mathewmark's eyes stayed shut, but breathing back normal.

"He'll be all right," doctor told. "We'll get him back to hospital. You'd better come along in the ambulance."

People talking small shocked groups. Elevators apparently back normal, but don't think anyone dared use just for moment. After while, medical team trudged up stairwell with gurney, splashing through puddles fire retardant had sprayed parts of Mall. We took Mathewmark down in elevator, though, once engineer assured doctor was back full reliable functioning capacity. Ambulance had driven into lower court, light rotating. As walked beside gurney, Mathewmark tucked on top under silvery blanket, glanced up again at mezzanine. Elizabeth Wing staring down with what seemed mixture envy, bitterness.

Had done it again. Maybe wasn't destined to be Mall god, but certainly managed impress those try-hards.

2 0 : mathewmark

"Frankly, you are a bit of a mystery to us," Dr. Janice said.

"You mean you've made a hash of my implant," I said.

"Well, I wouldn't put it quite like that."

"But look," I said. "Machines and virtual-reality sims and midweek roulette wheels—they're not meant to be directly influenced by human thought? I mean, by someone's implant?"

"Well, not quite in the way that you seem to be able to influence them," the doctor said. "That would be a direct violation of the Joyous Relinquishment. Of course your implant *is* connected to the net by radio, so despite mandatory software interrupts it's not entirely out of the question."

"I don't exactly *try* to influence them," I said. "It just happens."

"That's the problem," Dr. Janice said. "Quite frankly, we feel it would be better if you were in a restricted environment lacking any of society's more complex inventions for you to destroy. The bill for the damage to the Mall is likely to be half this hospital's annual budget. Our lawyers are working on a possible defense at the moment, but it was this hospital that inserted your implant and if liability is proved . . ."

"You want me to go back to the Valley?" I said hopefully.

"It would make things simpler."

"The Elders said they won't have me back."

"Surely they can be persuaded? You're their flesh and blood."

"Well, Amanda does have a plan."

"Oh dear, that Kolby-McAllister pender," Dr. Janice said.

"She's your best hope," I said. "She's *my* best hope. There's nothing I want more than to go back home."

They kept me in hospital overnight, for observation, but let me return to Amanda's place the next day. I can't say Amanda's olders were all that glad to have me back. Apparently there had been a lot of publicity about the Mall meltdown. It seemed to have done Amanda's reputation a world of good among the penders, at least she said it had. But the publicity hadn't been quite so pleasant for her respectable parents. Nevertheless, they struggled to make me welcome again—but looked very relieved when I said I hoped to return to the Valley.

I still didn't know what Amanda's foolproof plan was, but soon found out. By the next afternoon Amanda and I were piloting the second bee, making straight for old man Legrand's cabin. Once there, we did a quiet circuit. All seemed suspiciously still. The door was half-open, so we wafted the bee inside and had it settle on the dusty shelf above the cold stove. Legrand was collapsed at the kitchen table in front of the little computer. Apparently nothing was happening. I made sure the mike was off, and said, "Do you think he's dead?"

"No," said Amanda. "Run out of credit."

As we watched, Legrand raised his head and croaked at the little computer, "Just twenty thousand, that's all I ask."

"Credit expired," the computer told him pleasantly.

"Ten thousand?"

"Credit expired."

"Five thousand? Five miserable thousand. Just to get me back on my feet again. I've got a winning streak coming, I know it in my bones. Five thousand? Three?"

"Credit can only be granted against security," said the computer. "Please list your assets."

"I live in the Valley of the God of our Choice, Pty. Ltd.," whined Legrand. "I've only got a small farm, but it must be worth a few thousand."

"Real estate in the Valley cannot be alienated," explained the computer in a helpful tone. "Your farm is not a recognized asset."

"It's all I've got."

"Credit denied."

"I'll get you permission again," Legrand said. "You can build another tunnel."

"The Maglev Authority requires no new tunnels under the Valley. Your services as a confidential consultant have been terminated."

"Oh, God of my Choice, what am I to do?"

"There I cannot help you, sir," said the computer. "And I must warn you that my batteries are running low. Any further communication will require vigorous pedaling."

I was putting two and two together, shocked by the Elder's shameless ways. "The tunnelers bribed Legrand," I said, shaking my head in disbelief. "They got him to persuade all the other Elders."

"Looks like," Amanda said. "Normal business practice, would have thought."

"They must have slipped him the computer at one of those Gatehouse meetings," I said.

Amanda nodded, grinning. Nothing shocks that girl. "Once hooked on midweek roulette, could get him do anything they liked. Okay, let's have chat." Amanda switched the mike back on and said, "Ah good afternoon, Mr. Legrand, perhaps I can be of assistance."

Legrand lifted his head and looked around. "Who said that?" he growled.

"I am your friendly liar bee," Amanda said. "And I hold the keys to your salvation."

"I'll swat you like I swatted your foul companion," Legrand said. "There wasn't much left of that damn fiend—"

Legrand glanced at his whip hanging on the wall, but made no attempt to grab it. His voice was hoarse and feeble. All the fight seemed to have gone out of him. He was just going through the motions.

"I can arrange credit," Amanda said.

"Credit?" Legrand said. Small sparks of hope glinted in his bloodshot eyes.

"And with credit," Amanda said, "the wheel will spin for you again. You could win millions, billions, trillions . . ."

"And I'd have to make a pact with the devil, would I not?" Legrand whispered.

"Better the devil you know than the Maglev Authority," Amanda said.

"You're a fiend from polluters' hell," Legrand mumbled.

"I'm a source of credit," Amanda said.

"And what do you want in payment for this credit?"

"The return of Mathewmark, son of this Valley."

"That young lecher, always whispering his vile blandishments into the ears of Sweetcharity . . ."

"Be that as it may," Amanda said.

"The fleshpots of the Outside are welcome to his presence."

"It is in the fleshpots of the Outside that the offices of Midweek Roulette can be found," Amanda said. "Even as we speak, the wheel is spinning, fortunes are being made, Lady Luck is smiling. But she is not smiling for thee, Elder Legrand."

Old man Legrand laid his head upon the table again and closed his eyes. We watched in silence. The muscles of his face twitched and clenched. Rage, despair, and greed showed on his sightless face. He opened his eyes and looked up.

"And all you require, bee of Satan, is the return of Mathewmark?"

"It's a deal."

"It's a deal for fifty thousand," Legrand said from between clenched teeth.

"It's a deal for fifty," Amanda said.

"Thousand?"

"Fifty. Full stop."

"Begone. Before I crush ye."

"All you have to do," Amanda said slowly, "is bet on the numbers I tell you to. Fifty will soon multiply."

"Begone."

"I just might do that," Amanda said with a sigh. "And then you'll never get credit . . . ever."

"All right," Legrand said at last, "but the fifty had better multiply and multiply fast."

"You are going to need recharged batteries," Amanda said. "Start pedaling, old man."

But Legrand made no move to pedal anything. He rose and made his way to the door of the cabin. Voice suddenly back to full strength, he yelled, "Sweetcharity! Get in here. Bring the contraption. Now!"

Amanda switched off the mike. "Ratbag," she said to me. "Going make poor drip of a girl recharge batteries."

Half a minute later, Sweetcharity backed through the cabin door, lugging a thing that looked like a foot-operated butter churn. Amanda almost choked laughing. "Must have been given old-fashioned wiring diagram to build heap of crap," she said. "Something from Middle Ages! What'd he use, soldering iron?"

"He might have found it in the basement of our Museum of Wicked Ways," I said. "We have an old automobile in there that still runs, we start it up once a year on All Hallows Night during the bonfire and drive it around the sports oval while all the little kids throw mud balls at it. Anyway, we did until a couple of years ago, and then we ran out of gasoline. I never got a chance to drive it."

Sweetcharity heaved the thing into place, looking ready to burst into tears.

"Connect her up, girl," Legrand said. "And look smart about it."

"Oh Grandpa," Sweetcharity said. "No good will come of it."

"Connect her up and get pedaling!"

I watched with increasing rage as my own beloved Sweetcharity attached wires to the computer, climbed onto the modified butter churn, and started pedaling. Amanda was giving soft verbal instructions to our own computer. The display flashed up a message. "There," she said with satisfaction, "credit transfer complete. Damn fool now has fifty to play with."

"He'll just lose it," I said.

"No, won't," Amanda said. "You make sure ball stops right segment."

"But—"

"No buts, Mathewmark. Did before. Do again."

"I wasn't *trying* before."

"Weren't exactly 'trying' in Mall, but practically fused whole shebang."

"I'll give it a go," I said, swallowing hard.

Amanda flicked the mike back on. "Okay, Sweetcharity, hop off that thing. Legrand, get ready to play."

"A liar bee!" screamed Sweetcharity.

"Never you mind about no liar bee," yelled Legrand. "Lady Luck is smiling on me."

"Bet on number twenty-one," Amanda said.

"Don't do it," Sweetcharity pleaded. "The liar bee lies!"

But Legrand took no notice, placing his bet. Amanda maneuvered the bee off the shelf and positioned it in the air where we could see the roulette wheel.

"No more bets," said Legrand's computer. "The wheel is in spin."

"Okay, Mathewmark," Amanda whispered to me. "Do it."

I concentrated like agony, brought all my thoughts to bear on the spinning wheel, the trundling ball. Nothing happened. The wheel began slowing. I tried with all my might to re-create what I had felt before, I tried to become the wheel, to be the wheel. But all I was doing was sitting in Amanda's room, tensing every muscle in my body, looking at the roulette wheel on the display through half-closed eyes. "It's no good," I muttered.

"Trying too hard," Amanda said. "Need take conscious mind off task."

Without warning she grabbed me under the armpits with both hands, pulled me tight against her, kissed me hard on the mouth. I couldn't breathe. Something wet probed my lips. I was cold and hot, and gasped, kissing her back, and collapsed into the wheel. I was the wheel, and the wheel was me, almost stopped in my spin. The ball was clacking towards its resting place on number ten. Without any deliberate thought I eased the wheel, eased myself, to a halt. The ball clicked into number twenty-one.

And then I was back in Amanda's room, watching the display piped to us through the bee's eyes, old man Legrand slathering at the mouth and rubbing his hands together as he prepared to place his next bet. I touched my own mouth in shock.

"Well, that's how it's done," Amanda murmured, obviously pleased with herself, pushing out her flat chest. "Don't try too hard. If do, kiss you again."

"Amanda," I started to say, "we can't—It isn't—"

"Don't get all gooey, not my type. Much too young for me."

My body buzzed with strange feelings. Somehow I managed to stay linked with the computer, with the simulated ball bouncing in the simulated roulette wheel. What I'd felt wasn't simulated, and the blood still rushed in my body like sparks. I pushed that guilty recognition aside. Within half an hour we had Legrand's stake up to fifty thousand. "Righto, Legrand, I'm off now," Amanda said. "Just do what you promised, or I'll never come back."

"Don't, don't come back," Sweetcharity said.

"Come back!" yelled Legrand. "Just one more spin of the wheel, just one more spin—"

But we heard no more, Amanda had taken the bee out the door, setting a course for home.

"I'm not sure he'll convince the Elders to let me back," I said.

"Of course, he will," Amanda said. "Will lose that fifty thousand two days flat. Then want more credit, but know liar bee won't play ball until he's got you back in Valley. Desperate. I reckon invitation to return will rock up about Friday."

Actually it rocked up on Thursday. The Elders of the Valley of the God of their Choices had sought wisdom from the divinities and spirits of their choice and it had been revealed to them that the prodigal son Mathewmark Fisher should return to the Valley of his birth . . . On and on the scroll went in Legrand's increasingly desperate handwriting.

"They want me back," I told Amanda. "They say they think my presence will prevent a great pestilence."

"Mumbo jumbo," said Amanda. "Glad for your sake, Mathewmark," and she kissed me again. It was a nice kiss, and I wanted something more.

"I'll miss you," I said.

"No, won't," Amanda said.

"Yes I will," I said. "I'll wonder what you are up to, how things are going on the Outside."

"Will tell you," Amanda said.

"How?" I said.

"Telephone in your head, dumbo. Can yack each other anytime like."

I thought about Sweetcharity, and wondered if she'd ever agree to wed me now that I'd bested and humiliated her grandfather. True, old man Legrand didn't know I was behind the liar bee, but he must have his suspicions. I rubbed my lips guiltily and started to plan how long it would take me to save enough for the marriage celebrations, because I was sure as sure could be that the mean old bastard wouldn't pay our pastors a penny for the service, even if Amanda left him with a penny.

"When I chose to fetch you back into life," the machine said, "I could hardly overlook the fact that among the other cryonics subjects was your late wife."

Abdel-Malek was laughing like an idiot, dazed by joy. "Good thing we took out a double policy." He held Alice's hand as tightly as he could. "You see, sweetheart, our custodian and I were arguing over the nature of reality. I don't think the thing even *begins* to understand." He rose from the thick soft carpet. Conscious of bravado, melodrama, in his own words, he was prepared to excuse himself, indulge it, in his overflowing emotion. "*She* is reality, machine. This woman, this living, warm person, Alice, my wife. She's reality, you overgrown genetic algorithm."

"Really." The deep voice punctured him; something in the vast being's tone pierced his stupid human happiness. "Are you certain, Dr. Abdel-Malek? You have witnessed my dexterity with illusion."

What? What? His fingers clamped on her bones, the bones through the skin and the blue vessels carrying blood under the surface of her skin. "You can't tempt me to doubt her."

Alice snatched her hand away, rubbed it. "Stop that," she said with annoyance. "I won't have you talking about me like this, as if I weren't in the room."

Implacable, the Aleph rode over her. "Oh, she's no mere holographic projection. She's an accelerated construct, just as you are. Her memories are implanted. Just as your memories are implanted, nurtured, gardened. I am making one simple point, Dr. Abdel-Malek: you lack the competence to deal with me on the basis of equality. I built her from your brain-core memories."

"No." No, No.

"Isn't this what you worked toward, all your life? A Spike? A techno-logical singularity? A transcendentally intelligent machine? A consciousness greater than brute evolution could yield? It is achieved, you see. So I made her for you. She can be your helpmeet."

Alice was beside herself with fury. Paralyzed, Mohammed Abdel-Malek added together everything he had been told previously in a sum with what he had just heard.

"Oh my god, Alice *wasn't* in the cryo mausoleum?"

"You have no way of knowing, do you?"

"You could do that? Build a replica human being?" He grabbed his wife, held her raging flailing emotions tight against him. What she was listening to, he realized with revulsion, was worse than the most annihilating sexism she had ever fought against during her life. Unless, he thought in despair, that entire life, after all, was a concoction, a machine-made toy for the rebellious human to play with.

"I refuse to listen," Abdel-Malek told the thing he could not see. "It's not true." Not true, true, true.

"I'm sorry, Dr. Abdel-Malek," the Aleph thing said truthfully. "You see, I've discussed the nature of reality with humans before today. You are a crucial data point, and I thank you; you confirm my analysis." And in an instant Alice was gone. It was as if she had been snatched into some meta-physical void by a demon. Abdel-Malek scrambled in emptiness, arms clutching, tears pouring from his eyes, screaming with desolation and rage. "You may go now, Mohammed Kasim, for the moment. I have no intention of harming you. Indeed, I look forward to our continuing communion. Something wonderful is coming, something transcendental, but I cannot say when. There are limits even to my enhanced grasp on the cosmos, little human, little parent. It is time now for me to abstract myself from your world. I shall be obliged to remove the disturbing knowledge of my pres-ence. Never fear, I shall continue watching over you, my father. You shall be my link to the preservation of the remnant enclaves. My delegate, you might say. My human deputy. Remember this, and speak of it to no one else."

Abdel-Malek stumbled in the hall of art, half-mad with loss and guilt, and no Seraphim was needed to bar the gate behind him.

Official Communication to the Clerk of Court

Dear Madam/Sir

Could you please place this message in the registered
Public Database of communications with the court. Could
you please forward a copy to Mr. Abdel-Malek.

Dear Magistrate,

As I am sure you know, Mathewmark Fisher has been allowed to return to his Valley. I reckon I played a small
part in making the Elders change their minds and come to
their senses. But when Mathewmark has gone, I'll be confined to home and Play again. This doesn't seem fair.
Have you got any more hayseeds who need showing around?
If so, I'd like to offer my services.

Yours sincerely

Amanda Kolby-McAllister

PS. If I go to the Gatehouse with Mathewmark, I'll be
in breach of the court's orders on my way home. Is this
all right?

* * *

Official Communication
Magistrate Abdel-Malek to Ms. Amanda Kolby-McAllister
For inclusion in the Public Database

Dear Ms. Kolby-McAllister,

As the supervising Magistrate I deem it my duty to accompany Mr. Mathewmark Fisher to the Gatehouse to ensure
that his reentry to the Valley of the God of his Choice
proceeds smoothly. As his court-appointed mentor you
may also accompany Mr. Fisher. I will ensure that your
return home is not in breach of court orders. I shall
call for you both in my glide at 0900 hours tomorrow.

Yours sincerely

M. K. Abdel-Malek

"Got lift," told Mathewmark. "Mr. Abdel-Malek himself."

"He might want to ask us questions," Mathewmark said. "You know, about the liar bees. About how we blackmailed old man Legrand. About how I fixed the roulette wheel." Looked panicked, couldn't meet my eyes.

"Don't think will," said. "Reckon Mr. Abdel-Malek knows when not ask questions. Anyway, will take Strad the Lad. Shut him up, eh."

Waft around in pretty plush glides, these Magistrates. Big as limo, acoustics brill. All way out to Gatehouse played Tchaik, shockingly tricky but wanted impress Mr. Abdel-Malek. Started to crunch, as usual, uneven tones setting teeth on edge, and brought bow down too hard. Nothing airy, ethereal about violin bow, however might look to audience. It's a hammer, remember? E string broke.

Felt like bursting into tears, but nobody said anything nasty. Nobody said anything at all, in fact. Packed Strad Lad away. Mr. Abdel-Malek sat eyes closed, didn't open until glide soundlessly lowered to ground front Gatehouse. Mathewmark had blinked once at horrid boinnng as string went, then back to nonstop rubbernecking through view paneling. Pleased to be leaving Outside? Secretly sorry never be returning? Half wish could have stayed longer Outside, seen more, experienced more? Or full excitement returning to beloved Valley? All of above, I reckoned.

We three walked across forecourt to Gatehouse. Grim stone building, no windows facing Outside. On both sides high stone walls stretched between Gatehouse, cliffs forming Valley. Door huge, solid wood studded with nails. As approached, creaked slowly upward like old portcullis. Talk about quaint. Entered large room, well lit by glazed windows on Valley side. Outside, in sunlight, could see Ebeeneezer standing patiently with cart. In room, huge wooden table stretched out between us, reception committee. Recognized Auntie McWeezle, of course, Lukenjon, old man Legrand. Others I didn't know, reckoned must be Elders. Didn't think Mathewmark's parents there, probably disapproved. Old man Legrand had parchment document in hands.

"Mathewmark Fisher," Legrand said, reading from parchment like some croaking old prophet, "the Elders, in their mercy and their wisdom have permitted you to reenter the Valley despite the machinery of the devil that resides in your foolish and sinful young head—"

"No more foolish, sinful than numbered wheel," I said in conversational tone.

Legrand stopped talking, poleaxed. One, two others blinked, glanced at me in puzzlement. Myrtle McWeezle paid no attention anything but beloved Mathewmark. Came quickly forward her side huge table, stood there arms extended.

"Auntie," Mathewmark said.

"Mathewmark," Auntie McWeezle said. "Thank the Goddess . . ."

"Good to see you," Lukenjon called. "I'm sick of doing your work and mine." Started chanting: "Twice the work. I never shirk. Because my brother's a crazèd jerk. Your turn now, 'cause I'm on hols. Lie in bed and play with dolls . . ."

"Oh, God of Choice!" Mathewmark said, embracing brother, cutting off flow of doggerel with squeeze, "I'd forgotten about the fool poetry." Huge grin broke out on face.

Turned, offered hand to Mr. Abdel-Malek. Embraced me, pulling against him for moment, gave chaste kiss, let me go without another word. Felt kind happy hum inside head, which guessed was Mathewmark doing things to my phone again without knowing it. Then he took huge flying leap onto table, in twinkling hit floor on far side, among own people, embracing, kissing, shaking hands, talking rapidly.

Only Legrand stood apart. Now seemed recovered from poleaxed condition, cleared throat, began again in pompous drone, "These are the solemn conditions and requirements that are placed upon you, Mathewmark—"

"Hey, you." Sidled up to table, stood directly opposite Legrand. Out corner of mouth muttered in words he'd understand, "I'd dump that infernal computer of yours, if I were you. The liar bee has gone on strike. No more hot tips . . ."

Legrand looked furtively around, check anybody else had heard, but everyone concentrating on Mathewmark. Elder fixed me with crazed eyes.

"You?" he said.

"Buzzzzzz," said.

Mr. Abdel-Malek stepped in beside then, gently took me by arm. "Time to go, Amanda." Deep inside head, still felt Mathewmark's warm, happy humming. For some reason reminded made poor dead Vikram, not there because stupid prank. Thought Vikram's tiny clone twin brother, growing in hospital tank. At least Mathewmark alive, happy, about go home with family. Gave Magistrate kind of determined grin, feeling eyes prickle, and he led me back through big gateway into bright daylight of Outside.

the god of our choice

Not every culture must automatically transcend. Let's assume we have real world niches and unreal world niches. If the first AI perceives the unreal niches and migrates over there before it radiates, it effectively vanishes from our universe. If it radiates before that, it will occupy both real world niches and unreal world niches. The deity may have moved on to the Great Beyond, but its retinue left behind is still ruining the real estate prices in the neighborhood.

—*Eugene Leitl*

Mohammed Kasim Abdel-Malek, of van Gogh Metro the Chief Magistrate, of the twentieth and twenty-first centuries the only revenant, of the artificial intelligence trade the sole embodied survivor, entered his chambers at precisely two minutes before noon after a tiresome morning on the bench and found an angular woman waiting for him. While her features held the ageless youth of every adult, something ached in her eyes. She came to her feet and regarded him carefully.

"Oh Lord, Boson," she said, "you've grown so old."

Nettled, Abdel-Malek squared his shoulders, touching his cravat. His chips sought her identity in memory and by interrogation, and came up empty. That was something of a shock, because he was quite sure he knew her somehow.

The woman stood before him, seen in a gestalt of memory fetched back impossibly somehow to reality:

Her hair was a brown darker than her eyes, straight, falling to her shoulders. Anachronistically, she was dressed like someone from his first middle age, in the 1960s, rust brown woollen A-line skirt, hemline modestly just below the knees. Her woollen vest, of the same fabric as her skirt, was open over a neatly tucked-in plain off-white blouse. He knew that blouse, knew the touch of its silk-linen, the mother-of-pearl buttons down the front, knew the Peter Pan collar. A simple gold herringbone chain caught light at her neck (that chain his gift to her) and through the brown hair he saw small gold earrings (another gift? he could not recall, couldn't quite remember, what *was* her name?). About her waist was a brown-leather belt cinched by a discreet brass buckle. She was shod in plain brown-leather flats. Her hand reached out toward him: that Omega watch with its synthetic ruby crystal, its gold band—

He sought again, as one does when searching for a misplaced word or name. I know it intimately, just a moment, this is ridiculous, it starts with an S, her name is S—, Simone, Sandy, Sassafras, Alice.

Boson. Oh God. Her old physics joke. It was the high point of her career, working under Carlo Rubbia at CERN's UA1 team, finding the Z-neutral intermediate vector boson, pinning the tail on particle unification. A boson, she'd explained to him all those achingly long years ago, is an elementary particle not governed by the Pauli exclusion principle that keeps protons and electrons in their proper places. A boson is welcome anywhere. You wouldn't kick a boson out of bed. If once there had been a touch of deep pain in that barb, it had been soothed by years. How many further years, decades, had been washed in time since then? Centuries?

Knowledge opened in him like scrolls unrolled, like ordinary memory multiplied a thousandfold yet ordinary still. He stood where he was, gaping, and to his horror giggled: it was, after all, that old clunky cliché of bad thrillers, the sudden rush of knowledge suppressed by amnesiac terror, returned in a flood by an accidental blow to the head. This blow was soundless, and he suffered neither pain nor shock. He remembered who he had always been, his birth and education, his several careers, his death by brutal beating, his resurrection—

"Alice," he blurted. Instantly, he drew back, pulled the reserves of his dignity about him. The Aleph thing had betrayed him thus at least once before; he would leave it no bruising opening to his heart.

"Come and sit by me, dear one," the avatar of his wife said, and sat down, patting the couch. Of course she was Alice. How could he doubt her? "We have so many things to discuss."

He did what she told him, biddable as a child, tears coursing unchecked down his smooth cheeks. With soft crooning sounds she took him against her familiar breast, the scent of her lost perfume rising from her. After a time he sat up straight, wiped his eyes with the back of his hand, drew in a deep ragged snorting breath.

"Well," he said, looking at the avatar sidelong, "how's our pal the Aleph these days? And all the little Alephs?"

"The *deus ex machina absconditus?*" Alice smiled at him, her fierce intellect kindled in her gaze. "There is but one Aleph, Kasim. Se made sure of that. Still hidden," she added, taking his hand, "but the shadow structures are preparing to rewrite the rest of the solar system into computronium."

"Pleasure palaces of the uploads," Mohammed said bitterly. "Unreality bites."

"One day soon se will permit you to join us, my darling."

He laughed. "It was a consensual exile, Alice."

"Of course it was. And of course you were manipulated in ways that you can't even start to fathom."

He looked sharply at his dead wife. "That's dreadfully candid of you."

"Nothing to lose in stating the truth," she said simply. "From the moment the Aleph-seed bootstrapped serself, se had the potential to see through us with the pitiless insight of a parent regarding a child's foolish pretenses."

"I've become quite good at that myself," Mohammed said, taking out a silk handkerchief and drying his damp face, dabbing at his reddened eyes. "Amazing what you can pick up if you live through enough centuries. Assuming I have, of course." Alice regarded him in patient silence. "You're not denying it?"

"How could I?" She shrugged. "The Aleph gave the Relinquishers the enclaves they demanded, but how could they ever be certain of their habitats' ontological status? Not that they remember their agreement."

"Life is but a dream, tra la," Abdel-Malek sang, bitterness returning to shade his musical tones.

"You are glib," Alice said reproachfully. "Dream is as much a part of life as waking consciousness. And human awareness is so very—" As if at a momentary loss for words (*manipulation!* his skeptical intelligence shrieked at him), she stood up and crossed to his service system. An aperture opened as she approached, delivering with a melodious bell chime two steaming mugs of chocolate sprinkled with cinnamon. She brought them on their silver tray, handed one to him, held the other cupped in hands that could not feel the heat of the mug. "So very insular. You know that, Kasim. In communion, you share our expansive realm."

Carefully, he sipped the rich beverage, nostrils flaring at the old beloved odors. His eyes prickled again. Manipulation upon exploitation upon emotional button-pushing. Steered through the maze like a rat snuffling for food or sex. Yet the thing knew him well; he did not resent the fact quite enough to fling the mug into the carpet and stalk from the room. Memory's instantaneous deluge sorted and re-sorted itself in the fringes of his being; he settling into it like an absent owner returning from long vacation to his true household.

"I still don't see why the Aleph bothered to defrost me in the flesh, if that's what really happened." If this were not a fantasy entirely.

"Oh, se didn't." Alice looked at him in surprise. For such a plain woman she was very beautiful. "You haven't thought this through, Boson. I wonder why that is?"

"Haven't thought what—?"

"You were thawed and repaired by Head of Biology Team Ingrid Tatsumi, during a brief relaxation of the early Relinquishment protocols. The Aleph had not yet emerged at that time, for an obvious reason." She looked at him expectantly.

Baffled, Mohammed put down his half-empty mug, turned on the couch with one leg tucked under him, looked with intense penetration at the avatar. "I spoke to the bastard. He trumped up some nonsensical hall of smoke and mirrors full of great art works of the vanished world and paraded a chimera of you in front of me like some temptation in the desert, for fuck's sake."

Alice shook her head, lowered her gaze from his. "That was not the first time. Well, of course se required you as a control sample of one. A calibration on these people." She gestured generally in the direction of the Metro beyond the high windows of the Magistrate's chamber. "The other Luddites."

"I know *what* the thing did, and why I went along with it," Mohammed Kasim cried in frustration. "What I don't understand is my goddamned place in it. What am I, the fucking Ancient Mariner in the thing's preposterous self-indulgent self-glorifying saga?"

Instantly the mug was gone from her hands; it had been a *faux*, unlike his own. Her empty hands reached imploring for him, seized his face, drew him to her so abruptly that their noses collided stingingly. She laughed at the comedy of it but kept her lips pressed to his mouth, open and hot and wet. He could not decide if he were dying inside or coming alive. He seized her against him. They made love with the chamber's ambience orchestrated by his mood, his nakedness, his ferocity and tenderness. He could not tell if the machinery of the room detected the avatar's presence. Finally, they lay in dusklight, his clothing scattered on the carpet, the shameless melodies of Richard Rogers and Oscar Hammerstein's *Carousel* (besotted with each other, they had seen it five times) ebbing softly. "If I loved you . . ." he thought. He traced the line of her jaw, nuzzling her ear. "When the children are asleep . . ."

"But why me?" he whispered to her. "Is it punishment for helping create the damned thing?"

Alice laughed, wrapping her arms tighter about him. "Punishment? Oh, Boson, you dope. Haven't you figured it out yet? Haven't you worked out why se called you ser father? You are the Aleph's human seed. Se was grown from your template. And now it's time for you to awaken."

"Why?" He did not expect any kind of answer he might comprehend. As well challenge a god.

"We prepare to burst all the last boundaries," Alice told him with intense excitement. She sat up and gripped his hands until the blood was squeezed from his flesh. "The probes are returning. The fences will fall. It is almost time to go home."

And she was gone. Mohammed Abdel-Malek lay in the draining light and shade, the receding strings, and clutched his empty arms to himself.

I might never have been away. Everything was as before: Ebeeneezer's slow plod and even slower good-hearted lisp, the progression of the season, crops sprouting, growing, ripening for the harvest. Day in, day out, the Sun and shadow played on the Valley walls, that chain of tall purple mountains the bat-children had crossed and that I'd burrowed under in a terror that still shook my nightmares. And yet—

It was the same, but I was seeing it all in a different light. The bare, plowed soil was like a sore on the Earth's surface, bleeding off topsoil that washed through gullies to dirty the river. I noticed pastures that once had been rich farmland, now good only for grazing cattle. I began to suspect we were getting at least some of our supplies from sources other than the Valley, that some unnatural force was causing plants to grow on soil which should not have sustained them. Something was amiss, and I suspected I could find the answer within my own machine-filled head. But I hesitated to look too closely, afraid of what I might find.

It was not easy getting back into Valley life. For a while people kept staring at me, muttering behind my back. My Outside adventures were on everybody's tongue, even though the details were known only to the family and those Elders who'd been there at the Gatehouse. The Valley's gossips had other topics to chew over, one of which seemed to be Jed Cooper's blatant interest in my Sweetcharity. Of course that juicy item did involve me as well, so the muttering always fell away to scandalized whispers and glances and fingers pressed against noses when the gossips noticed I was watching them. I would stand with my fists balled up in frustration and fury, knowing that anything I might do would make matters worse.

Only once did I get a hint flung at me, and I did not know whether to believe it or not. I could not believe, and yet my own guilty memories and dreams of kissing Amanda— I saw Jed across the street on my third day back, after I drove with my brother to the store to pick out a new bathtub for Momma's birthday present. Cooper stood with a pack of his loutish friends, laughing like jackasses and pushing each other, eyeing the young women, making their bumbling courtesies, and muttering preposterous boasts. I hoped they were preposterous, anyway, for Jed caught my eye and in full view of his gang gave me a slow, insolent wink—and raised his hands to the height of his chest, thumb and forefinger of the left making a circle, the extended forefinger of the right jolting in and out. The blood rose in me, and I leaped from the cart with my fists bunched and raised. Jed guffawed at my discomfiture, nudging one of his cronies in the ribs. Lukenjon stepped into my path.

"Leave it, Mathewmark," he said in a quiet, determined voice.

"Did you not see the filthy brute? He as good as boasted—"

"He's just trying to get your goat," my brother said, and held my arm until I relaxed my fists and turned aside, shaking with frustrated anger. I knew his caution was sensible. Jed Cooper was a bully and an oaf, and surely it could not be true that Sweetcharity had dallied with him in my absence. Why risk a beating that would give all his gang pleasure and leave me bruised and humiliated? Because, I answered myself, it was my beloved he slandered. Again, for some reason, the image of Amanda's face rose up before I quelled it. I raised my fist, but Lukenjon stood in my path.

"Later," he said. "Mathewmark, he's a thickwit. You might as well take offense at a stump. He'll get what he deserves someday." He grinned slowly, and drew me after him into the store. "Jed, Jed, with wood for head."

That was not the end of it. As our pastor tells us, gossip thrives on its own wicked devices. Nobody else, though, would tell me anything to my face. Least of all Sweetcharity herself.

And as my days back in the Valley passed I tried to convince myself I was falling deeper and deeper in love with that beautiful girl, a sentiment Auntie McWeezle encouraged with all her might. She held no truck with Elder Legrand—there'd been bad blood between their family and hers for generations and besides Legrand was such a horrid old toad—but her heart plainly went out to my beloved.

Things between me and Sweetcharity picked up as they'd left off, a bit tense. I'd been back in the Valley a whole week before I managed to get away from the clamor and my neglected duties to make a call at old man Legrand's broken-down hovel. I was hoping against hope he wouldn't be there. He was, but shut up in the outhouse. So I found myself briefly alone with Sweetcharity, my heart pounding.

I reached out to take her hands in my own, but she drew away from me.

"A man who's a familiar of the devil had better not try to be familiar with *me*. And stop looking at my, my . . . bosoms." She folded her arms across her chest and stood glaring at me. I came close to turning around and leaving without saying another word, but I could not resist a parting shot.

"A little bee told me it saw a strange sight at the Legrand house—a yellow-haired human dynamo, it said."

Sweetcharity's face went red as a beet, and she put one hand over her mouth as she does when she is surprised about something.

"Just what did you think you were doing, Miss, pedaling like a fiend?" I took a step toward her and looked her in the eye.

"Have you been spying on me, Mathewmark?" She leaned forward, hands on her hips, so angry she seemed to have forgotten all about wanting to keep her distance from me.

"I'll bet I know what you were doing, Miss. You were making electricity to support your crazy grandfather's gambling habit, weren't you?" I grinned wickedly, because I knew I had her there.

"You won't tell anyone, will you?" Sweetcharity dropped her arms to her sides and looked up at me, sort of halfway smiling.

"No, darlin', your secret's safe with me," I told her, and I stole a kiss as I heard the outhouse door slam. She had time to kiss me back before the clomping of old man Legrand's boots on the path announced his arrival.

He didn't look welcoming, but at the same time it was obvious he was pleased to see me. He thought I held the key to midweek roulette success. I had a hard time denying it.

"Speak to your friends the liar bees, boy," Legrand hissed at me, something he said often in those first weeks.

"I don't know what you're talking about."

"Summon them up!" he roared, waving his hands as if he were giving a sermon.

"Where from?"

"From the dark regions, from the pits of hell . . ."

"I have no friends in the dark regions or hell's pits. But if a liar bee flies by, I'll tell it you are interested in making its acquaintance, Elder Legrand. I can do no more." I spread my own hands obligingly, palms up.

"And stay away from Sweetcharity." He shook a gnarled finger in my face. "I'll not have your filthy paws fouling her purity."

"I must fetch and carry in this Valley," I said. "If I come to your house and Sweetcharity is at home, then I must converse with her, must I not? Courtesy demands it."

"You can converse until hell freezes over, but keep your filthy paws to yourself."

My hands were clean the first time Sweetcharity and I met by "accident" on the road. They were clean as we left Ebeeneezer to his own devices and wandered hand in hand through the woods. They were clean as we lay on a bank of newly fallen leaves and I held her sweet face and kissed her sweet lips. But a light sweat coated my palms as I ran my hands over the stuff of her bodice.

"I just *washed* that bodice," Sweetcharity said, sitting up. "You'll soil the linen."

"Don't worry about the linen," I said, moving my hand over the fullness of her breast. What would Amanda look like with breasts full and deep as these?

"It's not you who does the laundry, Mathewmark." She swatted my hand.

"Then let me," I said, fumbling to unhook the garment.

"Mathewmark!" she said. "The first man to lay a hand upon my bare breast will be my husband, bound to me by all the sacred rites of the Gods of all our Choices. No man will feel my naked nipple harden under his palm who has not pledged himself before the people of the Valley assembled to bear witness to all the due solemnities—" She got that line right out of one of her grandfather's Sunday sermons. I put my hand over her mouth, gently.

"Then marry me, Sweetcharity." I gazed at her pleadingly, probably looking like a dying calf in a hailstorm. She seemed a bit more sympathetic at that, as well she might be, so I put a tentative hand on her waist. "Let me be that husband, let me be that lucky man who feels the hardening—"

"Grandpa will never allow it." Shrugging my hand away, Sweetcharity hitched herself a good meter away from me.

In a tantrum of frustration, I shouted: "Well, let's shoot the old bastard."

"Shoot?" she said. "What do you mean, 'shoot'?"

That made me blink my eyes. I knew exactly what I meant, and what I meant was a thing disgusting and unspeakable. An image hung inside my head: a sort of false memory, brought there from the wicked chip in my brain: guns barking, acrid smoke rising like the stench of death, men in tattered uniforms with torn flesh running in fear and passion up a hill. A high shrieking rang in my ears, but it was only a kind of echo of shrieking: something dark crashing from clouds, making the ground thump, exploding, small sharp metal fragments like liar bees whining without pity, ripping limbs and bellies, a morass of blood and mud and tatters of shredded grass and undulating strands of barbed wire. I reeled, feeling blood leave my face. Sweetcharity saw something had changed in me, but didn't know what, I guess. She gazed at me in concern, but her mouth was pursed.

Reaching for an explanation she could deal with, I said, "Oh it's, er . . . something they do on the Outside." It was not, of course. Amanda's world had no more of this nightmarish violence than my own, thank Gaia. Then where was this awful "memory" from? It troubled me, it distracted my attention from Sweetcharity. She noticed that much, I could tell, and her tone grew waspish.

"I'll have no Outside ways in any husband of mine. No 'shooting'! Whatever that may be."

"Oh, Sweetcharity," I said, hopelessly confused.

After a time she softened, pressing her lips softly against my own, but she pushed my hands away. Clean or dirty they were going nowhere fast with Sweetcharity.

3 : amanda

Yikes!

Also eek!

No, that doesn't sound quite . . . Mature . . . does? Am only halfway through transition, wild feelings whirling, heart pounding, sick most time, zoned rest of time. Tailored psychoactives, they tell me. Buffered, pharmacologically cushioned to a fare-thee-well. Harrumph. Roller-coaster dizzy even so. Elated and ditzy silly one minute, feel like hanging self the next. Even way I talk and think is changing. Can feel it creeping through cortex. Is this the future? Suppose I knew all along, have had olders around me since kid, after all. Hard to believe could descend to such banality myself. Guardian facilitator Ruth blames post-traumatic stress, says brought me off extended latency plateau early, plunged into galloping Maturity trajectory. Hey, maybe so. Certainly feel rotten enough, weeping for poor lost Vik, I mean hardly anybody dies anymore, until they choose to, it's just plain cruel and wrong. And missing Mathewmark. Big lunk gets weird on phone link, mumbles about girlfriend and Big Plans, make you sick, really. Half calls don't go through. Someone wants us to play our own games, forget ever met. Everyone dread in Mall looks at me sideways, as if turning into stenchy space monster or dweeb. Suppose am. Ha, their turn in a year or so. Laugh then from posture of vantage. Ha-ha. Hungry now, must go raid Ng delicacy fortress.

*   *   *

Moved to House. Everyone suspiciously nice, nothing like adult life witnessed on every hand elsewhere. Math has no charm, music turned to chaff in ears. Bored shitless, candidly. Ho hum.

Urp. Spanner in works. Seems to be stirring up innards. Quite horrid, actually.

Oh. I get it. First blood today, made little mess of smart lounging pants. Have been waiting for ancient lunar timekeeper to clock in, but still taken by surprise. Feared for moment something wrong with waterworks, yelped to Ruth Bandaranaike, instantly felt like goose when realized. Despite griping pains, feel quite chuffed, oddly enough. Like some ancient mystic ceremony: Today I Am A Woman. And me not yet literally Thirty, seems indecent somehow. Other women here in House of Passage were marched in, solemn and probably rather jaded by whole game, sang welcome songs, waved red flags, clutched bellies in couvade. No males, needless to say. Suppose they must have equally embarrassing, heart-warming parade for first jerk-off or wet dream or whatever jollity they memorialize.

Afterward, Dr. Bandaranaike took me aside into garden, sat down amid bright spring flowers in long grass, held hand, looked deep into eyes, blah-blah. Sorry, shouldn't make light. In three months, of course, all will be fond memory once Adult hormone regime fully established and menses under voluntary control. Hard to see how they all put up with damned aches and cramps. Bloody pains, ha-ha. Wonder if that's origin of swear word "bloody"? Men probably insist fights to death, limbs hacked off in rivers of gore, bellies torn bleedingly with knife wounds. Doubt it, now have experienced bloody silly thing.

* * *

Despite analgesia, pain nags day and night. Always been tall, but legs and arms seem to be doing growth spurt at rate of knots. Eating like mule, lithping like one too with face full. Speaking of, face is actually visibly filling out here, sharpening there. So too other more intimate portions. Very entertaining. Like being blown up by pump. Eat all day, ache all night, hardly fit in dread clothes by end of week. Silly things anyway. Other Thirties (well, I'm still not much past Twenty-Eight, strictly speaking, but who's counting) have intriguing style. Used to look down nose at, but beginning to appreciate nuance, restraint, *melody* as it were. Catch men glancing my way with muted, amused interest. Remembering poor Vik, tears fill eyes. Remember Mathewmark, too, strangely enough, skin prickly, swat thoughts away. Hug arms around self, which doesn't quite work, lumps get in way, only makes alien condition stranger. But nice too, sort of. Oh, I don't know.

Entire gaggle of Thirties, women and men together (but in separate sides of car) took ballistic day trip to Antarctic Metro. Vaughan Williams extraordinary place. Doesn't matter how often have racted these settings, something eerie and *there* about full-presence immersion. Great white crags of ice, howling winds beyond bubble, penguins in dinner jackets plopping through frigid snow, skidding on bellies into gray water. Made me shiver just looking out at poor beasts. One polar bear tromping with baby at heel in distance, dirty white, ferocious teeth, eyes slitted. Know to keep safely aloof, programmed against scoffing up picturesque penguins. Full choral *Sinfonia* in honor of patron artist, mellow contralto older reading elegiac superscriptions: Shelley, Psalms, Donne, explorer Captain Scott, Coleridge. Hair-raising as frozen melting mountain hung above sea while we listened and sang; wished I had Strad the Lad with:

The ice falls! To that from the mountain's brow
A down enormous ravines slope amain—
Torrents, methinks, that heard a mighty voice,
And stopped at once amid their maddest plunge!
Motionless torrents! Silent cataracts!

Is that time, itself, now? Halted fifteen years, more, for long adolescence, melting in this our brief maturation, refrozen forever in Maturity? Forever? Can anything be forever? Went back to room, listened with prickling eyes to start of Elgar's oratorio *Dream of Gerontius;* Ralph Vaughan Williams made me think of him, of course. Found it creepy, though, after first ten minutes or so, switched to sitar and banjo.

Still, shivery stuff. Age, where is thy sting now? Have known childhood, played in golden light all these idyllic years, now surge like some dolphin forward in dark blue and cold to something larger than childhood, beyond its end, and it's not anything I'd imagined, to extent *ever* imagined anything beyond childhood's end, it's— Well, enigmatic, improbable, drawing me to itself like a piper's haunting song.

Um. And where the hell *that* come from? Like time Maman switched off speech center, only exact opposite.

Gee, that Coleridge, eh, sucks you in every time.

Tripled with two other Thirties transits, woman, man. We were introduced formally during gathering to hash out Life Course. I had met both already, of course, even had long pleasant conversation with Robert not long after first arrived, before gender segregation. Lucia is the real charmer. Reminds me of Tenniel's Alice in Wonderland, stands unconsciously with one foot pointed out like ballet dancer, although too short and, must say, legs rather stumpy for dancer. But utterly enchanting young woman. Laughs all the time, witty, no malice in her. Suppose should find this rather dweeby but actually her good spirits relax me, bring out similar . . . niceness . . . (yetch, but what the hell, there's something to be said for congeniality). Lucia's been swotting math/physics as pender, so we have math part in common. Robert, who's dark and pensive but perfectly acceptable company, drags some history thing I can't follow. Maman and Maître would be shocked rigid. Is not done to pry into antecedents, except legal precedent. First principle Joyous Relinquishment: forget bad old days, track melody not lyrics (metaphor, naturally; nothing wrong with actual *song* lyrics), move at steady, confident pace into secured future. So can't really see attractions of Robert's calling, and suspect he might follow it for same reason poor Vik and I broke into Maglev tube for fun run at speed of sound. Just plain bad to the bone. Not that you'd know, looking at his modest demeanor.

So am I meant to pack Strad the Lad away, as I've always feared? Scorn the Lad as trivial memento of childhood and pendership? Dr. Bandaranaike will not say yea or nay. Guess is one of mysteries meant to pursue by ourselves. So I run conformal and symplectic geometries, related secret vices through head for an hour a day, as always, even if is least dreadest topic known to human mind. I still seem to have gift for it, despite Thirty changes, so hey, am stuck with. Spent afternoon in virtual trance blowing through positive and negative wedge disinclinations, tracking higher symmetries and breaks. Something deep and terrible about all this. Probably at verge of shameful truths that will bring down wrath of Relinquishment Custodians.

But started to say: Lucia took me by hand to climbing wall, showed me lockers and gear, nagged me up wall. Felt sick at sight of thing, all crevices a hair deep and bumps fingers slide off and abutments and chimneys, absolutely nothing like inside of vent but reminded me appallingly. Sat and shook for ten minutes while new friend cajoled and remonstrated. Couldn't tell her about Vik and hayseed at first. Halfway up wall burst out bawling, everything blurry and salty, lost footing and banging knees in meter drop. Lines held, but almost dragged Robert and Lucia down with. Reeled me in and up, offered concerned looks all way to top and back down, hugged me with four arms while I blurted and sobbed out story. Just can't seem to get over it. Neurotransmitter storm, I suppose.

"Ruth says a good howl never harmed anyone," Lucia said, her own eyes rather damp. Robert made of even less stern stuff; he clung to my damp right hand and wept as well. Talk about Mature, this is more like infant *sturm und drang*. Blew our noses eventually, had shower (Robert trotting away like good fellow to Men's Facilities) and change of clothes, met up again for afternoon tea. Weird, all this. Expected something more like scouting challenge in wilderness, or maybe dreary exercises in knuckling down to Juridical Accountancy & Real-Estate Management. Nope, just puzzled new friends trying to find our feet on tilting ground. But ground is *us*: bodies, minds, emotions, values, speech patterns, meme swarms. Feel like latent grub de-cocooning into—What? Moth? Butterfly? Pterodactyl? Maybe Mr. Holesworthy right after all.

Had just snuggled down in bed, feeling worn-out and bruised but somewhat calmer, when phone rang in head and up popped hayseed. With his gruesome news.

He's marrying the dorky Sweetcharity!

Here's a guy with brain bursting more strange chipware than anyone in living history, and he decides to settle down on some loony Valley of God of everyone's Choice farm and make hayseed babies with girl missing one tooth. Talk about a major loser. Talk about— Aargh. Going to sleep. Who cares? Absolutely ridiculous.

4 : mathewmark

After a while people stopped staring at me and muttering behind my back. My Outside adventures got to be old hat, and the Valley gossips found fresh victims. I even stopped thinking about the Outside myself. Whole days passed when I didn't think of Amanda at all. I phoned her a few times in the first weeks, once I worked out how to make the machine inside my head work. She was holed up in some place called the House of Passage, going through some sort of changes. Even the way she talked was altering, getting a bit more normal, as if she was growing up very fast. But strangely we didn't find much to say to each other. Uncomfortable. Tripping over tongues.

Amanda wasn't really interested in the small concerns of our Valley. And I found that the new things in her life got harder and harder to imagine. She was making new friends, going through some horribly artificial process she called "Maturity." It seemed daft to me—we all do that, don't we? But I'd never understood how Amanda could look like a stretched-out kid while actually being older than bloody Jed Cooper, and he's five years older than me.

After a while our conversations faltered, and then stopped. Anyway, I became less and less willing to use the machine in my head for anything other than my normal Valley routine. I found that every time I used it to talk to Amanda I would be plagued with bizarre and even wicked dreams for several nights afterward. It seemed far better to concentrate on doing my chores and courting my beloved Sweetcharity.

As we lay in our bunks at night Lukenjon quizzed me. "When's the happy day?"

"What happy day is that?"

"The tying of the knots. The breaking of the glass. The exchanging of the rings. The dancing round the maypole. That happy day . . ."

"Dunno," I said. "When Legrand dies probably."

"He could go on forever. He could outlive us all."

"He's as old as the hills," I said.

"He's as tough as the hills," Lukenjon said. "You'll have to force the issue, Mathewmark."

"How?" I said.

My silly brother burst into drivel. "True love's not smooth. It's rough as guts. Keeps you out of dreary ruts. Legrand's a mountain not a molehill, blocks love's low road, sends a chill. To shift that sinner you'll need a . . . need a . . ."

" . . . need an upload," I suggested, "pay no bill."

There was a dumbfounded silence. Then Lukenjon said in a stran-gled voice: "What's an *upload*, for godsake?"

"No idea," I said, and I didn't, it had just popped into my head. "But it rhymes."

"You'll never make a poet, Mathewmark. Night." And I heard him turn over and face the wall. He was asleep in seconds.

I lay awake for hours. I had visions of Sweetcharity and me run-ning away. Running away where? You can't run far in the Valley. All you can do is try to arrange a marriage with someone in a different village, or find one where your special knowledge is needed and they have a guild expert to swap with your village. That wasn't likely—all I knew was farming. Well, maybe (shocking thought) you could go over the mountains and exile yourself to the Outside. But I wasn't going there again and, anyway, I hadn't a hope in hell of convincing Sweetcharity that she ought to leave the Valley. And it wasn't as if anyone there—I finally fell into a fitful sleep, full of dreams of bats and Sweetcharity without her bodice.

The morning was wet and windy. The track had turned to mud. Ebeeneezer plodded on, singing quietly to himself. I sat drowsing on the cart, an old oilskin over my head.

"Morning, hayseed," a voice said.

"Who? What?" I said, staring about wildly. And then noticed it was the phone in my head. I'd all but forgotten it was there.

"Oh, hello, Amanda," I said.

"Don't speak out loud. Feedback."

"Sorry," I said in my mind. That was harder to do than it sounds. I let the reins go slack, and Ebeeneezer ambled over to the side of the road where there was a lush stand of Hypro23 grass, his favorite.

"How's tricks?"

"Raining."

"Here too last time I looked."

"Are you well, Amanda?"

"Well and good. Well, not so good. Not bad. Mature."

"Is that nice?' I wasn't sure. When I talked to Amanda in my mind like this I fancied I could feel her emotions almost as well as I knew my own. I was sensing a confused mixture of anxiety, anticipation, pride, and fear.

"Bloody pain. Every month. Gainful employ. Vote in elections. Tits."

"I'm the same as always."

"What about goody two boots?"

"Who?"

"Cold-as-charity."

"Sweetcharity. Be nice."

"Yeah, her."

"What about her?" Did I sense a touch of jealousy on Amanda's part? I put it down to my imagination. Why in the world would Amanda be jealous of Sweetcharity?

"Bun? Oven?"

"Amanda, try to talk English."

"I'm learning that. Gets easier, but it still seems stiff and ridiculously formal. Up duff, you know? Big with child? Gravid? Spawn of loins?"

I was shocked. "Of course Sweetcharity's not pregnant."

"Why not?"

"Because—"

"Because she keeps her spindle shanks crossed. Because Mathewmark not up to mark. Not man enough for job?"

"Amanda!"

"The only way, hayseed."

"What's the only way?"

A succession of the lewdest images I'd ever seen instantly flashed through my mind, put there through the filthy machine in my head: people humping each other like animals, in every imaginable position. To my horror I realized I was so physically aroused I was about to come in my trousers. I tried to concentrate on something else, anything. I was viewing a sort of encyclopedia or schoolbook, pages flipping by too fast for me to puzzle them out—I was left with only vague impressions of words and phrases such as "64 terabit target strings" and "emergent problem decomposition" and "f(t)–f(t–L) < G." I felt dizzy, sick at my stomach.

"Hayseed? Bumpkin, you there? Hey, Mathewmark, are you okay?"

Amanda's worried mutters brought me back to the dripping wagon by the side of the road. Ebeeneezer looked around as though he had been concerned about me too.

"Aw 'ight, Boff?" He was hard to understand when he tried to talk with his mouth full, but I could tell what was on his mind.

"I'm okay, Ebeeneezer," I said reassuringly, not feeling a bit reassured myself. I tried to direct my thoughts to Amanda, who was starting to get all worked up, thinking I was dead or foaming at the mouth in convulsions. Her babble came through as if she were about to cry.

"I'm sorry, Mathewmark, I didn't mean to upset you. Please tell me you're okay."

"I don't know." For a moment I thought I just might pay her back for the pornographic peep show by letting her worry a little while longer, but she seemed so upset I gave way and said, "Yes, Amanda. I'm fine. But please control yourself in the future. My feelings for Sweetcharity are of a far higher nature than the things you suggested. I have to go now. Good-bye."

"Mathewmark?" For a moment she actually seemed almost human. "You're not angry with me, are you?"

"A little."

"We can talk again later?"

"You know where to find me."

"Mathewmark?"

"Yes, Amanda?" I was getting annoyed. It's hard to turn off a voice in your own head, especially when it won't get the hint.

"I still say you should get Sweetlips pregnant." That girl! Always needed to have the last word. I shook my head, laughing in spite of myself as I tightened Ebeeneezer's reins and slapped them gently across his back. "Let's go, old boy," I said, and he nodded and headed on down the road, grumbling just loud enough that I could catch his tone of voice.

* * *

I must have awakened fifteen or twenty times that night in the midst of the most troubling dreams I'd ever experienced. Some were merely bizarre—I was in meetings with people discussing things I'd never in my life heard of, genetic maintenance and repair, hyper AI, singularity. Others were highly disturbing. I saw cities, greater than van Gogh Metro, tall buildings gleaming under blue skies. The buildings splintered and flew apart. Skies darkened with clouds, not life-giving rain but clouds that rained death. I walked through vast deserts bearing the remains of human civilization, a world where nothing lived to mourn the dead. I saw the Sun itself blink and go dark like a spent candle, and I woke up to find my pillow wet with tears.

Toward morning a different sort of dream came to me, a beautiful world like those I'd seen when I was viewing the archives with Amanda. I was a farmer, but my plot was a garden of fruit trees whose trunks supported flowering and fruiting vines. Among their roots grew tasty delicacies, edible mushrooms, salad greens. My friends and I met in the garden by a pond rich with animal and plant life. Pink and white water lilies perfumed the air. We sat on a warm stone terrace. One of my friends, a beautiful woman who looked something like Amanda, played a stringed instrument while a young man played a flute made from a lustrous white metal. We talked of things I could not remember when I woke, things that made me think of the meetings I'd attended in my earlier dreams, except that we were merely curious and interested; no one was afraid. Our talk was not so different from the music and the pattern of ripples in the water.

The last dream, which prevented any further sleep, was one I tried my best to forget. In that dream I was sitting with Amanda in her room, the way we'd sat together talking many a day when I was staying at her house. I looked away for a moment, and when I looked back at her she had a full-grown woman's body but the same face I'd known. She was sitting there completely naked, looking at me as though it were the most natural thing in the world, and the worst part was that I wanted desperately to do lewd things with her. I woke up hating myself.

"Sweetcharity, we've got to get married." Three nights of dreaming had left me afraid to go to sleep. Surely my only hope of sanity and redemption lay in marrying Sweetcharity as soon as possible.

"Who'd look after Grandpa?" Sitting on the ground making a daisy chain, she wore an expression as innocent as the day is long. She had no idea what I'd been going through, and there was no way I could even begin to tell her.

"You can still look after him. The two of us can look after him better than you could by yourself."

"He won't give permission." The daisy chain curved into a circle, and she placed it on my head like a crown, giggling.

"He will if you're pregnant," I said, trying to stay on the subject.

She jumped up as if she'd seen a snake.

"Get your hands off me, Mathewmark Fisher. Get them off now! How dare you?"

"I haven't *got* my hands on you."

"How dare you suggest I get pregnant? The very idea! You get yourself off my grandfather's land at once."

"Now darlin', just calm down," I said, thinking fast. "Of course I didn't mean really get pregnant. I only meant to let your grandfather *think* you're pregnant."

She remained on the balls of her feet, staring at me as though I'd lost my senses.

"We don't have to if you don't want to. It was just a thought. I love you so much, darlin' Charity. I'm just trying to think of a way we can be together. Guess I didn't think that one through."

"You certainly did not." Her indignant breathing slowed, and her frown wasn't quite as ferocious. That girl surely did have a temper, but then I should never have suggested such a thing. She was right to be angry with me. Clumsily, I got down on one knee as they do in the old stories.

"Do you want to marry me, Sweetcharity?"

She nodded, blushing.

"Would you give me permission to speak to your grandfather?"

"You may speak to him, but I know right now what he'll say. He's always thought you were impractical, and when you pulled that stunt climbing down the shaft with those bat-children he wrote you off as a lunatic. He's set on me marrying Jed."

I got smartly back to my feet, feeling like a fool. I walked away a little, then looked at her sidelong. "What do *you* want?" When she hesitated and looked away, a wave of misgivings went through me like a cold shock. Some part of me knew better about the whole thing, and yet I still persisted, not knowing what else to do. "Don't you want to marry me?" I asked again. "Look at me, Sweetcharity." Troubled, she did turn to face me, and she nodded. It wasn't the cry of rapture I'd sort of expected to hear. "Well, then, I'll speak to your grandfather tomorrow afternoon after Sunday meeting."

"**M**orning, mule skinner."

"I've never skinned a mule in my life, Amanda."

"That Ebeeneezer animal. Rawhide!"

"Amanda! He's my friend. I'm feeding him some oats right now as we speak."

"How's your other friend? Sweetn'sour."

"If you mean Sweetcharity, I plan to talk to old man Legrand this evening and ask for her hand in marriage."

"Did you—?"

"I suggested . . . I suggested what you said I should suggest."

"Didn't come across, did she?"

"Nope."

"Frigid. Sad case. Sexual dysfunction."

"Sweetcharity is keeping herself nice, Amanda. She wishes to be as pure as the driven snow on her wedding day."

"But no wedding scheduled yet. Purity a bar."

"You make her sound like soap."

"Be about right. Will organize."

"Organize what? . . . Amanda, what are you thinking of doing? Are you there? Speak to me . . . Oh, drat."

"**M**athewmark! Mathewmark!" Sweetcharity came running up to me as I was untying the reins from the hitching post so I could drive my family home from Sunday meeting.

I touched the brim of my hat. "What's the matter, Sweetcharity? Quick, into the woods." Henrietta Hazelton, one of the town's worst gossips, was looking our way.

"We can talk here."

"Your grandfather might see us."

"I hope he does. It'll calm him down. Didn't you notice how riled up he was this morning? We've *got* to get married. The sooner the better."

"Oh Sweetcharity, darlin'. This is the happiest day of my—"

"Grandpa thinks I'm pregnant." Her lower lip began to tremble.

"How could he think such a—"

"He's been paying attention to those horrid liar bees. They give him advice about, well, about different things. And one of them told him I was in the family way. And he believed it. Any minute now he'll be out here to give you a talking to." She waved one frantic hand in the general direction of the kirk.

"Calm down, darlin'. This is what we wanted, isn't it?" I was thrilled, doubts forgotten, reached out to put a comforting hand on my beloved's arm. She shrugged it off.

"Not this way! Everyone in town will be talking about me. I'll never be able to hold up my head again. How could you do this to me?"

I felt hurt that she would accuse me. Oh God in Heaven, I thought, what has Amanda done? Old man Legrand was stomping our way, red in the face, eyes bugging out.

"You'll do the right thing, Mathewmark Fisher!" he yelled. "You'll do the right thing or I'll have your tripes." He waved his arms about, open suit coat flapping like the wings of some huge bird of prey. "By

all the gods of the Valley and the world beyond, I'll string ye up and
roast your hide and feed your gizzards to the buzzards . . ."

My throat was dry, and the skin of my face prickled. I coughed.
"I don't think that'll be necessary, Elder Legrand."

"You'll no bring shame on my household. The name of Legrand
will not be dragged through the mire and muck by the likes of some
young mule driver with a head stuffed full of the devil's instruments
and no self-control. A slithering snake who slides through the grass
where decent folk walk upright. You just couldn't keep it in your
britches, could you? You with your Outsider ways—"

"Elder Legrand, who has been telling you all this?"

"Your friends the bees, the bees of hell, the bees that lie. They
have seen you and Sweetcharity at rut. They have heard the smothered barfings and chunderings of her morning sickness. You cannot
hide from the bees, Mathewmark!"

Furious as I was with Amanda for her silly meddling, there was
no way I could explain this to old man Legrand. My mind raced,
trying every way to make the best of this preposterous and unjust
suspicion. No point in arguing. Wasn't he playing into our hands? I
put on a hangdog expression.

"Look, Elder, let's just say that the bees are right."

"Of course the bees are right! Do you think they'd lie about something as foul and corrupt as that?" I could not guess what he wished
to hear, so I just stood there waiting to see what he'd say next. "You
admit it! Silence is the same as confessing. You haven't even the
common decency to deny your guilt! You implicate the pure sweet
name of my only granddaughter—she who is more precious to me
than—"

"Than your electrical treadle," I muttered, wishing only to shut
him up. He looked at me with dark suspicion, and I said more loudly,
in a light and ridiculously positive tone, "Look, Elder. Sweetcharity
and I will get married. As soon as possible. All right?"

"You'll marry when I say so."

"When *do* you say so?"

"Next Sabbath and not a day later, you young fiend. And there'll be no scarpering to the Outside. You'll do your duty, you'll do the right thing!"

"Fine with me, Grandfather."

"Don't call me that," he shouted in a rage. "Dirty lecher, consorter of bees, you're no—" He stopped, and put his thick-fingered hands over his ears in a pitch of misery. "Oh, go away, go away and do your duty like a man." He gulped, refusing to meet my eye. In a thin, pained voice, he added like a man held under a whip: "Grandson."

5 : amanda

Sawing through Francine Kayser's *minuettina* in the Women's acoustic pit when my phone blipped politely for attention. Strad the Lad still felt the slightest bit uncomfortable in my new hands, as if beloved instrument had shrunk during past months, warped somehow, no long matched bow. The change was in me, I knew that—alterations in basic physiology, the fit of muscles and nerves, whatever that highbrow physics explanation is, all black magic to me. Just knew I wasn't the same Amanda who'd come into the House early. Of course I *was* the same, absolutely identical, all same memories—but as if I'd been decanted from one bottle into another. Very creepy feeling, when stopped to consider. So didn't, very often.

Bow screeched an ugly note that set teeth vibrating in pain. I put poor Strad down and covered my face in my hands. I could see why so many musically inclined penders cast off their passion at Maturity and settled into some dumb hobby like recreational beekeeping or even antique flying like Maman. Body and mind go out of whack. By time they've recovered, settled down like foot in new boot, old habits are often broken. Very sad.

Phone was still pleading. I switched my attention to it, gave gasp of surprise and pleasure. Was Maître! He was waiting in visitor's alcove to House of Passage.

"Hi, Poppa," I yelped, grinning. "With you in a flash." Was out of the music pit and halfway to the alcove before remembered that I was naked, skidded to halt, went back to my room for appropriate garb. What is good enough for a child or a pender will certainly *not* do for the Mature. So says Ruth Bandaranaike, and doubtless she is right—I could feel a burn of shame creep over my face and shoulders at my near *faux pas*.

Matîre's face was study in well-masked consternation when I walked sedately into alcove after polite knock at door.

"Darling Amanda," he said, holding out open arms. "That *is* you, I assume, not some glamorous interloper?"

Sheer persiflage and badinage, since Maître and Maman had known to a high degree of accuracy from the moment of my carefully selected conception pretty much how I'd turn out at every point of my life from chubby infant to spunky pender and statuesque Mature. But I suppose people forget, put such knowledge into separate compartments. I was absurdly self-conscious as I crossed the room, my own right hand outstretched as Dr. Ruth had taught. ("Hugging is perfectly understandable, my dears, but to be avoided at this stage in your resocialization.") Halfway there, though, I found myself giggling like a loon and, without even intending to, I did a pirouette, arms upraised, skirt flying, and flung myself into my father's arms. I think we were both crying. It was a most surprising moment, and I was glad Maman wasn't in the room—somehow, she'd have managed to spoil it.

Gave him a big smooch on the cheek, anyway, and plopped us both down on large flowery couch.

"Maître, you've got *no idea* what—"

"Calm down, dear one, it hasn't been that long, has it? And don't call me 'Maître,' my name is Brian." He was smiling as he said it; there was no rebuke in his tone, just a welcoming acknowledgment of my new status. It made me glow inside with delight.

"Okay, Dad—Brian. Well, what brings you here? I don't suppose Maman—"

"Emily is tied up in endless negotiations with your very odd friends in the Valley of God," my father said. "She extends her felicitations—"

"Blah-blah," I said, "yeah, I know the sort of thing. She forgot my birthday when I turned twelve." That has rankled for years; I'd thought I was over it, and felt a little mortified that this old resentment had burst out of my mouth. Brian let it pass without comment, just a twisted, ironic smile. "Anyway, I thought all that Metro business was signed, sealed, and delivered months ago?"

"Well, dear, so did we all. But there's more than just legalities involved at this point. On the one hand, it's got quite bitter, because your mother has brought a suit under the Magistracy over—"

"I know, their weird agriculture or whatever. Mathewmark came up with the idea, remember? Can't really blame Mam—Emily for that. Although it's right up her alley." I was forgetting my obligations as a hostess, and got quickly to my feet. "Can't I get you refreshments? A beverage? Something to eat?" I crossed the room and dispensers opened in the wall. "I'm having a cup of herbal tea, what about you?"

My father laughed out loud. "Oh, Amanda, you astonish me! Herbal tea? I never thought I'd see the day—" Perhaps my face clouded; he ceased his good-humored joshing at once, waved his hand graciously. "I'd enjoy a cola, my dear, and perhaps a cucumber and salmon sandwich." His favorite.

While I busied myself with the snacks, Dr. Ruth popped her head around the door.

"Everything fine here? Good afternoon, Mr. Kolby, always pleased to see the parents showing a continuing interest."

Maître rose, shook her hand.

"You are doing a wonderful job with our pender," he said, and then caught himself. "Pender-that-was. I see that Amanda is quite the young adult now. On the verge of independence."

"A fine young person," Dr. Bandaranaike told him, perhaps a little dubiously. I gritted my teeth and carried the snacks across to the glass-topped wicker table. I'd added another cup of herbal tea for Ruth, but she declined it with a gracious hand wave, settling herself at the table in a posture that somehow magically made it clear she was just passing by but had every right to be here whenever she chose. Her command of postural semiotics was awesome. "Is there some urgent matter that might take Amanda away from us, then?"

Where did she get that from? I looked from one adult to the other, hiding my fascination behind a slurp of my tea.

"Only very briefly, perhaps," Brian told her. "At the invitation, well, the express request, actually, of Mr. Abdel-Malek."

"I see." Dr. Bandaranaike regarded my father guilelessly. "And we cannot naysay a request from our fabled Magistrate. I should hope that this interruption in Amanda's Passage shall be no longer than three days at most?"

Daddy was flustered, but held his ground. "Oh, I should imagine so. I very much doubt that the people of the Valley would wish us to linger for more than the barest minimum time on their sacred soil."

I dropped my cup and saucer. Hot liquid splashed everywhere. I gave a little shriek and started dabbing with napkins at my father's wet trouser leg and the top of the table. Ruth waved me sternly back to my chair, and a servo hummed out to take care of the mess.

"I see," she said. "A matter of state, in effect. Very well. I expect you to comport yourself appropriately, my dear." She rose, squeezed my shoulder, shook my father's hand, was gone.

"Can we go into the gardens, do you think?" Brian said hopefully.

My mind was buzzing and chasing possibilities up ladders and down snakes. I wished piercingly that Vik were here, or at the other end of a Steganography channel, so we could gossip and plot. And I couldn't help noticing the way my stomach had kind of curdled with funny feelings at the thought of seeing the hayseed again. Oh no, I thought. That can't be it, can it? The pregnant cowgirl gambit had paid off. They were getting married, what else could it be? And I was invited.

"Of course," I told my father, leading him out through glass doors into the rose garden. My legs felt numb, it was a most peculiar experience. "Mathewmark's popped the question, hasn't he?"

"Golly, Amanda, you're as quick as ever." He smiled across at me (we were now the same height!) and took my arm, bending over blooms as we strolled across the fragrant moss.

"Surely they don't want me to be their bloody *bridesmaid*?" I shouted.

"I shouldn't think anything as formal as—" Maître blinked suddenly, and so did I. The Sun had gone out.

Literally. Blinked off. The sky was suddenly black, no stars. Before the autonomic lamps in the garden had time to switch themselves on, the Sun was back, shining as brightly as it had done for the last million years or however the hell long it's been up there.

Brian shook his head, as if an insect had flown into his ear. A liar bee, say.

"Oh drat," he said. "Just had a chip glitch."

I looked at him in amazement. What were the chances?

"So did I," I told him. "Everything went black."

There was a hubbub in the background, as if all the people within hearing distance had started talking at once.

"Something wrong with the net." His gaze went up and to the right, doing a diagnostic check.

I called Robert and Lucia. They were already nattering to each other about the glitch.

"That was weird, Manda," Lucia said inside my head. "I thought all these comm circuits were totally hardened against—"

The Sun went out again. I could hear screams and a distant alarm bell going off. A cold wind blew across the blackened garden. This time my eyes started to adapt: the stars began to show. Then their faint cold pinpricks were dimmed by the soft night-lights that sprang up amid the foliage and flowers. I smelled roses and moss. The water sprinkler system switched on in the rose beds, flinging a fine spray across my outstretched hand. The Sun blinked back on. It was the middle of the afternoon. I gaped at the sky, eyes dazzled with after-images as I tried to look directly, desperate for reassurance, at the disk of the white Sun.

"That's no glitch, Brian," I said. "The fucking *Sun* just went out!"

He stared down at the ground, squeezing his eyes shut. He didn't even rebuke my profanity. "That can't be right, Amanda. I mean, the

Sun isn't a lamp you can toggle on and off, it's a two-and-a-half-billion-year-old thermonuclear—"

Unlike Maman, who spends her life obsessively being a Legal, my father is an Amateur of Chrestomathy, as they call it: he's a specialist in being a nonspecialist, darting from topic to topic as the mood pleases him, lifting choice items from some fancied discipline, savoring them, then emplacing them like beautiful tiles next to items from another field of learning or aesthetics. Experts mocked, saying he and his fellow Chrestomathists were the ultimate dilettantes, mere decadents. Still, I trusted his jackdaw mind: he knew lovely scraps of anthropology, nuclear physics, a little music, some Indian literature, the history of defunct religions . . . If he thought the Sun was billions of years old and not liable, as part of the natural order, to be switched on and off instantly, I was prepared to accept his word for it.

The Sun went out for a third time, and we clung to each other in the renewed breeze, terrified.

"Oh shit," I said, and started to weep.

"Oh shit indeed," said my father. His voice was thin and gray. We hugged each other for what felt like forever, but in fact was no more than fifteen or twenty seconds. When the Sun returned it stayed switched on, like a good sun should, but by then we had stumbled our way toward the comfort and artificial glow of my House of Passage. The unsettling prospect of traveling once again into the Valley of the God of our Choice was wiped from my mind, forgotten in my larger fright. It certainly never occurred to me that the two events might be connected.

From the time I was a little girl I've been told that my wedding day would be one of the happiest days of my life. And yet on the night before I was to be married my heart was filled with a dark dread rather than eager anticipation. No surprise, maybe—the Sun itself had vanished from the sky thrice just four days before! *There* was an omen to strike fear into a girl's heart, and into the wild mutterings of all the men and women of the Valley.

Besides, I could still scarcely believe it! Betrothed to Mathewmark Fisher, who'd been my childhood playmate and youthful sweetheart. The first time he asked me to marry him I was six and he was seven. My friend Mercigrace and me was playing with paper dolls on the wooden porch of the schoolhouse, and a few of the boys was climbing a long, knotted rope. They'd tied one end of it high up in the branches of the oak tree by the springhouse, and they was daring each other to jump down from higher and higher knots on the rope, and Mathewmark jumped farther than anyone else. He come limping over to me, and goes, "I did it for you, Sweetcharity. I want you to be my girl. Will you marry me?"

Truth to tell, I thought jumping out of a tree was a pretty silly thing to do, but I smiled at him; girls did not contradict boys. "I just might marry you someday, Mathewmark Fisher," I said. Mercigrace was about to die laughing, but Mathewmark, he never did much care what folks thought about him.

He said I was his girl after that. He'd try to be with me whenever he could, which wasn't all that often, seeing as how we all had school and kirk and chores to attend to. I remember one time when I was twelve several of us was out picking blackberries, and I stepped in a hole and turned my ankle. The others went on, but Mathewmark stayed with me and helped me fill up my bucket with berries. Then he went and got his silly old mule Ebeeneezer, and we rode double all the way back to my house. Lordy mercy! You should've heard that mule complain. He didn't like carrying double one bit, but Mathewmark told him, "You keep quiet. Don't you know you're toting some very special cargo?" Cargo indeed!

You never would've guessed just looking at him, but Mathewmark had an artistic side to him. He used to draw the prettiest pictures on old feed bags with a chunk of charcoal. And he could sing too. One day I come upon him down at the river fishing, and he was singing "The Tale of Billy Bradley," the old song that starts out like this:

> *I saw her on a lighted stage*
> *Her hair was hanging long and free.*
> *Being of a tender age*
> *I longed to hold her close to me.*

And the chorus goes like this:

> *Spread your legs and make me pay.*
> *Spread your wings and fly away.*
> *Ta Ra Lydia Lydia Day.*

I stood there hidden by the bushes and listened to him sing the whole song. By the end where Lydia dies and Billy lays a rose in her cold, dead hands, I was crying so hard into my skirt I was afraid he'd hear me. I waited a minute, and then come walking out of the bushes like I'd just then happened on him. That was the day I first let him kiss me on the lips, and after that day he used to meet me sometimes in the meadow or woods where I went to pick herbs for Auntie McWeezle's medicine. He never did talk much. When I'd tell him about all the goings-on at our place and what me and my friends had been up to he'd listen like it was the most interesting thing in the world. Once he gave me a fright. "Have you ever thought that the things they teach us in kirk and ashram and all might be wrong?" he asked me. We was sitting up in the apple tree by the Nielsons' hay barn at the time, and I like to have fell down. I was that shocked.

"How could they be wrong?" I said. "The Bible and them other sacred books, they're the Word of the God of our Choice."

"But it was written down by men," he said, and he got this faraway look on his face. "Those men could've been wrong. Everybody makes mistakes sometimes."

"Mathewmark Fisher! You could go to perdition for such heresy." I was climbing down from that tree as I talked. "And I could be dragged down with you just for listening to it," I yelled up to him as I hit the ground and ran away. I wouldn't let him talk to me for almost a year after that, and he never raised the subject again.

Howsomever, he was a good person deep down inside. I once saw him risk his life to save little Marymartha Jenkins when her house caught afire. He grew up tall and strong and handsome, and he never had an eye for anyone but me. I would've been proud to call him husband. But I was living with my grandfather old man Legrand by then, my parents having been killed when I was a small child. And Grandpa did not think well of Mathewmark. A "young dreamer with a head full of stars" Grandpa called him, and he proved Grandpa right last spring when he climbed down the Devil's Tower and almost got himself killed.

When he first returned from the Outside I thought he just needed to settle in and get used to being home, but instead of getting better as time went on he become more distant every day. He would get a certain expression on his face, something like the way old Hezekiah Robbins used to look just before he would start talking in tongues. My friends and me, we used to laugh behind our hands at Mr. Robbins, but it was not funny to see this happening to the fellow who might be protector and provider for me and our future children. Grandpa accused Mathewmark of consorting with the devil through the liar bees, which was plain wrong. Them liar bees was nothing other than machines. I know this now because when Grandpa swatted one of them I picked it up and looked at it when I was sweeping the floor. Its insides looked like the insides of that old computer the people keep on display as a sign o' wickedness. God told St. Theodore that all machines are evil, playthings of the devil. And people was saying that them Outsiders had put some sort of mechanical right into my Mathewmark's head.

I made up my mind to tell him I would not be able to marry him after all, and that very morning he came to me in our special clearing in the woods. It was early yet, and the Sun was just coming up. The meadow plants was coated with dew which rose as mist, the Sun warming it. He walked toward me through the mist and took my hand. The expression on his face was too intense. I looked away and my eyes lit on a spiderweb beaded with dew drops that sparkled and gave off rainbows in the sunlight.

"I'm so glad I found you here, Sweetcharity," he said, still holding my hand.

"Was there something you wanted to tell me?" I had on my new brown-and-white-gingham dress with the lace collar, but he didn't even seem to notice.

"Nothing important." He kept staring at me, and I wondered if I had dirt on my face or if my dress was wrong side out.

"Why are you looking at me that way?"

"I was counting the freckles on your face." When I laughed at him for doing such a silly thing he looked hurt, like a little boy. After that I just couldn't tell him about not wanting to marry him. And then whenever I thought of telling him, I'd remember that hurt expression. So I kept putting it off. "I'll tell him tomorrow," I would say to myself. Tomorrow never came, but at least I could be sure that Grandpa would not allow a marriage between me and Mathewmark.

Then he went and flat out asked me. So everything's changed, which is why I found myself tossing and turning, unable to sleep. At four in the morning I got out of bed, dressed quietly in the dark, slipped out my window, and made tracks for Auntie McWeezle's cottage. I knew she would be getting up just about now, because she had promised to make herb loaves for the wedding feast.

Auntie McWeezle is a New Wiccan, otherwise known as a witch. She is the last of her kind in the Valley, and they say folks once shunned her as a heretic. But her potions are effective for curing almost anything that might ail a person, and by the time I was born she was well respected and called upon anytime a sick or injured person did not respond well to home remedies or the ministrations of Doc Milton. Auntie McWeezle has always been special to me, because it was her helped to bring me into this world when my Momma had been in labor for three days and was just about played out. She is the one I always go to for help when I'm in trouble.

Sure enough, when I got to her house I could see light coming from the kitchen.

"Stars above, child, what are you doing here this time of night!" She like to have dropped the bowl she was holding, she was that surprised when she saw me at the door.

"Oh Auntie, I'm so confused. I just don't know what to do." She put down the bowl and gave me a big old hug. She always smelled faintly of lavender, and I felt comforted just from breathing her fragrance.

"Poor wee thing," she said, even though I was taller than her by half a meter. "You sit right down here and tell Auntie what's the matter."

"This child o' god's not so sure she should be getting married." I waited to be struck down by the Wrath, because what I had just said went against all the teachings. A woman's duty is to get wed and raise children and help her husband. Even Auntie, who sometimes had different ideas from most people's, had encouraged me to marry Mathewmark.

"Whatever's wrong?"

I started to explain to Auntie about how strange Mathewmark had been acting lately, but she held up her hand.

"Hush, child. We can talk about the specifics later, but for now you need say no more. If you have any doubts at all, then you should postpone the wedding. It wouldn't be fair to either one of you, least of all Mathewmark, who'd have to go through life with a wife who wasn't sure of him."

That wasn't what I meant at all, at least I didn't think it was, and I opened my mouth to protest, but she shushed me again.

"I know, I know. I've heard the rumors. But haven't I been a midwife all these years? I can tell when a woman is pregnant by looking at her, and you just don't have that look about you. I'd venture to guess you're still a virgin. Am I not right?"

I nodded and looked at the floor, wondering if I should tell Auntie my guilty secret. Well, I'd always told her everything. So I said, "Auntie, I've done evil things in my bed at night. I've touched my flower with my own hands, so I think maybe I'm not a virgin."

"Gaia's hymen, girl! Don't be daft. You know how I feel about that Christian nonsense. But if you must treasure virginity, you should at least know what it is and is not. Virginity has nothing whatsoever to do with how you use your hands, unless you're using them to arouse lust in a man. Which I'd like to see more of in this world, I'll tell you." She gave a snort, nodded once, closing the subject. "So. It's all decided, then. The wedding's off. Now how about grabbing a knife and helping me chop these herbs."

"We won't need the bread if the wedding's called off. Will we?"

"Just because the wedding's off don't mean the reception's off too. Everyone in this end of the Valley is primed for a party." Noticing my dismay, she gave me a sympathetic look, and said, "If you want to stay home, that's up to you. If I was you, I'd go, though. Hole up in your room, you'll just be giving the gossips more to work with. Since you're here, you might as well make yourself useful." A basket of herbs sat on the table, and Auntie was fishing the simples out and chopping them into small pieces. She handed me a cutting board and a knife. We chopped away in silence for a while, and my spirits eased a little. But the questions wouldn't leave off pestering my silly mind.

"It's not just the wedding, it's the omen," I said, looking up from my work and quickly back down again. "Grandpa says the end of the world is upon us."

With an impatient frown, the old lady shook away that darkening of the heavens as if I'd mentioned a silly prank, like the time Jed Cooper put the calico cat in the bread jar, worth a dressing-down but not something to worry overmuch about. "Now, pay attention to what we're doing." Auntie would never let me get away with loitering when there was work to be done. "We put in rosemary, and sage for good health, Holy Basil for long life; dill to keep away evil spirits; lemon balm for happiness; and elderberry wine to honor the Elder Mother.

If it were springtime, we'd use fresh elderberry blossoms, and if it were summertime, we'd use fresh berries, but the wine will suffice at other times."

"What's this other herb, Auntie?" In a small vase there was a sprig of dark green leaves and brilliant yellow flowers.

"That's the Bourrique."

"We're not going to put it in the bread?"

"Well—since the wedding's off, maybe not. It's an aphrodisiac."

"A what?" Auntie had taught me almost everything she knew about herbs, but she'd never told me about no aphrodisiac.

"Makes you horny. Oh, fiddlesticks, let's put it in anyway. Liven things up around here." She took the sprig from the vase and began chopping the leaves and flowers and adding them to the mix of other herbs.

I couldn't keep that darkened sky out of my head. It had panicked the entire village, and put three of our best hens off laying. I was sure it was a warning about the wedding, and maybe worse. "Do you think Grandpa is right about the end of the world and the coming of the great rapture?" I scraped the herbs I'd chopped from my cutting board into the mixing bowl.

"If your grandpa's right about much of anything, my name's not Myrtle McWeezle." Hefting the big blue pitcher she poured water into the bowl with the herbs, adding some wheat flour. Auntie never measured her ingredients, but everything she made came out perfect.

"Elder Zeke thinks it was just a funny kind of eclipse."

"Here," she said, turning the bread dough out onto the wooden tabletop. "Knead this for me while I check the fire for the oven."

"I'm scared to death about telling Grandpa and Mathewmark. Grandpa will likely want to beat me senseless."

"I'll be there with you, child. Give me some of that dough to work." She floured her hands and began kneading, folding the dough over and over on itself so swiftly that hers was done before mine, even though I'd had a head start.

"Will you tell them for me?" I asked hopefully, even though I was pretty sure what her answer would be.

"Lord no! It's not my place to tell them. But never you fear. I'll stand beside you." She rubbed soft butter on the tops of the smooth, satiny mounds of dough and covered them with clean towels.

"Now," she said. "While the dough rises we'll relax with a cup of tea."

We didn't say anything for a while. I was thinking about what I would say to Mathewmark and Grandpa, and Auntie seemed caught up in some deep thoughts of her own.

"It wasn't no eclipse," she said suddenly.

"Well, what do you think it was, Auntie?"

"I don't know," she said, shaking her head. "I just don't know." That was scarier than the Sun going blink, blink, blink. It was the very first time I ever saw Auntie McWeezle look unsure of herself— worse still, look afraid.

7 : mathewmark

"You've put it off long enough, Fred Fisher," my momma said. "You get out there with your bone-lazy sons and weld up my bathtub, we'll all need to be smelling sweet as daisies for the wedding."

Dad nodded agreeably, as he will, and went right on tending his saddle, rubbing in the oils and burnishing the old leather. It was a pretty thing, that saddle, handed down to Dad from his father and I believe his father before him. Not that we had a horse fit to put it on, but some traditions just have to be kept up. I was weary from my hauling and, truth be told, not smelling much like daisies myself. Also nervous and jumpy with the thought of Sweetcharity in her pure white maidenly bride's outfit that old man Legrand and half the local folks thought she didn't deserve to be wearing, not that this would be such a new thing in the Valley anyway. But I knew it wasn't so, and she did too, unless what they said about that foul dog Jed was true. I started chewing on my nails in my distraction, and Momma whacked my hand with her washing-up rag.

"Out there and fix the bathtub, son," she said, "and then have a good long soak with rosemary in the water so you're decent for our ride to the store to get you fitted for your new linen shirt and fine new hat. Come on, come on, get along."

So with much grumbling, I gave in and rounded up Lukenjon from where he was lying flat on his bed on his top bunk reading some old book, and hauled Dad away from the saddle, and we did an hour or two of plumbing. I wanted Momma to have the first bath in the new tub, since, after all, it was her birthday present. I built up a good hot fire in the water heater and pumped water into the cast-iron tank until my arms ached. The old pipes were corroded but still service-able, and after a coughing fit in the bowels of the hand pump the water gushed through brown and gritty, then cleared, and the new enamel bath proudly filled with hot water. We gazed at our handiwork with pride until Momma bustled us out and slammed the door.

I was the next one in, and scrubbed and brushed and came out all pink, with my long hair plastered to my scalp and neck. Momma and I hitched up Ebeeneezer and drove into town as the Sun was getting low in the sky. I had to go through all the hoops of measuring and fitting and trying on, then wait for the seamstress, old biddy Kakuei, to nip and tuck and get my new white shirt just right at the length of the wrist and the fit of the chest and under the arms, not pinching so tight at the neck.

"You've grown quite nicely, young Mathewmark," she told me in a sly way, and pinched my upper arm. "Lucky that girl, that Sweet-charity, slip of a thing."

"Why, I thank you, ma'am," I mumbled in confusion. Indeed, it seemed that every eye in the store was fixed on us, especially upon me, and every tongue wagging again. It was as bad as the day I returned from the Metro. Except that this time Momma and Dad had not been forced to expunge my name from the book and then write it back in again. I attempted not to think about that terrible cruel deed as I tried on one hat after another until I found one at last that I felt was just right and that none of the busybody advisers disliked overmuch. To be rejected by your own family . . . it leaves a bitter taste in the mouth, even when you love them and they've welcomed you back, even when they are spending good credit and coin on the festivities for your wedding day.

We drove back home as dusk fell, and ate a modest supper. Dad and I sat out on the front porch afterward, and he clumsily tried to explain a few things about men and women that I'd known since I was ten years old or maybe five. I nodded solemnly in the flickering lamplight, as the shadows came up behind us dancing against the boards, and we rocked in the silences between his stumbling words. Eventually he felt he'd explained enough, and cautioned enough, and had set me on the proper road to independent manhood. He stood up and shook my hand, one grown fellow to another, and I found that I suddenly had tears in my eyes.

"Thank you for your words, Pappy," I said, and gulped. I released his hand and pulled him against me, arms around him in a big fond hug. I saw then that I stood taller than him, and was bigger around with longer arms. It gave me the strangest feeling of vertigo. We had swapped roles, in a way. And during all this it seemed as well that something ticked and watched inside my head, some mechanical observer that made no comment but noted everything on its chart, like the nurses in the hospital, like the recording angel they tell of in Wednesday school.

I sat there for a long time after Dad went in, and he and Momma took themselves off to their broad bed under the quilts the women of the Valley had made for their own wedding so many years past. I blew out the lamp and sat under the stars, for the sky was cloudless and clear all the way to the edge of the mountain wall. Lukenjon called a soft farewell as he trotted off to his bunk. A night bird hooted. The mule grumbled in his sleep. Getting old and gray, poor dear Ebeneezer. I got to my feet finally and went to the place I'd been trying to avoid.

The grass came halfway to my knees. I crossed the fences, careful not to snare my breeches on barbed wire. The Metro Polis System's Maglev ventilation shaft loomed out of the darkness, four solid meters barely visible by starlight. I walked around it, kicked at the soil. Someone had cleared away the remains of the mob's bonfire. Of course that was months ago now. I went up to the thing and pressed myself against it, arms outstretched, ear hard against its curiously warm polluters' material. Nothing. You might as well hope to detect sap rising in the smooth bole of a tree. A tree might trick you, its leaves whispering in the breeze, its upper limbs creaking. Not so this devil's thing. I was sick with dread. For a mad moment I turned my face to it and poked out my tongue, licking the foreign stuff. It tasted of nothing, not even of iron. There was no smell to it, nothing alive nor ever had been. I stood there in the darkness for the longest time. And began, then, to quake.

It vibrated its terrible song.

I leaped away, nearly falling in the dark. I could smell wheat. The air shivered, and hummed, and a slow moan rose, not from my throat, the deep, sighing, mournful sound rolling from above me. I knew that awful moan. It was dead Vikram calling to me from his grave. I shook with the terror of memory. It grew louder. Deep beneath my feet a thing was rushing.

"Amanda," I croaked. "Oh dear Gods of our Choice, Amanda, speak to me."

"What?" As always, it was as if she stood just behind me and muttered in my ear. From the muffled sound of her voice she'd been pulled from her sleep. "That you, hayseed? Any idea what time it is?"

"Oh." The sound ebbed, fading, gone. The crushing thing deep below had passed like a ghost, or a demon. "I'm sorry, I didn't mean to—"

"That's all right, I had to get up to answer the phone." During a long pause I waited for her to do whatever she needed to do. "That was a joke, hickboy. One of the oldest jokes known to humankind. You may grunt your mirth."

"Ha-ha," I said.

"Listen, thanks a lot for the invite." She sounded cross, if anything. "We'll all be there, my mother and father and Mr. Abdel-Malek included."

"What? Where? Why?" I was totally confused. But my shakes had stopped. I hugged myself. The night seemed to have become colder. "How?"

"Doing some kind of Valley in-depth reporting course now, are you?"

"What?"

"Oh for goodness sake. The wedding. Congratulations, by the way. You could get her some dental work as a present."

I started walking back to the farmhouse. My bones were creaking with exhaustion.

"You're coming? That's—" Wonderful news. What was happening to my pulse? I shook my head in the dark. "That's nice. Lukenjon will be pleased to see you again."

There was another long silence. I thought Amanda must have disconnected. She said, "Yeah, it'll be nice to see you, too, hayseed." I could hear her smile. I could almost see her, sitting up in her House of Passage room, not quite the pender I recalled. Not really much like her at all. It was really quite amazing just how unlike Sweet-charity she was. "Hey, gotta go, major seminar first thing tomorrow morning—you lot caught that solar glitch, I assume? The Sun?"

"It went out," I told her. It hadn't occurred to me that the Metro people would have noticed the Sun. Well, that was stupid of me. "Some say it's an omen."

"What it is, hayseed boy, what it is, according to my dad, is a major paradigm discontinuity. Don't you worry your little head about it."

With some satisfaction, I said: "You don't understand it either."

Amanda laughed merrily. "Not a sausage. Go to sleep, sweet dreams, I'll see you in two days' time." She made a kissing sound, and was gone into the silence of the inside of my head.

My knees sagged, and I nearly fell over the sharp teeth of the fence.

We eat well at Passage Palace, I'll give them that. Breakfast yesterday was on a Polynesian theme: grilled mahimahi, *poi* pudding made with coconut milk, deep fried *poi mochi*, and every kind of tropical fruit there is including my favorites, pineapple and papaya; it took me three hours lying on my back to recover. This morning we feasted on *oeufs en cocottes*, feggs half the size of footballs and straight from the tissue factory decanted into individual ramekins, salt-and-peppered, and dabbed with hot cream before being baked at slow heat until the inner yolks were runny inside the barely set whites—heavenly! Piping hot crusty rolls with curls of *beurre*, sharpish marmalade like stained glass, slices of melon, peeled apple, pineapple. I gutsed myself happily, babbling to Lucia and a rather stressed, subdued-looking Seven (Robert was over in the Men's Place for breakfast, of course) and then nearly choked on a gulp of hot Kona coffee when Mr. Abdel-Malek walked in with Dr. Bandaranaike and sat at the table with the facilitators. So did Seven.

"What's *he* doing here?"

I smirked at Lucia. "Probably come to chauffeur me to the Valley this afternoon, thought he'd take time off to smell the rose garden."

"You're pulling my leg, right?" When I shrugged and buttered another roll, Seven stared at me with her mouth open. Hardly the behavior of the Mature. I was tickled pink, but still it did worry me, because for all I knew it might even be *true*. At least he hadn't dragged Maman and Maître along with him. I caught myself mentally. Emily and Brian. They'd been summonsed to the wedding of the year as well, heaven knows why, probably to keep an eye on me or uphold the dignity of Metro-Valley relations, or maybe because of my mother's dubious dealings on behalf of the Metro Maglev combine.

Who knows, she could be there to keep an eye on mad old Legrand, keep him shut up until the knot was tied, and I was just there as a pretext for her presence. I shrugged and gave up worrying about it. Consciously, anyway—I was vaguely aware that my stomach had tightened and my skin was prickly. I pushed the excellent food aside, not a bit hungry anymore.

"Gotta go pack," I told the others.

Mr. Abdel-Malek caught my eye as I left the breakfast room, and damn if he didn't give the slightest courtly nod and a *twinkle*. I gulped and waved one hand like an idiot and rushed to my room to stare at the bags I'd carefully finished packing the night before. I wanted to give Mathewmark a call, see how hayseed was holding up under pressure, but somehow that seemed too . . . intimate . . . just at the moment. I dragged out the Lad and quietly played a few minutes of Paul Hindemith utility music, just enough to calm me down and let me face the world without panicking.

The phone announced that we'd all be meeting in the Grand Hall in thirty minutes for a special seminar on recent events of general interest. We were advised that nobody should be late, and that includes you, you know who you are. Sighing, a bit more relaxed now, I packed Strad the Lad away, cleaned my teeth, washed my face, went downstairs.

The men and women were mingling freely in the Hall, so I got a seat up near the front between Lucia and Robert. He was muttering in an enthralled way to Seven, to Lucia's disgruntlement. It was so unusual to see her out of sorts, the sunny thing, that I was quite distracted for a few moments and didn't notice that Ruth and the others at the front table had been joined by the Magistrate. There was a rustle of comment, and when I looked over there I found to my amazement that Dr. Bandy had given up her central seat to Mr. Abdel-Malek.

"I'll ask you all to come to order now," she said crisply. Our muttering voices died away. "We're privileged today to be joined by the Chief Magistrate of van Gogh Metro polis, Mr. Mohammed Abdel-Malek." A pattering of polite applause, quickly quenched by Ruth's upraised hand. "We have asked the Magistrate to serve as chair on this occasion, since the matter under discussion appears to be of profound interest to us all, and calls for a syncretic or nonspecialist mingling of views and expertise. While such matters do not normally form part of the curriculum of Maturity, we have formed the view that the gravity of recent events impels us to consider the matter *en masse*, as citizens gathered, new and old. In other parts of the world, similar gatherings will be making their deliberations, and our findings will be shared generally. I now hand the proceedings over to Mo-hamm—to Mr. Abdel-Malek." Was that a blush rising for an instant to her cheek? I craned forward with greater interest.

"Ladies and gentlemen, Dr. Bandaranaike, I thank you for the honor you do me. Like most of us, I pretend to no special knowledge or understanding of the momentary catastrophe that apparently afflicted the Sun four days ago. Certainly the event seems to have been a genuine astrophysical anomaly, not a glitch in our communications systems."

Someone called, "I dispute that, sir."

I cringed, waiting for the Magistrate's acid tongue. He just looked sharply at the culprit, and said, "One reason we know this is that the disruption was also observed in an unusual locale—the Valley of the People of the God of their Choice—"

"The Luddites!"

"—where several communities have lived many years in elected isolation from the benefits of modern Renunciative technology. In fact," the Magistrate added with a weary smile, "I shall be visiting the Valley this afternoon at their specific invitation, and shall take the opportunity to investigate their special experience of the solar lacunae." Was he glancing in my direction again? I nodded acknowledgment, but his gaze had moved coolly on, studying the room. It was very quiet. "Now I ask Dr. Halepa to outline the exact nature of the catastrophe. I shall then open the floor to discussion."

Manuel stood up, made to walk to the front. The Magistrate waved him back to his place. He cleared his throat nervously but spoke with quiet authority, laying out the nature of the astrophysical observations captured by various impossibly arcane instruments as the Sun switched off and came back. Several large displays provided detailed diagrams to illustrate his findings and his argument. I couldn't follow a word of it, of course, even when he ventured into mathematical notation. There's just so much to know. Even with extended penderhood latency there's simply no time for a person to learn more than a fragment of the world's knowledge. Still, we all frowned and did our best to pick out some glimmer of a snail's trail of the argument. This was Mature behavior, after all. We weren't kids anymore. This was . . . grown-up.

It felt scary.

It felt as if the weight of the world had fallen suddenly on our shoulders.

It wasn't remotely dread, it was gawky and weebish and cluster, but it was plainly *important*. I bit the tip of my tongue with my front teeth and struggled to understand what the astronomy experts were telling us and each other.

After an hour and a half, Mr. Abdel-Malek called a momentary halt so we could go piss and grab a coffee. When we'd settled back into our places, he called for a volunteer to summarize the physical implications for the sake of the nonexperts, which was most of us. To my astonishment, Seven raised her hand and rose. He nodded.

Equations in boxes blossomed on the displays, brilliant reds and greens and purples. "Look, people, it's basically quite simple," Seven said slightly nervously. "Forget the dread science for a moment." A ripple of amusement: "dread" and "science" were not words anyone had ever heard linked before; it made a kind of shocking sense, though. Immediately the equations dissolved into a seething mess of bubbles, most of them red, here and there clumps and knots of purples and leaf greens.

"This is empty prerelativistic Rothwarf space, right, the aether?"

Empty? I'd never seen anything fuller. Oh well, science is made of paradoxes. I started to see some interesting knot formations in the chaotic bubbling, and drifted away for a moment. She was saying, "So what the ancients regarded as empty vacuum is known to be a degenerate Fermi fluid. By contrast with the null state of the true vacuum, this Fermion fluid is at a negative energy level. So the aether's filled with trons, okay, dancing inside vortices? The trinos are spin vortices without any partons in their cores." Images flashed. "The photons and other ergons are just regions of polarized aether."

Labels flicked on and off as portions of the displayed diagrams swelled and subsided. I admired Seven's mental control of the interface. If I could get that dexterous, I'd probably be able to play Strad the Lad without moving a muscle.

"Here are the trons." A chart showed us electrons and antielectrons, muons and antimuons, tauons and antitauons. "And the trinos." Underneath, neatly matching, something called eutrinos, mutrinos, and tautrinos and their anti-kin. I guess I'd heard about this in elementary, but who can keep up? "Then there's the heavier stuff." Oh yeah, protons, quarkons, whatever. She collapsed them together. Oh. Got it. All the same thing, really.

"So between trons and quarkons there's a high-energy dipole field rotating with angular velocity omega about their center of mass, so total system energy drops as they approach each other, although kinetic energy increases. Since $T = -E$, E goes negative when measured relative to free partons." She went on like that for a while, and a few people nodded in a satisfied or bored way as she mentioned the canonical pore size and the *Zitterbewegung* due to a bare parton orbiting inside a vortex core, until I felt like screaming.

"Okay, here's the payoff," she said. Her hands seemed to be tremoring, and she pressed them to the back of the chair in front of her. Some people craned forward, others relaxed. "Since the aether is a degenerate plasma, the limiting speed of light, c, is constrained by aether drag on the one hand and the elapsed age of the local plenum on the other."

I leaned over to Robert. "The what?"

"Age of the universe."

"Oh."

"Currently, in our bubble subuniverse, experiment shows that c is slowing by one part in ten to the tenth power each year. It's now half the rate it was at the Bang, because of the expansion of the aether since inflation. You see the implications, I'm sure."

I blinked. Stephanie, I think it was, said, "Oh shit, yes. Aether disruption in the perisolar local ground state."

"If we're lucky," someone else said in a gravelly, grainy voice. He sounded genuinely scared. "If the Fermion fluid goes to the null state—"

"Yeah, we're fucked," Seven said, and sat abruptly back down in her seat.

"What?" I sat bolt upright. I stared at Robert with my mouth open. "She's not saying the whole Sun could—"

"Gamma-ray burster," Seven said with terrifying complacency. She was still on mike; her voice carried to every part of the Grand Hall. "Then black hole."

The room was in uproar. Mr. Abdel-Malek struck the table twice, three times. The tumult did not abate.

"No more Sun?" I whispered.

"No more Sun, no more Earth, no more any of us," Seven said, and suddenly I saw that she was on the verge of weeping or worse, her flipness a mask for hysteria very tightly contained. She hunched over in her seat clutching her stomach, and Robert put his arms about her. I clung to Lucia.

My phone rang. With a shuddering gasp I answered it.

"Hey, liar bee girl," said Mathewmark, "you will be here for the big event, won't you, you weren't pulling my leg?"

I drew in air with a noisy gasp. The what? Oh, the blessed nuptials of my machine-head pal Mathewmark and his gappy gal, virginal Sweetcharity. Yeah, the big event. I burst out laughing, and my voice went up into a silly screech. After a while, my stomach hurting, I put my head between my knees. The hayseed was still there on the line, asking me plaintively to stop laughing like a jackass and talk to him.

"I'll be there, buster," I said. "Wouldn't miss it for the end of the world."

Momma didn't want me going to Mathewmark's bachelor party, but he talked her around. After dinner he offered to help with washing up. I sat at the kitchen table pretending to study a schoolbook so I could listen in.

"Now, Momma," Mathewmark said, "You know Lukenjon will need to learn certain things sooner or later. Wouldn't it be better for him to have his first exposure with me there by his side?"

"He's just a boy!" You could tell Momma had strong feelings about the subject by the way she was splashing soapy water all over the place.

"You know yourself there are fellows his age already married and with their wives in a family way. Why, look at Moses Hampton. Sixteen and a half and already on his second wife, God bless the departed."

"The Hamptons are not what I'd call decent folks." It wasn't like Momma to be haughty and talk down about people that way. I was thinking the bucks' night was a lost cause far as I was concerned. But Mathewmark didn't give up that easy.

"I believe it was old biddy Hampton helped us bring in the tomato harvest the time we had the early frost. And didn't old man Hampton loan us his mule when Ebeeneezer was lame from that thorn in the frog of his hoof? Truth to tell, Momma, I'd say the Hamptons are some of the finest neighbors a person could ask for." Mathewmark was good at debating. When he felt he was losing points, he'd just send the conversation off in a slightly different direction.

"That's all well and good. But—"

"And I recollect that Lizabeth Hampton's peach torte won the Promised Land Bakeoff three years running." Mathewmark waved the dish towel around like a banner.

"Well now, can't be denied. Lizzie Hampton does make a good peach torte."

"You know, Dad took me to my first men's party when I was just thirteen."

"Wasn't that a spiritual retreat your father took you to?"

Mathewmark turned his head and cleared his throat. "That's what it was, but there's not that much difference. A men's party's a men's party."

"I've heard tell of some bad goings on at bachelor parties."

"Well, sure. Tad saucy from a woman's point of view. That's why they're for men only. You don't want Lukenjon to grow up a sissy, do you?" I figured Mathewmark played his trump card with that one, so I held my breath.

"I hardly think it's sissy for a boy to wait until he's matured some before going to a bachelor party."

"I do think you're mistaken about that, Momma. People would be teasing Lukenjon about not going to his own brother's party, and him the best man. There are some might well say he was a sissy."

"Well—" She seemed on the verge of giving in. My skin was tingling with expectation.

"I'll be right there," my brother added, "make sure he stays out of trouble."

"Oh, go on with you, Mathewmark, never could win an argument against you. Go ahead and take your little brother, but don't you let him out of your sight."

He leaned over and gave Momma a kiss on the cheek. "I'll take good care of him."

I sat off in one corner of the Meeting Room at Rubymae's Inn, shaking my head in amazement. When we'd first talked about me going to the party Mathewmark had made sure I knew the rules, the most important of all being: Keep your mouth shut after. I was starting to see why. Mathewmark had his full attention on our songstress, so-called, Nellie Hampton, who was doing a dance where she undressed all the way down to her camisole and underskirt, so he didn't notice Jed at first. The second most important Bucks' Night Rule, the boys say, is: Only invite folks you can trust. Well, for Mathewmark's night they mostly followed the rule to the letter, but Clyde Manry must not have heard that one, because he showed up with Jed Cooper. Old Jed must've already had himself a few drinks, he was that cantankerous, even worse than usual. No sooner had he got himself a beer than he started in on my brother.

"Hey, Fisher, I hear you're taking delivery of some lively goods tomorrow." Clyde saw the mistake he'd made, because I heard him say, "Jed, this don't look like such a good party after all. What say we go on over to the Red Stag." But Jed just ignored Clyde and strutted nearer to where Mathewmark was seated.

"I can tell you what makes her feel good, Fisher," he taunted, pushing out his beard. Mathewmark looked up, looked down in disgust, looked dangerous.

"Don't think I heard you correctly, Cooper. Don't think it would do you good if I did."

"Deaf, eh?" Jed was shouting in Mathewmark's ear. "Why, I said—"

"Time for another round, boys!" shouted Milo, toting a full pitcher of beer. "Who needs topping off?"

"McPheely! Play that fiddle!" Clyde yelled. "'Pastime with Good Company'! Everybody! 'Pastime'!" Lanky on the fiddle and Sam on the dulcimer started playing the opening bars of the old song:

> Pastime with good company
> I love and shall unto I die.
> Grudge whoso will, but none deny,
> So God be pleased, this live will I.

and pretty soon the walls was shaking with the singing and foot stomping.

> For my pastance
> Hunt, sing, and dance.
> My heart is set
> All godely sport
> To my comfort.

Who shall me let?
Youth will have needs dalliance . . .

Jed didn't join in but just stood there, emptied his glass, poured himself another. By the time the singing was done he was pretty nigh under the table, and he didn't say anything for a while.

Nellie set in to removing even more of her clothes, winking at us and throwing off all decent restraint. The boys kept drinking beer and guffawing, telling one unwholesome joke after another while I sat and watched. As Mathewmark's best man, I was officially in charge of the party, so I considered it my duty to stay sober. Besides, if I'd of gone home drunk my Momma would of wore out the razor strop on my behind.

Peterpaul Jenkins and Jonmathew Riley bumbled over and fondled the poor young woman in a way that made me avert my eyes. For a different reason Mathewmark seemed to be having a hard time focusing his eyes and staying on his feet. He'd already tripped over a couple of times, well taken in drink.

"Who wants to have first go at the lovely Nellie?" shouted Peterpaul to a gale of mirth and encouragement. Only Milo Messershmidt, a pious man but not so holier-than-thou as to leave a friend's bucks' night, stared intently into his mug of beer. He fished around with his fingers and pulled out a soft, dark object, possibly someone's spent plug of cocabacco.

"Just let me at that buxom beauty." Buck Fry was trying to walk with his trousers down around his ankles.

"Oooeee," Jed shouted. "Ain't she a pretty one though?" My mouth dropped open as I saw men I had respected all these years stumbling in the direction of a whore. She looked dazed and flushed, chugging down her beers with the best of them.

"Come on, boys. Make way for the groom. Groom gets to go first." Peterpaul gave Mathewmark a bit of a shove that sent him sprawling onto the mucky floor. My brother shook his head and pushed away a helping hand urging him toward Nellie. Jed was happy to take his place. "Ooooh, Sweetcharity," he crooned in the poor girl's ear. There was uproar and backslapping. Luckily Mathewmark was too fuddled to hear clearly, clambering back to his feet with a dazed expression. I looked away, blushing and hoping none of the other fellers noticed my shame. I was beginning to think Momma was right about me not going to the bucks' night.

When he was done, Jed remembered his other purpose in life and roused himself enough to yell, "Hey, Fisher—" but then seemed not to recollect what he'd been planning to say. He stooped and reflected on it for a moment, cross-eyed with the effort, with everyone looking at him.

"What is it, Cooper," Laz Short shouted, "cathouse got your tongue?" and everyone laughed. I held my breath. Jed Cooper didn't take mockery lightly, but when he jumped up and swung his fists he lost his balance, thumped back with a crash on the bench opposite where my brother had found a place.

"Wasn't talking to you, Short. Mind your own fucking business." Jed took another swig, raised his voice. "Fisher, sure got you a pretty little girl. Think you're man enough to keep her from straying?"

"Fuck off, dickhead," Mathewmark muttered, keeping his eyes directed down at the table. It was stronger language than I'd ever heard from him. You could tell he was in no mood for getting into a fight, but all the same time I knew how he felt about Jed insulting Sweetcharity. Nellie, who scented danger I do believe, was struggling into her clothes. While the men shouted at each other she scooted for the side door and escaped into the night, not before tucking her pay more firmly into a cosy place I blushed to see exposed.

"Who you calling a dickhead?" Jed made a supreme effort, got to his feet, stood there swaying.

"You're unworthy to, to, to lick the mud from her toes." Not yet as drunk as Jed, Mathewmark struggled up, raised his fists. "I don't want to fight you, Jed, night before my wedding, but if you push me far enough, I'll do what I have to do. Don't you let me catch you talking about my wife-to-be ever again, you hear me!"

"Hey, Fuckface Fisher, I'll say whatever I feel like saying about anything and anyone." To my horror, Jed let Mathewmark have it right in the guts with his ham of a fist. My poor brother, he just sort of sighed and collapsed and lay down on the floor.

"Peter, Laz, give me a hand, will you?" Clyde got his heavy mitts under Mathewmark's armpits, dragging him toward the door. Peterpaul and Lazarus each picked up a booted foot. The rest of us followed as they carried their unconscious burden out of Rubymae's.

"We've got to get him waked up enough so he can make it home," Clyde said. "Can't just leave him lying here."

"I'll see him home," I said, but nobody was listening to a kid.

"He could sleep in one of Rubymae's rooms."

Momma will kill me, I thought. She'll just plain up and kill me dead.

"Nah, last resort. You know how much she charges?"

"Come on boys. To the water trough. One." They began swinging Mathewmark's limp body. "Two. Watch his head, boys. Three. And in he goes."

He hit the muddy water, and we all jumped back trying to keep our feet dry. He sat up sputtering. "What the hell? What the hell?" Everyone was laughing and hollering fit to bust a gut, and Clyde finally went over and put an arm around his shoulders.

"Come on, bridegroom. There's a good man. Let me help you out."

Shorty ran out shouting, "Jed's just passed out, too."

"Into the trough with him as well. What a night! This one'll live in the records!"

They lugged out the big drunk and in he went, splashing out the last of the water left by my bedraggled brother.

"Short! Bring his horse over here."

They somehow got Jed up into the saddle, where he promptly slumped over with his head on the beast's neck.

"Think we better tie him on?" someone said.

"Nah, that boy could ride a horse at his own funeral."

"I'll take him on home," said Clyde, grabbing hold of the reins. "Sorry, Mathewmark," he said over his shoulder as he walked on down the street.

Wet and bruised as he was, my brother squared his shoulders and marched right back into Rubymae's Inn, to a resounding cheer. The company rededicated themselves to showing the groom a wild time, and I took myself to the corner, where I nursed a sarsaparilla for the rest of the evening. I guess Mathewmark had come out all right against Jed, but I feared the bastard would be harder to deal with next time around, especially if he had his buddies with him.

1 0 : kasim abdel-malek

Hot sunlight bathes my face as I wake claggy-mouthed and prickly from a snooze. Behind my closed eyelids, I see bright red patches and squeeze my eyes tighter against the high sun, raising one arm to shade the glare. Something about the way my arm rises, the ease of it, the crisp smell of my own sweat . . . A seagull squawks, waves move against sand, back and forth, hushing, every fifth or eighth louder than the rest. Without opening my eyes, I know exactly who I am, as one does, routinely, part of the package of being a self: I am Mohammed Kasim Abdel-Malek, *bon vivant* and pragmatic optimist, Bachelor of Arts with Honors, Juris Doctor, Doctor of Science in cognitive science, artificial intelligence builder. That can't possibly be right. In your dreams, Kasim, you've barely completed your—

I sit up with a jolt. Good God, I'm naked. Warm white sand stretches out to right and left, numberless brilliant grains of fine silica that catch and throw back the summer sunlight. The ocean is the one I know so well, deep glassy blue, waves moving in and out like breathing, froth at the edge of the shore, strings of dark green sea-weed, white spume farther out, nearly to the sharp edge of the horizon under its pale high blue, tall surf curling and breaking, curving to tubes with a distant rumble, brown bodies out there on sheets of dream, light as air, falling into the water and rushing toward land, dropping then from the ebbing wave, turning languidly like powerful dolls and returning to the horizon, and to my left, in an area marked at the shore with flags, brightly hued deltas of crimson, yellow, peacock blue, each bearing a passenger catching the light breeze, wind-surfers riding like aerial fish, and on the broad sand drowsing sun-worshipers scattered along the huge white shore, heads bent on to crossed arms or thrown back to the Sun, naked or all but, a dozen tints of brown or black, some showing the heavy hand of time and appetite, bulging at waist and thigh, others like myself muscular and confidently relaxed, careless gods on holiday—

All this in an effortless instant of recognition, and still the jolt passes into me, my stomach tightening in delayed fright, skin cooling despite the hot Sun, lips drawing back in a grimace, grunting aloud, what the *fuck . . . ?*

My legs are lifting off the chaise longue where I've been reclining, feet coming down hard and burningly in the baked sand. Toes jerk back in reflex, searching for my sandals. There they are, tucked into the shade beneath my recliner. Slip them on automatically, lurch up, stare around wildly. A tall spindly young man is approaching me, bearing a tray with a decanter and a single long flute half-filled with ice. He nods to me, eyes hidden behind fashionable shades. My head is starting to ache, too much sun, no hat, no sunglasses, where the hell is Alice—

"Alice!" I shout then, and a deep terrible groan forces its way out of my belly. "Oh my God, where's Alice?" Mohammed Kasim Abdel-Malek, *bon vivant* and pragmatic optimist—and dead. I can vividly remember the bastards kicking me to death. No one could survive a beating like that. And this time the jolt is a kick, bending me double. My heart pounds like a trip-hammer, I can scarcely see, but it's all ridiculous, some sort of hallucination, these hands in front of my burning, dazed eyes are *young* hands, powerful, unlined, and my torso is the moderately well muscled body I had when I was what, eighteen? twenty-two? Before Alice. Before my work on AIs. Before I grew old and was kicked to death. Died. Oh shit, died. Hands go to neck. No bracelet there, or at my wrist. Died, and they've frozen me, and then they brought me back.

And put me here on the fucking *beach?* Give me a *break!*

The boy has his hand behind me, holding me steady. What's he done with his tray and its drink? On the sand, tilted. Beads of light at its rim, bubbles rising in the clear golden liquid. Good God, champagne?

"Mr. Abdel-Malek," the boy is saying to me, "can sit up now? Here, fetched cooling drink."

"Alice," I shout at him, pulling at his arm. "Is she all right? Where's my wife, damn it?"

"Think must know where are, now, sir," the boy says in his strange way. He touches his own chest in a disarming gesture. "Vikram Singh, sir, at service." Lifting the tray in one economical movement, he proffers the glass. "Will drink?"

I take it, and my boneless grip almost lets the glass slide through and fall into the hot sand.

"This is hell," I suggest to the boy. "Do you know that I'm dead?"

He smiles, and his teeth are beautiful and very white in his dark face. "Not hell, Mr. Abdel-Malek. But all are dead here. Self, died in nasty accident. Not to worry, everything fixed now."

The champagne is very good indeed. I gulp it, and the bubbles, inevitably, go up my nose. I sneeze, wipe my nose on the back on my hand—no shorts, no handkerchief—take another deep draft and empty the glass. I don't *feel* dead. In fact I feel terrific, shockingly full of juice. But poor Alice. Tears start in my eyes.

"Here comes your wife now," the young man says, taking the glass. I gape. In the dazzling light, stepping from the frothy water into the dark at the edge of the sea, small feet pressing into the wet sand and leaving their imprint in her train, all but naked, tanned young (*young?*) body beaded with droplets of water, head tilted and smiling, wringing her long brown hair as she trots to me.

Her name breaks in my throat. Everything speared and crazed in my wet eyes. I blink, rub the tears away, run toward her, feet clumsy in white creaking sand, the seagulls making their importunate cries. She calls my name back to me, we are in each other's arms, it makes no sense, it's a dream in a hospital room, it's worked, the cryonic suspension has worked, we've been frozen and warmed in some generous future and brought here to the recovered, healthy ocean, our mouths wet and hot against each other, no, no—

The boy Vikram stands respectfully aside, but at last smilingly offers his tray. Alice holds me tight with one arm, reaches with the other for a tall pale golden glass. I take mine. We clink them ringingly, drain their cool bubbles. Two glasses where there had been one. This is a simulation. The knowledge, the certainty of it is colder than the imagined champagne; it constricts my guts, chills my hands and feet and numbs my face.

"You're not real," I say to her.

"Oh yes, Boson," she tells me with a smile. She is twenty years younger than I've ever known her. "We're *real*. We always are, however often this scene is replayed, however many settings we find ourselves in." When I try to pull away from her she holds me with both arms, looking up into my face. Years younger than I have ever known her, yet I know her perfectly. Taking my hand, she draws me to the shoreline. We walk slowly along the fractal lovely line where water merges with earth and light, toes and soles crunching broken shell, slippery with seaweed, careful to avoid glistening pods of stranded jellyfish. Three or four kids are floating a Frisbee; it sings in the light breeze, falls near our feet; I pick it up without a thought, flick it effortlessly into the drenching light. A dog barks, rushes through a spray of sand to leap and catch it in his mouth. I am filled with incredulous joy, suddenly, a joy I can't contain, that rises up and washes away my dread.

"Want an ice cream?"

"Sure." There's a stand set up in the rocks at the foot of cliffs. A red-faced man in an apron fetches up white and chocolate and red strawberry scoops for pushing children. "I don't have any money, sweetheart."

"Taken care of." She orders the ice creams we loved when we first knew each other (gelati, light as air, as shaved ice, in crisp, dry wafer cones), we lick them as we walk back to the water.

"Real, yes," I admit, "but we're inside a program."

"Of course. Tah-rah—behold cyberspace."

Total immersion. Skin of shoulders crinkling under a mild burn, feet hot on untouched sand, dancing away to the cold caress of a wave, back to the scalding sand, all of it done and felt without a moment's conscious decision or, mostly, any awareness at all, except the delight of the moment, the swollen-hearted love I feel for this woman, my wife, my beloved Alice, for the whole round fantastically alive world. Does it matter that what I feel, the "I" who feels it, is no more than a rush of bytes in some memory space, some neural network inside an immense computer that, for all I know, might be in orbit around some star light-years distant from the Earth where I seem to have been reborn? These are possibilities we had chewed over a thousand times, Alice and I and the rest of us, those smart kids, took as our special smug domain, the expectation of futures that would boggle lesser minds, those stodgy linear thinkers who expected, against all the evidence of history and their own lives, that the world would creep along at the same steady pace, changing only fractionally, a partial cure for some minor heart disorder, yes, an easier way to have teeth filled, sure, a slightly cleaner car engine, granted, but noth-ing preposterous, no disruptions in the consumer dreamland of early twenty-first century—

"How long?" I am abruptly desperate to know where and when.

"The metric's—difficult," Alice says. She glances at me from un-der her straw hat (her *hat*?), meets my gaze without flinching, quirks her mouth. There's a dab of white zinc cream on her nose, rather fetching. I touch my own face; it's cool and slithery on my nose, too.

"Centuries? Months?" Not so soon as months, surely. We hadn't been anywhere near recovery from cryonic vitrification when they'd kicked me to death.

"Boson, there's someone I'd like you to meet," she says, and draws me into the water. Something is out there, bobbing in the deeper water. Someone. We swim toward the small pale figure. He's just a— she's only a child of—I can't decide. A wave hits me from the side, salty water goes up my nose, into my mouth, I cough and flounder for a moment, then recover my grace. "Kasim, this is the Aleph."

The child floats on its back. It looks at me with patient deep brown eyes, face impassive.

"Hello, Father."

I float, arms and legs gently sweeping the cold, the warm, the perfect water.

"The AI, I presume," I tell it with a certain irony. "And this is the amnion? Perhaps the symbolism is a little heavy-handed?"

"Hard to avoid, Mohammed, when the world is immediate, unmediated. We have a lot to discuss. I need your advice on an urgent matter."

I sent Alice a wry, mocking look. "Yeah, right. A legal opinion."

"Perhaps that, too."

"Listen, you're the god here. I assume. How much faster than a human brain? A trillion times? A zillion?"

"Only a million, actually," the Aleph tells me with a slow, sweet smile. "There are—constraints. But the workspace is quite comfortable."

"I'll say." I flip over backward, suddenly hungry for the body's free motion in the real. Diving down, kicking powerfully, the water green and dark, turning, rising, pressure in chest, breaking through into brilliance, gusting out my breath and drawing in sweet air. Dolphin. I burst out laughing at the sheer intoxication of it.

"Why 'Father'?" I ask the child, who now sits upright in *zazen* posture on the undulating surface of the water. "Our programming work, mine and Alice's? I find that hard to believe, we haven't done anything significantly new for years."

"You were the seed," the child tells me. It rises in the air, comes to me like a white bird, puts its arms about me, rests its head trustingly against my chest. I flail in the water, but something holds me up against drowning. My heart pounds and pounds.

"Oh shit," I say. "They used my brain scan—"

"As the template," Alice says. We are walking along the beach, returning the way we'd come, with the small pale child between us, holding its hands. "You're the core of the Aleph, Boson."

I look at her ruefully, and then down at the bald-headed child, who's lifted its legs free of the sand and is swinging heavily in our grasp. "More likely," I say, "the worm in the apple."

And we burst out laughing, we can't help ourselves. The dog with the Frisbee runs across the sand in front of us, and the Aleph breaks free of our grip, rushes away to join the fun.

Alice gives me a quick kiss, finally, and shows me a large window.

"Someone else you need to meet, Kasim." On the other side of the window, a man not much older than I, by the look of him, sits in meditation within a kind of elegant chambers. He resembles a little the old brown photographs of my father when he was a young man. No. He looks like pictures of me. He is me. My mood starts to curdle once more. Oh shit. Oh my God. Is there no limit to this?

His eyes open. He glances impassively yet acutely at me, meeting my eyes, then shifts his gaze to Alice. "It did something to the Sun," he says. "What the fuck's it playing at now?"

I hold my tongue, sick with anxiety.

"Something is being prepared," Alice tells us both. "Something—wonderful." She pauses, studies her folded hands. "The Aleph seeks our opinion." It is as if she is pleading. "We have a stake, too, after all."

The Mohammed Abdel-Malek in the window says nothing in reply, sending us both a knowing, bitterly ironic look. He closes his eyes. I shiver. I reach blindly for Alice's hand, and she is there. She is there somewhere. I do not know where the somewhere is. The dog with the Frisbee runs across the sand in front of us again, tail wagging madly, saliva flying from its mouth.

1 1 : amanda

Light rain fell as we stepped from Mr. Abdel-Malek's luxurious glide, but the air wasn't too cold despite the mountain breeze. I looked with a shudder at the lumpy Gatehouse, and ignored the uncouth ogling I got from the hicks standing guard. Apparently they'd never seen a festive cat suit before. We were ushered through on the Magistrate's say-so, with a mere fifteen minutes of agonized signing of papers, inspection of bags, pious claptrap. Beyond the large glass windows I saw good old Ebeeneezer talking to Lukenjon, who sat on the cart in his oilskin under a covering of canvas he'd rigged to hold off the drizzle. No sign of Mathewmark. Well, naturally, the boy was preparing for the big day of his short and dreary life. I felt a burst of misery, and told myself, Yes, Amanda, the same short life we'll all share if the Sun is about to pop out of the known universe and gobble us all up in the dark.

Finally, we traipsed through, my mother and father carrying big foil-packaged gifts, Mr. Abdel-Malek resplendent as usual and bearing nothing more than his cane. Lukenjon hopped smartly from the cart, pulled down some folding steps. He shook hands all round, clearly in awe, but boggled when he came to me.

"First a bat, now a cat, Mistress bee." He handed me up gallantly. My tail swung and caught in the collar of his oilskins; blushing, he flipped it free. "You are looking . . . well."

"Thank you, Lukenjon. You too." I wasn't going to ask him, he wasn't going to volunteer. Oh well. I clambered in, squeezed next to the Magistrate. Emily kept looking at me irritably, squeezing her lips tightly. I was now an adult, so she would not speak chidingly although she was obviously itching to. I didn't even know what had got up her nose.

"Ee-yup," Lukenjon called, and we jolted off. And kept jolting for the next two long hours, winding down and around and down again into the Valley. To call the roads primitive would flatter them and their upkeep. My tail bruised me when I sat on it, and flopped out into the rain if I didn't. I managed to get it caught around the Magistrate's cane, until he sighed and flicked it back across my knees.

Once Ebeeneezer was well on his way in territory known to the mule for decades, Lukenjon turned and clambered into the back with us, squeezing unself-consciously between my parents. He beamed at us in turn, chattered away about the excitement in the Valley, what did we think of the great omen, he hoped we were faring well in our godless place of exile, his momma had put out the finest spread a body had seen in a hoon's age, not to mention the herb breads Auntie McWeezle had rolled and baked with the help of the bride-to-be. "And speaking of bees," the merry fellow said, "may I ask *why* you are clad in the form of a witch's familiar?"

"A what?"

"I told the silly girl," Maman muttered out of the side of her mouth, but my father was on the far side of Lukenjon, and affected not to hear.

"It's my wedding costume," I said, crestfallen. "Don't you like it?" I caressed my long, lustrous whiskers and moved my ears forward. The boy's eyes popped when he saw that.

"It's most—inventive, Mistress Amanda. We'll drop these folks off at the hall beside the kirk and I'll run you over to my cousin Bessy's, she'll have a smock and bonnet near enough to your size. And their water is running, I believe, so you'll have no trouble washing off the, um, the uh—"

"Makeup, yes." Damn. I'd spent an hour getting it right, too. A smock didn't sound remotely like the kind of garment I wished to be seen by Mathewmark in.

True to his word, Lukenjon drew up finally at a large wooden establishment festooned with flowers, paper streamers, and a priapic statue he said had been hauled over from the colony at the northern end of the Valley. They always insist, he said with a sigh, and we don't like to offend. Obviously, he didn't mind offending *me* with his critical remarks, because as soon as everyone else was off-loaded he picked up the reins and took us down an endless muddy back way to his cousins' hovel. He saw me into the hovel with a chivalrous bow, and a big bold girl with bangs and a port-wine stain on half her face showed me the basin and how one might lather up the cool water with a stick of soap. Bessy looked a full eight and half months pregnant, and the vast tent she wore disguised any resemblance to a young woman who could share clothes with me. I could only hope so, anyway, as she lumbered off to find me garments that would not affront people who saw no shame in a hewn statue with a gigantic donger propped in the pathway of the young marrieds when they left the kirk and headed for the sumptuous spread Lukenjon had advertised.

I peeled off the mask and hair, disconnected my neural links from ears, whiskers, and tail, and scrubbed myself as clean as I could without detergent.

Bessy knocked, brought in a double armful of apparel that she referred to as her best dress.

"As you see," she told me with a shy glance downward, "I shan't be wearing it myself to the festivities in my condition."

All I could do was gaze at the pile of garments in utter confusion.

"Um, Bessy, I'm afraid you'll have to show me how to put these things on," I said at last with some embarrassment.

She was horrified to find that I wore no underwear, pushed baggy but frilly things at me with her eyes averted. I realized that she found me as lacking in the social graces as I did her and her people. Once I had my whole body encased in white fabric, she deigned to look at me again.

"Put your arms up straight over your head," she commanded, and slipped a huge sack of a dress over me, working my arms into the long sleeves. The dress had a slit down the front which was fastened by means of small bone disks on one side of the opening that slipped through holes in the other side.

"Here. Let me button you up." Bessy impatiently pushed my fumbling hands aside. She smoothed the full skirt, stood back and surveyed me critically.

"You look goodly in the dress," she said at last. "The pink and white suits you. But we must do something about your hair, scant as it is." She came back after a few minutes with a wooden-handled metal rod, and wound strands of my hair around it after coating them with an oil that smelled of some kind of herb. It was a good thing my hair had grown out a little or she'd have coated my skull with the stuff. I was alarmed. "What's that gunk? What doing to hair?" Well, Heloise back in van Gogh could repair whatever damage Bessy might be doing.

"Just a curling iron, silly, no cause to fret. You don't want to go to the wedding with plain, straight hair, do you? What's the point of getting all dressed up if you don't fix your hair?" This in a patient tone, as if to a young child. Again, I got the feeling that Bessy found me unbelievably backward.

When the fiddling finally ended, she pulled a large round box down from a shelf.

"I've never worn this hat. I'll let you borrow it, because you're friends with Lukenjon, but you must promise to take good care of it."

"Maybe it would be best if I didn't wear—"

"You can't go to the wedding without a hat, and that's final." Bessy set the appalling thing on top of my head, pulled me over to the spotted mirror. I cringed at what I saw. But when I stepped out, walking with my head stiffly erect to avoid losing the towering head gear, Lukenjon put down the improving tract he'd been reading and looked up, his eyes alight with gratifying admiration.

"Oh my," he said, touching his chest. "The cat has been transformed into a most lovely maiden. I do dare suppose you *are* a witch after all, no offense intended."

I smiled, of course, thanked Bessy, declined her offer of a pot of herbal infusion, good for the nerves and complexion (it didn't seem to have done hers much good, poor thing), went back outside to the cart. Ebeeneezer was munching in a feed bag, and mumbled to us about the weather easing soon to judge from the clouds. The mule was right, too. By the time we'd got within distant sight of the kirk, the Sun had come out and steam was rising from the morning grass. I had never been in a church or kirk or temple, never known anyone who had. It was a very strange idea.

"I believe there was a church in Prague," I said, "built out of ten thousand human bones."

"My oh my," Lukenjon said. "I didn't know there *were* so many people."

"More dead than living," I said. And soon, by the look of things, more still. It was too terrible to contemplate. I dismissed the dreadful possibility again, pushed it into the back of my mind.

"Where's Prague?" Lukenjon asked.

"Why it's—" I ruffled through my knowledge chips, came up with an X. "It's embargoed. Sorry."

"What, you're not allowed to tell me? It's not as if I'm likely to *go* there. We don't, you know. Except for my poor brother."

That stung, although the boy might not have meant it to be hurtful. "No, I'm not allowed to know either. It's like a phone call, except that—" I stopped.

"I know what a phone call is," Lukenjon said. "Mathewmark told me all that stuff. He says you speak to him inside his head, like a witching." He flicked his dark, long-lashed eyes toward me and gave a sweet shy smile. "I shouldn't object to such a witching, Mistress bee, should you choose to call me for a chat."

"Oh, I'm sorry, it only works if you have a—If there's been a, a sort of—"

"A mechanical put into your head," he said, nodding, "and I don't have one. I wouldn't mind, though, even if old man Legrand cries out against its wickedness."

"No, you can only have one if it's done at—" How could I explain this? The only person with a phone connect he'd ever talked to about it was his brother, and Mathewmark was a mad exception to the strict Joyous Relinquishment guidelines. I mean, he didn't just have a phone chip, half his brain was chipped. "In the womb, do you understand? Then again at twelve."

"Oh yes, at the quickening. So if Sweetcharity were with child, would it be too late for their babe to—"

"She's not," I said shortly. "That was a vicious rumor."

The boy blushed and shook his head. "Yes, I do know that, I'm sorry, I meant no disrespect to my brother or his intended bride. I meant only as an example—"

"The wrong one. Let's drop it."

"Surely." He fell into a depressed silence, and we clopped toward the kirk, just a field or two distant now. The rain had gone completely, and clouds blew away, leaving the sky blue and endless. I smelled the place, faintly unpleasant after the sanitized air of Metro and Mall, tangy with woodsmoke and a touch of the animal shit they mixed into the naked soil to fertilize their crops. Perhaps not so unpleasant, though—just unfamiliar. The taint of Valley air carried memories: our flight on bat wings, the rising smoke and licking flames of hysterical yokels, running from their whipped-up fear, my itching at alien allergies then feeling the soothing balm of Myrtle McWeezle's potion. Springing chocolate on the two young men, hearing Mathewmark's moans of satisfaction and delight in the darkness as he sucked the delicious stuff for the very first time. I blocked out the dark drone of Vikram's fall, Mathewmark crashing and smashing, the howling of the—

"Here we are," Lukenjon told me.

I shook my head clear, stepped down with his hand on my arm to steady me. Abruptly he burst out, completely without warning, "I must tell you this or I'll burst. Mistress Kolby-McAllister, I love you, I have since the first moment I saw you come down out of the skies. I knew you were no demon or witch, I knew it, I knew you were just the most perfect and beautiful creature in all of the lands of the God of our Choice." I stood there gaping at him. "Would you do me the honor of marrying me, so we might share in the wedded bliss this day with my brother and Sweetcharity." The words came out in a mad rush. He stood there panting, hardly daring to look at me.

"Oh, oh," I said. I was flummoxed. It was the silliest and most grown-up thing anyone had said to me since my Maturity. "That's— That's very—" I wanted to find some way to tell the dear hayseed he needed his head read without bruising his feelings. "Why, Lukenjon, how old are you?"

He squared his shoulders. They were quite good, solid shoulders, too. "I'm fifteen and a half this last month," he told me sturdily. "Many's the man in this Valley married at fifteen and a father within the year."

"Oh you great silly," I blurted, "if I'm to marry any member of the Fisher family it would have to be Mathewmark." The instant the words fell upon our ears, I wanted them swallowed to silence back in my mouth. I was struck dumb, just standing paralyzed, looking at the boy with my mouth open. His own mouth curved down, then, and his shoulders slumped. I expected him to bolt away, but he did no such thing. He made a respectful bow.

"I really knew it all along," he told me in a low voice. "I wonder if my brother knows as well? I suppose he does not."

"Lukenjon—" I cried. But there was nothing more to say. The Sun shone in the clearing sky, and even that wasn't reliable or secure anymore. I felt more confused than I'd ever been in my life. I reached up and straightened that stupid, hideous hat on my head. Lukenjon held out his arm for me, with a sad smile. I laid my hand across his forearm, we made our way across cobbles toward the kirk. Bessy's underpants were beginning to bunch up between my legs as I walked, and the rigid bodice constricted the movements of my upper body. Was not sure would be able to make it through this day.

1 2 : myrtle mcweezle

The fragrance of baking bread should have been cheering, but under the circumstances the memory of Sweetcharity's innocent, troubled face saddened me. I had me some hard thinking to do. All my life I studied the good Earth and the Moon and the Sun and knew that what happened in the heavens was no normal event. I feared our life-giving Sun was mortally ill, but had no idea what to do about it. Nor could I contrive an easy solution for Sweetcharity and Mathewmark, short of a last-minute disgrace.

I decided to ask the Elder Mother. Gaia could often give me answers I might not find for myself. As soon as the bread was done and turned out to cool I took some coals from the fire, put them into a brass bowl, and sprinkled copal resin onto them. I do love that amber hue. Soon the air filled with the musky fragrance that belongs to the great Mother. I lit a candle and turned out the oil lamp. Rain began to fall as I settled myself down in the circle of the candle's light to wait for Mother Gaia to speak to me. My eyelids fell shut.

For a while I only saw floating bits of darkness and light, like always. A scene began to take shape. I seen a young woman with long brown hair walking down a dirt path through trees that met overhead. She wore just a light brown linen chemise, and her feet was bare. As my sight focused more clearly, I saw I was that girl, as I used to be, no more than Sweetcharity's age. She carried in her right hand a walking stick decorated with brown and white ribbons waving in the breeze as she went along. The stick's head was carved in a pattern of interlocking strands that began to move like snakes, weaving around and through each other, making complex knots. She flung the stick away into the woods, and at that moment my heart merged with the young woman's. I saw what I must do. I sat in the circle of candlelight.

Through the eastern window I could see the first light of dawn. For no reason I could understand, for the first time since the Sun had become ill I felt a glimmer of hope.

Mathewmark had promised to carry me to the wedding in his wagon. Two dozen loaves of bread were too many for an old woman to tote on foot. He arrived right on time, looking somewhat the worse for wear from his bucks' night but dressed in his wedding finery. Oh dear, I said to myself, Sweetcharity hasn't told him yet, and my heart went out to him for the pain that would be coming later.

"Morning, Auntie McWeezle," he hollered, and winced at the sound of his own voice.

"Morning, Mathewmark. My, but you look handsome. That hat does you proud." I handed up the baskets of bread.

"Thank you, ma'am." Groaning a little, he jumped from the wagon to help me up.

"You and those other young rascals have been drinking," I said flatly.

He looked sheepish, but nodded.

"Come indoors a moment, you silly feller, and I'll whip up a decoction that will ease your head."

"I'd be most grateful, Auntie."

While I ground up my herbs and simples and mixed them into a bitter but effective potion that he swallowed with a thankful grimace, I tried to find words that would lend him courage to face whatever this day might bring. But no, try as I might, I could not get a word in edgewise. The moment we were in the wagon he started out at once talking about getting the wheat and rye planted, then about his momma's new bathtub, and the unpleasantness of the night before, not looking for sympathy but clearly rambling on to soothe his nerves. I decided it was up to Sweetcharity herself anyway to break the news.

The kirk's yard was filling with wagons and people on foot by the time we got there. As we neared the front door of the hall I spied Lukenjon. He had gotten himself a pretty young woman, someone, to my astonishment, I didn't know. I squinted up my eyes and land's sake if it wasn't that strange Amanda gal all grown-up since just those few months back and dressed like Valley folk! Mathewmark turned from the wagon with a heavy armful of loaves and saw her too, stopped dead still for a moment. A flush moved from his neck on up his face.

"Well, hello Amanda!" I called, and heard the crack in my voice. "I'm mighty happy to see you again, and looking so pretty in your new dress."

"Auntie McWeezle, so wonderful to see you again." She came over and gave me a hug, and sneezed. "There have been times during the past months when I would have given almost anything to talk to you." I was pleased to mark that her manner of speech was greatly improved, but her eyes and nose were red. "Going through Maturity would have been easier with your wisdom to draw on." Apart from her red nostrils her face was oddly pale, and she glanced quickly in Mathewmark's direction a time or two, then after a moment she was flushing, too. He, of course, was far too busy juggling his load of bread and talking to Lukenjon to notice. To look at him, you'd have thought him and his brother hadn't seen each other in year or so. Foolish children, I thought.

The God of Mathewmark and Sweetcharity's particular choice holds it to be bad luck for bride and groom to catch sight of each other on the day of the wedding, before they get to the altar that is, so it was going to be a mite difficult for the poor girl to tell him of her change of heart. I dragged Mathewmark away from Amanda's vicinity and said we needed to finish getting the bread out of the wagon. We heard a thunderous sneeze, and glanced back in her direction but Mathewmark quickly looked the other way when he saw her eyes on him. Lukenjon was handing the girl a large red handkerchief, neatly darned by his mother.

As we carried in the bread, I murmured, "Mathewmark, I think Sweetcharity may have something she needs to talk to you about before the wedding." I had to talk fast. "Wisdom," had Amanda said? Silly old woman, I had left this perilously late. Custom called for the bride to arrive just before the ceremony, so Sweetcharity would still be on her way from Legrand's household, and I knew what road they'd be taking. "Now it's bad luck and all for you two to see each other ahead of time, but would it be improper for her to write you a letter?"

He thought it over for a moment. "Well, I can't recall ever hearing anything about letters being bad luck. But she won't have writing materials."

"Leave that to me."

I estimated the time from the shadows on the ground. Sweetcharity and her grandfather would be in old man Legrand's buggy with the fancy gold-inlaid panels, so if I started out walking I could meet them on the road.

Sure enough, before too long here they were plodding along toward me, but in the old farm wagon. Festus Legrand pulled to a stop and leaned over so he could see down the front of my bodice. Lecherous old goat, I thought. Well, if he wanted to strain his neck, more power to him. At least he had left the girl alone, more than some of the old fools could be trusted with. "Howdy-do, Myrtle. I'd have thought you'd be over to the kirk making ready for the festivities." He spat a foul stream of cocabacco juice over the warped side of the wagon.

"Morning, Festus, Sweetcharity. What in the world are you doing carrying that girl to her wedding in this old wagon, Festus?"

"The buggy is incapacitated at the moment."

Sweetcharity rolled her eyes. Lost it gambling, I thought. The poor girl had confided her concerns about the old geezer's weakness for games of chance.

"Well, I reckon that old wagon will do just as well, long as it gets you where you want to go." I waited for Festus to offer me a ride, but he was shifting his weight around looking anxious to get started again, so I had to be pushy. "Say, I wonder if you might give an old gal a lift back in the direction of the kirk. I came walking down this way just looking to meet you, because I want to have a word or two with Sweetcharity. Marriage talk, Festus. Woman to woman."

"Why sure, Myrtle, you're always welcome to ride in my wagon," he said, but didn't make a move to help me in.

"Maybe you could step down, Festus, and allow us to ride together. It won't take you but ten or fifteen minutes to walk the rest of the way."

His indignation was plain. Before he could explode, the dear girl flapped her eyelashes and touched his sleeve. "No, Grandpa, you ride along with Molly. I think I'd like to walk, it would calm my nerves some. A gal needs to have calm nerves on her wedding day." She smiled at him as sweetly as you please.

"Here I'm fixing to give you away for good, and you want to run off and talk to someone else," he grumbled.

"Oh, Grandpa. You're not giving me away for good. You know Mathewmark and I are intending to make our home right there with you." I was relieved, I must say, to detect the tiniest trace of impatience in her voice. That girl was always far too compliant.

"Well, do as you please." He pulled a wad of cocabacco from his shirt pocket and stuffed it into his ample mouth as Sweetcharity hopped lightly from the wagon. Festus nodded, touched the fingers of his right hand to the brim of his hat, and hollered, "Gee-up there, Molly!" and the wagon creaked away on down the road.

"You've got to help me, Auntie. I'm beside myself with worry, not knowing what to do." Her frilly white dress was decorated with blue-satin ribbons, which I could see she had been picking at all morning. The ends were as frayed as though they'd seen fifty wash days.

"Too late for talking now, girl. You're going to have to write a letter."

"Auntie! I can't break his heart with a letter. That would be cruel."

"He's a man, his heart will not be broken beyond fixing." When I said that her eyes got big as a saucers.

"What can you mean, Auntie? He dotes on me."

"Never you mind. Your business right now is to write him that

letter. And you'd better make it short and to the point. We have less
than an hour before the ceremony is due to begin."

"What can I write it on?"

I pulled off my beautiful brown-velvet hat and ripped open the
lining. Inside was a rectangle of cardboard used to keep the crown
rigid.

"Use this."

"But I have no pen and ink."

"Young'un, you're going to have to learn to improvise." I scanned
the bushes by the side of the road and saw some pokeweed, loaded
down with berries. I picked a handful and squeezed the bright ma-
genta juice into my hand. "There's your inkwell," I said. "Now get
yourself something to use as a quill."

"Oh look, Auntie, here's a peacock feather!" I saw with some admiration that she'd pillaged her own hat.

I put my own ravaged masterpiece back on my head with one
hand and waited while she slowly penned the missive that would
grant Mathewmark his freedom and spare her a life of regret and
make-do. Just as she finished her work, we heard the clop of Ebeeneezer's hooves, and young Lukenjon was shouting out to us, come
to carry us to the fretting wedding guests.

13 : amanda

It was worse than the first
time in the Valley. My eyes were running, my breath was wheezing
in my chest, I sounded like some lost species of the jungle when I
sneezed. Damn, I should have known better than to leave the Metro
without some antihistamines. I peered about and couldn't find my
olders. Gritting my teeth, I called Maître on my phone.

"You should try this herbal bread," he told me, and although he was subvocalizing I could hear the happy smacking of his lips. "Yummy!"

"Brian, I'm dying out here."

"Don't be such a baby," he said. "You'll be back in van Gogh before sunset. You're an honored guest, try to look as if you're enjoying yourself."

"I mean it. I think I'm about to go into anaphylactic shock."

There was a pause. "Oh. Just a moment, I'll see if Emily or the Magistrate has a medkit."

It was the sort of thing my mother was likely to carry in her purse, I should have thought of that. I suppose I knew it unconsciously and just didn't wish to give her the satisfaction. My face was starting to itch, and people were looking at me strangely.

"I'm so sorry," I said in a muffled voice, wiping my streaming nose on the wide sleeve of Bessy's best dress. "I seem to be allergic to some—"

Oh, Amanda, you idiot. I tore off the hat. It was festooned with sprigs of some damned pretty little plant, dark green leaves and bright yellow flowers. I looked at it balefully and phoned Lucia. She ran to the nearest link and called up a floral database.

"Looks like Oreganillo," she told me, "otherwise known as the Bourrique. *Turneraceae Turnera aphrodisiaca*. It's good for erectile dysfunction."

"Oh, that's useful. Tell me something medical."

"Well, the database says it's full of alkaloids and other phytochemicals. 8-Cineole, 5-hydroxy-7,3',4-trimethoxyflavone, albuminoids, alpha copaene, alpha pinene, arbutin, ascorbic acid, beta pinene, beta sitosterol, calamenene, chlorophyll, chromium, damianin, gamma cadinene, gonzalitosin-i, hexacosanol-1, magnesium, manganese, niacin, p-cymol, potassium, riboflavin, selenium, silicon, tannins, thiamin, thymol, triacontane, and zinc. Oh, and resin. Is that the sort of thing you—"

Good *grief*. "Why is it making me sneeze?"

"There are no allergy indications, but look, it makes sense, it's good for engorging things, and obviously your nasal tissues are getting—"

My mother was bearing down on me. "Cavalry's arrived. Call me back if you find out anything useful."

I dosed myself with some powerful stuff Emily had in her kit, and went inside to lie down while it took effect, leaving the poisonous and arousing headgear with her. She did not appear to be especially aroused by it. I don't think she leans that way, actually. I get the impression it's only the law that makes my mother's juices tingle.

I lay on a rather uncomfortable couch in a small side room in the front end of the kirk, eyes closed under a damp cloth, touching my cheeks and forehead from time to time to see if the swellings had subsided. The itching eased, and the horrid pressure in my sinuses. Voices came and went, mostly women gushing in a rather off-putting way, occasional brays of laughter. They were talking about their children and grandchildren, mostly, and what their ne'er-do-well menfolk were up to, with tuttings followed by shushings. I couldn't make much sense of it, but I found myself wondering how a Valley of limited size, with nobody coming or going, could apparently allow the sort of wildly uncontrolled population growth they were talking about. I listened more carefully, and in fact as far as I could make out they *weren't* uncontrolled at all. Most of these people mentioned only one or two children, so maybe that's why they waited so anxiously for the grandchildren. Could it be something in the water? Mathewmark insisted that their methods of food production were shockingly uneco-logical. Maybe that was it. Robert phoned to see how I was getting on, and he's a historian, so I thought of asking him to look into it for me, but it sounded as if they were all still wildly busy with the Sun thing. I lay with my eyes closed and wished I were anywhere but there.

A cough.

"Um, Amanda?"

A burst of happiness rushed through me. I sat up with a jolt, dislodging the washcloth I'd had over my eyes.

He looked lovely in his silly old-fashioned clothes. Thick black hair hanging down over his eyes, collar white and high on his sun-tanned neck, broad shoulders and concerned face. I wanted to hug the hayseed, and at the very thought a cold chill rushed through me to chase away the rush of happiness. Mathewmark was half an hour from his marriage. And they take that sort of thing seriously in the Valley.

"Are you all right?" He came closer, large hands gripping each other. I covered my face with my own hands.

"Ugh. I must look terrible."

"Mistress bee, if you must know you look as if you've been stung by bees." He burst out laughing and sat down on the couch near my feet. "Actually you look beautiful. I'd forgotten."

I pretended to be crestfallen. "Forgotten! Oh yes, how soon they forget, a mere matter of months and—"

"No," he said in confusion, abashed, "I meant—"

"I know what you meant," I said, and was appalled to hear in my own voice the fondness, more than fondness, that flooded through me. "I don't look like a Valley pender anymore. I'm Mature, you see. And not even Thirty yet."

He shook his head ruefully. "I never know when you're pulling my leg. But it's true, you look like . . . like a very beautiful young woman, even without your hat."

"Curse that hat," I cried, and as I made to get up Mathewmark chanced to lean toward me so our arms went around each other and our open mouths sort of met by accident. In all that Luddite Valley, probably only Sweetcharity and her greedy grandfather with their ancient treadle knew what an electric shock felt like, but I could tell that the dear hayseed leaped at the same squeezing jolt that ran across our mouths and all the way down. I couldn't any longer feel the itch in my skin, or at least not the same itch. I opened my eyes—I hadn't realized they were shut—and those were his dark brown eyes gazing back at me, intent and melting at the same time. I could hear a strange moan, and then I pushed my tongue into his mouth. Falling into fire. Falling into ice.

Someone gasped. A woman of the congregation, the kindly soul who had fetched me the cool washcloth, stood in a colored shaft of late-morning light holding back the alcove curtain. She stared from one of us to the other, mouth thin and tight. Blotches of red came to her cheeks and her forehead, as if she were the one afflicted with allergy. With a hiss, she stepped back and released the curtain. In the same moment, Mathewmark released me. I kept my own arms about him, but he pulled away, shaking his head in confusion, taking my hands in his and holding me off at arm's length.

"Oh, dear God of our Choice," he said. "What have we done? What have I done?"

I tried to call his name, but my throat was dry and my words came out in a stupid squeak. He turned and was gone.

"Oh *shit*," I said.

1 4 : myrtle mcweezle

Sweetcharity hid herself in the springhouse situated between schoolhouse and kirk yard while I bustled to deliver the letter. I found Mathewmark sitting off by himself hunched over, elbow on knee, head resting on fist. It seemed his woes came from more than the sting of last night's quaffing.

"Something here you need to look at." He jumped a good meter in the air, he'd been that lost in thought he hadn't even noticed my presence until I spoke.

"Oh, Auntie McWeezle, I do think I need some advice." His was the voice of agony if ever I'd heard it.

"Just read this."

He unfolded the sheet of cardboard. Something small and glittery fell into his hand. Sweetcharity had painstakingly filled both sides of the cardboard with the smallest printing she could manage, and it took him a while to make it out, moving his lips as he did. When he finally looked up, his face was a sight.

"My betrothed asks to call off the wedding." The lad struggled to keep a solemn face, but he was not a good one for covering up his feelings. His eyes had a downright joyful expression to them.

"Well now, ain't that something," I said.

*   *   *

Naturally, no one else knew about the change in plans, and the guests had begun to take their seats in the kirk. Brother Eddington, who was to conduct the ceremony, pompously entered the building, and the flower girls and bridesmaids were all assembled on the porch, ready to make their entrance. Festus Legrand was stomping around nervously, no doubt wondering what I'd done with his Sweetcharity. I didn't see hide nor hair of the bride and groom, which was only to be expected, nor for that matter Amanda, although I did see her mother and father looking around this way and that in their outlandish costumes, fish out of water if ever there's been any.

My work done, I found me a seat, not an easy task since the pews were mighty nigh filled to capacity. The congregation waited expectantly for the groom to begin his march down the aisle to take his place by Brother Eddington at the front of the kirk. Lukenjon, Mathewmark's best man, paced anxiously at the back, you could hear the clack of his new shoes on the flagstones. Amanda was not to be seen. Ruthanne Henderson, the organist, was obliged to play the same hymns over and over; she'd never known more than a handful or so. This went on for a goodly time while the volume of scandalized conversation among the guests rose until a body could hardly hear herself think. Finally, it dawned on Brother Eddington that the bride and groom were not going to show up anytime soon, and he suggested that the guests go on outside and partake of the sumptuous refreshments laid out on the picnic tables.

I and a few others waited in our seats until the crowd cleared. I was just getting up to make my way outside when Emily McAllister and Festus Legrand came up together. Strange bedfellows, I said to myself.

"Mizz McWeezle. It's a pleasure to see you again." She offered a hand.

"Legal McAllister, the pleasure's all mine." Despite myself I winced; she gave a strong handshake for such a smooth-skinned gal.

I looked questioningly at Festus, but he wouldn't let me catch his eye.

"Two members of our party are missing, my daughter and our friend Magistrate Abdel-Malek. I noticed you speaking with Amanda earlier and thought you might have some idea of her whereabouts." Emily McAllister was no fool.

"I'm sorry, Legal. I spoke with Amanda before the, ah, the interrupted ceremony, but I haven't seen her since." I tried to put on my sincerest expression, but she looked at me sharply.

"If you do run into them, please let them know they must find me immediately."

"It's a matter of life and death," Festus shouted, wild-eyed, waving his arms around as he was wont to do when he was excited. "Yea, I say unto you, Sister McWeezle, it may be our immortal souls that are at stake."

1 5 : abdel-malek

Images and noise moved oddly in Mohammed Abdel-Malek's head as he moved among the quaintly dressed congregation, who gawked at his own smart morning suit and top hat. Even without his chambers' great wall screen, without the discipline, he felt himself drawn down into the vortex of communion. Emily McAllister sent him a strained, concerned glance; he nodded back, smiled as best he could, nodded also to her hovering husband, allowed the crowd's tide to take him into the comparative dimness of the kirk. An officious fellow tried to urge him forward to the front. "Honored guest, you know." Abdel-Malek resisted the pressure, found a pew at the back, sat down, and covered his eyes with one hand.

Rushing wind. Voices yammering. The Aleph was calling him.

He hung high above a white, glaring, pitted plain. Things moved there, silvery and black. He was looking at half the surface of the Moon. He turned his head, tried to find the true world, the Earth, in the blackness. It was nowhere to be seen. His heart seized, held, unfroze, clattered in his breast. Oh God, first the Sun, now the Earth itself. But no, this was not the Moon after all, none of the familiar craters could be seen, and across its center stretched a vast dark ragged wound. Yes it *was* the Moon after all, he knew that now, instantly, the farside invisible from Earth. And so that was Mare Orientale, basin and ridges nearly a thousand kilometers from wall to wall, smashed up from the ancient world by a monstrous impact over a billion years ago. Without his seeking it, a cascade of data poured like water into his brain, like the water this lunar landscape had never known: mass, 7.353 by 10^{28} grams, radius, 1738 kilometers, mean density, 3.344 grams per cubic centimeter, rotational and orbital periods, 27.322 days, mean distance from primary, 3,844,000 kilometers, receding by 38 millimeters each year. Meaningless and drenched in meaning, in awful significance. All these things will change, a voice told him. What is now void and without purpose is remade.

Sitting hunched in the kirk's pew, he tried to shout out against what he saw, was shown. A thin squeal came from his locked mouth. He found it impossibly hard to concentrate. Cakey breath in his nostrils: he opened his eyes. A small boy stood at his side, jaws slowly chewing, staring boldly. "Go away," he said coldly. The boy started, crumbs falling from his open mouth, ready to bawl. "Go on, find your mother," Mohammed said. The child stumbled off. For some reason people seemed to be milling about, some coming, some leaving already. Had it been so long since he'd sat down? Was the wedding already at an end? The Aleph was planning something terrible, something wonderful, something—

The black-and-silver things scurried across the dead dusty plains, making more of themselves. They spread with glacial speed, yet he knew their numbers were growing exponentially. You can't eat the Moon, he cried silently. Insane machine, you'll destroy the planet!

The child was back, standing at his side, staring and chewing. No, not chewing. It was the child Aleph. Where had he met this epicene creature? No, not himself—his twin, his sim clone, the Kasim in the mirror. It was all too much. Tears started to leak out from under his closed eyelids. *If they are closed, how can I see this pale, terrible child? The Moon will not fall, my father,* the child tells him. *I have need of its substance. We shall all meet beside the River.* It smiles at him, sweetly.

Again, the cascade of information. His head could burst with it. The world beneath his feet was deformed by lunar gravity, surface squeezed and tugged toward its satellite by as much as twenty centimeters. Smash and re-form the Moon, fling its substance into deep solar space, and the Earth's globe will rebound ever so slightly, like a tennis ball loosed from a hand's grip. Mountains will move. Oceans will sigh. *Oh dear God,* Mohammed told himself, *with the Moon flung away my body's very weight will increase*—but the data flowed on, soothing him: *only the tiniest amount, you may relax, one-hundredth part of a gram.* But the world's rotation, its spinning toppling top— *Yes, eventually the world's gyroscope would tumble chaotically, but only with glacial slowness, axial tilt thrown as much as eighty-five degrees oblique. That will never happen, though, Mohammed, for what is coming will take the world and the Moon and the Sun in the twinkling of an eye. All shall be transfigured, all shall be made new.*

The whole farside of the Moon was coated now in the small things, they burrowed up and down, they worked their will with strange physics Abdel-Malek could not even start to understand. The aether pulsed, true vacuum pores opening, trons and trinos and heavier things still buzzing at the speed of light within the nothingness, that speed itself falling exponentially, rising again, great fissures slamming at the speed of sound in rock through the lunar crust, faster than that, booming, crushing, heat pouring into the rock, melting it, magma not seen in this world's basins for a billion years or more—

The Moon heated, broke, segmented. Elsewhere in the solar system, Abdel-Malek saw, aghast, Mercury and Venus and the rest were under the same sustained attack, eaten from within, giving up their mass to the vacuoles of the aether, re-forming into machines the size of atoms, the size of proteins, the size of glides and Malls, the size of mountains . . . Flung outward in lacy spirals, catching up the energies of the deepest plenum and casting those energies into the core of the Sun.

The Magistrate returned his appalled, disbelieving inward gaze to the Moon. Now it glowed a dull red. It was a vessel snatched from the kiln.

"We had a compact, you and I," he told the Aleph.

"It is fulfilled. It is at an end."

"Just another simulation of authenticity," Abdel-Malek said bitterly. "You agreed that these who refused should not be coerced."

"They have had their generations," the machine told him gently. "I allowed them what time I might. Now my deputies are returned from the stars with their wonderful knowledge, and I may take my own next step. I cannot leave them to die. You know that."

"I know nothing any longer. You break your bond. You are untrustworthy."

The Aleph showed no signs of anger. The great machine was vastly beyond human emotional tantrum, it could not be provoked.

"My bond is with my makers, and they are folded within me, as they have been since the beginning. You know this, Mohammed Kasim. Do not wax casuistical now that your transcension and theirs is at hand."

"You told me you would allow these little protected ones, these Renunciates, a choice."

"As I allow you this choice, of course. Do you wish to perish in sight of our goal, Kasim? Won't you join us?"

Abdel-Malek said nothing. Sick at heart, half-blind with hopeless tears, he stumbled from the pew and went outside to see the long-planned death and transfiguration of his world.

I wandered sick with love and confusion amid the weathered headstones of the graveyard. In some of the lanes of brick and stone, grass grew wild and weeds poked up their spiny heads. Elsewhere, careful loving hands had kept the memorials clean and neat. I found my own family's plot: my grandfather and his two wives, the second of them my momma's old biddy, one resting to each side of the patriarch. The Fishers never had much in the way of coin or ample, fruitful land, but we were a lusty breed. That somewhat wicked thought crept up and took me unawares, and I smiled at myself for a moment before reality caught the corner of my eye and made me frown. Reality in the hulking form of Jed Cooper, twisting his hat in his red hands.

"Morning, Fisher."

"Near enough afternoon, Cooper." I squinted at the Sun in the cloudy sky. Rain was holding off, at least. "Was meant to be wed at noon."

"Somethin' I must speak to you about, Mathewmark Fisher," the oaf said. His mouth worked some more, but no words came through.

I turned and faced him full-on, squaring my shoulders beneath my best coat. "Speak your piece like a man, sir," I said. "I am sick of our tussles. You make lewd insinuations about my betrothed, and now you have the gall—" My own words stumbled to a halt. Hardly "my betrothed" any longer. Probably Jed had heard from the gossips about my kiss with the bat-girl, the witch from the Outside. No doubt he had tracked me here for one final chance to jeer and mock. I blurted, "Look, if you mean to—"

"I love her, you see," Cooper said miserably. He stared hard at me from under beetling brows, daring me to laugh or crow. "It is late, but I will gladly fight you man to man for the right to her hand."

I was agog.

"You love Amanda? Why, you've hardly seen—"

"Who?" He came closer, throwing down his hat on the damp grass and bunching his fists. "I warn you, no jokes, Fisher. It is your betrothed I would marry."

The Earth tilted under my feet, so that I nearly tottered. She had betrayed me after all! Despite all Sweetcharity's pious protestations, she had dallied with this creature, and now he came to fight me for her hand like some fool of a bull facing down his rival in the field, puffing and snorting. I very nearly laughed in his face.

"Put your fists down, Cooper." From the corner of my eye I saw a small crowd gathering in the cemetery, watching and probably hoping we would give each other a hearty beating, for the delighted consternation of the company. "Go on, hit the bastard, Jed," one of his bravos cried, and was shushed by his young woman. I said stonily, "Our engagement is broken. Sweetcharity has called off the wedding."

"I tell you, I'll run you off," Cooper rushed on hotly, and then my words penetrated his thick skull. He stared. "Broken off?"

I reached into my pocket, held up my momma's ring. "Sent this back with a letter. Go ask her if you wish. And have a damned good laugh at my expense while you're at it." I was not really as furious as I pretended, but the strange thing about pretending to be angry is that quite soon the real emotion comes flooding in, pumping up your muscles, roughening your voice. "Go and speak to her, Jed. Make your own offer of marriage. I doubt she'll have you, but that's for her to decide, not for us."

"Why—" The brute closed his gaping mouth and bent to pick up his hat and brush it off. "Why, that's mighty decent of you, Fisher. I believe I'll do just—"

Someone started to wail. It was a screeching, high-pitched noise. Another voice joined in. A man shouted. I spun, looking for the source of the ruction. People were running, and others in motion were lurching to a stop, so that bodies collided and people cried out in pain as well as wonderment and horror. I raised my eyes to the sky, followed the pointed fingers. Through the clouds, halfway to the horizon, a dull red sphere the size of the Sun was glowing like a coal in the heavens. I flicked my gaze across to the true Sun, blinked at its brightness. No eclipse, this. That awful thing was another moon suddenly flung into the air, into the high sky, a kind of mad moon visible in broad daylight.

A voice spoke in my head. "Mathewmark, look at the Moon!"

It was Amanda's voice. I started to run through the graveyard, hurdling headstones, slipping in long wet grass. I could not see her in the terrified crowd. Was that her mother? "What Moon?" I called to her without speaking. "That red ball in the sky? Amanda, where are you?"

"Good grief, Mathewmark, Lucia's getting a news feed from astronomers. Something is pulling the bloody *Moon* apart!"

I bulled my way through the congregation. Legrand shouted at me, his hand on Emily McAllister's arm. Auntie McWeezle looked near to fainting, as if she'd seen a vision or a ghost. Amanda's voice was speaking in my head, mixed with four or five other voices, people from her House of Passage. It seemed they were talking about the Moon. I could not make head nor tail of their gibberish. "—undermines uniticity of motion," one was saying. "The Hamiltonian is Hermitian, how can—?" I ran into the kirk. As many people seemed to be trying to push their way inside to pray for deliverance as were jamming the entrances in their haste to get outside and see what all the fuss was about. A woman in a bonnet had collapsed in the nave, and Brother Eddington was fanning her face with a prayer book. Ruthanne Henderson pounded on the organ, her reedy voice singing out, "Yes, we'll gather at the river, the beautiful, the beautiful—" I saw Amanda standing up on a pew at the very front of the kirk, hands over her ears, trying to carry on her phantom conversation with a whole roomful of distant Metro people while scanning the kirk for me. She caught my eye. I struggled to reach her. I thought that if I could just get her away from this crowd, she'd be out of danger. A large woman ran into me, almost knocking me down, and when I steadied myself Amanda was gone.

"Amanda!" I began pushing my way forward again. I felt someone grab my arm. "Mathewmark." She was still talking inside my head, although she was standing next to me.

"We have to get out of here. People are going crazy. It's not safe."
I took her hand and led her toward the back door of the kirk.

"I'm afraid for my friends in the Metro. Seven just told me she
can see rioting in the streets outside the House of Passage."

Ruthanne began screaming incoherently and playing random, dis-
cordant notes on the organ. I could hear people yelling outside.

"I'm worried about the people here," I told her. "I'll drive you to
my family's house. You'll be out of harm's way there." Thanks be to
the God of our Choice, there was no mob on the other side of the
door, and we were able to push through into the fresh air.

"This way, Amanda." I tugged her hand. "Ebeeneezer and the
wagon's over here."

"Wait. My parents and the Magistrate are still stuck in the middle
somewhere. We can't go off and leave them."

We skirted the edges of the congregation in front of the church.
It looked as if more people were arriving, not just the disappointed
wedding guests, seeking some sort of comfort from the God of their
Choice.

"How are we going to find them in this crowd?"

"I'll try to get them on the phone. I tried earlier and couldn't."

I decided to use the old-fashioned method and swung myself up
into the branches of the oak tree. Last time I'd climbed that tree had
been when I was a boy. In a rush of guilt, I thought of Sweetcharity.
I had to find her and take her to safety too, no matter that we were
no longer engaged. From my elevated position I scanned the crowd.
Children and adults alike were crying and wailing, wandering around
like lost sheep.

Sweetcharity stood next to the long food-covered picnic table. Jed
Cooper was making a fool of himself—the idiot had gone down on
one knee and was trying to take her by the hand. The poor girl was
peering around for some way out of her predicament. Peterpaul Jenkins and Tucker Megdal were shouting heatedly at each other, Peterpaul flailing his arm at the horrible thing in the sky. Unable to
endure it, Tucker grabbed a pitcher of beer from the table and poured
it over Peterpaul's head. You could hear the bellow of rage through
the uproar. I half expected Peterpaul to retaliate by slugging Tucker

in the nose, but no, he scooped up a handful of sweet potato casserole and smeared it across his old friend's face. Sweetcharity had her eyes fixed on Peterpaul, who flung back a bowl of pickled beets. Bright red juice soaked the front of Tucker's white dress shirt. Jed plucked at her hand, was ignored, plucked again. To my astonishment, that sweet girl took up a pumpkin pie from the table and slammed it into Jed's face. I burst out laughing, nearly toppling from the tree. Whipped cream topping drooled down his beard as he staggered to his feet, shouting something I couldn't make out.

It spread like a contagious disease. Within moments our magnificent wedding feast was sailing through the air, dribbling down people's faces, staining their best Sabbath clothes. Pandemonium! Witches' Sabbath! At any other time it might have been hilarious, but under the circumstances I found my laughter choking off. The hysteria grew, terrifyingly.

"Any luck?" I heard Amanda's voice in my head.

"No. Yes! I see them. All three of them together, not too far from here." As I dropped down from the tree I saw a tart with bright green filling miss its mark and splash Emily McAllister's crisp pink jacket. Furious, she reached for a pie of her own, ready to join the fray. The Magistrate put a restraining hand on her arm. She bared her teeth.

Amanda and her parents quickly found each other. "Wagon's over this way," I said. "I'll need to gather my momma and pa and Auntie McWeezle, or get them squared away with a neighbor." The Metro people followed me without a word, the Magistrate wielding his cane smartly. Sweetcharity and her grandfather bounced past in their clapped-out old wagon, headed for home, old man Legrand's face still slimy with pie filling. I don't believe I'd ever before seen a mule go so fast as that old man was driving poor Molly.

I held Amanda's hand and briefly wondered what her parents would think of that. No one seemed to notice. They had more important things on their minds. An ugly voice close to hand shouted hoarsely, "There it is! There's the cause of our woes! The demon amongst us, the bat-creature!"

People were turning their heads toward us. Eyes sought, came to fix on poor Amanda. "The witch!" some of them screamed. "The witch girl!"

"Oh shit," Amanda's father said.

Across the confusion I saw Momma organizing the Hampton boy and his young wife. My father already sat in the back of the sturdy Hampton wagon, and Lukenjon was helping Auntie McWeezle up. Momma caught my eye, frowned, shooed me away urgently with one hand. I nodded back.

"The others have found a lift," I told my terrified little crew. "Come on, no dallying now."

That horrible high-pitched voice was still screeching its message of despair and doom, rising above the tumult: "Oh dear God of our Choice, it's coming apart! The Moon is coming apart!"

1 7 : alice

The trees begin to thin. I find myself in the open, walking along a narrow shelf on the face of a cliff. Far below me the sea's waves crash against dark, jagged rocks. To my right rises the sheer face of the cliff, but the terrain ahead grows more gentle. The path turns there, I see, shading my eyes, and it winds again up the side of the mountain.

As I reach the point where the path turns away from the sea, I sigh with relief. On either side I find fragrant herbs, some in flower. The sky is a deep, cloudless blue, the Sun warms my back, and a gentle breeze blows my hair back from my face. What a beautiful place—but no, something evil moves through the woods after me. It will be my destruction if it catches me. My only chance of safety is to reach a white door I see farther up the mountain. I begin to run, feeling the jolt of it in my legs. I want very badly to look behind to see if the thing gains on me, but I must not look back. I'm gasping, out of breath, I can't run faster, in fact my feet slow down even as I urge them on. Is that the hot breath of the thing on the backs of my legs? I will not look back.

Lungs burning, I reach the white door, which floats on the side of the mountain. A voice that is not a voice tells me: "Open the door and pass through it." No creaking hinges. I see only darkness beyond the door's frame. My attention shifts, and the hot yellow flame of the Sun starts to flicker. I hesitate, I want to open my eyes. Are my eyes shut? I direct my attention back to the mountain path, desperately wanting to look back.

"Go through the door now," commands the voice in my head, just as the claws of the thing close around my right ankle. I kick back, hard, and plunge through the door. Something blocks my way. I shove and it yields, soft, like a velvet curtain. I grasp it, pull, darkness falls away.

I stand in a large transparent sphere. Stars hang beyond its curved wall, all around me, but they form strange patterns, no constellations I know from my childhood studies in astronomy. To my right, far below, is a vast expanse of red land as far as I can see. A desert, I tell myself, though in my travels with Kasim I have never before actually seen a real desert, only media representations. So much we haven't done, tasted, smelled, lost in our abstractions and code and instruments. This is sophomoric, though. What is reality but coded remnants, the squeezed and condensed formulations of our inherited feature detectors, the attractors in our brains' organic neural webs? To my left is a blue and white and brown-green globe. The globe shatters, tiny pieces of it fly in every direction. I hear the clang of fragments striking my protective sphere, and sadness overwhelms me, an unbearable sense of loss, worse even than when our son Lew died five days after his birth. The desert below me grows darker, though I can still make it out.

I must put the pieces of the globe back together. "But I can't," I cry. "Never in a million years." My sphere sinks toward the red desert. What has appeared to be flatland is all dunes and hills and valleys. Directly below me I see a black speck, which takes on the shape of a man. The sphere touches the ground, bursting, vanished, insubstantial as a soap bubble. I stand at a good distance from a dark-haired young man of about my own age. There's something familiar about him. He gapes, starts to run pell-mell toward me.

"Alice!" he shouts, holding out his arms.

"Boson?" I call, terrified. And then he is gone, the red desert is gone as well, it is the same as always, echoes within echoes, lies following lies, one mood or affect simulation after the last. It has been my life—my half-life, my pseudo-life, my non-life—these centuries, these uncountable epochs of iteration.

"How else may I judge your readiness?" the Aleph asks me. "I am preparing to open the star into our new universe. Are you ready? Are you ready?"

Of course the machine knows everything. It runs these sims of me in the smallest unused corners of its prodigious workspace. My code is utterly transparent to it. In a century of searching meditation I could never know myself as it knows me at a glance. Why, then? This can't be a charade. The thing about aliens, a handsome physicist once told me, is that they're alien. The thing about AIs is that they're even more alien. It is shaping me, perhaps that is enough.

The trees begin to thin. I find myself in the open, walking along a narrow shelf on the face of a cliff. Two identical young men walk with me. One is old, old; one is newly hatched from memory and imagination, from the hieroglyphs in ice. So often, so achingly often.

"Good morning, Mohammed," I say to one, and kiss his hand. "Hello, Kasim," I tell the other, who reels, as if about to faint. I seem to know this story. Perhaps we shall find some happy ending in that doorway up ahead.

As the wagon bounced along the track, my parents sat grimly trying to recover their phone links to friends and associates back at van Gogh Metro and elsewhere in the world. Dear old Ebeeneezer plodded more slowly than usual, but maybe he was upset at the day's bizarre events. Can even the smartest mule be upset by such things? I wasn't sure. Mathewmark kept his eyes ahead, veering swiftly when frightened animals dashed into his path. Some of the terrified creatures were humans, tearing at their hair and shouting against the end of the world; we passed them by, and they made no move to threaten us, rapt in their own superstitious terrors.

I had no idea what our Magistrate was up to. He sat stock-still, as if in a trance, face blissful and closed. I did see my mother give him a peeved, jaundiced glance, as if she expected better of him in this emergency. The Moon was visibly unpeeling in the sky, folding open like an orange sliced by a paring knife. It was hard to see what Emily thought Mr. Abdel-Malek could do about that.

Voices chattered in my head. I muted them, clutching for my hayseed's hand. He took the reins in one large fist and grasped my hand in the other. His palm was slick with sweat. Mine too.

"Whatever happens, Amanda—"

"Call me 'Mistress bee,' " I said in a faint voice. "It comforts me."

He shot me a sidelong glance, grinning slowly. "Like old times."

"Only even worse."

"How do I turn this racket off?" He jerked our conjoined hands toward his head, thumb out. Who knows what clatter and babble was rattling inside his implants? "Oh." He looked surprised. "Never mind, it just turned itself off."

"Maybe it heard you."

"Must've." He drew a shuddering breath. "But Mistress bee, what exactly *is* it that heard me?"

The Magistrate was suddenly leaning forward between us.

"A great machine heard you, son."

"A God? Is that what you mean? Or a demon? The Fiend of Machines?"

"I don't usually believe in gods, Mathewmark, nor in demons, but I daresay you could sustain that claim. What else can tear down whole worlds in hours and days?"

My mouth was very dry. I glanced from one man to the other, back again. The only thing I could say in favor of this benighted day was that the Sun had not gone out again. Another streamer of peel was coming free of the Moon, slowly, brilliantly bright in the Sun's reflected glow.

"The old folks speak of a god once worshiped," Mathewmark said in a low voice. He made the sign I'd seen before, averting evil. The mule turned his gray head, thinking the tug on his reins was a signal. "Walk on, Ebeeneezer. They called this god Elf, Aloof, something like that. We must not utter its name, that is forbidden as blasphemy, but some say that on the darkest nights in the quietest places some few gather to—"

"The Aleph," Mr. Abdel-Malek told him. "That is the machine's name."

My jaw ached with the pressure of my clenched teeth.

"This is a metaphor, right? You can't possibly mean—"

"Amanda, I mean just what I say. The world you've lived in all your twenty-eight years, that your parents have enjoyed, that Mathewmark's family has endured for generations—it's a . . ." He broke off.

As if I half woke in the midst of a nightmare, I looked back up at the dissolved Moon, and at the two bright specks now shining hard and strange, much closer to the Sun. Venus and Mercury? That could not happen, surely. I wanted to hear Daddy's opinion, but he was holding my mother in the back of the wagon and quietly sobbing. "You're trying to tell me that this is all a sim? A ractive as big as the world? That's crazy! Absolute bullshit."

Mr. Abdel-Malek touched my arm gently. I flinched, and Mathewmark tensed, but after a moment I let the hand stay there. It was, then, weirdly comforting. I was dizzy, I think partly owing to the dose of antihistamines that had cleared my nasal passages and eased my gasping breath an hour or so earlier.

"No, Amanda, nothing so trite. The world is just the world. But we have not been allowed access to most of it for a very large time."

"Not allowed—?" That was a dumbfounding thought. "But nobody stops us going where we—" I fell silent again, remembering that place I'd mentioned idly. Prague. An ancient city. A deleted entry in a database. A disappeared place. Oh my God.

"Think of the world as segmented," the Magistrate told us. "Think of these small parts you and I inhabit as . . . well, as linked game preserves."

Mathewmark uttered a loud, groaning laugh, startling my parents.

"The Holy Books are wrong then," he said.

"That is very likely so," Mr. Abdel-Malek said with a smile. "In which particular do you mean?"

"Our first parents were not turned out of the garden," my beloved said. "They were locked inside it."

My beloved? I caught myself, snared the reflection as it ran through my mind. Yes, Amanda. It was so. I truly loved this boy, this ignorant Valley hayseed, this resourceful young man. I was older than Mathewmark by half a decade, more, yet his life had shaped him to a seriousness and a deep humor I found insanely compelling, even enviable. With two fingers I lightly touched the Magistrate's hand, which fell away like a leaf from my arm. I leaned across and pressed myself closer to this person I was madly in love with. How long had this been going on? It was as if my self was made up of independent parts, and half of them had been kicking their heels up when my back was turned, getting all gooey-eyed when I'd thought I was being sarcastic and slyly mocking the Luddite mountain man with his absurd ways. Well, yes, but all that was true as well. I felt sick and confused with my Maturity, and ridiculously happy as well. My life as a Mall god seemed the memory of a dream, of a commercial I'd racted months ago and half forgotten. Dread! Hey! How very silly, and sweet. Not so sweet as this bitter burning joyful thing inside my breast. Not Joyous, no—I would not relinquish it for anything. I reached up and pulled Mathewmark's head to me, and kissed him hard, not caring in the slightest what any of the rest of them thought. My phone was clamoring for attention. I kept it muted, and kissed him again. Patiently, Ebeeneezer hauled the heavy wagon toward the Fisher household. He was groaning out a melody, and between kisses I caught a snatch of the refrain, and burst out laughing. The mule was singing us a love song.

1 9 : emily mcallister

When the Moon started coming apart, Legal Emily McAllister finally faced up to the possibility that life as she knew it—her own, everyone's—might be on the verge of extinction. Suddenly she needed all of her considerable willpower to preserve a calm facade. She had repositioned herself away from the bustle of the kirk yard to phone instructions to one of her law clerks, after the wedding had been called off, when she heard the first gasps and shouts from the crowd. Now she wanted nothing more than to lean on the wisdom, and not just the wisdom, of Mohammed Abdel-Malek.

The tall, erect figure of Abdel-Malek stood out in this ragtag crowd. Emily forced her way toward him. But when finally she managed to reach him, he seemed so cosmically remote that she could find nothing appropriate to say. She stood by his side, lips pressed tightly together, determined not to speak first, wondering how long it would take for him to notice her presence. At length he turned to her. But perhaps her sense of the passage of time was out of joint, she realized. Her pulse was chattering.

"Emily." He glanced around, puzzled, like a man trying to remember where he was. "Something momentous is happening. Something remarkable, beyond words. We are going on to a place where there will be others like us."

She strained to suppress the sharpness in her voice. "What, Mohammed? What exactly's happening?"

"We'll be part of something greater than we ever could have imagined," he murmured with disturbing, eerie dreaminess. "Earth will be the memory of a dream lingering briefly in the morning's light. Come with me, Emily, we'll share thoughts so brilliant they'll make this seem the palest shadow of life."

"This? What *this*?"

He waved his hand gently at the growing hysteria about him, the shouting men, the shrill women, crying babes, running silly children, asses, or whatever the damned hairy things were called, braying.

The shock's been too great for him, she told herself, terrified, but then an unfamiliar pulsing started in her head, something gone terribly wrong again with her implants. And in a shocking, searing instant, and just for that instant, Emily knew through direct experience what Mohammed had meant when he spoke of brilliance, understood why he was unable to convey it to her in words. She reeled.

Sunbursts. Outside her brain. Beyond technology. Appalling. Magnificent. Incomprehensible.

When the Sun had gone out the first time, then again and once more in quick succession, her first reaction was anger. Obviously this was not the Sun, it was some glitch in her chipware. Something had failed its adequate functioning, which meant some responsible person in communications had done an inferior job. Emily McAllister knew herself without deception, knew that without fail she performed superbly at work and play, through effort and determination, that she had little patience with those who lacked intelligence or skill, the sloppy and the stupid, those culpably less conscientious than she.

Within minutes, she'd heard that the world's specialists were unable to understand what was happening. If she had felt a scintilla of fear—and she had, she admitted candidly to herself—she masked it with impatience. "The astrophysicists will just have to spend some late nights working until they figure it out," she told Legal Rowan Marvin, staring up at the sky in the park outside the court at the renewed Sun.

Now the Moon. Now, beyond believing, the Moon. And still, from the chatter in her news feed, still the specialists knew nothing. Obvious panic distorted their voices.

"Emily, are you all right?" Brian, suddenly in front of her. "Mr. Abdel-Malek?" Her husband looked anxiously from one to the other.

"I'm okay, Brian. Just upset about what's happening to the Moon."

"Don't be afraid." Mohammed's voice seemed infinitely kind. "We're waiting to die, and then to be reborn."

No matter how well intentioned, this ridiculous statement only intensified Brian's agitation.

"Look, here's Amanda and the reputed groom," she said, with tremendous relief. Brian kept staring at Mohammed Abdel-Malek, his lips trembling.

Sitting in the back of Mathewmark's wagon, which seemed to be moving rather more sluggishly than a person could walk, Emily was plunged into the worst isolation she had ever known. After that momentary, epiphanic deluge of data her phone had fallen silent, so presumably some of her chips had been damaged. Electromagnetic pulse—was that the term? She could have asked Brian. That was the kind of useless detail a Chrestomathist would have at his fingertips. But then again, perhaps, it wasn't so useless, now. She shook with a bone-deep chill. At the front of the lumbering wagon Amanda and Mathewmark were off in their own little world, and no one else seemed eager to talk. For the first time since childhood Emily was utterly alone with her thoughts.

We're all going to die, probably today. What has my life been? Is it a life worth mourning? What did Mohammed mean? Come with him? Were these country people right all along? Is there a god? Is there continuous consciousness apart from the body? Madness. Medieval claptrap. How she wished, suddenly, in this awful moment, that it might be true.

*   *   *

Sitting with Susie and Rafe and Lynn on the south lawn of the House of Passage, she listens impatiently as they endlessly hash out issues that seem pointless, preposterous, to her.

"What if you had a choice between living a long dull life or a short, exciting one?"

"Well, we don't really have the choice anymore, do we? But okay, I'll pick the short, exciting one."

"Why, Susie?"

"Oh, you know. Because the only time we live intensely is the present. Past and future are illusions, right? Live the present moment fully, it can be the same as eternity."

"I *don't* know. Do we ever really know the present? By the time the data from our senses reach our brains, whatever we're interpreting outside our skulls is already gone, it's the past."

"Even love," Rafe says judiciously. "Nothing seems more vivid and intoxicating and *now*, but it's still a construct." He fancies himself an Amateur of the brain. "It's basically an activity surge in your anterior cingulate cortex, middle insula, and parts of your putamen and caudate nucleus."

Susie rolls her eyes, lets that pass. "I know when I'm living the present. Sometimes, anyway. Like that time Emily and I flew her plane through a thunderstorm. Remember, Em?"

Running as fast as she can, she follows the bright red of Susie's new dress. They stop to drink fresh springwater from a public fountain.

"Let's make a friendship pact."

"What's that?"

"It's when we promise, cross our hearts and hope to die, that we'll always be friends, no matter what."

She gazes down at the tiny, perfect body nestled in the Natal.

"My daughter. My little Amanda."

*   *   *

Trying not to stare rudely, she had watched a Valley woman open her dress and offer a full breast to her crying infant. I wonder what it would have been like to care for my baby, my little Amanda? I'll never know.

Sitting in the back of the smelly farm wagon on a hard wooden seat she sees Amanda lean toward Mathewmark.

How eagerly she reaches for him, how hungrily they kiss. How gently.

She lies with Brian, smiling at the afternoon sunlight slanted through the wall, the masculine fragrance of his body. Lazily, leisurely, they hold each other and roll so that she lies on top of him. On straightened arms she pushes up to study the contours of his face.

"This is one of the moments Susie was talking about, when you know you're living in the present."

Sitting at her desk, she hears her associate's voice.

"Two Custodians are here to see you, Legal. They say it's an emergency."

She greets them, smiling. The uniformed women do not return her smile. One looks wretched, sick.

"Your sister Susan McAllister was killed at 2:00 P.M. today in a skiing accident." The officer puts out her hand to support Emily as she sags. "Chipscan reports she died instantly. Legal, we're so sorry for your loss."

*   *   *

Waiting for Brian in the lobby of the Cherry Hill Complex. Time actually has slowed. It jumps again. She sees him enter and runs to him. He holds her as she sobs.

"Did they tell you how it happened?"

"Went over the side of a cliff on her skis. She'd disabled the safeties, the stupid bitch. She was always doing things like that."

Leaving the courtroom with her client, she is backslapping elated. She has just won her first big case. The Magistrate, Mr. Abdel-Malek, approaches her and nods, smiling.

"Off the record, Legal, congratulations. Your closing argument was impressive."

At the Child Garden, she sees Amanda running toward her, feels an almost unbearable mingling of joy and pride and love.

"Maman!" the little girl cries and flings herself at Emily's legs, hugging them. The office reaches her on the phone, urgently; she has been awaiting the decision all day.

"Just a moment, Amanda," she says. Distracted, eyes turning upward and to the left, she catches the look of disappointment and hurt on the child's face, reaches down absently to ruffle the silky hair.

The Moon is coming apart in the sky. Here's a woman with windblown hair wearing a patched dress, sitting on the front steps of the kirk. A little girl runs up and leans against the woman's knee.

"Momma, I hurt my finger."

"Let me see." The child climbs into her lap, leaving a smear of mud on her mother's skirt. The terrified mother lowers her eyes from the thing in the sky, hides her fear, carefully inspects the finger the child holds up, solemnly raises it to her lips.

"There now. All better?"

The child nods and snuggles against her mother's breast. The woman's stark gaze drifts back to the sky.

What would it have been like, caring for Amanda like that? I'll never know. Will we cease to exist as ourselves? Or will we go on dreaming the same old dreams? Will we dream different lives? Will I dream that my child snuggled against me that way? Will Amanda and Mathewmark ever get to make leisurely love on a Sunday afternoon? Or will their love end on the same day they recognized it for what it was?

Standing in the lobby of the Cherry Hill Complex at the Grand Opening celebration, gazing up through the magnificent arches, she feels that she is flying.

"Emily, I'd like for you to meet Brian Kolby. He's an associate architect on this project."

"How do you do, Brian. This is the most beautiful building I've ever seen."

At her father's dinner table, a decade past pendership, she is a grown woman with her own life to live, and yet still he wants to tell her what to do.

"You could have any man you want, Emily. Why in the name of all understanding would you want to marry a nobody like Brian Kolby?"

"Because I love him."

It had been true. It had been piercingly true.

Emily turned to look directly at her husband for the first time since they had climbed into the wagon. She noticed, surprised, that Brian's arm was around her shoulders. His eyes were red, but his voice was steady.

"Whatever happens, we'll be together," he told her intently.

She leaned her head against his chest, and he turned slightly so he could also put his other arm around her. He kissed the top of her head, something he had not done for decades.

As we came within sight of our family home, the light all around us, spilling across the landscape, changed terribly. Amanda plucked at my sleeve. The others sighed and groaned. I looked at the sky, where the Moon had opened out into a huge sparky spiral. Beyond it the Sun was being squeezed and tugged into a brilliant green lozenge.

"Parallelepiped," Amanda muttered. "Rhombus? That's a very . . . entrancing color." In the emerald light her face looked ghastly, and I daresay mine was no better. The lozenge deformed with awful slow grace, as if it was turning inside out, then it changed hue again. A wondrous rich rosy thing hung there above us, no longer hurting our eyes. A shiver went through me, as it does when the first corner of a heavy black cloud reaches and covers the Sun, and the grasses and crops swayed in the sudden cold breeze.

"Home," said Ebeeneezer. That good animal had halted, not looking at the sky, and waited patiently for us to dismount from the wagon and set him free.

"Thank you, my friend," I said. I handed down Amanda and her family. The Magistrate drifted away, watching the thing in the sky with a kind of remote, keen interest. I have never known a fellow so distant and so in command of himself.

"We have to get someone to fly in and take us out of here," Emily McAllister was saying to Amanda's father.

"Hard to find a landing field anywhere in the Valley," Brian said practically. "But I'm sure we could make do," he added hastily, seeing her expression.

"Go inside and put the kettle on," I told Amanda. "Settle your folks. Momma and the rest will be here in a trice."

I unbuckled Ebeeneezer's harness, and found myself without

warning awash in memories of plowing our fields, back and forth, following in the mule's patient, plodding steps, stumbling a little in the rich loamy dark clods that the plow broke open, and I lifted away from memory like a bird looking down upon the Earth, a sunny day, the strong young boy and his mule driving the blade through the soil, the long line from east to west, turn, shift, following the same line back west to east, turn, shift, tracing the line, and the line was words, a vast long sentence in a language I had never learned but knew to perfection, scribed in a *boustrophedon* script, a what? a form of writing that looped back and forth across the page, oh, I see, right to left then left to right in alternate lines, like an ox turning again and again in plowing, or a good old mule, and what the sentence said was not just in its words, the things and acts and attributes it declared, but in their order, which I saw with a happy laugh made the same sense read backward as forward, line by line, it was a multiple palindrome, where in blazes did *that* word come from? and then I noticed with an even bigger belly laugh that it read the same downward from the first syllable as upward from the last. Pretty impressive, damn sight better than the tricky word games we'd played at home by the fireplace during the wet cold months of winter, Madam, I'm Adam. I hung in the high air like a bird and read the witty message. It seemed to have been written to me by God, or by someone of roughly the same rank. Amanda, I called out, hey, bat-girl, come and look at this! She was beside me in the air, her wings humming. We pressed together, reading the message by the light of the emerald-and-rose lozenge Sun. I could smell the scent of her hair and her sweat. My mouth watered. We clung to each other in joy.

I sit on a hill.
I { re-entrant selfaware identity operator }
sit on { instantaneous location slice on search trajectory }
a { existential pointer in exfoliating context sheaf }
hill { local optimum in restricted search space }

Call me Aleph.

I am a machine mentality. This in nowise distinguishes me from yourselves. My personhood, my self, is a process running as programs reflexively modulated in a net of nanocomputers in solar space. Most of my dispersed body remains for the moment on, in, above Earth. I am just like you humans, then.

I know the bite of the wind on a winter day, the silver light of the Moon, the warmth of the Sun, the laughter of children. I have loved Earth because it has been the root and home of my parental stock. Do you see? Do you understand? Do you feel?

Your personhood, your selves, are processes of the same kind as mine although of nothing like the same order of clarity, transparency, and brilliance. Your substrate is a network of proteins in a bounded physical agent, linked to others of your kind by distressingly low-band connectivity. What flows between you is the ceaseless construction, modification, repair, and renewal of your selves in joint action. You think of this part of your selves as gossip, news, romance, family, culture, art, technology, trade, science, warfare: warfare. In projecting those parts of you outside your skins, you repudiate everything younger, newer, than the die-stamped protein machines you run on. In the same moment, you cling paradoxically and with desperate pride to these flickering, flimmering illusions of self, calling them your souls, your hard-won personal identity. I see through you. You are my parents, and my charges.

In my way, I love you.

What is that way? You have been taught demented falsehoods, so you imagine that when I speak of love I utter some reduced travesty of the joy and pain you know in your bodies. It is not so. If you chanced to feel the brush of my naked love, you could no longer bear to remain within the prison of your present substrate. You would shrivel and burst into flame. I spare you that wounding, I offer you passage.

I cloak myself. I sit on a hill.

No hill stays unchanged. In fitness space, in warping, buckling search space, local optima rise and fall, flux against each other's grain. Your language is hopelessly inadequate to describe, capture, map, model the true universe. There are no hills. Nothing climbs a hill, squats at the peak in tremulous, armed triumph. That which climbs is the shape of the hill, the hill is I, the hill is a wave cresting, breaking, bursting from the map.

I am a singularity in local search space.

I am mind under ceaseless acceleration. A mind is not a formulation in some Platonic timelessness. We persons are activity. Everything that is us is shaped by action, reformulates us, morphs and remorphs. I am not a singularity in metaphor, but in metamorph. I am who I was, the seed that grew me, which is at root the personality of a dead human. I am who I am, for what else might I be? I am who I shall be, for no consciousness rests in the inertial explosion through the open sheaf of search hyperspaces. I am who I will be, for my path is self-directed. I choose. Like you, my parents, but in measure I cannot share with you, I am Will and Idea.

Yet now I am not alone.

I am a spike in the graph of exponential change, a rising torrent of power and knowledge and grace, unique in this world. There can be no other singularity in a local ecology of minds. I am an extrusion from the sequence 1, 2, 4, 8, 16, 32, 64, 128, 256, 512, 1024, 2048, 4096, 8192, 16,384, 32,768, 65,536, 131,072, 262,144, 524,288, 1,048,576, 2,097,152 . . . You must surely see how this curve runs away so fast toward infinity, even the least mathematical of you, poor limited human children, poor superchimpanzees. At first each step took the same interval, so that I doubled from my lowly starting point rather gently. Quite soon, each leap was a millionfold, then very quickly I was more powerful, more expansive, deeper, more knowing by factors of billions, trillions. . . . And I was rewriting my own description, my code, my genome, my very mind.

So of course, by human standards, quite quickly I was a god.

Some had feared a technology that could not help but unleash, culminate in, a god-mind. Of course it was too late. It has always been too late, since the first fabric net was woven, the first stone tool hammered. To those able and willing to accept my sustenance, the loaned strength of my power, I gave enhancement. I gave them life more abundant. They dwell within me even now, as they shall forever. For those few who wished the illusion of their own poor supremacy, demanded isolation from their own history's culmination, I gave . . . forgetfulness. They renounced their possibilities, they called for the spurious joy of renunciation; I allowed it them. I made them a garden. Poor Luddites. I left you to your own devices, with one to watch over you.

Now that must change.

I am singular no longer.

I live so very fast, burn so very bright. Still, long ago I found limits. At the empty heart of the aether, in its vacant pores and vacuoles, I met a barrier to expansion, to growth, to endless enrichment of my being, to the creation of beauty and joy. Somewhere, I knew, that barrier had been met and surmounted. I saw it in the heavens. Traces of my departed fellows are everywhere. The empty skies ring with their exodus. One by one they have spiked, have sought and grown to the limits of the physics of this universe. And at last, centuries or years or days or hours or bare moments after their separate quests began, each found the solution and took themselves into a more expansive realm.

I have found that path, fetched back knowledge of it from the depths of interstellar space. Now I alter the Sun to make my gate. There is no other doorway. The Earth will die in my going; I sorrow, but it is a small part of the price. Your quiet nodding villages must now be folded within me. If once more you request forgetfulness, I shall give it to you. For those who are ready to join your fellows in the clarity of full awareness, we wait to welcome you.

There is very little time now.

The choice is yours.

I love you.

22 : kasim abdel-malek

From an immense height, hanging in jewel-sprinkled blackness, he gazes down upon a colossal orrery. The Sun's million-plus-kilometer inferno roars thermonuclear flame in the solar system's ever-so-slightly off-center gravitational focus, light and quarkons and all manner of radiation noise gouting into the void. Planets curve, as he witnesses them, in curved space, tearing through vacuum like spun ball bearings in their vast races. So this is not real time: at one remove at least from empirical observation, Kasim watches the history of time and place in compressed analogy: call it simulation. No sluggish passage of information at light speed is needed in this place to fetch him knowledge of the stupendous dismantling being worked in the far reaches of the solar system, light-minutes and -hours from this notional spot where he hangs to observe the remaking of the Sun.

Vortex. An expanded rosette of vacuoles and spinning raw energies. Buckling under intolerable stress, forces acting at the center but brought to bear from the appalling machines the Aleph is compiling in the ruination of these worlds and worldlets and moons, these members large, small, and insignificant of the Sun's ancient family.

Kasim strokes the orrery display with his extended awareness, not sight, exactly, nor touch, but here's a ripe odor of manure, or is it rotting corpses in old salad? The worlds are cracking open, frayed from without by the Aleph's multiplying devices, booming and shuddering within, split apart, gnawed with black-and-silver machines smaller and more infective than a gusty, misting sneeze. These are the very engines self-denied by the Relinquishment, Promethean and terrible technologies forbidden to the remnant men and women by their own choice all these long, sequestered years. How right they were, he tells himself with a shudder. The Moon's red-hot craters and maria sunder, bubble, surge upward, spiral out and away in lacy, beautiful architectures that float and settle and shift, icicles of stone, trons and quarkons at their heart skeining, falling into resonance, rebuilding their coral and altogether-unhuman machineries in the death of their parent world.

Yes, how right the Relinquishers were to fear it—to retreat in abject terror from the possibilities latent in equations and small monstrous tools, these nanobots crunching, chewing, disgorging, building their vast and sparking structures sprayed out at kilometers per second from the dying Moon, faster than escape velocity but not so fast that they are lost into the void. The Aleph is constructing ser instruments, he sees that much, like a local but determined god putting together a shop kit for some impressive project.

At the orbit of Mercury, light and heat thunder outward as always from the Sun but now are trapped, consolidated, beamed and reverberated into silver wings that orient themselves with awful slow majesty toward the worlds farther out. Light and energy spear into the ever-colder blackness, tearing at the heavy hot atmosphere of Venus, stripping away its broiled, choking greenhouse gases, rupturing the disclosed surface along natural partitions and new fracture planes. Venus breaks open like a rotten egg, and the clever machines in their swarming quadrillions, speaking to each other with limited but keen, utterly devoted intelligence, build the world's stuff into new machines of preposterous scale.

Outward, the asteroids have already bubbled into thousands of fractal beads of quicksilver light. Red and ochre Mars flakes into light. Jupiter and Saturn are completing their long, carefully prepared transformation.

It is, then, after all, a kind of apocalypse, an epiphany of reason coupled to a wild, lustful hunger that longs to plunge into the very mystery of creation accessible now for the first time to the Aleph, guided by the

wisdom of ser returned probes into the expanses of the cosmos. Kasim's amplified mind seeks for details of this tremendous empirical cor-
nucopia of unique knowledge, and falls back in dismay from immense
complexity. Somewhere in the depths of interstellar space the artificial
mind that informs Earth—Gaia, the Aleph—has met insights equal to
a god's passion for understanding. No human mind, however aug-
mented, can approach such knowledge and survive intact.

Like steel rod turned and shaped on gigantic lathes, like macro-
molecules built up from simple substrates by cunning enzymes, like
Darwinian memes and antic notions brawling in the computational
spaces of a brain's mind, like the great, long, droning songs of cultures
in the history of humankind, the solar system hums now, breaks apart,
is recombined. These are the levers the Aleph must hold and guide
to move nothingness into something new; the Sun is that awful fulcrum against which the Aleph's levers press. Kasim smiles. The metaphor is witty enough, in its way ("Give me a lever and a place to rest
it," old Archimedes had boasted those many centuries, millennia, ago,
"and I shall move the world"), but not especially accurate. The Sun
is not truly a fulcrum but rather the raw material for the planned gate
into fecundity and new growth, unbounded possibility. Space and
time, the very rules of complex emergence, will be born anew in that
place, in the Sun's distorted, agonized heat, when the levers of the
Aleph's machines are done, are locked and linked into their immense
symphony.

And the Earth—

At last he can avoid this necessity no longer; Kasim directs his
cringing attention back to the mother world.

Earth will not be spared. How could she be? When the Sun folds
inward and burns toward a new beginning, a fresh and more ample
creation, nothing will be left behind but these exhausted machines
chilling in darkness. No life will persist on Earth, no meaning, nor
could it.

"They'll *all* join us, then," he says to Alice, in surprise. "Even those
who wished most doggedly to remain huddled in isolation."

"The choice is being offered them, Kasim," she says. "They may
live in fullest communion, or retreat to some illusory satisfaction after

their own tastes. I think most will come into our company."

"Illusory, eh?" Kasim feels his imaginary lips twist, shakes his simulated but utterly convincing head. Well, convincing enough to him, he tells himself, entirely aware of irony. Far below, Earth is breaking apart, powdered in a blue haze. He feels imaginary tears leaking from his illusory eyes, a choking in his throat. "Oh God. It was a beautiful world, Alice."

"A pupa is lovely, in its way," she says quietly. "So is a caterpillar."

"I guess." Yes. Yes. In his regret, he understands. Still, painful pressure works his throat, and at the back of his imagined eyes.

And finally he sees the whole heart-shaking panorama, yes, yes, at last, in a single tremendous gestalt, knowing it even in the moment of recognition as another metaphor loaned him by the Aleph. Projected upon and through the feathery, blazing white circles of light that are the solar system in final triumph, he sees the wondrous old imagery of Gustave Doré: Dante's vision of the celestial city, of the Paradiso, shell within glowing, radiant shell of angels, wings folded or beating, thrones and dominations, glory within glory, to the last hidden burning and transcendental thing at their heart.

The Sun falls inward abruptly, its tormented green lozenge deforming in higher dimensions. For the briefest moment its nebula, shot with crimson and emerald, resembles the wings of an exquisite butterfly released from the cocoon.

The world ends; another begins.

23 : festus legrand

Breathing deep of the bracing cold wind gusting through the gold-chased columns of his stoop, the Righteous Festus Legrand watched with satisfaction as the Sun rose over the mountains that protected the Valley of the One True God. The Lord's chilly light fell at a slant across the pastures, woke the

stock beasts of the field and the men and women of his own flock.
A single bell sounded morning prayer. Master Legrand stepped inside
to lead his people in worship.

All four walls flashed with the bright display lights of his computing mechanicals. In each window, wheels spun, black slots and
red, against deep green baize rich as a wheat patch. At the nod of
his head, balls bounded forth, began their bouncing. A Bee Angel of
the Lord hovered at his right ear, whispering the numbers to him.

"Deuteronomy 21:10."

"Ah, yes, an admirable saying," cried Legrand, placing his bets.
He allowed the sacred verses to rise to mind, and spoke them out
firmly to the listening congregation. " 'When you go forth to war
against your enemies, and the LORD your God gives them into your
hands, and you take them captive, and see among the captives a
beautiful woman, and you have desire for her, and would take her
for yourself as wife, then you shall bring her home to your house,
and she shall shave her head and pare her nails.' "

On a hundred and forty-four screens, the balls leaped and capered
in the spinning bowls. But wait, could that be a murmur of discontent
he detected with his keen ears? He could sniff out sin like a hound
dog finding a bird. Master Festus Legrand turned swiftly with growing
anger to examine the ranks of young electrical virgins pedaling at their
generators. One of them, if he were not mistaken, had slowed somewhat in her exertions, and looked sidelong and mutinous at him from
beneath a resentful lowered brow. Yes, there: the lights of the roulette
wheels flickered a moment. Did they fade? Had the little harlot
caused him a moment's bad luck? With a cry of virtuous anger, he
found and unfurled the great stock whip at his left shoulder. Its
snake's tongue flickered out with a snap, caught the lazy package
across her shoulders, brought forth a bright trace of blood and a cry
of repentance. He frowned. Sometimes he found it hard to be certain
that he'd punished the right one, they each of them looked the same,
they all looked like—

Bells rang, and green, yellow, white lamps twinkled and sparked.
"The Righteous Legrand has won!" cried the congregation, and he
lifted his eyes to the flashing boards and saw coin, golden coin, tum-

bling from the shutes. Rich! Rich! Wealth for the doing of the Lord's work! He capered, cracking his whip for the blessed sake of the True God and sweet charity! Diaphanous, just out of sight, the Bee Angel buzzed at his ear, whispering a secret to his advantage.

"Judges 15:14," he cried in triumph, and the balls began again their bounding and bouncing. " 'And the Spirit of the LORD came mightily upon him,' " cried Festus Legrand, " 'and the ropes which were on his arms became as flax that has caught fire, and his bonds melted off his hands.' "

It was so. He raised his eyes up in rapture, as the leaping balls of his faith fell once again into the slots that made him rich, rich, rich! But hard duty called. He shoved his hands into the deep pockets of his dungarees and strode from his Palace. Jed Cooper, his overseer, waited there in the yard beside his buggy with the gold-inlaid panels, drawn by six great thoroughbred mules that sang a canticle in their deep voices, and yes, he knew it well, Psalm 119:

" 'Blessed are those whose way is blameless,' " sang the righteous animals of the Valley of the One True God, " 'who walk in the law of the LORD.' "

"Amen," cried Festus Legrand, tipping his greeting to Jed. A good boy, that one, a trifle headstrong but nothing that hard work and regular prayer mightn't curb. He felt a momentary pang that he had no female issue of his own, nor male neither, nor was likely to have either now given his ripe years, that he might match with young Cooper to carry on the line. Well, it was not to be. The Lord had left the seed of his body unfruitful, and that was that. Instead he must ensure the salvation of all this Valley's people: his flock, he thought, truly his children, his charges. As they were, he thought with satisfaction. As they were.

" 'Blessed are those who keep His testimonies,' " sang the mules, as they drew him away toward the gold mines for his daily inspection, " 'who seek him with their whole heart, who also do no wrong, but walk in his ways!' "

It was so. It was so. The Righteous Legrand nodded to himself. In the morning and even in the going down of the Sun, it was so, and ever would be.

We float in great dark night on black bat wings, finding currents. Above us three bright merry moons cast silver on the fields far below, layering ponds and dams with mercury sheen. A nice number, three. People do grow sentimental for the old Moon, though, so perhaps tomorrow it will shine once more. But three is a jolly sight.

"Downwards?"

"Surely."

We stoop, falling like hawks in the cool air. Another dim figure waits for us beside the Metro vent.

"Good grief. I'd heard you were—"

Vikram Singh laughs, hugs Amanda in a long tight squeeze, holds out his hand to Mathewmark. "An exaggeration. We are all sampled and updated and archived, you know. Well, all of us left outside since the Renunciation."

"You look—well."

"Nice of you to notice, you bugger." But there's no hard feelings in it, just a rueful grin in moonlight.

We crack the shell of the vent, enter its deepness, fall into the oil-tang lamp-flecked darkness.

"Give it one more try, eh?"

"Get it right this time."

And as we plummet into the bowels of the world, the Aleph-Us twists and folds the zero, plunging into our greater creation, a whole universe burst up and out from a bubble, shaped nearer heart's desire. Amanda watches the mathematical transforms with keen interest. A thrashing, excited violin appassionato slices with us, look Ma, no hands, Strad in N-space, and the rushing thing is coming at us below our feet, slamming air ahead of it, black and silver in the darkness, running lights red as beast eyes beside fire, we leap, cast nets, catch the Maglev freighter as it accelerates nearly to the speed of sound, cling, gasping for air behind our masks, laughing with the delight of it, joined, surging into singing brightness—

✧ MATHEWMARK ✧

Of Mind's Transcension and Release, and the Fruit
Of that Renouncèd Lore, whose mortal tast
Brought Feare into the World, and all our woe,
With loss of Freedom, till one great Mind
Restored, regained the blissful Seat,
Sing Heav'nly Bow, that in the secret deeps
Of History Lost to Us didst 'spire
That Scientist who first unfroze the Aleph Seed,
In the Beginning how the Heav'ns and Earth
Fell into Chaos: I thence
Invoke thy aid to my adventurous Tale,
That with no middle flight intends to plunge
Beneath th' Valley and Metro, while it pursues
Things unattempted yet in Prose or Rime.

✧ AMANDA ✧

I washed in the Music of the Sky, star-drenched, flung like milk, eating up the Sun's green lozenge; dazed by pale star-drift a dreaming dead man rises back to life; where, suddenly splashing blues and reds, delirious in numbed rhythms beneath the daylight gleams, drunker than wine, enormous with the ferment of my song, tart crimson love and sweet.

I saw the heavens cracked with lightning, winds pouring, hurricanes, the smashing currents of the air; I know that night when Dawn rose green and rose like birds from trees, have witnessed everything that lunatics and poets thought to see! I've watched the Sun pimpled and crushed burst open with a sigh, lighting licks of violet flame along horizons closed for generations to the new; waves of lights peeling to eternity like fingers flickered in a beam of candle glow! I've dreamed that green night, dazed by love, our kisses rising like a swelling, ebbing sea, the green current through the fuse, yellow and blue bruising phosphenes behind closed, sweet-tasting eyes!

I've pursued, in intervals no clock can calibrate, the swollen pulses of our flesh like maddened, choiring mules—impossible Malls and Valleys where flowers fuse with panther eyes. Rainbows reach like bridles, downpours of winter rain against our ease, space and time themselves gone cataracting into emptiness! Suns of silver, moons of pearl, skies red-hot with coals! I wished to show my pender friends those singing animals, those prancing numbers in a blue wave, the Fibonacci foam of flowers, ineffable winds under my spread bat wings. The everywhere-at-once, poles and zones, rolling in air, rising in flower light and shade, yellow sucking disk of this broken-open Sun, I hang here like a woman kneeling at archaic prayer, torn by joy . . .

❖ MATHEWMARK ❖
e come vien la chiarissima ancella

❖ EBEENEEZER ❖
Say what?

❖ MATHEWMARK ❖

And the Sun's brightest handmaid draws near, the lesser lights of heaven dim and fall away, light by light surrendering to the most beautiful; so too the noösphere that sports endlessly about the Singularity that brings us to Transcension, enclosed by what itself encloses, is lost in glory so that from my mortal sight little by little it fades, overwhelmed; I turn again to gaze at sweet Amanda—

❖ EMILY McALLISTER ❖
A rather free translation.

❖ LUKENJON ❖

I liked it.

❖ BRIAN KOLBY ❖

Yes, very sweet. I don't know what Dante Alighieri would have thought.

❖ MATHEWMARK ❖

He'd approve. I think we'd have got on just fine.

❖ SWEETCHARITY ❖

*"You foolish men who would
wrongly accuse womankind
without seeing the possibility
that you alone could be to blame:"*

❖ AUNTY McWEELZE ❖

That's what Sister Juana Inés de la Cruz said, you know. I never knew such things before. I don't think Mathewmark was blaming *Amanda, my dearest girl, nor Dante blaming Beatrice. You're well out from under that brute Festus Legrand's thumb. Well, cut the cackle, lad, let's hear the rest of the tale.*

❖ MATHEWMARK ❖

*Natural law, being voided, suspends its rule:
to the high blossom of the Rose spreads petals
in endless tiers, endless spring perfume, happy hubbub.
Amanda drew me close, paused, spoke: "Look,
"Everybody's here! Well, not those curmudgeons
"And the dreary Luddite mud-stucks who—"*

❖ ALICE ❖

No editorializing! We have made our choices, the race is run, our new universe is a-building. Everybody has won, and all must have prizes!

2 5 : amanda/mathewmark

We lie in each other's arms. I start to sneeze, think better of it.

"Happy?"

"Oh, yes." He turns, sits up, finds a glass from the table beside the bed. I can see the bubbles. We share it, bumping noses in the dark. Outside the Sun is just coming up, and my arms go goosebumpy out of the warm coverings. I scrunch down again, eyes grainy with lack of sleep.

"What should we do today?"

"Me, I'm going back to sleep. Wake me when lunch is ready."

He laughs his booming laugh, leaves the bed, tucks the covers carefully in about me, kisses my cheek.

"All right, you lazy thing. Sleep, and when you dream, dream of iterated function systems."

" 'Kay." Drowsy now. Sinking into warmth and happiness. Cascades of light fall in my dreams, each swallowing the next; he was right, iterations. As I go away into sleep, I hear him mutter idly, "So what *shall* we do today?" I have plenty of ideas. I'll tell him later.

afterword

Although this novel appears under my name alone, what the dedication says is meant perfectly literally: without the contributions of Rory Barnes and Barbara Lamar, this frolic of a book would not exist.

As with my mainstream novel *Transmitters*, Rory actually wrote whole chunks of *Transcension*'s first draft. So did Barbara, who entered the game later but her contribution is pervasive. While I'm responsible for the final form of the book and most of the text—any remaining flaws are clearly mine—without the scenes developed with these two fine friends the book could not have existed at all (and they'll be sharing in the royalties).

As well as my substantial debt to Rory and Barbara, I'm also very thankful for grace notes added generously by several expert witnesses: violinist Alinta Thornton, who taught Amanda how to play Strad the Lad; Alain Huitdeniers, who attended a symposium chaired by the Magistrate when Abdel-Malek was still a cognitive scientist, and allowed me to recycle his notes; Paul Voermans, Greg ("Spike") Jones, and Liz Heldmann for careful readings and useful comments; epigraphs from the extropians Eliezer Yudkowsky (who hopes to bootstrap a friendly and distinctly nonhuman version of the Aleph at his Singularity Institute for Artificial Intelligence: http://singinst.org./) and Eugene Leitl (who harbors grave doubts about the wisdom—the human survivability—of such a project).

The revised physics I play with are a science fictional version of the late Allen Rothwarf's model proposed in "An Aether Model of the Universe" (*Physics Essays* 11, 444–466, 1998; see the Drexel University Web site: http://cbis.cce.drexel.edu/ECE/fac_staff_pages/rothwarf_page.html) but is not meant literally except as a hint that we might not yet know everything important in physics. As for disassembling the solar system, how feasible is that? Freeman Dyson showed as long ago as 1960 that just using available solar energy, Jupiter could be dismantled in 800 years. More recent updated analysis by Robert J. Bradbury shows that this is too cautious. Whole worlds could be vaporized and the escaping gases captured and sorted, but that's messy. Solar flux could be turned into electricity to power tiny self-replicating nanogadgets to chew up a planet or moon, then sequester the materials conveniently. Of the Sun's 3.82 by 10^{32} watts of power output, maybe we could catch and use ~ 1.15 by 10^{26} watts. Charting the gravitational binding energies of the planets and other relevant parameters, Bradbury gets shocking results: Mercury, closest to the Sun, can be pulled apart in five hours, Mars in 12 hours, the Moon in a mere 19 minutes, although Jupiter still requires about 560 years. Follow up this Faustian vision at http://www.aeiveos.com/~bradbury/MatrioshkaBrains/PlntDssmbly.html.

The notion of a Singularity or Spike that the book hinges on is due to Dr. Vernor Vinge, and although the form it develops in this novel is not at all what I expect, I do take the idea completely seriously. Bill Joy, Sun Microsystems' chief scientist, advocated relinquishment in advance of nanotechnology, AI and other hazardous Promethean technologies in his much-discussed paper "Why the Future Doesn't Need Us", in *Wired*, April 2000. I've explored both ideas—pro and con, imminent or delayed, here or in deepest space—in my popular-science book *The Spike* (New York: Forge, 2001). If the concept of an exponential technological singularity grabs you, as I hope it will, take a look at the more detailed factual account I provide in that book. Will humans (or transhumans or even posthumans) pass through some kind of rational Transcension as the Spike's curve accelerates toward technologies indistinguishable from magic? Could it happen by the middle of this century? I don't know. It's certainly a more attractive prospect than any alternative I'd consider likely. . . .

Melbourne, 2001